End of the Beginning

Book 1

By Meg Castro

This book is a work of fiction, the events are fictitious. Any similarity to a real person, living or deceased, is coincidental and not intended by the author.

End of the Beginning All Rights Reserved © 2022 Meg Castro

Cover Image © 2022 Mark Lieberman

No part of this book may be reproduced in any form or by an electronic or mechanical means, including information storage and retrieval systems, without permission from the publisher, except by reviewers who may quote brief passages.

Version: 1.3

ISBN: 978-8-9865595-0-6

Published by: Meg Castro/Bohlander House Press Dover, NJ USA

Www.bohlanderhousepress.com

To the Real Lady Feathrye, Heathyre:

This has been a work in progress since our junior year English class. We weren't sure if we would ever see this published and here it is. Thank you for putting up with my ideas since we were 17.

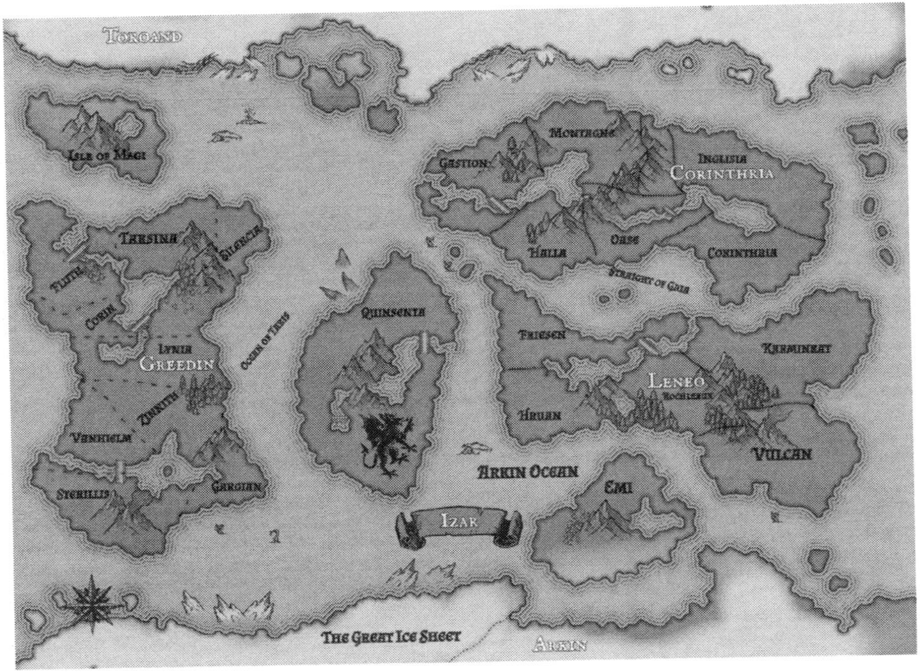

Chapter 1

The streets of Emi City were quiet as the wind and ice bore down on the island city. The city was surrounded by mountains, scattering most of the towns and villages along the coast or on the mesas of the mountain range. Along the highest peak were the old watchtowers that were still functioning to watch for storms. They had been lit the last few nights, warning those out on the water to be careful. Emi City was the capital of the island of Emi and a major port for the island and those that lived on the arctic tundra of Arkin. Winter storms were common in Emi, but not like this storm. The storm felt as if it was filled with fury, with ice that felt like needles piercing exposed skin. Those who were foolish enough to brave the ice storm burrowed in their fur cloaks as they moved quickly to their destinations. Chimneys had smoke billowing out of them as the street lanterns were constantly being relit from the wind that tore through the streets. They said the god Arkos was furious; the storm was his anger, that the people of the arctic continent of Arkin were paying for his wrath.

One of the few people out on the streets was heading toward the old mining district. Taslan Strum had come on the last boat from Vulcan. The crossing over the Arkin Ocean had been rough. Prior to the storm ports all around the continents of Leneo and Emi had shut down because of dangers roaming the sea, the storm was just another cause to ground all ships. It was not just the storm grounding ships but rumors of creatures lurking the sea.

Creatures that were spoken of only in tales that, for some, had been long forgotten, were making appearances, destroying ships, and killing crews.

The man hurried down a narrow passage, pulling his hood tighter around his face as the wind whipped at his dark brown hair. His hazel eyes were taking in everything around him, cautious of the storm and of those that could mean ill. He squared his shoulders against the wind as he moved. His thoughts were running all over the place, from his business being here on the island to the odd things happening all over the globe. He had been near port looking into some of the strange situations that were arising when he got the call to come here.

As he neared where he needed to go, Tas wondered if the others would show. It had been a promise made on their graduation from the academy that, when they were needed, they would come to the one in need. He found the door with the black rose nailed upon it. A symbol that death had come to this house. Grief hit him as he knew this house, knew the inhabitants as well. This was like a second home for him. Laughter could often be heard from behind the door, yet today there was only silence as he stared at the black rose. It took all of his strength to raise his fist and knock on the door of the home of his boyhood friend, Arngrierr Thodeson.

The door opened, and he was quickly embraced and then brought into the warmth of the front room.

"Tas, you came," the younger man stated as they hugged tightly. His blonde curly hair pulled back hastily.

"How is he?" Taslan Strum asked as he shrugged out of his ice coated cloak. Thierren Hass took it and hung it near the fire.

"He hasn't been sober since I arrived," Thierren warned, his green eyes full of concern. "Edelberg should be here soon."

"I got the last ship," Tas stated as he hurried to the fire that was going in the hearth.

"Edelberg went to make the official identifications," Thierren explained softly. "He arrived yesterday."

No sooner had the words left his mouth than the door opened, and a burly man walked in, his reddish-brown beard the only thing one could see from the hood. "It is done," Edelberg said as he shrugged out of his cloak. When he spotted Tas, he let out a shout, then hugged him hard enough to lift him off the ground.

"When we heard the ports were closing, we feared you wouldn't be able to make it," Edelberg stated as he shook snow out of his red hair and beard.

"I came in on the last ship," Tas repeated.

"Then we are all here," Thierren sighed.

They each nodded and followed Thierren into the back of the house. Sitting at the table in front of the kitchen hearth was a large man. When standing, he was over seven feet. It was said his family were descendants of an ancient race long forgotten or he was simply part giant. His black hair was so dark there were hints of blue to it, his skin tan from birth and from being outdoors. His pale eyes stared blankly at the fire.

Tas walked toward where Grierr sat. They had roomed together that first year at the academy, with Edelberg and Thierren rooming across the hall from them. The two were like brothers, there were moments one could imagine them having an entire conversation without saying a word. Thierren had prayed that once Tas joined them, things would get better. That this nightmare would be over.

"We're all here," Tas whispered to Grierr as he kneeled on the floor before him. "We heard your call, and we came."

"They're..." Grierr began, his voice breaking as the rest of the sentence died on his lips. "Why them?"

"We will find the answers," Tas promised his friend.

"You see everything!" Grierr yelled as he bolted up from the chair, causing Tas to scramble away from him. "Did you see this?"

Tas said nothing and held his hand to stop Thierren and Edelberg from interfering. Tas stood ready for whatever Grierr would say or throw at him. Preparing his senses, Tas then erected a magical barrier to separate himself from Grierr.

"You could have stopped it!" Grierr roared as the surrounding air cracked with energy. "They would still be here!"

Spells bounced off of the barrier as Tas held it. Tas grabbed his staff from his pack to help increase the power of the barrier as it deflected the spells. When Grierr used one of his fireballs, Tas prepared himself for the heat from it. A flash of cold air greeted him and Thierren standing between them, with his staff raised high.

"ENOUGH!" Thierren yelled, as he stood between Grierr and Tas.

Grierr growled at him, but kept his hands to his sides.

"We should never use fire when one's emotions are strong or when indoors. Fire should only ever used to..." Thierren began in perfect imitation of their Elemental Magic professor.

"To warm or melt but never to harm," Grierr recited as he snapped out of his haze. "I... Tas..." Grierr stammered as his legs trembled.

Tas moved quickly as he saw Grierr buckle, with Edelberg rushing over to help him. Grierr clung to them as sobs shook his body. Thierren watched to ensure that Grierr would not wield magic before he moved about the kitchen. He placed a large pot on the wood-burning stove top, activating the runes that Grierr had enchanted into it to keep the fire hot enough to cook but protect little hands from being burned. He added a broth from the pantry, then added his own touches to it. As he activated another rune to let it simmer, he placed a kettle on the burner next to it.

Thierren walked to his satchel and rummaged through the teas he had. He found the one he was looking for. It was his own recipe; it would calm the nerves and mind without leaving one feeling drugged or put them to sleep instantly. He pulled out another tin for himself, Edelberg, and Tas. Walking to the shelf where Luna had kept her collection of teapots, he picked out the one he had gifted her last year at the Winter Solstice. He found a tea strainer, then prepared the calming tea in it. He grabbed another tea pot and put theirs in that. Once the tea pots were ready, he poured the steeping hot water into them. While the tea steeped, he grabbed earthenware mugs from another shelf and some honey bread that a neighbor had brought over yesterday.

Edelberg and Tas had gotten Grierr back into a chair. Once Grierr was settled, Edelberg helped Thierren bring the tea pots over. Thierren poured the tea for Grierr and handed it to him. Grierr sniffed it.

"What's in it?" Grierr asked as he tried to figure out what Thierren had put in it. Having a healer as a friend came with some benefits.

"It's my blend," Thierren assured him. "It will help calm you, but it won't cause you to fall asleep instantly and it won't numb you."

"You perfected it then?" Tas asked Thierren. He knew Thierren had been working on a calming draught that did not cause drowsiness or numb emotions.

"Yes," Thierren answered.

"I'll still feel?" Grierr inquired. While he wanted the pain to be gone, he needed to feel his love for his family that had been ripped from him.

"Yes, your emotions will be calmer, allowing your mind a rest," Thierren promised. "I might have to strengthen it for you, but we'll see."

Grierr nodded and took a sip. He could taste hints of lavender and chamomile in it, along with just a bit of mint. There were other herbs in there, but he couldn't identify them. He sipped it again and watched his friends getting their own teas ready, Edelberg teasing Thierren about how much honey he put in his own tea. Tas poured cream into his tea before settling next to Grierr.

"I should apologize for the fireball," Grierr said to Tas.

"There is no need," Tas brushed it off.

"Thierren, this is good," Grierr informed Thierren.

"How do you feel?" Thierren asked him.

"And here we go. Someone has slipped into healer mode," Edelberg joked.

Thierren rolled his eyes at the redhead. Grierr took another sip before answering. "It is quieting the rage and the pain, but it's all still there," Grierr realized. "I feel like I can breathe for the first time in days."

"Good," Thierren answered. "I didn't like how the calming tonics were more of a sleeping potion that seemed to shut down emotions. Yes, the patient could sleep, but once they woke up, the onslaught of emotions would be there. I wanted a potion that would help calm but also allow the person to process the feelings so that their sleep is more natural than if it drugged them."

"It also doesn't taste like perfume or bark," Grierr added.

"Could I have a sip?" Tas inquired.

Grierr went to give Tas a sip, but Thierren stopped him. "No," he stated sharply. "Tas, there is an ingredient you are allergic to in it. I have made one for you. It's in my bag."

"Kava?" Tas asked as he thought of calming herbs that Thierren would use.

"A hint, but enough that I fear you could react," Thierren admitted.

He would never admit to himself that one reason he became a healer was because of Tas's severe allergy. The knowledge that no one had tried to produce alternatives beckoned Thierren to learn, if it was possible.

Edelberg talked while they sipped their tea. He told Grierr stories of his family back in Friesen. Edelberg was the youngest of five siblings and tenth in line to the Royal Throne of Friesen. He often was relieved when one of his siblings had another child as it kept him far from the throne. As he told them a story about his youngest nephew trying to catch a pony, Thierren checked on the broth. He poured a small bowl of it and set it in front of Grierr.

"You have nothing but alcohol in you," Thierren reminded him. "Eat it slow. You need to rehydrate your body."

"Thank you, Thierren," Grierr whispered.

Tas and Edelberg traded tales back and forth of their royal families. Tas was the youngest of four. His grandfather was currently King of Quinsenta, the Dragon Kingdom. Grierr ate while Thierren watched him. Between the broth and tea, Grierr tired. When Grierr had trouble staying awake, Thierren declared it was time for Grierr to sleep. Tas helped him upstairs and into a bath. He stayed until Grierr was asleep in bed before he returned to the kitchen.

Edelberg was helping Thierren prepare a meal for the three of them. It would be a quick stew added to the broth that Thierren had made for Grierr.

"How is he?" Edelberg asked as he poured Tas a glass of red wine.

"Asleep," Tas answered, sinking down into a chair. He had only just been in this kitchen a month ago when he checked in on Luna while Grierr was in Arkin. "He bathed and managed to not drown himself. A few more tears before he finally fell asleep."

"He should be asleep for the rest of the night," Thierren said. "I'll set a mug of tea next to him in case he wakes up. I never know how his body is going to handle something."

"I was telling Thierren that I will sleep down here tonight," Edelberg informed Tas. "People have been coming to pay their respect at all hours. My hope is the storm keeps them away. As it has, I would like not to risk him waking up."

"Not with this being the first night he has slept in a bed," Thierren added.

"Should we keep watch on him?" Tas asked as he got up to help Thierren serve the stew. He made Thierren sit while he dished out the stew.

"No, he should sleep through the night. If he wakes, he will be able to fall asleep with the second mug of tea," Thierren answered. "I do not think he will do anything rash, but we could ward the room to alert us if he does."

"That would work," Tas said. He ran a hand over his face. "Do we know the cause?"

Edelberg looked at Thierren who nodded. "The same as his aunt," Edelberg said quietly.

Tas reached out and squeezed Thierren's hand. "At least I could assure him they felt no pain," Thierren replied. His Aunt Tabitha had died a few months ago under the same circumstances. He had been there when the autopsy had been performed on her.

"We should all turn in once we finish," Edelberg replied as he tried to hide a yawn. "The next few days are going to be long."

Tas nodded, already dreading the days to come. They were going to notify the Council of Magi about this new attack, then explain to Grierr what the three of them had been working on for the last year. That was a conversation that might go wrong.

Chapter 2

Tas was the first to wake the following morning. It took him a few moments to realize where he was. Over the last year, he had been on the move researching strange tales around the world for the Council of Magi. That year of travel had him adapting to being in new places. He had taken the tea just before bed that Thierren had made for him, allowing him to sleep with ease. Grierr had been right. The new tea allowed one to still feel their emotions, but it allowed them to move past them so that they could sleep or function. There was no numbness, no feeling of exhaustion. Tas left the study where he spent the night on a travel cot. Thierren was asleep in the small attic room. They had converted it int a room for guests and a playroom when the weather was poor. Tas could not stay up there, as he had many memories of playing with Grierr's children.

      He looked in on Grierr. The giant of a man was still asleep, snoring, in fact. Smiling sadly, Tas shut the door and made his way downstairs. Thankfully, his frequent visits to the house meant he knew what steps to avoid from waking Edelberg who was asleep in the living area. Of the four of them, Edelberg was the lightest of sleepers. Something they had learned in the third year when the four roomed together at the academy. Tas saw Edelberg had kept the runes activated during the night, keeping the house warm against the bitter cold. He headed into the kitchen and saw through the large windows that the storm had calmed down, almost as if it was tired of Grierr's emotions. The ice had turned to snow during the night and the sun seemed to come out in certain spots.

Tas walked to the glass doors that led to a small courtyard area. It contained earthen pots that, in spring and summer, would burst with herbs and vegetables, toys would be everywhere. Except, this summer there would be no children laughing or afternoon tea outside because it was too hot indoors. Tas felt his grief hit him like a wave crashing on the shore. He steadied himself with a hand on the doorjamb.

"Luna, you were the glue, what are we going to do..." Tas asked the empty kitchen.

Grierr's wife was a force of her own. She was tall, almost the same height as Tas, which was just over six feet. Luna was one of the few that could go toe to toe with Grierr when he was in a mood. She had a way to calm him down, to soothe him without treating him like a child. In fact, she would not marry him until he stopped drinking. He had been sober a year on their wedding day. Over the years he would have a beer here and there, a glass of whiskey when Tas came, and that was all.

Tas felt a hand on his shoulder. He turned and saw Thierren standing there. Tas had not realized he had been crying or talking until Thierren pulled him into a hug. Edelberg came into the room. He nodded to Tas before getting the kettle going. They would all need caffeine to get through the day. Once the kettle was on, Edelberg joined the hug, causing Tas to chuckle.

"Group hug without me?" A deep voice rumbled.

They looked up and saw Grierr standing there. Thierren motioned, and he soon joined them, his arms wrapping around the three other men. The four stood there, letting the hug, the knowledge they were all there, help them with their grief. When the whistle of the kettle started, they broke off, each going about getting breakfast ready.

"The weather is letting up," Edelberg informed them as he got the mugs ready for coffee and tea. "The wind has calmed, and the ice turned to snow. I'll go out later to help with cleanup."

"If anyone is ill, let me know," Thierren instructed Edelberg as he warmed some honey rolls on the stove.

"I will pass the word on," Edelberg promised.

Grierr sat down in his usual chair and looked around the kitchen at the chairs that were empty. Tas squeezed his hand.

"Hans, the innkeeper, he was at the dock when I arrived last night," Tas began. "He said if it's too much being here, he has an apartment empty for us. No one would know where it is. He rents it out, and it's not attached to the inn." Grierr nodded.

"You let us know what you need us to do, what you need help with, and when you need time alone," Edelberg told Grierr.

"Can one of you talk to Hans?" Grierr finally said. "I don't know if I can stay here and not lose my mind."

"I'll go with Edelberg after breakfast," Tas promised.

"Can you get word to her parents?" Grierr asked. "I ... have I talked to them?"

"They were here when I arrived," Thierren stated in a calm voice. He handed out the plates with the rolls on them. "They were keeping gossip mongers from entering. When I arrived, I sent them to their home so they could grieve in peace. I told them we would get word to them."

"Please do," Grierr replied. He looked at his friends. "How did they die?"

"Are you sure you are ready for this?" Edelberg asked cautiously.

12

"I need to know," Grierr said, his voice cracking.

"You are not the first to arrive home to find their family dead where they lay," Thierren said quietly.

"Who else?" Grierr asked as he reached out to grip Thierren's hand.

"Aunt Amelia," Thierren answered.

His aunt was one of the few of his family that he cared about. She was a witch who worked as a mid-wife and healer. He had studied with her when he was learning to become a healer. Like Thierren, Amelia was also an outcast. No one in his family spoke to her except for him.

"When?" When Grierr was on Arkin, information did not reach him with the ease it would have if he were on Emi.

"Two months ago, before Winterfest," Thierren stated. He pushed his chair back and walked to the windows. "I was not there. Her apprentice, Emaya, was. It was late. Both had turned in after preparing for the Winter Solstice the next day. Emaya is a light sleeper. She saw this dark cloud of black mist surrounding the house. It entered through the cracks under the door, swirled around her, then left. She watched it float up the stairs a moment later. It was as if time had frozen. The mist vanished and time continued."

"That is what the magistrate tried to explain to me," Grierr whispered. "How? What is it?"

"We don't know," Tas answered. Grierr looked at him with a questioning look. "We can stop when you need a break."

"Continue," Grierr said.

"Back in the fall, Edelberg and The Council of Magi asked me to look into some odd rumors that were circling within the Magi Community," Tas explained to Grierr. "Vanishings, healthy people dying while they slept, monsters that don't exist appearing."

"What we found was that whatever was happening was not targeting sorcerers, but those who are closely tied to them or the magical community," Edelberg continued. "When we heard of the dark mist that brought instant death, we asked to bring Thierren in to see if, by examining the bodies, he could determine the cause."

"Could you?" Grierr asked.

"They feel no pain, nothing. It's as if they go to sleep and don't wake up," Thierren tried to explain. The findings in the medical community were still confusing. "As if whatever this mist is, it extinguished their life in between breaths."

"And what of magical creatures or the elemental nymphs and spirits?"

"They are just as concerned as we, for they have seen the mists and watched it take out a herd of animals while ignoring them," Edelberg answered. "They have also seen creatures that should not exist rise from the oceans and slip out of caves."

"This is insane," Grierr informed them. He ran a hand through his hair. "But I have heard some of this from the villages here and when I am on Arkin. Rumors of things that we have not seen in history are roaming the tundra, families vanishing."

"No continent is free of it," Tas replied.

"Is there not information on what has started this madness?"

"And that is where we will stop," Thierren said. Grierr went to argue. "No. You need time to digest what we have told you and allow us to get your messages to people."

"We will have this conversation today," Grierr warned, his voice almost rolling like thunder.

"We will," Thierren assured him. "At this moment, there are things we need to do to prepare to get to the apartment. We can discuss things tonight."

#

They finished their breakfast and changed for the day. Edelberg and Tas placed warming charms on the cloaks and were ready to brace the storm. The wind was not as bad as the day before. The snow was falling slowly as they observed the street that Grierr's house was on. As they made their way to the center of town, Edelberg noted that there were others doing the same, making note of the damage and what paths would need to be cleared. A few nodded to Tas as he walked with Edelberg.

"They seem to all know you," Edelberg noted. He knew Tas visited more frequently than he had, but he did not realize how much more until seeing how many people seemed to know Tas.

"I help when I'm here," Tas replied with a shrug.

"I guess I didn't realize how often you came here," Edelberg replied.

"Once a month if I could," Tas admitted. "The months that Grierr was in Arkin, I would stay for a week at a time if I could help Luna."

As they neared the town center, several people were talking near the town hall. They were being instructed what to do. Tas headed toward them, with Edelberg following. The older man in the center of the group smiled when he saw Tas.

"Mayor Tomlin," Tas greeted the white-haired man. "This is Edelberg. I don't know if you remember him or not."

"How could I forget Lord Edelberg?" Tomlin chuckled as he shook hands with the red-haired man. "How are things in Friesen?"

"Good," Edelberg replied with a grin. "Everyone is doing well. I came wondering if I could be of a help?"

"Actually, yes, one roof collapsed because of the weight of ice and snow," Tomlin explained. "We could use all the help we can get to secure the remains of the roof."

"I will gladly help," Edelberg promised.

"Tomlin, Thierren said if anyone is ill or injured, to send word to him," Tas informed the mayor.

"I am sure we will need him as we clear out from this storm," Tomlin said. He then grew solemn. "How is Grierr?"

"Functioning," Tas answered.

"I feel that is all we could ask for," Tomlin answered. "If he wishes for another place to stay, we can find something."

"Hans has already offered," Tas assured the mayor. "Actually, I should meet up with him before his tavern is busy."

After saying goodbye and parting with Edelberg, Tas headed towards the inn. He saw Hans was shoveling paths with the help of some of his workers and regulars. Tas whispered a heating spell to apply to the shovels, along with a lightweight charm. The men looked startled until they spotted Tas walking toward them.

"Taslan!" Hans said as he set his shovel down. "You ease our backs with those spells."

"Anything to help," Tas replied. "How did we fare here?"

"The main market area seemed to survive, mostly. A few stalls will need some repairs, but nothing major," Hans answered. "We will know more once we are dug out. What can I do for you?"

"Spread word that anyone who is ill or injured should send word to Thierren," Tas replied. "We also would like to take you up on your offer."

"Yes, absolutely," Hans said. "I'll grab the keys from inside. I had a feeling and had some of the basics stocked."

"You are a good man, Hans," Tas said.

Hans nodded and headed into his tavern. Tas got a whiff of soup simmering on the stove and coffee being made from within that tavern. It seemed Hans was going to be feeding those who needed a warm meal today. The man returned a few moments later, handing him the key. Tas thanked him again before making his way back towards Grierr's home. When he arrived, he saw bags and crates packed and were stacked near the door.

"He has been busy," Thierren informed Tas.

"It's keeping his mind active," Tas replied. "I'll take some bags and make the way to the apartment. Word has gone out to come to you for any ailments."

"And Edelberg?"

"Is helping with a home that had a roof collapse," Tas replied.

Tas ignored his soaked boots and leggings as he made his way back out into the cold. The apartment was a good ten-minute walk from Grierr's place. It sat above the tailor and grocer, with windows facing the ocean and town. Tas unlocked the door and set the sacks down in the foyer. He entered the apartment and walked around. There was a large central room with a fireplace. Tas went to the fireplace first and got a fire going in it. He warmed his hands as he hung his snow sodden cloak on a peg next to the mantle. His boots came next and the woolen stockings he had on under his leggings. They both went in front of the fire. The floorboards were cold, but he would make do while he saw about getting things set up. He found the kitchen in the room's corner; it had a wood-burning stove, a sink with well pump, as well as some wooden counters. There was a chest with cooling charms on it for perishables. A few shelves contained the basics. It was enough.

Footsteps were coming from the stairs, and soon Thierren came in carrying a crate and some packs. He brought them toward the table that separated the kitchen area from the main room.

"We should get the stove going as well," Thierren suggested. He walked toward the stove while Tas unpacked what he brought. Some went into the chest with the cooling charms on it.

Grierr entered with the rest of the items. Tas went over and helped by taking some bags from him. There was one that Tas recognized as Luna's. Grierr held on to that with a white-knuckled grip.

"I haven't gotten further than the main room," Tas explained. "There is a sleeping room off of the main room with two sets of bunk beds and a small bathing room."

Grierr nodded. Holding onto the woven bag, he headed to find the sleeping chambers. He found it, then set the bag down on one of the bottom bunks. He sat down on it and held the bag in his lap, unsure of what to do next.

"Thierren just ran out," Tas said as he entered. "The local healer asked for his advice on something."

Grierr nodded. Tas sat down next to him. Grierr held onto the bag as if it was his lifeline. "I took tokens to remember them... I can't be in that home, but I don't want to be away from them."

"I wish I could help, that I could take some of the pain from you," Tas admitted.

"Even if you could, I don't think I would want you to," Grierr replied. "I should go to the temple to complete arrangements."

"Do you want me to come?"

"No, I'm going to take her parents with me," Grierr answered. He squeezed Tas's shoulder before he stood up. "Perhaps you can find out how long until we can leave."

"That I can do," Tas promised.

Grierr stood up and headed out of the room. Tas followed him. Before Tas headed to the docks, he grabbed the loin of pork out of the chest. Tas placed the pork in a roasting pan. He then went about peeling and cutting up carrots and potatoes to go into the pan with the pork. Once he seasoned the vegetables and drizzled cooking oil over it, he placed it in the oven. Placing a few charms on the stove to keep the food and home safe, Tas pulled on his woolen socks, boots, and his cloak.

The wind had gotten strong again, and the sky turned gray. There was a feeling in the air that another storm could hit them. Tas hurried to the dock where he saw the manager of the dock talking to someone. They both stopped when they spotted Tas.

"I'm not interrupting, am I?" Tas asked. Not everyone was comfortable with sorcerers.

"Master Taslan, I would like to talk to you," the Dock Manager informed him.

"Of course," Tas said.

He followed the man to the small building that contained his office. Jareth closed the door, then motioned for Tas to take a seat.

"What have you heard about what's going on in the waters?" Jareth asked Tas.

Tas studied the man. "Are we discussing weather or...?"

"Or."

"I think a glass of whiskey would help this conversation," Tas suggested. Jareth went to a small cabinet and unlocked. He took out the

19

whiskey he used to celebrate the signing of a contract or the toast of a new ship. He poured them both a good amount.

"Thank you," Tas said as he accepted the glass. "I could only get passage by promising my personal protection of the ship. Since it originated from Emi, they were eager to accept my help."

"I was curious how you found a ship that would brave the waters," Jareth admitted. "Your companions arrived before many of the ports essentially shut down."

"What are you hearing?" Tas inquired.

"Monsters that are only talked about in legends, monsters no creature has ever described before," Jareth replied. "Ships returning with no crew and the signs of claw marks on the sterns, masts torn clean off."

"That matches what I was told when I was trying to find a ship," Tas confirmed.

"You realize this means supplies will stock up or run out?" Jareth replied.

"They won't," Tas told him. "I sent word to my grandfather before I left the mainland. He will speak to the dragon herds that live in Quinsenta to see if something can be done."

"That is what I was going to ask of you, if perhaps they could be of service," Jareth replied.

"It will take planning. They cannot carry as much as ships and some species can't do long treks," Tas informed him. "But they are a creature that will help when there is need of them. They do not shy from a sense of community."

"Yet many fear them," Jareth said.

"Piss one off and you pose the threat of being their dinner. I think a healthy dose of fear mixed with respect is the best attitude amongst people when dealing with dragons."

"Very true," Jareth replied. "If I can be of any help, reach out to me. I have names of the other port experts, if that would help?"

"That would actually," Tas said. "We are staying at Hans' apartment near here."

"Then I will have a list sent there," Jareth replied. They finished their drinks.

When Tas stepped out of the building, it had snowed again. Pulling his cloak tighter around him, he made the short walk to the apartment. He heard voices as he climbed the stairs and smelled the scents coming from the roast. When he entered, Edelberg was filling Thierren in on what he learned while helping around town. They both stopped when Tas entered.

"Where did Grierr go?" Thierren asked.

"To the temple with Luna's parents," Tas answered as he hung up his cloak.

"Where did you go?" Edelberg asked Tas.

"To the docks to discuss when we could get passage to the mainland," Tas replied.

"And?"

"I will explain it all when we are all here," Tas informed both of them. "In the meantime, another storm is blowing in, so we should make sure we have everything we need in case we're snowed in."

"I'll check the wood supply," Edelberg answered. "I'll also bring up a few armfuls, so we have plenty in here."

As they prepared for the incoming storm, the snow came down harder and the wind howled. Edelberg piled up enough logs to get them through the night and a good part of tomorrow. The storm shutters were closed tightly. Grierr uncovered extra blankets from a small closet. If it were too cold in the bedchamber, they would all sleep in the main room. As the sky darkened, they heard heavy footfalls come up the stairs. The door opened and Grierr entered with a gust of snow. He closed the door then helped Edelberg drape a blanket over it and secure to minimize any drafts.

He walked to the fireplace and warmed his hands. His cloak was hanging on the peg near the fire. They were quiet as they completed dinner. They poured drinks, Grierr going for water instead of wine or whiskey. They did not speak of anything heavy during the dinner. Instead, Thierren and Edelberg filled the table with tales of what was going on in Emi. Edelberg had helped craft some rough sleds for the children to use on one of the hillier streets. Thierren caught a patient lying to a healer, hence why he had been called out. Once the food was gone, dishes cleaned, Tas poured them each wine or whiskey.

"If we are to leave, Emi, it will not be by boat," Tas warned them all.

"Surely the weather can't be that bad," Grierr stated.

"It's not the weather that is keeping the ships in ports," Tas replied. "Do you know how I reached Emi?"

"You paid a captain, and they brought you here," Edelberg said.

"No," Tas replied. "I had to ensure safety of ship and passengers by using several charms that would make us undetectable to anything."

The three stared at him. "Why?" Grierr asked.

"What did the two of you see or hear on your journey here?" Tas asked them.

Edelberg and Thierren looked at each other. Thierren spoke first. "The prices have increased," Thierren recalled. "The sailors took armed shifts at night or when the sky was gray. Paying passengers did not go to any part of the ship that would have them be outside. There were whispers among the sailors of monsters, ships vanishing."

"Same," Edelberg said. "In fact, they said they would reduce my rate if I would be part of the armed watch. I asked what we were looking out for."

"What did they say?" Tas asked.

"Your worst nightmare come to life," Edelberg recalled.

"There was a ship attack off of Vulcan," Tas began. He held his glass between his hands, staring at the contents. "It was in sight of the harbor. A monster not previously known came out of the waters. Its tentacles surrounded the ship, cutting off any thought of escape. The entire crew was ... eaten. The strange part is that after it killed the last crew, the creature seemed to send the ship back to the harbor. Almost like a warning."

"When did it occur?"

"Two days before I left for here," Tas replied. "The ship that agreed to take me is based here in Emi. They were desperate to return home."

"So, we have a mist that kills people tied to the magical world and sea monsters that are killing sailors," Grierr summed up.

"Throw in weird weather forecasts and Greedin's climate altering, and that's about it," Edelberg agreed.

"What's going on in Greedin?"

Thierren paled. He was raised to never speak against the Gods, that they were infallible and to talk ill of them would anger them more. Tas went to speak, but he spoke first.

"A Volcano has formed in the southern tip of Greedin," Thierren began, his voice neutral. "In the southernmost province of Greedin."

"Volcanos do not just form out of nowhere," Grierr argued.

"I am aware of that," Thierren shot back. "But a mountain that starts erupting lava when it has never done is hard to ignore."

Thierren grabbed his whiskey and took the contents down in one gulp. They all stared at him. Thierren was not a whiskey drinker. He stuck to wine and ale if he was going to drink.

"Thierren," Tas said gently. "You, okay?"

"No, I'm not," he said, standing up. His emotions and thoughts were all over the place. "Because we have reached the portion of where I now have to talk about how the Gods I worship, the Gods that are supposed to protect my people, my homeland, are instead turning against us and killing us all because they are angry at each other! So no, I am not all right!"

They were all taken aback by his outburst. Thierren was normally the calm one. He rarely let his emotions get out of control.

"Do you believe it's the gods?" Grierr asked.

"It's the only things many can think of," Edelberg answered as he watched Thierren pace. "Who else that walks among us can control nature, create volcanoes, create a mist that kills?"

"Why Greedin?"

"There have been rumors, tales of unrest for the last two decades," Thierren replied. He sounded exhausted. "They talk about infighting. When an offering is made, it is as if the opposite happens than what a person asked for. The Priests try to cover it up with us not being faithful to our gods."

"How are they doing with that?" Edelberg inquired. He knew Thierren had issues with religion because of how he was raised. Thierren was never one to talk about his family or childhood.

"Not well," Thierren admitted.

Grierr sat there, taking all in. "Tas, are you saying that our enemies are the Gods of Greedin?"

Chapter 3

Edelberg needed to get away from his three friends. He needed a change of scenery; he needed noise and entertainment. It would help ease the restlessness that was building in him. After telling Tas he would head to the tavern, Edelberg bundled up and headed out into the freezing night. It was a quick walk to the tavern; he could hear laughter as he neared it. Smell of food and ale wafted from the doors, he stomped his feet to shake off the snow from his boots before he approached the bar. Hans spotted him and pointed to a stool that was free at the end of the bar.

Edelberg nodded and headed toward it. The ale was already waiting for him. He shook the snow from his beard before he took a sip. The tavern was nowhere near full, but it was good to be around people. Talk of death and wars nonstop for days could sour one's mood. When a small plate with fresh bread and cheese appeared, Edelberg smiled at Hans.

"How are they?" Hans asked as he cleaned some glasses.

"Settled in for the night," Edelberg answered. "We're keeping Grierr sober."

"Quite a few of us remember what he was like when he was well into his cups," Hans stated. "It's good he has friends like you to help him."

"What's the talk around town?"

Hans sighed as he looked around to make sure they settled everyone with their orders and the few staff he pulled in for the night were good.

"Talk of angry Gods and Demi-gods, feuds among them that are spilling into our realm," Hans replied. "Whispers that it is stirring up the spirits of long ago who are now coming out to see and judge."

"None of which is good," Edelberg sighed.

"That it is not," Hans agreed. "The storm, we know it is Arkos mourning for those lost on his island. But the monsters that haunt the ocean, those are not his."

"What do you know about that?"

"Sea serpents that can take down an entire ship in minutes, a creature that can cause fire to burn water as it consumes ships," Hans replied.

"And the mist?"

"We heard rumors from friends and family on the continent, but it had not struck here," Hans admitted. "We hoped Arkos' protection would keep it from us."

Neither spoke for a few moments. Hans went to fill an order while Edelberg cut himself some cheese. He watched the other patrons as he ate. Long ago he had promised Grierr that he would not bed any female here, reminding Edelberg that Grierr would have to deal with the heartbreak after he left. It was tempting to ignore the promise he had made, but he knew now was not the time.

#

Tas had woken up close to three in the morning. Edelberg had returned around midnight, for Tas remembered him stumbling into the top bunk of the bunk they were sharing. Looking around the room at what could have woken him up, Tas spotted Grierr was not in his bed. Getting up, Tas pulled on his cloak, then headed into the main room. Grierr was at the stove pouring himself some tea. The fire was going strong in the hearth and in the stove. Neither spoke to each other as they both went about preparing their tea. The storm was still raging outside.

"What time did Edelberg get back?" Grierr asked Tas.

"Around midnight," Tas answered. "Both you and Thierren did not even stir when he entered."

"You were always the light sleeper," Grierr reminded him. "Thierren could sleep through anything unless he's watching over a patient."

They fell into silence as they sipped their drinks. "You said you have a contact in the rebellion on Greedin," Grierr stated as he watched the snow fall.

"I do," Tas answered. "Their leaders are part of my network."

"You and your spies," Grierr chuckled.

No one would ever suspect Tas to be the head of a network of spies that helped him with his work for the Council of Magi. Grierr stared at the steam rising from his mug. "Thierren seemed surprised by this."

"We haven't talked in a few months," Tas answered and sipped his tea.

Grierr nodded as he studied his friend. It was not like Thierren or Tas to go a few months without communicating. "Do you want to talk about it?"

Tas shrugged. "His family is putting pressure on him again to take up a seat in the council for their province," Tas replied.

"I thought his cousin sat on the council," Grierr replied.

"He did until someone learned that he was taking money from the Cult of Prophecy and the traditionalist sect," Tas answered. "This means the pressure is back on him and more so to raise their name out of scandal."

"And that led the two of you to stop talking. Why?"

"He told them no," Tas stated, and saw the flash of surprise on Grierr's face. "He had about two months left of his advanced healer training. He would have had to stop, and he refused. I had just been visiting him a week before, which meant they pulled the 'I'm a bad influence' line on him. I told him I would cut off communication for a while so he could deal with them."

"Don't get angry when I say this," Grierr began. When discussing Thierren with Tas, conversations could get heated and tense. "What we are going to be undertaking, the people we are going to be going up against, this is going to be the hardest on him. At some point soon, he is going to decide on which path to follow."

"You heard him after dinner. It was one of the first times he spoke against his parents and their beliefs," Tas pointed out. He knew what Grierr was saying.

"And are you prepared for what could happen if he chooses his family over this?" Grierr asked his best friend, the man who was more like a brother than a friend. "Tas, I am not saying this to be an asshole."

"That would be Edelberg," Tas commented, trying to ease the tension that filled the air.

"Which is why I'm bringing it up without him around," Grierr replied. "You are my brother in all but blood. That is why I worry about what could happen if he leaves."

"I...do not know how I will be," Tas admitted. "I have thought about it..."

"But you are a hopeless optimist," Grierr smiled at his friend.

"I am."

They sipped their tea while watching the storm rage below them. "What am I going to do without them?" Grierr asked quietly.

"I don't know," Tas answered honestly. "We'll take it one step at a time. I'll be there with you even if you throw an occasional fire ball at me."

Grierr had to chuckle at that. "Lu would have my head if she knew I tried to summon fire against you," Grierr said with a sad smile. He looked at Tas. "Do we know any of the others that were killed that way?"

"Just Thierren's aunt, the other victims have been more attached to small sects, the majority have been associated with the witch covens. It is only recently that those connected to sorcerers are being killed," Tas admitted.

"And the Council of Magi asked you guys to look into it?" Grierr asked, shocked. There was a portion of the Sorcery Community that did not like to include witches in their population or in protection. "You know some views on witchcraft."

"They were outvoted."

Grierr nodded. "What are your feelings?"

Tas knew what he was asking. He set his mug down and watched the snow for a few moments before talking. "If we do nothing, we will watch the world fracture until we recognize nothing, until the chance to survive is gone," Tas answered.

"And if we attempt to fix it, go up against Gods?"

"We will help to ensure that all the races will survive."

"The cost?"

"War against the Gods."

"No small task," Grierr commented.

"Is war of any kind ever a small task?" Tas inquired. He picked up his notes and looked them over.

Grierr stood in the front room. He was watching Tas, who was going over maps and notes while mumbling in the language of Dragons. Tas rarely noticed when he spoke in the language of his homeland, Quinsenta. In school, it would drive them crazy, for when they would go to copy his notes, they would be half in common tongue and half in Dragon.

"I was half expecting you to come flying in on your dragon," Grierr stated.

"Bart hates the cold," Tas replied and looked at his friend. "Besides, people remember bright red dragons flying overhead."

Grierr had to laugh at the image that popped into his head. Tas was a Dragon Talker, a rare trait. Quinsenta was the land of dragons. It also had elves, dwarves, humans, and goblins. The country had two rulers, the King of Dragons and the King for the country. The human ruler would bond with the Dragon King, forming a mental connection between the two. But a Dragon Talker was different and only occurred when a dragon hatched from its egg the same moment a baby was born in Quinsenta. Only two or three a generation might become one, and they would become trainers, or ambassadors. Tas was a sorcerer which made his bond even more unique, and the current king was his grandfather, so when it was learned that he was a Dragon Talker, it seemed to confirm the intimate relationship between the two thrones.

"I remember when he came to the academy the one time because he got bored and missed you," Grierr recalled. "Gave the headmaster a near heart attack when a teenage dragon suddenly lands in the main courtyard."

"Only to learn he's basically an oversized puppy."

"That spits out electricity when angry," Grierr added.

Grierr paused before he spoke. "I was on the mainland; I go once every three months to make repairs for the villages there. They give me spices, rare minerals, gifts for Luna and the children. For ten years, this is what I did. I would bring with me goods, letters, packages from Emi to them as well. I went for two weeks each time, sometimes shorter, sometimes longer."

A log snapped, and a few embers spilled out of the fire. They watched them crackle before turning black. "One warrior had made a practice blade for Jared. He had asked my permission on my last visit, and I had given it," Grierr continued. "I couldn't wait to see his face when I gave it to him. A few days later, I had this nightmare. I was near a stream, and I was following it to this beautiful glen. I heard Rowena's giggle and Robert teasing her, I heard Jared asking when I would return, and Tomas babbling away. But they weren't there. I could hear them, but I couldn't see them. Then the sky went black, the field turned to snow. I hear a scream, the cry of a child, then silence. I didn't want to look, by the Gods, Tas, I didn't want to look. But I did, and they were there, floating in the water. Death had already taken them."

"Grierr, you don't have to do this," Tas said gently.

Grierr shook his head. "I have to do this," he argued. He watched as another log burst into flames. "I transported home, haven't done that since Luna was pregnant with the twins and she went into labor while I was away on a job. Landed in the street outside of the house, I saw the magistrate talking to the neighbors. He said something to me when he saw me there, tried to keep me from going in. I pushed them all aside and went inside. They laid all lay curled together as if sleeping. No one should know the feeling I felt, the emotions tearing through me now. We need to stop this."

"We will try," Tas promised.

Chapter 4

Three days later, after the storm had ended, they met with Luna's family. Today would be the day to honor Luna and the children. Together, they would make their way to the path that would lead them to the temple of Arkos. One could see it from anywhere on Emi. It was a reminder to the inhabitants that their God was there, watching them, protecting them. They had met Arman and Greta at the base of the trail, both ready to lay their daughter to rest in a place of honor. They followed the path up, passing the monks that kept the eternal flame lit. Each nodded as they continued. It was early afternoon, and they stopped for a quick lunch before continuing up the rest of the way. Greta had packed them a light lunch to eat for the trek to the temple. The temple was often only used for worship on high holy days. The rest of the year, it was a learning place for monks and priests.

There were legends that the tomb of Arkos and his family was hidden somewhere within the temple. The legend stated that they could only access it through a private chapel that only those descended from the God could use. Not even the High Priest and Priestess would dare access the family chapel without a descendant with them. A priest could go their entire life without seeing the inside of the chapel. It had been hundreds of years since there was even a rumor of a descendant being alive. A cult had hunted many of Arkos's descendants to the near extinction of his line. Tas never paid much attention to the legends. As they ascended to the top, he noticed how the monks bowed as Grierr walked. How some made a holy symbol of Arkos as he passed them. Greta and Arman did not seem phased by this, or if they were, it appeared as if they had seen this before. When they reached the summit, they stared at the white temple before them. There was a large center dome done in light blue with a smaller gold colored dome on either side.

"It's stunning," Edelberg stated as he took in the large white structure. He had read about the Holy temple of Arkos, the first of the children of Gaiaa to descend from the heavens to the earth. Arkos had settled on the island of Emi and the arctic continent that became known as Arkin.

Grierr said nothing as he led them through the silver doors and into the main chamber. They lined wooden pews in rows before a larger statue of Arkos. Here was where the community came for the high holy days, for weddings, funerals, and other special occasions. The temple also served as a refuge in times of trouble, with hidden doors that went into the mountains. The monks that took care of the temple stopped and bowed before Grierr. Tas, Thierren, and Edelberg looked at each other. While none of them were experts of the Arkon religion, they knew enough to know that monks normally did not bow before anyone but one of the high priests. And they knew Grierr was not a priest.

They headed to an ornately decorated door. It showed the marriage of Arkos to his bride, Elidi. Grierr took out an old key that he had in his pocket and placed it in the keyhole. One of the High Priests walked toward them.

"You honor us, as always, Arngrierr," The Priest stated. "You have our deepest sympathy."

"Thank you," Grierr replied. "We are ready."

Grierr unlocked the door, letting the small party into the room. Candles and torches lit on their own. It was a small room, but the artwork that decorated the walls was stunning. There was a family tree painted on one wall where it showed the lineage of Arkos. Tas noted how many of the names had been crossed out over the years to show they had died. There was only one branch that seemed to be current, and there were five fresh black lines through the names. There was one name had not been crossed off. It was a name that Tas knew very well.

Greta and Arman brought forth the urn that contained the ashes of their daughter and grandchildren. They placed it on the altar that was placed in front of a painting of Arkos. Grierr placed an offering next to the urn. He bowed his head before he took a seat in the pew. The others followed suit while the High Priest said a silent prayer before Arkon's painting.

"We assemble on this day of sorrow, our Lord, to bestow upon you the souls of Luna, Jared, Robert, Rowena, and Tomas," the Priest began.

Tas paid little attention to the service. His focus was on Grierr. His friend was doing everything in his power to not fall apart. Luna's parents were leaning on each other, both silently crying. Thierren also was monitoring Grierr while Edelberg seemed to take in all the artwork and decor.

"We ask Great Arkos to allow your descendants and their beloved mother to be welcomed in your embrace," the Priest finished.

Thierren shot Tas a look at the closing prayer. Grierr was going to explain what was going on at some point. They all stood. The priest explained they could take all the time they needed; he walked to Greta and Arman to explain how they could enter the sacred chapel they were in.

Grierr sat for a few moments staring at the Urn before he stood. He walked to a wood panel that was carved with Arkos' famous white dragon. Taking his pendant out from under his tunic, he shoved it into the panel.

Edelberg went to make a joke, but the panel glowed, then moved, revealing a circular stairwell that went down. The moment Grierr entered the stairwell, the torches lit. When Edelberg entered last, the panel slid closed without a hand touching it.

They took the stairwell down and stared as they entered a large chamber. Ancient artwork decorated the walls. Tas walked over to them, touching the details. It showed the creation of the world, the birth of the six children of Gaiaa and the Universe. There were six panels that showed how each child went off to find their own place. There were shelves carved into the walls which carried ancient texts and scrolls. Tas held back the urge to want to see what the shelves contained. Thierren laid a hand on his shoulder, as if he knew what Tas wanted to do.

Their focus then fell to the center of the room. There was a bronze statue of the god Arkos sitting on a simple throne. He wore no ornamentation, no crown or staff. On his left index finger was a simple band showing his marriage to his wife. Tas studied it, waiting for the statue to breathe because of its lifelike details.

Grierr walked to the statue and kneeled before it. From his bag, he then brought out a small box he placed at the feet. Bowing his head, he laid a hand on the urn and then on the knee of the statue.

"I ask of you, our Protector, to watch over them in their eternal sleep, to grant them peace," Grierr whispered. "I ask you as our guide, to help them find their way to fields of Evermore."

Grierr kissed the box, then looked up at the statue. "I ask you, my ultimate grandfather, to watch over us as we embark on this journey. It is unknown what we will face, what we will learn," Grierr continued with a tear running down his face. "Please help me, guide me from my grief, from the darkness I see."

Tas gasped, taking a step back, for he swore the statue moved. Thierren and Edelberg followed him as they stared in wonder as a man emerged from the statue. He was taller than Grierr, with darker skin, long black hair, and green eyes that saw everything.

"Why must you always kneel?" the man asked as he raised Grierr to his feet before embracing him. He then looked at the three men behind him. "These are the three."

"They are," Grierr answered. "They heard my call and came."

"I am impressed," the man said as he stepped forward. He studied each of them and smiled gently. "I am Arkos and my several times over grandson has chosen the three of you as his worthy companions. Sometimes we often forget or ignore the promises we make when we are young when called upon. Yet each one of you came to his aid, overcoming your own obstacles to do so. I am honored by that."

"We… do not know what to say," Tas said, almost speechless.

"Arngrierr will explain the need for secrecy," Arkos told them. "I see in each of you great qualities that will aid in the days that come. These are dark times, dark days. The death of my blood has angered me in ways I thought was not possible."

"Then the storm was caused by you," Tas realized.

"Yes, I apologize for the rough sea crossing, Dragon Talker," Arkos stated, as he studied the taller of the three men. "I see wisdom in you. You are wise beyond your years. Yet you get frustrated when others do not see things the way you do. Be patient with those who are stuck in their ways."

Arkos moved to Thierren. "You are often the one who keeps peace amongst your friends," Arkon noted. "You wish to solve the world's problems with peace and not violence."

"I do not believe that peace can be achieved through war. No party wins, no one becomes great because of it," Thierren answered softly.

"War does not make one great, nor does it declare a winner," Arkos agreed. "Yet sometimes it is the only way to show another that the path they have chosen is dangerous. Blood will be spilled, there will be battles. You must brace yourself for what is coming, know that peace is not always the way. The ways of old will change and you must change with that. Can you walk a path your blood will not support?"

"And if I cannot brace myself for that?"

Arkos looked at him sadly. "Then it will destroy you in the end." He laid a hand on the young sorcerer's shoulder before moving onto Edelberg. He smiled at the burly man. "You are a battle mage, a rare class that uses their skill with weapons and merges it with their talents. Just remember, the blade is not always the answer. Rushing in headfirst sometimes results in the head's loss."

"My teacher often told me that," Edelberg laughed.

"Your humor will be needed," Arkos informed him. "Keep it even when things get bad."

He then turned to Grierr and smiled sadly. "If I could have stopped it, I would have," Arkos said softly. "But they were gone before I could even touch them. Do not drown in your grief, do not let your thirst for vengeance cloud your vision. I will protect them, and they will be honored."

Grierr nodded as the god kissed his forehead. They watched silently as he merged back with the statue. No one spoke as they headed up the stairs. Arngrierr locked the door when they went through it. Greta and Arman were sitting in a pew, staring around the room. They both stood when the four entered.

"We will watch over Emi," Arman promised his son-in-law. "You are family. Do not forget that."

Grierr nodded. He took a key from his pocket and handed it to Greta. "This unlocks a passageway into the mountains," he explained. "If there is no alternative, use this key and bring many with you. The caverns will hold the population easily."

"What if you need it?" Greta asked as she held the key close to her.

Grierr looked at the altar. "The mountain will know who I am and will let me enter," he assured her. "Do not let anyone know you two hold the key."

"Your secrets are safe," Arman told him.

"I know," Grierr said. He stared at them both. "He will welcome them as his own, though it means nothing to us. I would ...."

His voice broke. Greta reached up and hugged him tightly, rubbing his back. "I know," she whispered. "Being honored among the gods is a true gift, but it will not replace our loss."

"You will look out for him?" Arman asked Tas.

"I will try," Tas answered. "What we are about to do will not be easy, but I will try to make sure he gets into no more trouble than needed."

"That is all we can ask," Arman replied. "He has been a son to us long before they ever married. This will not change."

"Good," Tas answered. "Do I need to get anything to Aten?"

Arman removed an envelope from his pocket. "He is studying in Silencia at their observatory," Arman answered. "We tried to send word, but do not know if it reached him."

"We will get it to him," Thierren promised. He took the envelope and placed it in the pocket of his tunic.

They made their goodbyes, then exited the temple. The monks and priests bowed to them as they left the building. They began the long trek back down the mountain. They would arrive at the base of the mountain as night fell. No one spoke as they descended the mountain. Tas took the lead with Edelberg in the back, Thierren keeping a close eye on Grierr. Unlike the trip up, they did not break for food. The street lanterns were just being lit when they emerged from the trail. Silently, they made their way to their small apartment. The soup that Thierren had left simmering made the space smell inviting.

"We should eat, then go to sleep," Tas stated as they took their seats.

"We can finish packing in the morning," Edelberg agreed.

"Do we know yet how we are leaving the island?" Grierr inquired.

"I have a feeling your grandfather will help with that and if he doesn't, I'll call out to any that are near," Tas answered.

Going to sleep that night was easy. They were all exhausted from the hike to and from the temple, as well as emotionally drained from the events of the day. Thierren and Edelberg both woke up at the same time the following morning to see that Tas was already up and out of the room. Thierren slipped out of his bunk as Edelberg went through his morning stretches. He expected Tas to be in the main room, yet all he saw was the fire going in the hearth. He could hear voices coming from outside. Looking out a window, Thierren saw why Tas had gotten up so early. A beautiful white dragon with gold accents had landed at the docks. Smiling, Thierren grabbed his cloak from a hook and headed down the steps.

The dragon was lying on the ground; it focused its bright blue eyes on Tas, who was gushing over it. He was rambling in a mix of common and Dragon.

"You are beautiful," Tas said in the language of Dragons.

"I have never seen one with gold accents," Thierren stated as he joined Tas.

It startled Tas for a moment at Thierren's arrival. "And you won't," Tas answered. "She is the companion of Arkos."

Thierren stared at Tas in shock. Tas was smiling like a kid waking up on the first morning of the Winter Solstice.

"And who is this beauty?" Edelberg's booming voice inquired.

The dragon seemed to roll its eyes at the loud voice. When Grierr appeared, the dragon moved to sit on its hind legs and bow. Grierr bowed his head to the dragon.

"They sent her to help us make up some time," Tas informed his friends.

"We are to ride on that… dragon," Edelberg stammered. He was not much for flight, he preferred land and ocean.

"Ignore the bearded man," Tas suggested to the dragon. "He gets ill in the air."

"I do not," Edelberg yelled as he marched toward the dragon. He swore the dragon snickered as he climbed on.

Chapter 5

The dragon landed on the outskirts of Port Leno in Vulcan, allowing the four of them to slide off its back before taking to the skies again. They let Edelberg have a few moments to steady himself before entering the bustling port town. Edelberg had never been a fan of traveling by dragon. Once he was ready to move, they headed to the nearest tavern. The *Old Oak* was packed as they opened the door and immediately encased in noise. Edelberg and Thierren went to get a table while Grierr and Tas went to talk to the innkeeper.

"Any rooms for the night?" Tas asked.

"If you don't mind the bunk room," the innkeeper replied.

They heard yelling from the taproom. Tas turned and saw a short female carrying a tray of mugs above her heads as she kicked a stool toward a patron who was stumbling around.

"Elias, you leave now, or I will drag you out by your ears!" the female roared.

"Ah, Heathyre, you know I don't mean it," the man seemed to beg.

Her hazel eyes narrowed at him. "Come back when you're sober," she stated, and served the rest of her drinks.

"We're investigating the dangers that are occurring in the ocean and around us," Tas said quietly. "Do you know of anyone that could help?"

"She'll be able to explain things," the innkeeper answered, gesturing to the bartender, who was currently dragging a man out of the bar.

Tas nodded and headed into the taproom as Grierr paid for the room and food. He joined his companions at the table. Edelberg filled him in on how the patron that got kicked out tried to grab a feather out of Heathyre's hair and she elbowed him in the stomach before dragging him out. Grierr sat down a moment later.

"I'm told you are asking questions," Heathyre stated as she appeared at the end of their table.

He had pulled her light brown hair back in an intricate braid with feathers woven into it. Her corset and woven top highlighted her curvy figure, knowing just the right amount to show to ensure good tips.

"We are also going to order ale for all of us, as well as the dinner special," Grierr assured her. "We are not here for trouble."

She laughed at that, a full out laugh. "The troublemakers always say that." She studied the four men in front of her. "Will you need extra helpings this evening to counter any mana spent?"

They greeted the question with shock. They enchanted their staffs to look like walking sticks or not to even be noticed by passersby. They wore nothing that said they were sorcerers.

"Yes," Thierren stated. He pointed to Tas. "He will. Irons and carbs, he conversed with a dragon the entire flight over from Emi."

Heathyre arched her eyebrows at Tas. "An impressive talent," she stated. "I'll be back with your ale and a basket of bread. Your meals should be ready in twenty."

"Thank you," Grierr said.

Tas followed her retreating figure. A hand on his brought him back to reality. Thierren's eyes were studying him.

"She's... unique," Tas answered. He watched the server carefully as she moved through the patrons and tables. Her laughter came easily, it seemed, yet there was something about her that told Tas she was not a regular being. Yet he could not seem to see what she was. "I can't place it."

"Friend or foe?" Edelberg asked.

"Friend," Tas answered. His ability was unique, he knew that. The ability to know if someone meant harm had saved him many times, just as knowing they could trust someone in a moment of time. It was rare he came across a being where he did not know what they were.

"You can't just do that with every person we meet," Thierren hissed at Tas. He never liked it when Tas flaunted what he could do.

"It has its uses," Edelberg argued. He knew Thierren had never been comfortable with Tas's ability to read people. To be fair, Tas never abused his ability, just in situations where they needed to know if there was danger.

Thierren shot Edelberg a look as Tas studied him. "Yet you didn't stop from telling her I could talk to dragons," Tas pointed out. He looked at Grierr. "What are your thoughts?"

"They are wary," Grierr stated after a quick gaze around the room. He might not be able to read a person like Tas, but he could notice the energy of a room. "But not so much of strangers, but of what could be brought here, of what other troubling news could come."

"Would they withhold information until they know we are not a threat?" Edelberg inquired.

"They want to ensure we are trustworthy and mean no harm toward someone they know," Grierr answered. "Just like we need to know who can be trusted. One word to the wrong person and our mission will be over before we have time to realize what happened."

"Don't give Tas an excuse to use his abilities," Thierren groaned.

It was not so much that he disapproved of what Tas could do. Thierren feared what could happen if people knew what he could do. He knew what people like his family thought of magic, of people with unique abilities, and such. When his parents realized he was a sorcerer, they believed it was a curse, an omen that showed they were not pious enough. His affinity with healing magic helped ease some of their discomfort, but they did not fully accept his life as a sorcerer.

"Just because you are uncomfortable with it doesn't mean he or any of us should stop using what we have been born with," Edelberg argued.

"You don't see me telling you about every herb in your drink or food," Thierren threw out.

"I would hope if you sensed poison, you would," Edelberg argued.

"That isn't the same thing."

"It is. You would warn any of us if there was poison in our meal or drink," Edelberg informed him. "Just like Tas would alert us if someone meant ill toward us."

"Enough," Tas said, his head spinning with the two bickering.

Thierren went to say something, but did not when Tas sent him a look. Tas hoped it was the stress they were all under that was causing the two to bicker. Thierren and Edelberg had always had a playful bickering relationship. But this was different. There was a strange tension between the two. He saw Heathyre getting their tray together and hoped the two would not start bickering before she arrived.

Heathyre made her way back with ale and fresh bread. "What questions are we asking?"

"Before I left for Emi, I heard of a captain who had lost his crew," Tas said carefully. "We would like to speak with him about it."

"Why?" Heathyre inquired as she set down their mugs and breadbasket.

It was Grierr that spoke. "The Council of Magi sent us to look into all the horrible things that have been happening," he answered. He felt the kick under the table he got from Thierren. "I just lost my family to the Black Mist."

"We will add a candle to our shrine to the Great Mother," Heathyre said with a bow of her head. "In the morning, I will leave instructions to where he lives. He is a good man. We have become protective of him and do not take kindly to anyone that will mean to him ill will."

"We will be respectful," Tas assured her. "We are searching for answers and information. Not to punish those that are the victims."

She nodded, then turned and set her watchful gaze on Thierren. "Your friend would not have been able to scan me if I already hadn't done the same to him, nor would I give this information out if I didn't think I could trust any of you."

Thierren tried to speak, but she continued. "I don't know if I trust you," she continued. "Of the four, you have a hesitancy in you that makes you the unknown. I am trusting my friend to you. Do not make me regret that decision."

With that, Heathyre turned and left to head back toward the bar. No one spoke for a few moments.

"I like her," Edelberg finally said.

"You like any female," Grierr answered.

Edelberg just laughed at that. It was true; he loved women; he saw no reason to settle down when he did not have to produce an heir or a spare to continue on his family line. The mood at the table eased, as they all had to chuckle. If that were his purpose at the time to ease the tension, then he would be glad to do it.

"Heathyre!" a regular called. "Tell us a tale."

Heathyre set her tray down as the barkeep nodded to her. Grabbing her lute before heading to the stool in front of the hearth, she sat down and tuned the small instrument. Some nights she would take requests, other nights she would ask the crowd to get a feel for what they wanted. But tonight, she knew the tale she wanted to tell.

"Many listen to the tales that are spread from modern tomes," Heathyre began as she found the notes she wanted. "They forget the tales of old, tales passed down from the stars, from the spirits that roamed the land long before the gods descended from the heavens. I am going to tell you one of these tales."

Tas and Grierr looked at each other, then shared looks with Edelberg and Thierren. They got comfortable in their seats, ready to hear what tale was going to be told.

"Gaiaa had seen her children all leave the heavens to find their place in the world below," Heathyre started. "It was during these early days when a star seemed to fall from the sky. Three separate tribes saw the star fall and went to find where it landed. As it fell, it split into two parts. Two horse tribes went to find the shard that fell on land while a sea-faring tribe went to search for the shard that fell to the sea. The shard that fell to land had split in two upon impact. When the horse tribes found it, each tribe sent four of its people to take each shard to the Holy Shrine of Gaiaa. The shrine sits at the foot of the volcano here in Vulcan.

"While they traveled overland, the sea-faring tribe searched for where the other piece landed. They found it laying in a crater on an island they had never seen before. The chief sent four of his best warriors and scouts to bring the shard to the shrine unknowing the other two tribes were heading there as well. It took months for the journey. The seafaring tribe arrived first. They set-up camp, wanting to wait until the Summer Solstice to present their gifts. Soon, the representatives from the horse tribes arrived. The sea farers shared their meager supplies as the eight travelers had run low on their own. While they waited for the longest day, the twelve bonded over their journey to arrive here. Once the day arrived, they gathered at the door of the shrine and waited to present their gifts to the statue of Gaiaa.

"When it was their turn, they presented the three shards as one group. The statue took form, and a woman emerged from it. She gently motioned for them to stand as she thanked them for her precious gifts. She kissed each on the forehead, giving a blessing to them as well as a gift. From these twelve came the first sorcerers. For many, this is where the tale ends," Heathyre stated.

She took a moment to accept a mug of ale to wet her parched throat. It allowed the patrons to move if they needed to, as well as drinks and food to be refilled. After a few moments, Heathyre picked up her lute and picked up her tale.

"Gaiaa took these three shards back with her to her home," Heathyre began. "Gaiaa stared at the home that had once been filled with laughter and voices. Now it was quiet, as all her children were out finding their purpose. While she was proud of them, she was lonely. Taking the three shards that had once been a star, Gaiaa decided she could form the shards into something more than what they currently were. She breathed life into each one. From each shard, a daughter was born.

"But they were not ordinary children, for they had been once part of the universe. Each would grow to possess an ability that would have leaders and rulers seeking them out for consult. The oldest daughter saw events of the past, allowing her to warn those who came to her to not repeat the mistakes from long ago. The middle daughter saw the present, allowing those to know what path they were currently on. The third daughter saw the future. Yet it was not one future but the different paths a person could take. She became the most sought out of the three sisters. She relished in the praise and adoration she received from those who came to her. The three sisters had once been close and always with each other. The youngest sister did not see that she was pushing her sisters and mother away as her fame spread. It was not until she lost it all did she realize what she had done, but it was too late by then."

With that, Heathyre set her lute down, signifying she was done with the tale. "What happened?" Someone yelled from the crowd.

"That is a tale for another day," Heathyre answered. "And I have drinks I need to serve."

As she headed to the bar, Heathyre turned and nodded to the four sorcerers in the corner. Tas lifted his mug to her before taking a sip.

"You think she told that story because we were here?" Edelberg asked.

Thierren stared at him. He mumbled 'moron' under his breath. Tas elbowed him in the side. "Most likely," Tas answered. "That version is often told; the Prophecy Cult doesn't like it."

"How come?"

Tas shrugged. "They don't really like any version of myths that show discord amongst the Gods, spirits, Demi-gods, or the Fates," Tas said. "Or that is the theory I came up with. To them, everything must be harmonious. Tales of discord could cause questions to be asked."

"Questions can be dangerous," Thierren said softly. He knew that all too well from his own upbringing. "It is late, and we need to be up early if we are to meet with this captain."

#

True to her words, when they came down the following morning for the breakfast that was offered, a note was waiting for them. Tas took it from the innkeeper as they headed into the taproom. The only people there were those that rented rooms for the night. They were treated to bread, eggs, and fresh fruit. Once they were situated with their food and tea, Tas finally opened the note. He raised an eyebrow as the language was not Common. Heathyre was giving a hint as to her origins, yet still revealed nothing.

"Everything all right?" Thierren asked Tas.

"She wrote in the old language," Tas answered. "I have to translate it in my head."

They let Tas translate the note with Grierr helping when he had trouble. Tas and Grierr were better with languages than Edelberg and Thierren. Thierren double checked his medical satchel. If they were going to be walking about the port, he could pick up any supplies he needed. Grierr drew a small map of the port city from memory as he identified where they would need to go.

"Let's finish eating," Tas said as he folded up the note and slid it into his pouch.

The wind of the ocean was freezing as they stepped out of the inn. The port was already bustling as stalls and shops were getting ready for the day. Despite Vulcan being a country with volcanoes, it was not the red hellscape many expected. The country had learned how to live around the destructive forces, using the black stone to build their homes and buildings. Because of this, they made very few buildings of wood. It filled the farms with fertile soil, bringing a bright green to a dark ground. Most towns, cities, and villages did not lie near the volcanoes. Those that did were a good day's walk from them. Dwarven and human stone masons around the volcanoes had built trenches to bring the lava flow toward the ocean as best they could. Geothermal energy created from the volcanoes heated many of the homes.

It was one of Tas' favorite countries to visit. It was a shame that he could not bring his friends to some of his favorite parts, like the hot springs and the observation towers that watched the volcanoes. They pulled their lined cloaks tighter around them as they headed toward the main avenue. It was a ten-minute walk from the inn to the location that was on the note.

"Tas, you're the academic," Thierren began as they walked.

"Says the man who is a healer, medical doctor, and a licensed surgeon," Grierr commented.

Thierren rolled his eyes at his back. "Before I was interrupted, I wanted to know your thoughts on the tale from last night."

"It's the one that they taught us at the academy and most covens tell," Tas commented. "Why?"

"You must have dug deeper," Thierren stated. "You would not be happy with the ending where the cause is unknown. There has to be more."

"He has a point," Edelberg agreed.

"If there is more, and I have searched for it," Tas began. "I have not found it. There is very little surviving material on the Fates of Gaiaa, as they are named in academic circles. People have been searching for what caused the sisters to fall out with each other. What was it that led the youngest to lose control?"

"And nothing?" Grierr inquired. "Isn't that odd?"

"Very," Tas agreed. "But as Thierren pointed out last night, we know a certain group that for centuries has tried to erase any signs of discords among those they feel are above all that."

They were all silent for a moment, then Thierren spoke up. "The Fates are supposed to be guides and some say judges for Gods, spirits, and Demi-gods," Thierren pointed out.

"That is said to be their roles," Tas agreed, curious where Thierren would go with it.

"If the Fates of Gaiaa are no longer a unit, wouldn't that mean the balance was off, that they could not judge those that mis-step?" Thierren asked.

"In theory, yes," Tas agreed.

"So, if they can't judge, could that be why certain beings are out of control?"

Tas stopped walking as he digested what Thierren had just said. He turned and looked at Thierren. Part of him wanted to hug him for what he had just realized. Instead, he could not help but laugh. Edelberg and Grierr had also stopped to watch Tas.

"Did Thierren possibly figure out the answer to one of your questions?" Edelberg asked Tas.

"One that has been driving Tobias and I crazy for the past few months," Tas admitted. "Thierren, what would I do without you?"

"Be poisoned by a healing potion because you weren't paying attention," Thierren answered.

"Well, that is true," Tas admitted. "Remind me to contact Tobias later."

They continued on their way until they came across a street of whitewashed row houses. Each had tiny yards in front of them. Tas went up the front steps of number 15, as he raised his fist to knock the door opened. An average height man stood there; his blonde hair bleached in sections

52

from being outside most of the time. His skin was tan, making his pale colored eyes stand out. He wore a simple woolen tunic and leather pants.

"Heathyre said you would arrive about now," he stated as he opened the door. "I'm Jonah."

"I'm Tas. The men behind me are Grierr, Thierren, and Edelberg." Tas introduced them to him.

Jonah nodded, then stepped aside so they could enter his home. "Did she explain why we want to speak with you?" Tas asked as they entered the small foyer.

"Ay, she did," he answered. He motioned them to follow him toward the back of the house.

He brought them to the kitchen, which was quite cozy. "Tis the warmest room in the house on days like today," the man informed them. "Take a chair. I have tea and coffee beans."

Edelberg asked for coffee while the rest were fine with tea. The man put a kettle on, then went about scooping the beans into a grinding machine.

"Captain Jonah," Tas began.

Jonah stopped him. "I was a captain, but just call me Jonah."

"Not a captain anymore?" Thierren asked.

"Hard to be a captain when you have no ship," Jonah replied, as he finished grinding the beans. "Not sure I'd be able to captain a ship again."

"Did they punish you?" Tas inquired. He knew some dock bosses would not take the loss of ship and goods well.

"No." Jonah poured the ground beans into a cloth, then tied it closed. He placed it into a glass pitcher of sorts. "After what I saw, what I lived through, I don't know if I can ever be in charge of a ship again. Especially not with the seas being as they are."

"How are the seas?" Grierr asked.

"Odd things have been happening," he answered as he watched the kettle. "It's not just here that the stories are coming from, but all around."

"What are the stories saying?" Thierren inquired. Antique maps were framed and hanging on the walls of the room they were in. There were old sea faring tools mixed in with books on the floor to ceiling bookshelves.

"Ships being turned back because they couldn't move further out to the ocean. Tales of sea monsters that forced ships to turn around or captains to abandon ship. They say that the God Taris is angry. There's a lot of that these days. Angry Gods have taken their anger out on us."

"And one of his creatures attacked your ship," Tas stated.

Jonah looked at Tas carefully. "Why do you want to hear my tale?"

"Nothing you tell me will surprise me, not now, not with everything going on," Tas assured him. "The Council of Magi has asked my friends and I to learn about what is going on."

"Are you all sorcerers?"

"Yes," Tas answered. "We are not here to discredit you, but to prevent things like this from happening. We have each witnessed something that has no explanation as to why the Gods would do this."

"Thank you," Jonah stated. He poured the boiling water into the pitcher with the coffee. He set it and a mug in front of Edelberg before getting the mugs and tea for the rest. "I… it still seems a dream."

"Take your time," Tas assured him.

"Do you have any family?" Grierr inquired.

Jonah chuckled at the questions. "Nah, the water is my life. Not fair to raise a family when I spend most of the year on the water," Jonah stated. "I was orphaned and was taken on as a cabin attendant when I was a wee lad. Worked my way up, became a captain, got my ship. Wanted nothing more than that. The ocean, the water, there is freedom to it."

54

"It's how I feel in the air," Tas stated.

Jonah studied the man for a moment. "You're a dragon rider?"

"I am," Tas answered. "There is freedom as you soar through the clouds that I am sure is like how you feel on the waters."

"That is very true," Jonah agreed, and stared into his tankard of water. "The ocean has always been kind to me. I give my blessings when they are due, and I studied the charts of the water and the sky."

"What do you do?" Grierr inquired. From the size of the man's arms, he did not think this was an ordinary angler.

"I deliver goods," Jonah replied. "I sail from Emi all the way to the top of Greedin. I even bring goods to that island of wizards."

The four friends looked at each other. This man knew the water better than the four of them combined. "Tell us what happened, friend," Grierr encouraged. "We will not think you are crazy about whatever happened."

"What good is it to speak of such a thing when nothing will come of it?" Jonah inquired. "This world has gone mad, the Gods fighting their own battles, forgetting about us, the people that serve them, that honor them."

"We are going to end this misery, or try to," Tas said softly. "This chaos, it needs to stop. The gods need to remember what it is like to not be honored by man, but to aid us in return."

"Dangerous words to be spoken at such a time," Jonah noted.

"Any words spoken now can be deemed dangerous if heard by the wrong ears."

Jonah looked at the four men before him. Each was different, not just in how they looked, but in how they came across. "Your other two buddies talk little, do they?"

"We talk when talk is needed," Edelberg stated. "But Tas and Grierr have been doing just fine without our comments."

Jonah studied the frailer of the four who had yet to speak. "You aren't sure about this madness, about this quest thing you are on, but you go because they asked you," Jonah observed. "And now you come here and wonder if I am going to help or just ignore what is really going on in this world. You hope I send you all on your way, because it means that this cannot be real."

"You know nothing of what you speak," Thierren said. He was not sure how this man, a man with no talent, could say such a thing to him.

"I watched a sea monster, a monster that has never been drawn, rear itself out of the dark waters of the ocean," Jonah began. He unrolled the parchment that held the sketch of the creature he saw and showed it to them. "I watched as it ripped my crew apart while I tried to get them to safety. I watched as it all but laughed at me, while it made sure I watched in horror as it devoured the sailors who were more like family than blood could ever be. These Gods, they're done with us, they no longer care if we get hurt in their war. We are just cannon fodder to them."

"How many limbs?" Tas asked as he studied the drawing.

"Nine in total," Jonah answered, a slight shudder running through him as he remembered it all vividly. "You do not see him coming, for his scales are the color of the ocean. The moment he comes out of the water, there is no noise, no rushing of water off of him, not even a wave to show that something has emerged. All becomes quiet and when you finally see him; you know that death has found you."

The table was silent as his words sunk in. "There is no such monster as one with nine limbs," Thierren began, hearing this went against what he had been taught. It warred with his thoughts and beliefs. "What he speaks of is impossible."

"So is a black mist killing my family," Grierr said softly.

"A black mist?" Jonah inquired. "Word of such a thing has trickled down here. It picks its target, leaving some alive and others dead."

"Another scare tactic," Edelberg mumbled. "Just like your monster. Scare the strongest from what they love."

"This is madness," Thierren stated, almost slamming a fist on the table. "They wouldn't all abandon us."

"That it is," Grierr agreed as he stared into his mug. "And a few short days ago, I wanted nothing to do with any of this. I wanted to be left to my grief. But I made a choice, a choice that each of us must make on their own."

"Are you really going to try to end this cursed nightmare?" Jonah inquired as he looked at the water in his mug.

"Yes," Tas answered.

"Then I want to join," Jonah replied.

"Why?" Tas asked.

"When I look out on the water, all I see is blood," Jonah answered. "I hear my men screaming for help. I feel the fear slide over me all over again. I want no other captain to feel this way. I need to find my way again."

"This isn't some simple journey through the woods," Edelberg warned the captain. "We will go up against Gods and the nightmares they throw at us."

"What can you bring to our travels?" Thierren asked. "What we are doing is no easy adventure to brag about later."

"I know the seas, I know the skies," Jonah informed them. "I know routes that are not shown on maps. I might not wiggle my fingers and have something happen, but I have a brain and can use a compass."

Jonah walked to his desk, where he pulled out a series of rolled out parchment. He motioned for them to come and join him. Untying the strings on them, he unrolled maps of the globe. They gathered around his desk to see the map he had laid out on the desk.

"You are going to want to make your way to Greedin," Jonah declared as he studied the map. "This means you will need to make a path across land until you reach Hruan. From there, we could take a ship to Quinsenta. As of the moment, tis the only port that is allowing ships to move from."

"That's a lot of land to travel," Edelberg noted.

"It is if you only follow the known route," Jonah commented. He then pulled from a shelf another rolled up parchment. This was thinner, almost like rice paper. He unrolled it and laid it on one of the maps.

"Where did you get this?" Thierren asked in awe as he stared at what he had marked on the map. Any cult would kill to get their hands on such a map if just to destroy its existence.

"Dreams," Jonah informed him. "This is the path of the original Watchtowers."

"Watchtowers?" Grierr asked. He recognized the symbol from the one etched on the watchtower of Emi.

"What are they?" Edelberg asked, confused about why his friends were staring in awe.

"Nice to know you failed to pay attention in history," Grierr commented.

"Before we were countries, when Tribes roamed the world, Watchtowers marked safe roadways," Tas explained to Edelberg. "They meant that the road was watched and protected. Those traveling would be safe from ambush. However, most of the trails have been lost to time. There are only four known Watchtowers. This map could change all of that."

Grierr studied one trail on the maps. "I know this route," Grierr replied as he traced a finger along a route. "My family used it to escape from the cultist centuries ago."

Jonah nodded. Edelberg looked at the man before them. "You see things that others cannot," Edelberg stated.

"People may not see them, but it does not mean they have vanished completely."

"He would be an asset," Grierr pointed out.

"We would bring a mundane on a journey that could endanger him," Thierren pointed out. "It would be dangerous to consider this."

"Even without him, it is dangerous to consider any of what we are doing," Tas pointed out.

Thierren said nothing as he stormed from the room. Tas watched him leave. "Jonah, I apologize," Tas began.

Jonah held up a hand. "He has the right to voice concerns," Jonah stated. "I cannot wield the power that the four of you have. It would honor me to join your mission, but also understand what dangers that could pose."

"What Jonah can bring to the journey, I feel, outweighs the concerns of him not wielding magic," Grierr stated.

"I agree," Edelberg replied.

"Grier, Edelberg, will you help Jonah get ready?" Tas asked them. "I will meet you at the inn."

Tas then followed the path that Thierren had fled. There were several places in any city or port town that Tas would be able to find him: a library, observatory, the highest hill, or a museum. Tas never used his abilities when it came to locating Thierren for he knew the man would hate if he did. Knowing there was a well-known research library in the area, Tas made his way toward it. He found Thierren sitting on a bench in front of the building.

"Used your ability to find me?" Thierren asked.

"No, just years of knowing you," Tas answered.

Tas was not even sure how to start this conversation. Something was going on with Thierren. He had sensed it since he arrived back at the island. It was as if Thierren resented the fact that he had shown up, that they had all shown up to help Grierr. They sat in silence, watching as people went about their business.

"Are we seriously thinking of doing this?" Thierren asked.

"You were on board back at Grierr's house. Now you are concerned?"

"We are talking about a war with people more powerful than us, which is bad enough," Thierren pointed out. "But now you want to bring on a mere mortal who has no ties to us."

"We need someone who knows the land and the waters," Tas replied. "He does."

"We just met him, and you are recruiting him already."

"He belongs with us."

Thierren glared at his friend. "Because your sight tells you?"

"So that is what this is about," Tas realized. Tas could read people, knew when they were lying or when they were telling the truth. Of the four of them, Thierren had envied the talent, saw it as another gift given to Tas.

"The Great Tas Sturm off on a mission of importance," Thierren replied, with a hint of sarcasm in his tone. "You could do this all on your own. I mean, history will only remember you, anyway. The rest of us will be forgotten. We will fade from history, but they will never forget you, the great Taslan."

"I never asked for any of this," Tas reminded him, trying to keep his temper from spilling out. "If I could, I would give them up."

"That's what makes it worse," Thierren yelled, several heads turned toward where they say. Thierren quieted his voice. "You don't get how lucky you are, how many wish they could do what you do. And yet you would toss it away."

"You are right, it is a gift," Tas commented. "But it is a curse as well."

"How could it be a curse?"

"Because I know you are lying to me, to all of us," Tas stated, turning to face Thierren. "I know you are holding something from us. Something that could kill one of us, if not all of us."

"You know nothing of what you are talking about," Thierren said, his voice coming out harsh.

"Because you tell us nothing!" Tas exclaimed out of frustration. "We have known each other since we were ten and yet what I know of your family is almost that of a stranger."

"Because not all of us come from fairy tale settings," Thierren shot back.

Tas felt the rage build up around him. He could smell the sea air close in around him as he tried to calm down. There were no words that could be spoken to ease the tension. Instead of adding to the fight, he turned and walked away. Tas walked back to the inn. He found Edelberg exiting the main doors as he approached.

"I was just about to come find you," Edelberg stated. "Thierren being an ass?"

"I used my talent to read our newest member," Tas answered.

"Ah," Edelberg sighed. "So, it ruffled Thierren's feather once again. You are important."

Edelberg studied Tas. It had been a while since he saw Tas this furious with someone, especially with Thierren. "What we are about to do is dangerous enough. We don't need infighting or doubts to hinder our progress," Edelberg agreed. He rested a hand on his friend's shoulder. "He might have been the first to arrive at Grierr's, but he didn't want to go. He didn't want to answer the call."

"How do you know?" Tas asked him.

"He told me," Edelberg answered. "He said with him answering the call, it gave his family more power over him."

"He knows more than he is telling us," Tas stated.

"He could, but we cannot do anything about that now," Edelberg advised. "For the moment, we need to focus on what happens in the morning."

"Do we have what we need?"

"Jonah introduced as to some merchants he is friendly with," Edelberg said as he guided Tas into the tavern. "We have all our supplies; Jonah is already plotting a course to Greedin. I left him and Grierr discussing routes. Let us see what he and Grierr have planned for us. Thierren will return when he is calmer."

Chapter 6

Upon Tas returning to the inn, he learned that while they were out, a private room had become available. This allowed them to stay in the private room instead of the communal bunk room. Tas had a feeling that Heathyre had something to do with the arrangements. They covered the table in the center of the room with maps and measuring tools as Grierr and Jonah went over the routes they could take. While purchasing their supplies, most ports had been shut down throughout the continents of Leneo, Corinthia, and the Northern section of Greedin. The risk of sending ships out into the waters was too great a cost at the moment.

    Over a roast, ale, and fresh bread, they discussed the best paths to follow. The routes would have to be overland with the few river or lake crossings they might have to make. Thierren had returned before the food arrived. He apologized to Jonah, who assured Thierren the words did not hurt him. Thierren could help with some routes from the rumors he heard, helping to narrow out more.

    "When do you need to be in Hruan?" Jonah asked Tas as they completed plans.

    "Shortly after the Spring Equinox," Tas answered. "The President is having a discussion of the troubles occurring and wants to make plans on what to do."

"With water routes out of the questions, could we take Dragons?" Edelberg asked. He was not looking forward to having to travel by foot or horse.

"Too much attention," Tas said with a shake of his head as he paced the room. "We don't want to draw attention to our movements."

Thierren was going through his supplies to see if he needed herbs or bandages. "Not drawing attention would be good," Thierren agreed.

"I'm not walking across three countries," Edelberg informed them.

"Fine, we'll carry you in a litter," Grierr stated from the map. He looked up at the red-headed man. "We're taking horses and a carriage, most likely, and it's only one continent at the moment."

"Fun," Edelberg groaned.

"Then you can walk," Grierr suggested as he refilled his mug with water. "I'm sure the horse would be relieved to not have to carry your bulky frame."

Edelberg mumbled a few curses at him. Thierren finished with his pack and walked over to the table. "What route are we thinking?"

"Well, all routes go through Rochleaux," Grierr replied.

"Cutting through Parrin would be the best place to stop for supplies and information," Jonah added, referring to the capital of Rochleaux.

"We can grab the Royal Highway from Parrin to the border of Hruan," Grierr explained. "We don't have to move around mountains, which will save some time."

"We should be careful there," Thierren said gently. He did not want another fight breaking out. Despite not knowing where he sided with things, he knew it was foolish to ignore the rumors he was hearing.

"What have you heard?" Tas inquired as he studied Thierren.

"Nothing really," Thierren answered. "Just whispers, rumors swirling. Emaya has family there. She was worried about them."

"Rochleaux is a pretty calm place," Tas stated. He studied Thierren. He had not been getting much news out of Rochleaux.

"It is," Thierren agreed. "Emaya has been growing concerned the last few months. Communication between her and her family was becoming slower and slower. Their letters would discuss laws that were being passed, but parts of the letters have been censored so Aunt Amelia and she could not see what they were about."

"It matches what I have heard as well," Jonah commented, studying the map. "Some businesses have been complaining of goods taking longer to arrive from Rochleaux, or being limited to how much they can order. Shipments being seized to be searched for anything that could be deemed magic."

"Why?" Tas asked Jonah.

"From what I heard, which are rumors, Rochleaux created a program to register those that fall under their category of Magical. The problem is, shortly after being placed on the list, the people tend to vanish."

"They're cracking down on the magical community?" Edelberg inquired.

"I don't know," Thierren admitted. "I am just telling you what I know. I think we should be careful."

"Thierren is correct," Jonah agreed. "If we are going to pass through the capital, we should be prepared for a hasty exit."

Grierr leaned back in his chair as he thought about the information that had just been revealed to them. "Jonah, are you aware of any shipments that need to be delivered to the capital in Rochleaux?"

"I am sure there are. Why?" Jonah asked as he studied the tall man before him.

"See if you can plan for us to perhaps bring a small shipment by carriage," Grierr suggested. "This would give us purpose as to why we are going into the country without raising too many questions."

"I'll talk to a few of the vendors I know and see what they can set up for us," Jonah replied. "They should be in a tavern near the docks."

"I'll go with him," Edelberg suggested. "We can grab wagons and horses on our way back."

"If the general store is still open, I'll grab last minute supplies," Tas agreed. "This way, we can leave first thing in the morning."

Within moments, the three men left, leaving Grierr and Thierren alone in the room. In a port town, shops and businesses were open later than in most places. Grierr had a feeling that the three would be gone for a little bit. This would give him time to gauge how Thierren was handling their new addition. Thierren had always been wary about trusting newcomers. Grierr suspected it had a lot to do with how he grew up.

"Jonah seems to be a worthy addition to our group," Grierr stated. Thierren just shrugged as he began to collect his things to pack.

"It has been the four of us since our first year at the academy," Grierr noted. "We had other friends, sure, but at the core it was us."

"Your point?" Thierren inquired, looking up from what he was doing.

"That it has been a long time since we have allowed another entry into our small group," Grierr pointed out. "And really, with how I was in Emi, it has just been the three of you. Now there are five of us."

"I'm not jealous," Thierren stated. He did not trust people. His parents were always suspicious of outsiders and what their intentions were.

Anyone that was different was someone to watch. They would frown down upon Jonah, as he was a laborer and different.

"I didn't say you were; I was just saying that it's been a while since we let someone in our group," Grierr replied. "We are all going to have to get used to this, too, being together again for more than just a few days at a time."

"Are you really okay going up against our Gods?" Thierren asked suddenly. His voice filled with confusion.

"They took my family from me," he said in a choked voice. "My entire world changed in that moment. My joy, my heart, it was all taken from me because they felt like it. Why wouldn't I fight against them?"

"So, for vengeance," Thierren inquired. He was not trying to be cruel; he was trying to figure out his own thoughts. He knew Grierr would understand this, or he hoped he would.

"No, I fight so no one else has to endure what I have, so no one else has to bury their children," Grierr answered. "That is why I fight."

Thierren looked at him, not sure what to say. "I do not know where I stand," Thierren admitted. "That frustrates Tas. But I feel at war with myself."

"Thierren, for now you can get away with not knowing why, but at some point, you are going to decide," Grierr informed him. "And that decision has to come from you. It can't be from any of us."

"Those were not the words I wanted to hear," Thierren stated.

"This is war, Thierren. The time to coddle is over."

Grierr turned and headed to his own gear. He had his own bag to go through. Letting himself into the room, he headed toward his bags. Opening the front pack, he pulled out a small sack. He closed his eyes as he felt the weight of it. It contained his wife's favorite pendant, a toy soldier of his son, a stone that Rowan had found and treasured, and other reminders of what he once had. He slipped the sack back into the pocket when he heard the door open. Thierren slipped in without saying a word. When Tas returned with Edelberg and Jonah, the tension between Grierr and Thierren still hung in the air. Tas looked at Grierr who just gave a quick shake of his head. They would talk about it later.

"We have goods to bring," Edelberg informed them. He slapped Jonah on the back, causing the ship's captain to stumble forward. "His friend is sending word to his contact in the city that the goods will come by wagon. We have a signed letter from him stating we are employed by him to bring the goods. And Tas could secure enough to get us to the capital."

"Then I say early to sleep, so we are up before the sun," Grierr stated.

All agreed. Jonah would meet them at dawn near the stables attached to the tavern. He bid them goodnight before heading to his own home. Grierr rolled up the maps and placed them in their holder before he finished packing his things. Edelberg was singing as he double checked his own belongings. Soon, they were done with their chores and headed to the bunks to catch sleep.

#

Before dawn, the five men made their way to the stable where the horses and wagons were waiting. Heathyre stood there as well. She had been talking quietly with Jonah as the four emerged from the inn and headed to the stables. After giving Jonah a hug, Heathyre walked toward Tas. He was surprised when she handed him a large basket.

"Fresh bread, cheese, and salted meat," Heathyre informed him. "I included names of people to trust in Rochleaux, and places to avoid."

"Thank you."

"The road ahead of you will not be easy," she warned. "But I believe the stars are right and this group could be what we need."

"What else do the stars say?" He asked.

She smiled more to herself than to him. "Words you are not ready to hear yet," she said. "Be safe."

Tas watched her walk back into the tavern. She had to be one of the strangest yet most sincere people he had ever met. He walked over to one of the wagons with the basket of food and placed it with the rest of their supplies. They had three wagons filled with goods to be delivered. Edelberg would take the lead wagon with Grierr in the back. Thierren was taking the middle wagon. Jonah would ride with Edelberg in case they ran into trouble with their route. Leaving Tas to float between the other two wagons. He was not sure how receptive Thierren was going to be to him, so he would start with Grierr.

The port town was just waking up. The bakers were already firing up the ovens, as well as the blacksmiths. The docks were becoming alive as ships were getting ready to fish along the shores. They headed onto the main road that would bring them out of the town. Their final destination would be the country of Hruan, which was a good two-week ride ahead of them if the weather held out. From there, they would either take a ship to Quinsenta or Tas would call Bart to get them. No one was sure if Emi and Vulcan were the only two countries hit.

Around noon, they stopped for lunch and to let the horses rest for a bit. They all needed to stretch and move around or they would be stiff when night fell. Edelberg got out some bread and cheese for lunch while Tas brought the horses to a stream. He tied them to a branch, giving them enough room to walk around and eat the grass. Jonah pulled out of the map of the continent of Leneo. He marked where they were and then placed a star to where they headed.

"We have about thirty leagues before we hit the border of Vulcan and Rochleaux," Jonah noted.

"And in plain speak, that is what?" Thierren asked.

"90 miles," Grierr answered. "It's going to take us about three to four days to get to the border if we don't push hard on the horses."

Tas studied the map. "It should only take three days to get to the border of Rochleaux and Hruan once we leave the capital."

"We will need more supplies there, possibly trade in the horses," Grierr added. "We can also learn about anything major that is going on in the other kingdoms."

Jonah calculated the distance from Parrin to the capital in Hruan.

"It should be another six days to get from Parrin to our destination in Hruan," Jonah answered. "If we hit bad weather, I know a few routes that will get us to Parrin with little issue."

"It's early spring. The weather should be mild," Thierren pointed out.

"And Emi shouldn't have had a major ice storm this late in the year," Edelberg reminded Thierren. He then looked at Jonah. "I can help with some of the routes once we near Rochleaux."

Jonah nodded as he rolled up the map and tucked it away. He bit into the bread before he spoke again. "You each have accents," Jonah noted. "Edelberg I can place. Friesen?"

"Yes," Edelberg answered, impressed. "You do a lot of runs to Friesen?"

"My ship was one of the few that could handle the Strait of Gaiaa," Jonah answered. "Friesen is a beautiful kingdom."

"That it is," Edelberg agreed. He then motioned to Tas. "Tas, or Taslan, is from Quinsenta if you didn't figure that out since he talks to dragons. Grierr comes from Emi and Thierren hales from Greedin."

"How did you all meet?" Jonah inquired, though he knew what the answer might be.

"We all attended the Academy of Sorcery," Tas said. "Grierr and I were roommates. We met Edelberg in our alchemy class, and Thierren we met in a history course our first year. We roomed together throughout the rest of school."

"And you remained friends all this time?" Jonah asked in awe. The four nodded. "I am envious of that."

"Why?" Thierren asked. He did not understand how a man who traveled the world would be envious of friendship. "You've explored the world."

"Which means little time for placing down roots," Jonah pointed out as he bit into a piece of cheese. "I lost what friends I had when my ship was torn apart. Even then, I might have known some of them for only a few years. A sailor's life can be very transient."

"And you would prefer roots?"

Jonah chuckled at the question. "Before the attack, I would roll my eyes at such a question," he admitted. "I had everything I wanted. A good ship, good sailors, contracts waiting to be filled. The attack, it took all of that from me. Now I have nothing. No ship, no crew, and there are no contracts because no one will risk the waters out of fear of what other creatures are lurking. That is not such a life to live."

They were all quiet for a few moments. "Coming with us gives you purpose again," Thierren realized.

"It allows me to help ensure that no captain will have to know what it is like to lose their ship, their crew to a monster," Jonah replied. "Even if we fail, at least I will die knowing that I did not sit back, that I tried to help. That's better than sitting at the tavern day in and day out with no direction what to do now."

"Wise words," Tas stated.

"You know why I am here. Why are each of you doing this?" Jonah inquired. He knew Heathyre had trusted the four men, or she would not have sent them to him. This was only the start of their journey, and he knew little about each of them.

"My reason is the same as yours," Grierr answered. "I lost my family to the black mist. No one should know what it is like to bury their children, their wife."

"You have my deepest sympathy," Jonah replied, with a slight bow of his head. "Though no words will ever heal the grief you feel."

"The Council of Magi asked Tas and me to look into the rumors of the black mist, of what is going on," Edelberg answered. "The more we looked, the more we heard. We both knew there was no walking away from this. We have to do something."

"And you?" Jonah asked Thierren.

"I lost my aunt to the black mist," Thierren answered. "I want answers. But at war with what we are going to do, anyway."

"It is good to question," Jonah noted. "Sometime the one that doubts, that questions, helps the rest see a larger picture."

Thierren stared at him in surprise. "I keep hoping that there is a way to solve this that isn't a war that will reshape our very world," Thierren admitted. "I also struggle with what my family will do if they learn of my involvement and with what I feel is the right path."

"When I was a young captain, I had a sailor who you remind me of," Jonah informed him. "He joined my ship because he wanted to explore the world before he decided if he should follow the path his family laid out for him or if he should follow his own path. He had asked me before he left my ship if I could decide for him. He worried about displeasing his family and what the decision would do to him. Maybe I should have, but what I know is at some point we must make our own choices."

"And now you sound just like the rest of them," Thierren groaned.

Jonah laughed at that. "Then I am honored to sound as wise as the likes of you."

Thierren looked at Jonah for a moment. "What happened to the sailor?"

"He chose the path his family wanted, and he regretted that decision but would not turn back from it. It changed him. I no longer recognized the man he once had been."

#

They arrived in Parrin during a spring rainstorm on the first day of the month of Saltus. The Spring Equinox would be in two weeks. Stable hands rushed to get the horses into stalls while Tas paid for their keep. They hurried into the local inn, where straw was scattered across the stone floors to keep the mud and water at bay. The innkeeper noticed them and approached them with a smile.

"Come, we have fires going. Stew is bubbling," the innkeeper told them. "There is a drinking room in the back if you wish some ale to go with the food."

"Maybe later tonight," Grierr answered. "We need rooms for one, maybe two nights?"

"Let me see what I have. I'm Harold," the innkeeper replied. "This storm has caught many by surprise."

They followed the older man to the large desk, where a book sat in the center. A roll of thunder shook the building. He ran a finger over the pages to see what rooms were still open. "There is the bunk room," he noted. "I also have two adjoining rooms that share a small living area."

"Washroom?" Edelberg inquired. He would kill for a bath at this moment. They were all muddy and in need of baths after several days on the road.

"This one has its own as well," Harold answered. "Each year I try to update a bit more. I have two suites with indoor plumbing and at least a public washroom on each floor."

"That's impressive," Grierr admitted. "We will take the room. If we need it for longer?"

Harold flipped through some pages. "You can have it for the week, if need be," he told them. "I'll put a hold on it for now. If you need it, you have it. If you don't, just let me know."

"That's reasonable," Tas agreed. He handed him a bag of coin. He was handed two sets of keys. Tas took one and Edelberg took the other.

"Stew will be on all day," Harold informed them. "Dinner starts at 6 and goes until 10. The kitchen in the drinking room serves basic fare until midnight. If you want laundry service, leave the bag outside the door in the morning. Breakfast is from dawn until nine in the morning. It's basic fare, but it will give you a good start to the day. I take it you settled up with the stable already?"

"We did," Tas answered.

"Then I will let them know what rooms to put your things in."

"We need to purchase some supplies where are the best places for that?" Grierr inquired.

"The town square," Harold replied. "That is two blocks north of here. You will find your basic needs there and more. For the horses, you can talk to the stable hands and then can get you whatever you want."

"Thank you," Grierr replied.

They headed toward the stairs, then went up to the third floor. Their room was at the end of the hall. Tas opened the door, letting them into a small living area. There was a small table that sat four, a short wooden couch, and two chairs situated around the stone fireplace. A newer looking door led into the washroom complete with toilet, sink, and tub. The two bedrooms each had two bunk beds and then one full size bed. Everything looked relatively clean for the most part.

"Grierr, Thierren, and Jonah," Tas began. "Why don't you three stay here? You can dry up and look over the map. Make a list of what we might need. Edelberg and I will go look at the square and see about gathering supplies."

"You won't hear me complaining," Thierren stated, relieved that he would not have to go out in the rain.

"That's a first," Edelberg mumbled. He pulled on a fresh cloak, then followed Tas out of the door.

Tas dragged Edelberg out of the room before he could start in on Thierren. Jonah went to the fireplace to get a fireplace going. Grierr and Thierren both grabbed dry clothes and went to the second room to change. Neither cared about changing in front of the other, as they had shared a dorm for so many years that it was not unusual for them. Once in dry clothes, Grierr took over Jonah's spot by the fire so the sea captain could change into dry clothes. They hung their wet clothes on the hooks about the hearth so they could dry from the heat of the fire.

"Edelberg has been a bit on edge since we left Emi," Grierr commented.

"We've all been on edge," Thierren replied.

He did not want to get into a conversation about Edelberg right now. The two had a huge fight a few months ago. Both had said things that could not be forgotten. For Thierren, it had diminished the level of trust he had for Edelberg. Thierren was not ready to forgive Edelberg for what he had said.

"You're closing yourself off from us again."

Thierren nodded. "I have a lot of thoughts I need to sort through," he answered.

Grierr understood what he meant. Of the four of them, Thierren could become overwhelmed with emotions and thoughts. This had led to massive panic attacks back in school. One way he learned to cope was to take a step back and work through his thoughts, his emotions, then when he could grab one of them to talk to. It was often Tas, Grierr, or their other friend, Kaidan.

Jonah came out with his own wet clothing to hang. As he was hanging up his items, they heard a loud commotion from downstairs. The three looked at each other, unsure of what to do. Without a word, they each made themselves busy in the rooms, making it clear they had just arrived and were settling in. Thierren took the moment to find a well-concealed place to stash their staves and anything that would shout out they were sorcerer. When Jonah noted what he was doing, he helped Thierren conceal the items. Once hidden, Thierren cast a charm so that the items, if found, would appear like regular items or would simply blend into the hiding spot.

The loud pounding on their door had them taking deep breaths. It was Jonah who answered so that Grierr could activate a rune that would make people see him as being shorter than he was.

"Yes?" Jonah asked as he opened the door to see three soldiers standing there.

The other doors opened, and occupants were being escorted out of their rooms in a rough manner.

"We are here to do an inspection. All occupants must report downstairs," a soldier informed them. "Grab nothing. Leave all of your belongings here."

Jonah, Thierren, and Grierr followed the soldiers down the stairs and into chaos. Grierr was the first to notice the captain, who seemed to have some difficulty keeping control of the patrons of the inn. He motioned to Thierren to look. Thierren nodded, then spotted Harold. Slowly, the trio moved to where the innkeeper was standing.

"They are here claiming to look for anyone that is deemed magical," Harold informed them in a low voice. "The list for who qualifies keeps getting longer and more ridiculous."

Thierren looked around the rooms. "Could we open the tap room and put families and those staying over in that room?" Thierren asked Harold. "Then those that came into the tavern for a meal or drink can stay in this room?"

Harold studied the trio. "Let me speak to the captain."

The inn keeper made his way to the captain. They watched as he talked with the captain; it was an animated discussion. It appeared the captain was not happy with suggestions about how to organize things but saw it was a solid plan. Quickly, he began to give orders to his soldiers on how to separate the people in the tavern.

Thierren noted a man sitting on a stool with a bloody nose and bruising around his eye. Not thinking, he went right to the man to help him. Soldiers grabbed him by the arms.

"He is injured," Thierren protested.

"And why are you concerned?" A soldier snapped.

"I'm a doctor," Thierren stated. "I swore an oath to aid those in need."

The soldiers looked at each other. One let go of him and went to speak to the captain. He returned in a few moments. "If you have a medical bag, I will escort you to retrieve it," the soldier informed Thierren. "We will set up a room for you to treat any that need it. But those that resisted us will go last on the list and you are only to patch them up."

Thierren nodded. He was shoved forward as the soldier followed him back to the stairs. He knew that Grierr and Jonah were watching him to make sure he was safe. The soldier stayed close to him as Thierren entered their rooms and grabbed his bag that contained what he needed to do a quick medical exam.

"I need to inspect it," the soldier informed him.

Thierren handed him the bag, warning him to be careful. The soldier just rolled his eyes as he opened the leather satchel. He took the items out with some care, placing each on the table. They closely examined each item before the soldier motioned to Thierren that he could pack his bag up. Once Thierren finished, they escorted him back downstairs to a small private dining room. The captain was standing there.

"We have secured you a room," he told Thierren. "As well as some of my soldiers to assist you."

"You are too kind," Thierren said. He knew very well the soldiers were there to watch him.

Chapter 7

Tas and Edelberg were mentally exausted from dealing with the shopkeeper. It was quite obvious from the few hours they spent ordering supplies that there was more going on in Rochleaux than the rumors had led them to believe. The Lord Chancellor was keeping a close eye on everything: contracts, inventories, names of those who bought massive quantities of certain things, wagon and carriage rentals, animal feed. It was not just the magical community he was locking out. He was offering rewards to citizens if they passed on any information about a citizen being magical. Of course, if a citizen knew of someone who met the requirements and did not tell, they would also be punished for not telling. The Royal Family had all but vanished. Some whispered that they were prisoners in their homes. Silently, the two men walked back to the inn. On other trips, they would meander, checking in shops for different things they each might want on their journey.

When they turned the corner to the inn, they saw an entire patrol out front. The frazzled looking inn keeper was hurriedly talking to a soldier. Edelberg and Tas approached.

"Reasons for approaching?" A guard inquired.

"We are staying here," Tas answered.

"They are guests, their names are in the book that your captain has," Harold answered from where he stood near the door.

The guard studied them for a moment. "Enter, but you are to report to the captain to confirm your identity."

Tas nodded and headed into the inn, with Edelberg following. They spotted Grierr and Jonah standing in the doorway that led into the dining hall. All those who were staying in the tavern had congregated there, either by force or for comfort. Grierr spotted them. His shoulders relaxed as he motioned them to follow him toward the fireplace.

"What is going on?" Tas asked.

"Inspection," he answered. "They arrived about an hour ago. They took the book and are going room by room."

"What are they searching for?" Edelberg asked.

"Anything that can be used as a tool used for magic," Grierr replied. He saw one of the kitchen helpers enter with a tray of steaming soup. "There is a young mother in the corner with a toddler and baby."

"I'll bring warm milk and I believe we have some cookies in the back to keep the young one happy," the helper said. "Anyone else?"

"They took her husband out."

"Harold will see to her," the helper told him. "Your friends have returned."

"This is Ivy," Grierr introduced her to them.

"Tell your other friend the two he sent to the kitchen are now resting. Both had a full bowl of broth and the tea he sent."

"We will pass on the word," Grierr promised.

"You've been busy," Tas replied as he realized that Jonah, Grierr, and Thierren had indeed been busy while Tas and Edelberg had been gone.

"Ivy and a few of the kitchen staff have been helping to keep everyone calm, or as a calm as possible," Grierr answered. "They had arrived shortly before the guards did, so they have been getting food and warm drinks going."

"Where's Thierren?" Tas asked.

"He worked out a deal with the captors to tend to the injured," Grierr replied. "The soldiers aren't too gentle in their interrogation technique."

It was then they heard Thierren yelling. Tas looked at Grierr who nodded for him to go. Tas hurried down the hall where he saw Thierren arguing with guards. An older man lay on the floor, trying to get up as a soldier examined a crutch.

"That is not a magic staff!" Thierren was arguing with the captain.

"And are you an authority on magic staffs?" The captain inquired.

"No, but it is obvious to anyone that this man needs it to walk," Thierren said. He saw Tas enter. "Can you help him up?"

Tas nodded and headed over to where the old man lay. A guard stepped in front of him, blocking his path.

"We have not searched you," the guard informed him.

"He is registered to my suite," Thierren told the guard.

"Then why wasn't he here when we arrived?" The captain asked.

"Because another companion and I were getting travel supplies," Tas answered. "We only just returned a few moments ago."

"And you are part of this one's medical team?"

"Yes," Tas answered. He was not sure what Thierren had told the captain, but he would go with it.

"He can assist," the captain informed his guard.

The man moved away, allowing Tas to assist the man. He kneeled next to the old man, who, up close, did not look as fragile as he appeared to be. Tas softly informed the man what he was going to be doing. With help from the old man, he could get him on his feet and sitting on the bench.

"What is his name?" The captain asked Thierren.

"I'm sure if you check the guest log, you find he is in there," Edelberg said as he entered the room. He had heard the conversation from the hallway.

"And who are you?" The captain asked, staring at the redheaded man as he entered. Red hair was not a common color in Rochleaux.

"Edward," Edelberg answered. "You will find my name in the book along with theirs."

The captain eyed him, but instead of arguing, he looked at the book. "Which room did you say you were all in?"

"Here, let me help," Edelberg answered as he walked over. "Keeping names and room numbers straight has to be daunting."

"You do not know," the captain grumbled.

Edelberg touched the book, going through the log until he found their room. "Right here," he pointed.

"Ah yes, one of the updated suites," the captain answered. "I will need your paperwork just to verify."

"Of course, I have all of ours right here," Edelberg informed him as he reached into his side satchel to pull-out slips of paper. "I'm the organized one of the lot, so I'm always stuck holding the paperwork."

While he talked with the captain, Thierren could approach the older man, finding out where his injuries were from the fall. Thierren glanced at Tas, both realizing that Edelberg was using one of his talents on the captain. Tas gave room for Thierren to work while he also monitored Edelberg. They were playing a dangerous game right now. Edelberg rarely used his talents unless he saw no way out or if it was the only way to get information. He had always said that even if he were the heir to the throne, he would have abdicated, for no leader should be able to persuade a person's mind to their will.

"I believe we are all set, gentlemen," the captain finally spoke. "I will let the innkeeper know we are done with our inspections."

"Thank you," Edelberg answered.

No one in the room spoke as the guards left. Shortly after, Grierr entered with a frantic-looking woman about their age.

"Grandfather," she gasped as she rushed to his side.

He patted her hand. "I'm fine, dear," he assured her. "These kind young men helped me."

"We can never repay you," she told him.

"No payment is needed," Thierren told her. "I would suggest getting him out of the country."

"You can tell he is special," she smiled.

"Just because I know things doesn't mean I'm a 'magical being' or whatever our Lord, whatever he calls himself, says," the old man grumbled.

"Even if we could leave, we have no money to get us out, nor a visa to allow us past the borders," she answered.

Edelberg looked at Tas, then at Thierren. "How many are we talking?"

"The two of us, my husband, and my daughter," she answered. "I'm Amira and this old grump is Kade."

"A pleasure," Thierren replied. "The guards did no more damage. I have some ointments and teas that will help with your aches and mobility."

"Are you staying in the inn?" Edelberg asked Amira.

"Yes, he had an appointment with a surgeon this afternoon," Amira informed them.

"I take it the surgeon tried to sell you on a procedure that won't help," Thierren guessed.

"It will kill me before it would help me," Kade commented. "Knew he was a fake the moment we entered his place."

"Your husband and daughter?"

"Are being entertained by another family in the taproom," she replied.

"Give me a few minutes," Edelberg replied. "Tas, can I use your globe?"

"Does one of your brothers have the receiver?" He asked.

Edelberg nodded. "Yes."

"He's going to help us," Kade stated to his daughter. "They all are."

"I am enjoying the helpless old man act you played earlier," Thierren informed the old man as he closed his medical satchel.

"Most people see a cripple and assume we are all idiots, so I go with it," Kade replied. "Drives my daughter crazy as well."

"How is your friend going to help us?" Amira asked the gentleman.

"My name is Tas. The man treating your father is Thierren," Tas replied. "Our friend Edelberg knows some people across the border in Friesen. I have a device that will allow him to communicate with them to find out if he can, in fact, help you."

"You four also put on quite an act," Kade chuckled. "I'd like to know that trick your friend did that had the guards leaving."

"You wouldn't believe us if we told you," Grierr replied, reminding them he was in the room. "Since you two have everything under control, I am going to check on the innkeeper and others. I'll send her husband and daughter to you as well."

"If they have roughed any more up, send them to me," Thierren called to Grierr. Grierr nodded as he left the room.

"How long have things been like this?" Tas asked the father and daughter.

"Things became odd roughly a year ago," Amira replied. "The parliament was passing laws that were giving the Lord Chancellor more and more control. We saw less and less of our royal family. Six months ago, there was a protest as laws restricted those that were deemed magical creatures. There was also a demand to see the royal family. The Chancellor, well, he said he was speaking for them, that he was only following their royal decrees."

"Doesn't sound like them at all," Tas stated. He knew a few members of the Royal Family; his brother had once dated the middle daughter when they were younger. He was adding more questions to ask when they reached Hruan.

"It doesn't," Kade agreed. "After the protest, crack downs began happening. Curfews, closing the borders, limiting how much can be purchased at a time."

"Then the roundups," Amira continued. "The decree claimed they were rounding up those they deemed as 'magical creatures' to be placed in a safe location due to what has been occurring in the world. They said it was preemptive measures so that others would not harm members of the magical community."

"Rumors are traveling faster than thought," Tas commented.

"Whatever is happening in Greedin is seeping out to involve us all," Kade stated. He noted a pained look on the one name Thierren's face.

"I take it no one hears from anyone they have rounded up," Tas inquired.

"No," Amira answered. "Anyone trying to aid anyone deemed magical or caught protesting the restrictions also vanishes."

A gentle knock alerted them to someone entering. Jonah came in with a tray of food. "Forgive the intrusion, but Harold wanted to make sure we were all fed," Jonah explained. "I am Jonah."

"He is traveling with us," Tas informed him. "Jonah, what do you know of the restrictions on goods here in Rochleaux?"

Jonah sighed for a moment. "It should not affect Rochleaux like the coastal countries," he stated. He looked at Amira. "Did the restriction on goods start at the same time as the decrees or later?"

Tas gave Amira a reassuring nod. "I could understand the restriction on how many supplies can be bought at a time after there was a surge of people trying to cross the borders," Amira stated.

"I assume that with shipping at a standstill, the Rochleaux caravans have been in high demand?"

"Yes," Kade stated. "Recruiters were going to every able body to help with new shifts and routes."

Jonah nodded as he thought. "This would mean profit for the kingdom, as well as showing a helping hand to neighbors," Jonah stated.

"Your point?" Thierren asked as he sorted through his supplies.

"That if the kingdom is picking up the shipping slack, then placing a restriction on their own people for goods makes little sense," Jonah answered.

"It's on all caravans now," a deep voice stated.

"Amos," Amira said as she went to her husband. Their daughter went to her mother easily. "This is my husband Amos and my daughter Lyra. These men are..."

"Helping those they can," Amos noted. "The taller one is ensuring everyone is eating in the dining room."

"You said they were restricting caravans now?" Jonah asked Amos.

"Jonah was a ship captain," Tas explained.

"Then I am sorry for whatever horrors you have seen," Amos told him. "To answer your question, about two months ago, they handed the restrictions out to the warehouses. I run one. Any caravan that was passing through our borders was to be sent to the nearest military barrack. If Rochleaux was a stop on their route, then they would need to quarantine for two weeks."

"Quarantine from what?" Thierren asked incredulously. "Despite all the other hells out there, there is no plague or pestilence out there that would call for such a thing."

"I'm going to take a guess and say that it's to make sure that whoever is driving the caravans is not on their list of who needs to be protected," Tas theorized.

"That is our thought as well," Amos agreed.

"Restricting caravans will decrease what you are earning," Jonah noted.

"Could the Lord Chancellor be trying to ensure that there are enough supplies for rougher times?" Thierren suggested. He was trying to find a logical explanation that wasn't the Chancellor trying to take over the kingdom.

"Trust me when I say that is not an issue," Amos replied. "You are asking the same questions we have been asking for months now. Some have dared to bring it before the Parliament."

"What happens to them?" Thierren asked.

"You don't hear from them again."

Their conversation was interrupted when Lyra shyly walked over to them. "Grandpa said you made him better," she said to Thierren.

Thierren crouched down in front of her. "I did," Thierren assured her. "But I have a huge favor to ask of someone who could help me."

"I could help," Lyra said.

"Can you make sure that Grandpa uses his crutches and takes the tea I told him to use each night before bed?"

"I can!" Lyra exclaimed.

"Now this is very important," Thierren said in a very serious tone. "He needs to drink all the tea. So could you make sure he does that, because I know sometimes we don't always enjoy taking all our medicine?"

"Grampa hates having to take medicine," Lyra whispered to Thierren.

"Well then, I guess asking you for help is perfect because I'm sure you can help him take it."

Lyra nodded her head before she ran to her grandfather. "I'm going to help you."

"That you are," he chuckled.

The next person who came through the door was Edelberg. He closed the door behind him and put a ward to conceal what they were talking about.

Tas looked at Edelberg. "Well?"

"They will leave with us in the morning," Edelberg answered. "When we get to the cross-roads Micah will wait for us to bring them to Friesen."

"You mean... we can leave?" Amira asked in shock.

"Yes, I handed the letter to your husband. It has my family's seal on it. Anyone who confiscates it will declare war," Edelberg told her. "My brother Micah is the one who will meet you."

"Do I want to know what he was doing near here?" Tas asked.

"The same thing you have been doing but for the royals," Edelberg answered.

"Micah is one if Edelberg's older brothers," Thierren explained to the family.

"He's what, seventh in line?" Grierr asked.

"No, he's down to 8th because of Nora's son," Edelberg reminded Grierr.

"Then who is ninth?"

"Micah adopted a baby he rescued on his last mission," Edelberg answered. "That's what got me down to tenth."

"I'm going to meet a prince?" Lyra asked in awe.

"Yes, you are," Edelberg informed her. "He's my older brother. We're two years apart. He is going to go with your parents and grandfather to a pretty neat spot to take a vacation."

Grierr motioned for Amira and Amos to follow him. Tas joined them as well. "Micah will have his own men with him, but you won't see them," Grierr explained quietly. "He runs intelligence for Friesen."

"Where will we be going?" Amos asked.

"You will stay at one of the Royal Properties for a few weeks to recover, then you are going to be going to Gastion," Grierr explained. "They are already taking in those fleeing from here."

"How do you know all this?" Tas asked.

"Edelberg caught me up when he was done with the call," Grierr answered. He turned to Amira and Amos. "Do not worry about supplies, but if you have any animals, we need to know so we can make preparations for them."

Amira looked at her husband, who nodded. "We brought our valuables with us," she admitted. "We feared what would happen and wanted to be ready in the event they tried to take my father."

"We can never repay you for this," Amos told them.

"No payment is needed," Tas assured him. "We took a vow to help those in need or in trouble."

"Now, why don't we eat then? I think someone might do a story time after the meal," Jonah suggested.

#

It was near midnight when the five of them were alone in their suite. They moved Amira and her family to a room closer to theirs. Thierren was pacing the main room as Edelberg poured them drinks, Grierr pouring himself spring water instead of alcohol.

"None of this makes any sense," Thierren began. "How have things fallen apart this quickly over such a large area? Why separate the magic population?"

Tas, who had finished writing a letter to the Council of Magi, cracked his neck before speaking. "According to the mighty Lord Chancellor, the belief is that if all those with magic are in one spot, then the threat to the general population will be less."

Thierren stared at him, but it was Jonah who spoke. "That's... barbaric."

"It is," Thierren agreed. "But it shows that the Chancellor is frightened. He believes the only threat at this moment is those in our community. If he groups them together, then perhaps he believes the mundane is safe. He also is using that fear to gain more power and control."

Everyone in the room looked at him. "But it's not just the magical community," Tas argued.

"I'm aware," Thierren agreed. "However, the belief is that it is for the greater good. In his mind, a few lives lost are easier to explain than lives of thousands."

"How can you even say that?" Grierr stated, staring at Thierren as if he did not know him. "My family, what happened to Jonah? None of them would fall under magical creatures, yet my wife and children are dead. Jonah's crew is dead."

"Our enemies will say that they are…"

"Don't you dare say that they are casualties in a greater game," Jonah snapped, surprising everyone. "I am sick of hearing that my crew died because of some greater thing. I am sick of hearing that their sacrifice will grant them eternal peace in the land of the dead. What about my peace? I close my eyes and I hear their screams; I see them being ripped apart; I hear them pleading for my help while it held me as a prisoner. I watched them be slaughtered. I had to tell their loved ones they were dead. So don't you dare say that they are casualties, and the Gods will honor them. It's your way of trying to ease your own soul, but it does nothing for those grieving, those mourning."

Thierren stared at him. He then looked at his friends, his gaze falling on Grierr's last. Grierr looked him in the eye, and he waited for his friend to defend him. "My wife is dead," Grierr stated. "My children are dead. My line has been hunted for a thousand years because a religious cult deemed us an abomination. I have been told all my life that their deaths were a sacrifice for the greater good. Death is not a greater good when it comes before you are old. Burying a two-year-old is not something I should take with pride or find peace in."

"And starting a war against the Gods we should take lightly?" Thierren threw back. "A war where we will sacrifice countless lives in order to save the innocent?"

"We did not start this war, they did," Edelberg declared as his fist slammed on the table.

Chapter 8

They left at dawn, Amos carried a still sleeping Lyra, while Grierr helped Kade down the stairs. Jonah and Edelberg had been the first up to ensure their supplies and wagons would be ready. Both Amos and Jonah pulled in some favors the night before to get what they would need for the journey that Amos' family would be taking. It would be a two-day ride to the Crossroads. Once there, they would either meet Micah or wait for him to arrive. Tas was hoping Micah would pass on the information to him they could use. It had been common for the two to share information when they learned they were working on a similar assignment.

No one spoke as they moved through the quiet streets of the capital. They had made a small bed in the back of the second carriage for Lyra to sleep in. Edelberg would ride in that wagon in the event they came across any trouble. Grierr and Tas were in the lead wagon with Jonah and Thierren on horses to track the path up ahead.

"I don't want to talk about it," Tas had said once they were on their way. Grierr nodded, and they rode in silence.

Once Lyra was awake, the moodiness that still lingered from the night before was forgotten. Instead, it was replaced with Lyra going from wagon to wagon, asking a million questions, and having the sorcerers patiently answer each of her questions. One could find even Thierren entertaining her.

"He is really annoying me," Edelberg mumbled at one point.

"Edelberg," Grier said gently.

"What I'm just saying is he either figures out what he wants or he's going to piss one of us off bad enough that we kick him out of the party."

"Harping about it will not help," Grierr reminded him.

Tas let out a sigh as he watched Thierren make flowers dance around Lyra while they had stopped for lunch. "At Hruan," Tas said finally.

Both Grierr and Edelberg turned to look at him. "Why then?" Grierr asked.

"We are meeting with a few people to discuss intelligence," Tas explained. "Most likely, from that information, an unofficial summit will be called in Quinsenta. Once we are in Quinsenta and behind doors discussing what is going on, there will be no turning back for any of us. This gives us all the time to sit down and talk about what's going on."

"And what if he goes with his parents? We just let him?" Edelberg asked.

Grierr shot Edelberg a nasty look as he saw Tas's features harden. He noticed scents of the ocean as if they were at a beach somewhere. Tas was angry.

"Then it is his choice," Tas answered. "I would rather he leave us before we reach Quinsenta then betray us once we are started."

"Do you think he would betray us?" Grierr asked Tas.

"No, but Edelberg does," Tas said and walked away.

Grierr turned and looked at Edelberg. "You are going to have to learn to deal with whatever has always made you distrust Thierren."

"You honestly don't know what it is?" Edelberg asked Grierr.

"No, enlighten me." Grierr never knew how Edelberg's mind worked or why he held a grudge toward someone. He had given up figuring it out back in school.

"It's because of how he ignores what is right in front of him because he believes too much of his own parent's bullshit to realize that Tas is utterly in love with him. That his career, his values are more important. That the world is crumbling around him, but he's so self-centered all he cares about is himself!"

With that, Edelberg stormed away, leaving Grierr speechless. It was not the revelation about Tas's feelings; he had known since their days back in the Academy. What surprised him was Edelberg.

"Are you all still furious with me?" Thierren asked Grierr. He had watched both Edelberg and Tas storm away.

"And if we are?"

"What I said last night, it was out of line," Thierren answered.

"Are you saying that because you mean it, or you know it's what we want to hear?" Grierr asked.

"Look, I know I screwed up. I know the bullshit I said is exactly what my parents would say or one of my brothers," Thierren answered with some anger in his voice. "And I get pissed at myself every time I hear their words coming out of my mouth."

"Then why do you say them?" Grierr asked. "Do you believe them?"

Thierren was silent. "I don't know what I believe anymore."

"You keep saying that, Thierren," Grierr said wearily. "We aren't in school anymore. People are dying. At some point, you are going to have to decide what you believe and who you want to be."

"I can't lose him, or any of you," Thierren whispered.

"You are going to lose him if you don't decide," Grierr warned. "He will support whatever decision you make."

"Jonah said something similar to me," Thierren replied.

"That must have hurt coming from someone like him to talk so openly with you," Grierr taunted.

"I am not like them," Thierren stated.

"Then stop acting like them," Grierr suggested. "Now I need to check on Tas before he causes a storm to burst out on top of us."

Thierren watched Grierr walk away from him. The letter he had received from his parents that had found him in Emi still burned in his satchel. He had told no one about it. About the matches they had found, about the position they could get him at a reputable clinic, how he could raise their name to the highest it could be. On paper, it sounded simple: marry the pretty girl with ties to old money, work for a world renowned healer, get your name published, live the life many would dream of. Yet at this moment it felt more like chains than any dream, for they would force him to be someone he was not. He had promised his parents that he would only stay for a few months to ensure that Grierr could move forward without aid. They understood the need to be with his friend after such a tragedy. Yet the cost of going meant once he returned, he would choose a bride and follow the path they laid out before him. They would chain him to Greedin for the rest of his life. Any trip to his see his friends would have to be a lie. At that point, what would another lie be for him to tell?

He heard Jonah whistle, letting them all know it was time to get back on to the road. There was a campsite. The old man knew that if they reached it by nightfall it would keep them well protected until morning. Grierr forced himself to move. He helped to get Kade up on a wagon bench, then took the reins. Amos carried a sleepy Lyra to the next wagon. He noted

Thierren took the driver's seat on that one. This left Edelberg and Tas to patrol as they followed Jonah. The old man was good company. He would share tales of his life, but there were often moments of silence that were comfortable. The silence gave Grierr time to think about what he and they were all going through.

"You are all wrong," Kade said at one point.

"What do you mean?" Grierr asked.

"About being betrayed by a friend," Kade answered.

"You can see the future as well, old friend?" Grierr inquired.

Kade laughed at that. "Only the Fates see the future," Kade chuckled. "And even she only sees the many paths one can take in our life."

"So, how are we wrong, then?"

"I would say you are all about to be meeting one of those paths," Kade assumed. He studied Grierr.

"If we are at a crossroads, then why are you saying we are wrong?" Grierr asked him.

"Because once one goes down a wrong path, it is very hard to find a better path," Kade answered. "I've seen it happen several times before. I often sit back and watch, but... the four of you have something special."

Grierr turned to look at him for a moment before looking at back at the road. "So, what do we do to not go down the path?"

"Learn to listen to what the other is saying," Kade stated. He gave Grierr a look that said to not speak. "You are hearing what the other is saying, but you are not listening to what each other is saying. Thierren is in a similar situation that you are in."

"How can even compare the two us?"

"You have lost your family, and now you are fighting to ensure no one will know what you went through," Kade replied. "Yet by him moving forward with this quest, he is risking doing just what you want to prevent. Death will not be separating him from his family. He will walk away knowing that he will never be allowed back. It is a decision that will take immense bravery and support from the very people who are pressuring him to make a choice."

Grierr went to argue but stared at the old man. "The four of you are caught up in your own reasonings, it is hard for you to see what the other is going through," Kade went on. "When one becomes isolated, they withdraw and feel their only way forward is on their own."

Grierr fell silent as he thought about what Kade had said. His grief was very real. His family was torn from him. He will never see them again except for his dreams and memories. Yet Kade was right. What they were asking of Thierren was to walk away from his family, knowing it would mean he was disowned. There would be no going back for Thierren.

It was near dark when they reached a densely wooded area. No one questioned Jonah, as he seemed to find an unseen path. From what Grierr could tell, this had been a forgotten wood cutter's path. Grierr had gotten down from the wagon to guide the horses in by foot. They walked for almost a good mile before they came across the remains of a camp. The cabins were still standing, some completely overrun by overgrowth. Edelberg unsheathed his sword and followed Jonah as they went cabin by cabin. There were two that were inhabitable.

The cooking pit took a bit of work to get it working. The fire started up just as the sun was setting and the cool night air given them a chill. Amira and Thierren spoke quietly as they got food ready for dinner. Tas entertained Lyra so she would not get in the way as the adults secured the camp. Grierr dug through his satchel and pulled out several stones. He brought one over to the fire pit and placed it among the stones.

"What is that?" Amira asked.

"It's a rune stone," Grierr explained. "This will make it so that the smoke will not be detected. I'm going to get the fire going in both the cabins and will use the same stone in them so we can be warm during the nights."

"That will be wonderful," Amira agreed. "How do you do it?"

"It's his talent," Thierren answered. "Each sorcerer usually has a skill or talent for something. Grierr, here, can blend runes into items."

"What is yours?" Amira asked.

"Healing," Thierren replied.

"A worthy skill," Amira said as she had heard a hint of regret in Thierren's reply. "My father has commented that his leg has not felt as well as it does in a long time. I would say it's more of a gift to those you heal."

Grierr smiled at the woman as he headed into the cabins. Edelberg was laying down defense wards around the area that would alert them if anyone crossed them. Amos was gathering branches so they would have fire throughout the night. Grierr set a stone into the small cast-iron stove, then used some twigs and branches he brought with him to get the fire going. Once it was going, he charmed it to stay low, burning for a bit. He did the same in the other cabin.

He heard the call for dinner and joined everyone at the table they had made. The horses were taken care of, tied to the small paddock area that had the remains of a barn. They had water and hay and seemed quite content to munch on the area. Jonah was coming back up the path they had taken.

"There is no trace we came through," Jonah informed Grierr.

"How do you know of these places?" Grierr asked as he walked to the table with Jonah. "Is it a pull? Do you see it in your head?"

"A bit of both. The pull directs me and when I am near, I see it in my mind," Jonah said simply.

They both sat down and took the bowls of a simple stew with some bread that was handed to them. The conversation was good as they ate. When they were close to finishing with dinner, Amira had Amos brought some water from the stream so they could wash the dishes and then themselves.

"While you settle in, my companions and I need to discuss our plans for after we see you off," Grierr stated. Three sets of eyes stared at him. "Jonah, you are more than welcome to join us?"

Jonah studied him for a moment. "I think I will help Amos bring up water, then tend to the fires to warm the cabins for sleep."

Grierr nodded. Jonah would stay with the family in case they needed any protection during the night. Grierr stood up and headed to the cabin that he would share with his three friends. He stoked the fire, adding more kindling to it so that it would get warmer. He heard his friends come in one by one. Edelberg was the last and shut the door.

"What's going on?" Tas asked as he sat on one of the cots.

"Us," Grierr said, pointing to each other them. "We have been arguing since Vulcan. The tension is getting thick and we need to figure out a way to end this tension before it gets worse."

"It's not that bad," Edelberg replied.

"It is that bad," Tas countered. "What are you proposing?"

"That we talk to each other and actually listen to what the other is saying," Grierr said. "Because that's the problem. We aren't hearing what the other is saying."

"Look, we know what the problem is," Edelberg said as his eyes landed on Thierren.

"No, we actually don't know the problem," Grierr answered as he stood to his full height and looked at Edelberg. "The three of us have been assuming since school what we think Thierren's family is like. We have never asked him to clarify, or to explain why joining us means walking away from his family. And all we are doing is pushing him away from us."

"Thierren hasn't been forthcoming either," Edelberg argued.

"Thierren is in the room," Thierren reminded them. His arms were folded across his chest. He looked at Grierr. "I... what is it you are suggesting?"

"We each explain why we are doing this, and you explain why you are hesitant," Grierr suggested. "Even if you decide in the end to leave, we will at least understand your decision and respect it."

Thierren raised in eyebrow, he looked doubtful that was the case. "Fine."

Tas stood up first. "My vow to the Council of Magi," Tas began. "I swore to protect those of Magic as well as protect the mundane from magic used wrong. I also know people who have been wronged by the Greedin Gods and some stories are horrific. I want to see justice for those whose lives have been destroyed."

"I promised Tas he would have my blade and my staff," Edelberg said simply. He did not elaborate, as he often was a man of a few words for discussions like this.

Grierr sighed. "I have to do something, or my grief will rip me a part," he admitted. "Do I want to fight Gods? No, but I have witnessed what this group is doing to those not under their domain. I wonder what they are doing to their own people?"

"And now it's time for Thierren to bare his soul to you," Thierren said almost bitterly. He ran a hand through his hair. "Because if I don't, then the cold shoulders, the thoughts that I'll betray you all, will be true, right?"

"You won't betray us," Tas stated.

"Really? Because Edelberg thinks I will," Thierren countered.

103

"And Edelberg can be an asshole," Tas reminded him. "And he is being an asshole about this. I know you, Thierren. You wouldn't betray us."

"Using your ability on me?"

"Never on you," Tas said, almost as if it pained him.

Thierren stared at him. He turned to look at Grierr. "What do you think?"

"I think you would leave in the middle of the night so you would not betray us," Grierr answered.

Thierren had to laugh at this. It was an insane situation he was in. He could walk out the door and not look back. They were giving him the perfect out, the perfect reason to return to his family, to tell them he was finally agreeing to what his family demanded of him. Thierren got up and walked to the door, and laid a hand on it. Tas and Grierr did not move, did not say a word. Edelberg smirked as if he was right. Thierren looked up at the rafters and mouthed a simple charm that would make this conversation to be remain unheard by anyone or any being.

He let his hand fall a way then returned to the cot he had been sitting on. Edelberg stared at him as Tas tried not to grin.

"What do you know of my family?" Thierren asked as he opened his rucksack.

Grierr and Tas looked at each other for a moment. It was Tas that answered. "We know they are part of a traditionalist sect in Greedin. That your father is a clerk in Lycan's capital, working for the provincial leader there. You have an older brother and a younger brother; your mother is pious. Your being the first sorcerer in your family has raised your family's status. You do not agree with all their views."

"That's a good summary," Thierren agreed. He took the envelope out that contained the letter from his family and handed it to Tas. "What do you know of the Malfinites?"

"That it's a crappy name for a cult," Edelberg commented. He paused, then looked at Thierren. "Shit, really?"

"What are the Malfinites?" Grierr asked as Tas was reading the letter.

"Thierren can correct me if I'm wrong," Edelberg began. His brother Micah had a run in with a group of them. It was the only reason he knew anything about the group. "They are a very conservative branch of the Traditionalists. Where Traditionalists view the children of Gaia as true Gods, the Malfinites believe Malforin is the one and only God. That to worship any other God is blasphemy."

"There are monotheistic religions around," Grierr pointed out.

"Yes, but the Malfinites take it to an extreme," Edelberg answered. He looked at Thierren. "Your family?"

"Some of the founding members of the order come from my family," Thierren answered. Edelberg let out a string of curses and paced the room. "They believe the only way to serve Him is to devote your entire life to Him. You marry not out of love or even for an alliance, but to ensure you will have children. They train the children from an early age that they are the army that will come to the aid of Malforin in time of need. A portion of your wealth is to be donated to the temple every month. If you are wealthy, it means you are in his high esteem. If you are poor, you are not pious enough."

"That's... insane," Grierr stated. It reminded him of the cult that had virtually eliminated his entire family line. "What about His children?"

"We view them in high regard. We see them as His messengers," Thierren explained. "Not quite like the cult that went after your family. They

105

would see any sign of discontent attributed to one of his children as a sign of you bringing dishonor to him."

"What is your family's plan?" Grierr asked him.

Tas had finished the letter and was staring at Thierren. "For him to return after Grierr is done grieving, so he may select from one of the brides they have chosen."

"You are forgetting about the position at the clinic where I will be working with a renowned healer," Thierren added bitterly.

"Well, then I am glad that my grieving is taking longer than planned," Grierr stated. Thierren sent him a grateful look.

"If you went back and told them no, what would happen?" Edelberg asked Thierren.

"Best-case scenario, they will send me on a retreat to confess my sins, to find my honor, and return to the path that Malforin has set forth before me," Thierren answered. "Enough food and water to survive, freezing cold baths, mandatory prayer, and solitary confinement."

"Worst case?"

"They poison me in my sleep and claim I died while I slept," Thierren answered.

"That sounds almost better than the retreat," Edelberg commented. He hissed when Grierr elbowed him.

"The poison is slow acting, and I would still be alive as they burn me on a pyre," Thierren added.

"Never mind, retreat sounds great."

They all had to chuckle at Edelberg being absolutely grossed out. "If you were to not return?" Tas asked quietly after a moment.

"They would kick me out, declared an enemy to the cult," Thierren answered. "As for my family, they would strip me of the family records, and they would live their lives as if I never existed."

"This is all wrong on so many levels," Grierr said.

"Tas," Edelberg said. "You were right. I am an asshole."

"You guys didn't know," Thierren admitted.

"Why didn't you tell us?" Grierr asked.

"Well, you never asked, and when we graduated, we all went on our different paths. I thought for a time that I had gotten away from their plans," Thierren admitted. "Then my cousin and older brother messed up really badly so that in order to save our name in the cult, they placed me forth. I have a higher standing than they did because I am a sorcerer, so it would undue any of their damage."

"How many Malfinites are there?" Tas asked.

"A thousand at most, spread out between Lynia and Halla."

"We can handle a thousand pissed off cultists," Edelberg stated.

Grierr had skimmed the letter that Tas had read. "There are only female options on here?"

"Yes, because unless you know something I don't, two men can't conceive a child," Thierren added.

"Good thing you like both," Edelberg answered. He dodged the elbow that Grierr was aiming at him.

"Not helping," Grierr warned him. "If you don't return, what happens to the brides?"

"They will actually have a better chance at a higher match because they had been chosen for me," Thierren said. "Despite that, I won't exist anymore in their eyes. It's a fucked-up system."

"So, let's say you decide to join us," Tas began. "We are going to go to Greedin. What should we expect if we run into one of these people?"

Thierren stared at him. He had to think, for most people did not walk away. "I don't think we're looking at duels in the streets," Thierren replied. "I know of one person who walked away. They didn't kill him, that I know of."

"We check his food and drink for poison," Grierr said to Tas. "I could fashion a rune for him to wear that would light up if poison is detected."

"I can get word to the Rebels if he chooses to walk away. They can figure out areas for him to avoid," Tas agreed. "I can have them delve into the cult as well, see who we need to be careful of, if there are any leaders we need to know about."

"We'll mention it to Micah," Edelberg added. "He might know some information about it. If he doesn't, he will within a month. He'll probably have a spy in place within two months."

Thierren stared at them. He had not even decided, and here they were planning on how to keep him safe.

"What if I choose to return?" He asked.

"You aren't getting rid of us that easily," Grierr stated with a chuckle. "We'll produce ways to kidnap you. Willingly, of course. No matter, you still have a vow to the Council of Magi, and if we use that to steal you a way a few times a year, then we will."

"Look, I'll be pissed if you choose to return to them," Edelberg admitted. "They are not worthy of you. You deserve to live your life as you want to. But if you feel you have to do this, as long as you aren't passing over information to them about what we are doing, then I think I can respect why you would return to them."

"Knowing you will never see them again, it is not an easy thing," Grierr said softly. "They are your family. Whether they are worthy of being called that, it is not an easy decision. We will try to respect your decision if it is to return to them."

"That is all I could ever ask for," Thierren admitted. For the first time in years, he felt weight leave his shoulders. Knowing they would stand with him meant more than the words they were saying.

Chapter 9

Micah listened to everything that Tas had been telling him. He stood with his arms folded across his broad chest, his light brown hair pulled back in a plait. Two daggers hung at his hip. His people were keeping watch and helping the family move their things. Thierren was giving instruction to one of Micah's men about Kade's health. Lyra was charming the rest while Edelberg and Grierr helped rotate out supplies. They were dividing up what would go with Lyra and her family. Jonah stood watch to make sure that no one would interrupt the party.

"What I know of the cult is troubling," Micah confided to Tas. "The idea he is even entertaining the idea of leaving is a testament to the friendship the four of you have."

"So, you know little?" Tas asked, feeling lost. If, between their two networks, there was little information, then it did not bode well for getting a sense of the situation.

"They rarely associate with those outside of the Traditionalist sect, despite much of the larger sect wanting to distance from them," Micah answered. "There are two communities that I know of in the Lycan region of Lynia that are just Malfinites. Any outsiders are treated with distrust. There are rumors of outsiders vanishing during a stay there."

"I had a feeling of that," Tas admitted.

"I'll find out more if I can," Micah promised. He then handed him a bundle of letters. "Letters from your Rebels, the Council, as well as your mother."

"Thank you," Tas replied as he accepted the letters.

Micah looked at where Thierren was talking to his men. He noted Edelberg was glaring at the healer. "They're fighting?"

"Edelberg has had an attitude since we left Emi," Tas admitted.

"His moods have not been the best lately. Quick to temper," Micah replied. "He'll dodge questions he doesn't want to answer. Mom was relieved when he told her about his mission with you. She feels better knowing you'll be keeping an eye out for him."

Tas arched an eyebrow. "That's not a good sign," Tas stated.

"I know," Micah agreed. "Could be why he is sending Thierren glares. If Thierren questions his moods, he would see it as a threat."

"My thought as well," Tas agreed. He looked through the letters really quick and froze at one of them.

"Oberon sent it to the palace," Micah informed him. "Don't worry, your people, my people, and your grandfather's people have all read through it. Your sister-in-law has a copy for her file."

"What does he want?"

"From what my network is saying, he's telling people you are playing hard to get, that you are nervous of the attention it would bring to you, you aren't ready for the world to know, the list goes on," Micah answered.

"Can I burn it?"

"Do whatever you want with it. We just wanted you to know he's getting ... more aggressive."

111

"Because I don't have enough on my plate right now," Tas groaned. "Can you send a message to Cora? Let her know we talked and for her to switch around some of her people she has in the Lynian palace."

"She'll take orders from me?"

"I will let all my chiefs know you are my voice while I'm saving the world," Tas assured him.

"You going to tell me how you got spies in Lynia's palace?" Micah inquired. He had been trying for a few years to get some in that place.

Tas motioned toward Thierren. Micah raised an eyebrow. "Really?" Micah asked.

"He rebels against his family in ways that can't get traced back to him," Tas replied. "He finally told us last night the full story. He risks a lot just being with us."

"The Traditionalists have never taken well to outsiders," Micah agreed. "Anything else?"

"No, I'll update you once we meet up with Kaidan and get to Hruan."

They joined the rest of the groups. Lyra was sad to leave them, but excited by her new friends. Micah promised to get word once the family was safe. The five waited until they could no longer see the party. They were down to a wagon and three horses now, which meant they could move faster than with the two wagons. They would be rough camping tonight, meaning there were no hidden spots for them to use.

Jonah and Grierr rode ahead to locate an ideal spot for them to camp. They wanted a spot off the road and where they could easily get away if Rochleaux guards found them. They rode until the moon was high in the sky. They made camp a distance away from the road where there was a small brook they could use for water. They set up the tents around a small fire and had salted meat and the rest of the bread from earlier in the day. No one spoke while they ate.

Once the meal was done, Grierr unrolled the map on a log for them to study. They needed to reach Hruan before they ran out of supplies.

"The main trade road we know is going to be watched," Thierren stated. "This means paperwork is going to be needed."

"I can do my trick with a few people but if it's a full unit, I don't know if I can keep up the facade," Edelberg admitted.

"The more people there are, the more drain on your power," Tas added. "It would take days for you to recover if you had to manipulate that many."

Jonah was pulling at his chin as he studied the map. Grierr handed him a pencil. "What do you see?"

"There is an old Watchtower still intact near the Hruan border," Jonah replied, as he marked its location on the map. "It's a different entry point than the trade route. Many don't use it because you can only get a few horses through at a time. It's a narrow trail cut through the mountain range."

"It looks like there are a few minor roads that head toward that area," Edelberg noted. "We wouldn't have to cut our own path."

"If we get caught by a patrol, it would be suspicious," Thierren warned.

"Maybe not," Tas replied. "The Watchtowers fall under the Council of Magi protection. I can inform them I heard a rumor of one and need to see if one still stands so the council can be informed."

"That would work," Grierr agreed.

"Rochleaux might not be a fan of magic, but most people know to not anger your Council," Jonah added.

"The route looks like there are plenty of woods for us to find cover at night," Grierr noted as he studied the map.

Once the route was confirmed they headed back out onto the road. Without the family, they could move faster and travel past sunset. Though the constant chatter of the little girl was missed as they rode. There were very few travelers on the road as they moved off of the main highway. If they passed a wagon or a person, the person had their head down and paid no mind to anyone else. This just confirmed how many things had changed in the country.

"What did Micah tell you and Jonah?" Grierr asked Tas as they took their turn on the wagon.

"There is a group of refugees hiding out in the woods," Tas stated. "Hence why we need to get to the Watchtower."

"We would need to wait until we can get a sorcerer to stand guard at the tower once we get them there," Grierr pointed.

"Not if there is already a sorcerer with them," Tas said with a hint of a smile.

"Who?" Grierr inquired.

Tas smiled at him. "Kaidan."

"This is going to be interesting," Grierr agreed.

It had been a while since he saw Kaidan. Kaidan Hunt had gone to the academy with them and was in their larger group of friends. Of the four of them, Kaidan had been the closest to Tas and Thierren. They followed the same path back in school and both worked for the Council as representatives. Grierr had not seen Kaidan in a few years, but they had written letters to each other during that time. It would be good to see another friend of theirs. Yet deep down, Grierr wondered how Thierren and Edelberg would feel about seeing Kaidan again. Edelberg had always been distant with Kaidan and with everything going on, he was not sure how Thierren would handle another person in their group.

They stopped well after sundown and had a cold meal. Instead of setting up their tents, they rolled out their bedrolls and slept under the night sky. Edelberg had set wards to alert them to any trouble. They woke at dawn, eating another cold meal before feeding and watering the horses. They only stopped for lunch or to give the horse a break. Edelberg had gone to scout ahead and rushed back, warning of a patrol. Jonah took out the map, studying it before he found a path they could take. It would be slow, as they would need to guide the horses through the woods. The wagon they broke down, making it look like bandits had come by that section of the road.

"We might need your skill," Jonah said quietly to Tas as they walked deep into the forest.

"Why?" Tas asked.

"The last time I walked these parts, there was a small herd of dragons that protect this area," Jonah answered.

"Then I will send out a message that we are here and mean no harm," Tas replied.

He stopped for a moment and took hold of the staff that was strapped to his back. Holding it in his hand, he focused on the surrounding area. The staff would allow him to widen the area for his message to be heard. The others had stopped to watch. It was rare they got to see Tas try to contact a herd of dragons. The air about where Tas stood seemed to be alive as leaves floated about him on a breeze that only affected him. Jonah watched Tas with an odd expression, remembering a friend from long ago that had the same raw power that Tas was harnessing.

"They would like to meet us in a clearing near here," Tas said as the leaves fell to the ground. He looked at Jonah. "They said you would know which clearing."

"Aye," Jonah answered.

Edelberg and Thierren were in the rear as they began moving again. "Why does he have to be hot when he does shit like that?" Edelberg asked Thierren with a grin.

"I thought you only liked women," Thierren pointed out.

"I'll try anything once," Edelberg admitted. "And when Tas looks like that, it's tempting."

"Not him," Thierren answered as he picked up his pace so that he would walk with Grierr. Edelberg was cackling behind him.

"Everything all right?" Grierr asked, noticing Thierren looked mad.

"Just Edelberg being his crass self," Thierren answered.

It was all Thierren had to say for Grierr to understand. The two walked in silence as they followed Jonah. It was near nightfall when they emerged out of the forest into a clearing that was like out of a fairy tale. Flowers bloomed everywhere. You could hear the noises of animals and insects filling the air with music. They heard a stream running through the clearing. Tas gasped and pushed past Jonah as he walked toward the center of the clearing.

The air shimmered for a moment as Tas approached, and then a large forest dragon appeared. His scales were a deep green, his body was slender, his legs and arms long and muscular. The dragon had folded his wings close to his body as his dark eyes watched them as they neared. When the dragon spoke, it was like a rumble of thunder, yet only Tas would understand what was being said.

Grierr stood next to Jonah. "You knew a Dragon Talker once," Grierr stated.

"Once, many lifetimes ago," Jonah admitted. "Your companion reminds me of him."

"You are not quite what people think you are."

Jonah chuckled. "I am what people need to think I am," he answered with a slight grin. "A guide, a protector, a friend to lean on."

"You are no sorcerer or witch," Grierr noted.

"There were other beings that walked this world before the Gods descended from the heavens," Jonah reminded him.

"Some said they vanished when the Gods arrived."

"Some did, some stayed, others watch, but we have always been around."

Their conversation ended when Tas let out a laugh as the dragon rubbed its snout against him. It was the dragon's way of marking the person as safe, so other dragons in the area know he is not prey.

"This is Verde," Tas introduced them with a huge grin. "He welcomes us to rest tonight in the clearing. We will be safe here. We can hunt as long as we do not kill a mother animal. In the morning, he will bring us to the refugees."

There was another rumble. "He said to not enter the forests unless we are called for," Tas added.

"How come?" Edelberg asked.

"It's his home. There are a few eggs that just hatched, so the mothers are nervous of strangers," Tas answered.

"There are plenty of small animals to trap here in the field," Jonah commented. "We will be fine in the clearing."

The dragon gave a snort, then headed towards the shadows of the forest. Tas was smiling at the retreating dragon form, as if in a daze. Grierr sighed and motioned for Jonah to follow.

"He's going to be like that for a bit," Grierr informed Jonah. Edelberg and Thierren joined. "Thierren, you want to take the bow and go with Jonah? Edelberg and I can set up tents and get a fire going."

"Why Thierren and not me?" Edelberg inquired.

"Because I don't trust you," Grierr said. Edelberg made a face at that. "You'll try to find out how strict the dragons are and then Tas will have to convince them you will taste horrible roasted."

Thierren had to laugh at that. "I'll get my compact bow from my pack," Thierren answered as Edelberg flipped him off.

"Come on, let's get the horses tied up and the tents up," Grierr said to Edelberg.

The horses had remained calm at the sight of the dragon and were currently munching on some grass. Grierr spotted a few trees in the field that they could tie the horses to. While he took care of the horses and monitored Tas, Edelberg got the tents from their packs. There was a clearing in the field that would be perfect for a fire as there was a circle of earth with no grass to catch fire. As Edelberg set the last tent up, he saw Tas had constructed a fire and was getting it going.

"How's the head?" Edelberg asked him.

"They are letting me hear their song," Tas informed him. "So, it's crowded, but it's wonderful."

"Are there words to it?"

"Not in the way you think," Tas answered. "It's words, but with impressions and feelings mixed in. Their language is more intense than just words."

"Horses are happy and content," Grierr stated as he joined them. "I see you've returned to our reality."

"Partial," Tas replied.

"They're letting him listen to their songs," Edelberg added.

"So, if he stares off into space, we know why," Grierr replied with a chuckle.

They heard voices and saw Thierren and Jonah were talking; it seemed as if the two were getting along better than they usually did.

"He is a fine bowman," Jonah informed them as he held up several rabbits. "I have not seen many hunters be able to take down such small animals with as clean a shot as he."

"Thierren was top rated back in school," Edelberg agreed.

Jonah grabbed a knife from his pack. "I'll clean these by the stream, then we can eat."

Soon the rabbits were skinned, and roasting on the open fire with a few root vegetables they had. The stars were bright in the sky, and they took turns pointing out constellations and the stories behind the formation. Jonah knew many of the older variations. It was determined that Edelberg had the least knowledge of stars and constellations. Tas was quick to remind them that Edelberg had gotten the lowest score in Astronomy out of all of them back at school. When the food had been eaten and the fire banked, they took turns washing in the stream before retiring to their tents. No wards had to be set out, no turns at watch. They were safe here in the clearing.

They woke after dawn, where they ate bread and cheese. They packed the tents up; the fire extinguished by the time Verde returned to them. Grierr retrieved the horses while the dragon spoke, Tas translated for Jonah, who had his map out and was marking their course on the map. Edelberg tied their packs to the horses while Thierren checked his medical supplies to see if he was low on herbs. One dragon had informed Tas they could help replenish medicinal herbal supplies.

Grierr noted that Tas and Jonah were done with the dragons when he saw Tas scratching one on the chin. Jonah headed toward where he and Edelberg were.

"What's the plan?" Edelberg asked.

"The dragons will stay invisible. They will be on alert for any patrols," Jonah explained. "Apparently, they have spotted an increase a few weeks ago."

"They gave you the path to follow?"

"I have it marked out," Jonah answered. "Tas will be in constant communication with the Dragons."

"I'll guard him," Edelberg told Grierr. "He'll be out of it if he has to keep up with all of it."

"Who will take the rear?" Grierr asked.

"What about Thierren?" Jonah suggested.

"What about me?" Thierren asked as he joined them.

"Edelberg is going to be guarding Tas because Tas has to be in contact with the dragons," Grierr explained. "He usually takes the rear. Jonah suggested you."

"I'm not great with a sword," Thierren stated.

"But you are with a bow," Jonah replied.

"He's right, you are," Edelberg agreed.

Thierren stared at his friends. They never had him take rear before in any of their travels. "If you all trust me to do it."

"I trust you," Tas said as he walked toward them. "Thierren will take the rear. Edelberg will guard me. Jonah will take lead as normal with Grierr being look out."

Grierr took the horses that they would lead, Tas climbed on, for it would be easier for Edelberg to guard Tas if he were on a horse and being led. Soon they were on the path. Every now and then, there was a shimmer between the trees. Grierr realized it was the dragons that were guiding them. They made no noise, which was odd for how large they were. One would not know that they were there if you did not know what to look for.

"I forgot how draining his gift can be," Thierren said as Grierr checked on him.

"We usually only see him with Bart," Grierr agreed.

"Do you remember when Bart had a dragon cold and almost burned down the astronomy tower?" Thierren chuckled.

"Headmaster Tobias wasn't sure if he could expel a dragon," Grierr remembered. "That was until Bart helped the workers rebuild it in half the time."

"He was so conflicted," Thierren agreed. He then looked at Grierr. "What do you think we are going to find when we meet up with Kaidan and the refugees?"

"I do not know," Grierr admitted. "Micah wasn't sure how many were with Kaidan, just that it was getting hard for him to keep them safe."

"Getting a large group to the Watchtower is going to be tricky," Thierren pointed out.

"The good news is Verde confirmed the Tower was in good shape and could house the size of the refugees," Grierr replied.

"We still have to get them there."

"Can you try to be optimistic?"

"That would be out of character for me," Thierren stated with the hint of a smile.

"True, and we couldn't have you be out of character."

They stopped at noon for an hour. Tas had eaten some morsels, then fell asleep under a tree. They let him sleep for a bit. Jonah and Edelberg scouted out the area to make sure the area was safe. They knew the dragons were there as well, but also wanted to let the dragons know they could help, too.

Thierren woke Tas up when Jonah came back, explaining that they spotted riders in the distance. A dragon confirmed that there were riders a few miles behind them. Thierren helped Tas to the horse and onto it. Once Tas was secure, Edelberg climbed up after him in case they had to ride hard. Knowing there could be a patrol out there made them all tense and silent, Thierren had his bow ready as he spotted a dragon keeping pace with him.

"It's bandits," Grierr informed Thierren when he rode back toward him. "A dragon got word to Tas."

"I'm not sure if that's worse or not," Thierren replied.

"One dragon is going to mess with them. If it was guards, they would stay away."

"Better them than us," Thierren decided. He understood why the dragons would not want to mess with Rochleaux guards.

Just in the event the bandits got away from the dragons, Thierren had his bow ready should he have to fight. He saw Edelberg had done the same thing with his sword. Tension rose to prepare for an incoming attack. The dragons were moving closer to them between the trees.

It was the blood-chilling scream that had everyone freezing. Thierren looked to where the scream came from and felt his heart stop. Edelberg was catching a screaming Tas as he seemed to fall off the horse while holding his head as if he were in agony. Edelberg laid him down gently as Thierren heard his name being called. He was already off the horse and grabbing his medical bag; he ran to where Tas was convulsing on the ground.

"What happened?" Thierren asked Edelberg as he kneeled down next to Tas.

"He was mumbling, then tensed up moments before he screamed," Edelberg answered. Panic heavy in his voice.

"Any spells thrown out from the woods?"

"Nothing. The dragons picked something up the moment he screamed," Edelberg replied. "What do you need?"

"Keep him on his side," Thierren instructed as he examined Tas.

Jonah came over, kneeling down next to Tas. "I can help," Jonah informed them.

"How?" Thierren inquired. He did not mean it if the question came off in a doubtful matter.

"I can connect to his mind," Jonah explained them.

Thierren stared at him. His family would say that this type of person was delusional, abusing the law of nature. But he was not his parents, and this was an emergency. "Do it," Thierren said. "I need to know what happened."

Jonah nodded. "He needs to be on his back."

Edelberg looked at Thierren for confirmation. Thierren nodded. Edelberg rolled Tas onto his back. Jonah took a deep breath, placed his hands on either side of Tas head.

"If I pass out, ignore it," Jonah informed the two men.

He closed his eyes after that and entered Tas's mind. The images were chaotic, so was the language being whirled around. It was as if Jonah had entered a tsunami occurring in Tas's mind. There seemed to be this black slime that was trying to take up root in his memories and in his magic. The moment Jonah saw it, he immediately pulled himself out of Tas's mind and forced himself to vomit.

"He needs something to purge his system," Jonah ordered as he tried to bring up more of his stomach contents.

Thierren did not argue and rummaged through his bag. Jonah stumbled to the ground and rushed toward where Grierr was standing with the dragons.

"I need to speak with Verde," Jonah stated.

One dragon moved forward and seemed to nod its head. "If I place my hands on your snout, could we communicate?" Jonah inquired.

The dragon moved so its snout was right to Jonah. Jonah placed his hands on either side.

Have blood dragons returned? Jonah inquired.

There was a sense of shock floating through the dragon. *We have heard rumors. Until this moment, I did not wish to believe them to be true.*

We need to get Tas to the camp, or he will not survive the night. They now know he is a Dragon Talker and will taunt him.

Agreed. I will take him and the healer he is connected to. The other dragons will ensure you and the others will arrive safely.

Jonah removed his hands and looked at Grierr. "I will explain everything once we are safe. Tas needs to leave immediately," Jonah informed him.

Grierr did not hesitate as he ran to his friends. Whatever conversation they had was quick. Soon Edelberg was carrying Tas towards where Jonah was standing.

"I'm going with him," Thierren stated.

"Verde will take you, we will follow," Jonah told him. "Keep purging him. If black ooze shows up, ask Verde from one drop of his blood, boil it with your healing tea, and force him to drink it."

Thierren felt his blood go cold. He knew the remedy. He had come across it in an ancient healer's tome. There was only one thing in the world that would cause such a reaction and people thought the monster never existed. Thierren nodded and climbed onto the dragon. Edelberg handed him Tas, helping to get the unconscious sorcerer onto the back of the dragon. Thierren bid his companions goodbye. Within moments, they were airborne.

Chapter 10

Thierren was exhausted. His bones ached, his brain was working through so many scenarios. None of those scenarios were helpful as to what was wrong with Tas. If Kaidan was at the camp, he knew he could have helped in figuring out what was wrong. Kaidan might not be a full healer, but he had some skills and would be helpful. As Verde descended, Thierren spotted Kaidan standing there in the landing area with a group of men. Only from the air could one see how massive the camp was. They arranged tents of all sizes and colors in rows. There were wagons that were doubling as shelter or a work area. In the center was Kaidan, waiting for Verde to land with two men carrying a stretcher waiting with him.

When Verde landed, Kaidan was quick to help get Tas onto the stretcher, instructing the men to bring Tas to Kaidan's tent. He then helped Thierren get down, pulling him into one of his signature bone crushing hugs.

"You look like shit," Kaidan stated as he looked over at his friend.

"So do you," Thierren answered as Kaidan kept an arm around his shoulder.

That was the end of their reunion as they hurried after the men. His focus was on Tas and the vial of blood that Verde had gifted him during the flight. As long as Thierren was holding onto Tas, he could communicate roughly with the dragon. Something he had learned on the flight and seemed to give Verde a good chuckle. Kaidan's tent was larger than some others. It reminded Thierren of a tent a general would have in battle. Upon entering, he saw it was arranged very much like a general's tent.

Tas was already being moved to a long table under Kaidan's instruction. This allowed Thierren to be right at his side. His pulse was weak, his coloring had gotten worse during the flight. The more concerning part was the veins around his temple were turning black. Thierren swallowed back the panic, focusing on what he needed.

"I am going to need boiling water, a bowl of cool water, and rags," Thierren instructed as he checked over Tas.

"Call for Moira," Kaidan yelled one of his men.

"Right away," one man said, rushing out of the tent.

Within seconds, a young woman entered. "What is needed?" She asked.

"Is Lysander still here?" Kaidan asked.

"He's still on patrol," Moira answered.

"Thierren, this is Moira, one of our healers. Give her the list," Kaidan stated.

"Boiling water, bandages," Thierren began listing off all the items he would need. "Blankets, buckets."

"Any potions or tonics?" Moira asked him. Thierren shook his head. "Should I call for Lysander to return?"

"I'll handle that part," Kaidan said.

Moira nodded, then quickly left the tent. Kaidan pulled his dark hair back with a leather string, then pulled off his vest, so he wore a basic tunic underneath. "What do you need me to do?" Kaidan asked.

"We need to strip him out of his tunic. He vomited during the flight," Thierren stated. "He was vomiting mid-flight. It's black and smells like death."

"What is going on?" Kaidan asked as he helped strip Tas out of his outer vest and tunic. They got him on his side, then draped a blanket over him. The black goo on the tunic was a weird consistency, almost like tar.

"The only theory I have currently is unbelievable," Thierren answered. "One of our companions, his name is Jonah. He seems to know. We did not have time to discuss our theories."

"Who's this Jonah?" Kaidan could sense the panic in Thierren. If he kept asking him questions about what was wrong, what they could do, he could keep Thierren focused on what needed to be done and not the panic.

"We met him in Vulcan," Thierren stated as he took a waste bin and placed it next to the makeshift bed. "He was a sea captain, watched his men and ship be destroyed by a monster. He joined our quest."

The flaps to the tent rustled, and Moira entered. She had braided her hair back already and put an apron over her brown homespun dress.

"I have everything," Moira answered. She handed the kettle over to Thierren. "What else?"

"Two other of our friends will arrive with another gentleman," Kaidan told her. "They will want to come right to my tent. Bring them here, then can you take over my role?"

"Of course," Moira agreed. "I'll have our cook reheat dinner for them all. Tents?"

"Set up already, the one next to mine," he answered.

Moira nodded. "I'll handle it. Send word if you need me."

She looked at the healer; it was clear he had training in his movement. "Do you need anything?"

"I'll have Kaidan send word if I need anything else," Thierren stated. He turned to look at Kaidan as he washed his hands and readied what he needed. "If he starts to be sick, you are going to hold him. He will start to thrash about. Just hold him so he doesn't fall off."

Moira slipped out of the tent, leaving Kaidan and Thierren with Tas. At the moment, Tas was lying motionless on the table. His color was graying, his breathing labored. Thierren added the blood to the tea and mixed it as Verde instructed him.

"Are you almost done?" Kaidan inquired as Tas seized up.

"Yes," Thierren answered. "Can you get him sitting?"

"Not on my own," Kaidan admitted. He was ready to call for help when the flap opened.

Edelberg came rushing in. Grierr and Jonah followed him. Thierren instructed Edelberg to go on the other side and help Kaidan get Tas sitting. Grierr would help hold him up while Jonah kept his legs from kicking out. Once everyone was ready, Thierren used a spell to loosen the jaw so he could open Tas's mouth. He poured the tea into Tas's mouth, making sure they were small sips. The four men holding him kept him as still as possible as his body tried to fight the tea. Thierren kept trying to get as much of the tea down Tas's throat as he could. Tas was groaning as he kept forcing him to drink. Grierr trying to keep Tas from turning his head away without hurting him. When the last drop was drank, Thierren wanted to collapse.

The others lowered Tas back to the table. They were all silent as they waited for something to happen. Thierren checked Tas' pulse and temperature, finding relief in the steady rhythm of his heart and the coolness of his forehead.

"I set up a tent right next to mine," Kaidan said. "We can move him there. There's a street to wash up in, and dinner is being reheated for all of you. I'll have my men move him. The four of you go wash and take a moment."

"That would be appreciated," Grierr agreed. They were all exhausted and starving.

Grierr motioned for Edelberg to join him. They had left all their gear with the horses. They were given direction to where their belongings were. It took one trip for them to bring everything to the tent that Kaidan had set aside for them. They set four camping cots up in each corner. There was a camping stove in the center and two long tables on either side. The tent flap moved, revealing Jonah and two men bringing in Tas on a stretcher. Grierr got a cot set up for them to transfer him onto. Once Tas was placed on his cot, they covered him with a blanket.

Grierr studied his friend, while it seemed as if he was out of the woods. It was unusual to see Tas so still. He felt a hand on his shoulder and saw Thierren standing there.

"He is never this still," Grierr stated.

"Kaidan said we could wash up since we're covered in black ooze," Edelberg reminded them both. "He'll stay with him."

Thierren only then realized the state of his clothes and agreed that washing and a change of clothes would be a good thing. They grabbed their packs to bring with them, following one man who showed them the bathing spot. There was a small waterfall that the refugees used that fed into a natural spring. Thierren stripped and dove right in, going for the waterfall. Grierr found the deep section and stepped into it. He focused on washing off the grime from the road and from Tas. He saw Thierren was leaning against the stone wall of the waterfall alcove. His shoulders were shaking. Grierr knew Thierren was going to need some time to get himself together. His reaction was not just because it was Tas. That made it more intense. It was because

Thierren used his powers as a sorcerer to help his patient. Meaning he took on some of the pain, some of their anguish. Yet Thierren did not recognize it as a gift. Most healers, even if they were sorcerers, could not do what he could.

"I'll keep an eye on him," Edelberg assured Grierr.

Grierr finished with washing. He dried off, then put on basic traveling clothes. Slinging his pack on his shoulders, Grierr braided his hair as he walked. He would have to do a widower's braid at some point with beads for each child he lost as well. Perhaps when they got to Hruan he could have Kaidan's mother do it. Many citizens in Hruan followed Arkos as their main God and held many of the same traditions that Emi did.

He entered the tent and saw Kaidan was getting a fire going in the stove. Kaidan stood when Grierr entered. Grierr set his bag down on one of the cots then walked to Kaidan. The old friends hugged.

Kaidan clasped Grierr's forearm, then touched his hand to Grierr's forehead. "You have my grief, my sorrow, my love," Kaidan stated. It was a traditional phrase given to those in mourning in Hruan.

"May it ease their journey," Grierr said quietly.

"My family has lit lanterns in our family shrine for them," Kaidan said as they took a seat at the table.

"I will thank them when we reach Hruan."

"They would like to see the four of you," Kaidan answered. "You can tell them I found my path."

"I will."

The flap to the tent opened and the female from earlier in the day entered carrying a tray of food. "More is coming," she said to Kaidan as she brought the tray to the table.

"Good," Kaidan stated.

Moira stood up, and for the first time, studied the tall male before her. "You're an Arkonite!"

"Why don't we say it louder?" Kaidan groaned. Though Grierr had never told them, they all knew, for it was the only way to explain his height, his features, and lack of family. "Not sure the whole camp heard you," he teased. Moira blushed.

"And you are not a witch nor a sorcerer, yet you do not hear me declaring what you are or aren't," Grierr stated in a calm voice.

"Moira, this is Grierr," Kaidan began. "He is a friend of mine from the academy. Grierr this is Moira. She is one of our healers."

"Are your friends coming?" Moira asked Grierr. "I apologize for my outburst."

"You aren't the first to be surprised upon seeing me," Grierr assured her. "The many forget about the Arkonites. As for my friends, they'll be here shortly. Jonah was just heading there when I left."

"How's Thierren?" Kaidan asked.

"I don't know," Grierr admitted. Thierren had always been good at concealing his emotions, making him hard to read.

Moira busied herself with setting up the food she had brought in. By the time the rest of the food arrived, so had Jonah, Edelberg, and Thierren. Kaidan handed Thierren a steaming mug of tea and had him fill his plate first.

"Moira, these are Edelberg and Thierren and their companion Jonah," Kaidan made the introductions.

"Did you and Kaidan know each other prior to the camp?" Edelberg asked her as he took a seat next to her.

"No, we met by chance," Moira stated. "I had a small group and was trying to find a place to get out of a storm. We each thought the other was a group of bandits."

"When we realized we were helping the refugees, we joined forces," Kaidan added. "We met a third group. They have another healer. Between him and Moira, they can treat most of what we see."

"How do you communicate with the dragons?" Jonah asked.

"You knew we were coming," Thierren realized. "You were waiting for us."

"We learned early on how to communicate by drawing messages in the dirt or we light a certain bonfire for emergencies," Kaidan explained. "They sent word to the dragon that watches over us, and he informed us that Thierren would arrive with Tas and that Tas was sick. Three others would follow."

"Clever," Jonah answered. "Most do not realize how much dragons can do."

"Well, when one goes to school with Tas, you have the advantage of learning about dragons," Kaidan argued.

"Why is that?" Moira asked.

The friends looked at each other. It was Grierr that spoke. "Tas is a Dragon Talker from Quinsenta," he explained. "His dragon stayed on campus while we were in school."

"What ails him?"

Thierren let out a sigh. "We don't know," Thierren admitted. "We have a theory, but Jonah and I need to discuss it more to figure out what happened."

"A curse or spell?" Kaidan asked. Though he knew of none that could do what was happening with Tas.

Jonah looked at Thierren, who nodded. The healer was exhausted and was letting Jonah take the lead on this. "We believe he was attacked through his connection with dragons," Jonah explained. "Like Thierren said, it's a working theory that we have not had time to really delve further into it. At the moment, it is the only thing that makes sense, but its implications are ... troubling."

"How so?" Kaidan asked.

Thierren looked almost dead on his feet. When he stood, Grierr grabbed his arm to steady him as his legs swayed. "I think I need sleep," Thierren admitted to them all. He could feel the exhaustion heavy on his bones. "Jonah, will you be fine with explaining it all?"

"Yes, go rest," Jonah agreed. "We can handle everything else."

Thierren nodded. He bid good night, then headed past the screen where the cots were. He toed off his boots before collapsing on the cot closest to where Tas lay.

"What happened?" Kaidan asked after he erected a charm around them to keep their voices from bothering the two sleeping men.

"Verde was leading us here. Tas was in communication with him and the herd," Grierr explained. "After lunch, we were riding. Edelberg had Tas on a horse with him in the event of a bandit attack, so this way Tas could stay connected to the herd. All of a sudden Tas made this noise as if he was being tortured. The rest falls to Jonah and Thierren for knowing what to do."

"What do you know of Blood Dragons?" Jonah asked. There would be no way of making this conversation easy.

"They are creatures of legends," Edelberg said, ignoring the look on Grierr's face. "Some believe they never existed but used as a warning to avoid areas, to protect sacred spots."

"There is nothing sacred about them," Jonah commented.

Moira stared at Jonah as the words found meaning. Jonah studied her. "What do you know of them?"

"As Sir Edelberg stated, creatures of legends," Moira stated. Jonah arched an eyebrow at her, so she continued. "The God Leo, while being the god of the hunt, was a tinkerer, an inventor."

"You don't hear that about him," Grierr commented.

"There is a lot that has been lost over time," Moira admitted. She accepted the tea that Edelberg had refilled for her. "He was known to experiment with animals to see if he could create different versions of them, if they could be infused with magic."

"That's almost barbaric," Edelberg stated. "And crossing a lot of lines, if he was a sorcerer, he would violate our laws."

"He was often in trouble for these creations," Moira continued. Jonah had given her a nod to keep going. She had a feeling he would take over if he felt he needed to add to what she knew. "The first rumor of a Blood Dragon was during the Tribal Wars. They believed it at first to be the spirits of the dead tribes coming back to wreak havoc on those who betrayed them. Their fire, it wasn't real fire, but it poisoned the land that it fell on. People who had been burned by it died slowly as if it poisoned their bodies from with in."

"Leo created them," Kaidan realized.

Jonah nodded. "He had a laboratory somewhere on this continent," Jonah took over the tale. "Here he would work in peace, often on how to aid humans, elves, and dwarves. Yet now and then, an invention would go wrong. He would destroy it. They said he would throw whatever failed into the Volcano of Vulcan. One of his creations was he wanted to create a hybrid dragon that essentially could be controlled by dragons."

"Tas would say that is a terrible idea," Grierr replied. "One does not control a dragon, but learns to live with its quirks and habits."

"Leo learned this as well. He threw his creation into the volcano and it is rumored that out came the first Blood Dragon," Jonah continued. "Leo was appalled by what he had created and vowed to destroy the creature. He spent the rest of his time on this earth destroying each and every one. Before he returned to the heavens, he destroyed his workshop and all his notes so no one could recreate them."

"So how does this lead to Tas?" Kaidan asked.

"It's rumored that Leto, the god of illusions and tricks, found his uncle's old workshop and restored it, along with all of his notes."

Grierr cursed under his breath. "Meaning he found out about the Blood Dragon and most likely has created one," Grierr stated. "Bloody hell."

"What do they do exactly?" Edelberg asked. "How do their burns poison people and ruin the ground?"

"They bring destruction," Moira answered. "They breathe a blue fire that can destroy anything in its path. Its blood poisons the land if it spills on it. Their claws are poisonous, so if they cut you with one, your blood will become corrupted. It is a slow and painful way to die if you don't wish to be turned into a blood sorcerer."

"But Tas is stable," Edelberg pointed out.

"Thierren used dragon's blood," Moira realized.

Jonah nodded. "Verde offered some of his blood when he realized what was going on with Tas. Thierren mixed that into the healing tea that he gave Tas."

"Unless you want to become a blood sorcerer or die, the only known cure is blood given freely by a dragon."

"Are you a Dragon Talker too?" Moira asked him.

"No, I'm just a sea captain."

"Jonah, a Blood Dragon did not attack Tas," Grierr pointed out. He had seen no monster in the area they had been in.

"Not physically," Jonah answered. "I ... there is a record of a Dragon Talker who had been attacked mentally by a Blood Dragon. They can corrupt the mind, poison it against itself. They use that link between a Dragon Talker and a dragon to change the mind."

"The black ooze that Tas was vomiting?" Edelberg asked, shuddering at the memory of watching it come out of Tas's body.

"The corruption," Jonah said simply.

Chapter 11

Thierren went for a run when he woke up the following morning. There had been no issues during the night and after the amount of energy he used on Tas, he now needed to run off the rush that came to him the next day. On his run, he saw Edelberg was working with the group of people who were acting as guards. Jonah and Grierr were probably discussing strategy with Kaidan. Once Tas was well enough to move, they would have to start the journey to the watchtower. There was an urgent sense they would need to move due to the increase of soldiers that were patrolling the highways and investigating the woods. The dragons and other creatures were doing an excellent job of keeping the soldiers from getting too far into the woods.

    As he entered through the hidden entrance to camp, he slowed down to talk to the two people who were keeping watch. He had seen nothing or felt nothing in his run around the perimeter. They thanked him for his information, from there he walked toward his tent. Thierren spotted Moira standing near the hospital tent as if she were waiting for him.

    "I just checked on him while you were out," Moira informed him.

    "Was he still asleep?" Thierren asked, accepting the mug of water from her.

"He had just woken up. I hope you don't mind, but I explained everything to Lysander. You have not met him yet, but he is the other camp healer," Moira replied.

"That's fine," Thierren answered.

"He has some additional information," Moria told him. "His clan had spotted a creature that resembles a Blood Dragon last fall. They quickly moved locations and researched their history on them."

"I would like to talk to him," Thierren stated.

"After you change and have breakfast, come to the medical tent. We can talk, and you can meet the few patients we have in there?"

"That would work," Thierren agreed.

Thierren bowed his head and finished the walk to the tent. He entered through the flap and saw that Tas was sitting in a chair at the table where Jonah, Grierr, and Kaidan were looking at a map. Tas still was pale and had a faint gray pallor to him.

"You should rest," Thierren informed him.

"Any more resting and moss would grow on me," Tas protested. "I'm just sitting."

Thierren arched an eyebrow at him. "He is," Grierr assured Thierren. "Though he needs frequent reminders."

"You are the worst patient ever," Thierren almost growled. He went to his pack and grabbed fresh clothes to change into.

They had a privacy screen to change behind and a pitcher of water and towels to clean with. When he was clean and in his travel tunic and leggings, he joined the others at the table.

"What do we have?" Thierren asked.

"How long until Tas can move?" Kaidan asked.

"Three days at most," Thierren figured. "As long as he doesn't spike a fever in the next 24 hours. Your other healer, Lysander, might have more information on Blood Dragons."

"Several of his clan are part of his group," Kaidan answered. "His sister, Rhea, is their leader at the moment. She informed me they had a potential run in with one last fall."

"I'm going to speak with him and Moira after I finish eating," Thierren replied. "What are our plans so far?"

"We are planning to filter out into three groups," Grierr explained. "Jonah has identified three paths we can take to the Watchtower. The group is too large. We will draw attention."

"We are going to split the six of us amongst the three groups," Kaidan took over from Grierr. "Grierr will make a runic stone that will alert the others if they have found trouble or when they have reached the Tower."

"How are we splitting the groups?" Thierren inquired.

"We are placing you with Tas," Grierr assured. "You are the only qualified healer to deal with his sorry ass."

"I am coherent," Tas reminded them.

"Lysander or Moira should go with Grierr," Thierren suggested, ignoring Tas. "His group will need someone who knows something about healing."

That had Tas chuckling as Kaidan tried to keep a straight face, but finally lost it when Grierr flipped Thierren off. Edelberg walked in on Tas and Kaidan cracking up while Thierren and Grierr were staring at each other.

"What did I miss?" Edelberg asked.

"I was just informing Kaidan that Grierr's healing skills have not improved since school," Thierren stated.

"What healing skills?" Edelberg asked, confused. This comment had Tas and Kaidan erupting into a new fit of laughing.

"Moving on," Grierr said, trying to sound serious. "Tas and Thierren will lead one group. They will have the route through the woods, as this will give them the most cover. Jonah and Kaidan will take the next one over the old wood cutters trail. They could run into some bandits, but it should be pretty easy. I, Edelberg, and Rhea will take the old highway. We could run into a few minor patrols and bandits, so we will have to make ourselves not look like refugees. We can figure out which group Moira and Lysander go with, but a healer in each group would be good."

"How are we going to hide the refugees?" Edelberg asked.

"In plain sight," Rhea said as she joined them. She had her bright red hair pulled back into a complicated bun and wore her basic leather uniform. She most likely had a dozen knives on her.

"Rhea," Kaidan said with a hint of a smile. "The one sitting is Tas. The tallest one is Grierr, Edelberg is the one with the beard, and Thierren is the blonde. You already met Jonah."

"I have heard a lot about all of you," Rhea grinned as she set down bread, cheese, and some salted meats. "Our cook has an idea. It's a bit out there, but it might work."

"What did Tolk suggest?" Kaidan asked her.

"Painting some wagons to look like a traveling group of musicians and entertainers," Rhea replied. "They are more common in the area, going from town to town. Because of the current state of affairs, they are going to look a bit more run down as no one is really okay with strangers at the moment."

They all wanted to point out a flaw, but stepped back to think about it. Tas spoke first. "You could bill Grierr as part giant and Edelberg as a strong man," Tas stated.

"It's crazy but it could actually work," Edelberg agreed as he pulled at his beard, thinking of the potential the idea had.

"I guess we'll call a group lunch and find out if any of our people have talents that could waylay the patrols," Kaidan answered. "If you can fill in a bunch of people with actual talents, it will be more believable."

"I will get word out that we will eat as a large group today," Rhea stated. She looked at Thierren. "When you feel the urge to run again, some of our new recruits, as we are calling them, would run with you."

"I'll keep that in mind," Thierren told her. "If you will all excuse me, I need to change. I promised Moira I would head over once I've eaten."

"If you need Jonah, he's helping with the horses," Grierr told him.

Thierren nodded as he headed behind the screen to change into leather travel pants and a green homespun tunic. He ignored his hair before grabbing his medical satchel and headed out of the tent. The hospital tent was located across the path from Kaidan's tent. It was large. They had brought together several tents to create the space. It impressed him when he entered, seeing a pitcher with soap to wash hands upon entering. Cots seemed to be hidden behind screens or blankets hanging from the roof of the tent. He spotted Moira talking to an elf that had the same bright red hair as Rhea. Moira looked up and nodded to him.

"Lysander, this is Thierren," Moria introduced the two men.

"A pleasure," Lysander stated as they shook hands. "Kaidan told me you have serval medical degrees?"

Thierren nodded. "Your training?"

"Our clan's healer," Lysander answered. "When we had to split the clan up because of new laws cracking down on Elves in Rochleaux she gave me the clan's healer tome. She said she had it memorized and I would need it more."

"That is a gift above anything," Thierren stated. "My aunt trained under a clan healer. The knowledge of your people is immense, especially with herbal remedies and battlefield care."

"What of you, Moira?" Thierren asked her.

"I was raised on a small island," Moira answered. "Ours was the only village. Our village healer taught much of what he learned to me. Then, in my travels, I would stay with other healers and learn from them."

Thierren nodded. "Moira said your clan had a run in with a Blood Dragon?"

"Yes, last fall, before the harvest moon," Lysander recalled. "My sister is one of our lead hunters. She was leading a group into a section of woods we always hunted, for we could get the most game to be salted for the winter months. You can ask Rhea for the details of the meeting, but the area they usually hunted looked as if a blight of some kind had plagued it. The ground was black, the vegetation was all rotten. The animal carcasses looked as if acid had boiled them. We teach the lore of the First Age as a warning when we are young. They teach us of Blood Dragons, and the Great Hunter Leo's fight to destroy the creature he created. Rhea, and the elders with her, recognized the sight for what it was. It had been the nesting grounds of a Blood Dragon. They returned and the following morning we packed up and headed to our winter camp several months early."

"Does any of your lore talk of how to heal a person if they had been attacked whether physically or mentally?" Thierren asked as he jotted the information down in his journal.

"The notes in the tome states those that have magic in them have a higher chance of survival," Lysander told him. "I would show you, but unless you can read Elven, and the water dialect of it, you would not understand it."

"I can read very basic Elven," Thierren admitted, surprising the Elf in front of him. "But not enough that I could read a clan tome. I trust you."

"The records show that during the First Age, those that were natural witches, seers, or sorcerers seemed to survive the initial burns," Lysander explained. "The 'mundane' died after several agonizing hours. It took many years for a treatment for those who survived. Even then, those that survived the initial burn had a poor chance of survival."

"Unless they turned to blood sorcery," Moira commented.

"Not necessarily," Lysander argued. "We only hear of the successful ones, but many die during the ritual as their body cannot handle the poison and then the influx of mana that enters them."

"We learned something similar at the Academy of Magi," Thierren recalled. "There is a theory that those who survive the ritual actually have some small amount of magic in them. That is why their body can handle the mana that comes into them. But the power is so small it goes undetected."

"That would make sense," Lysander agreed. He quickly jotted down a few questions he now had about blood magic. "Anyway, the treatment they developed, I believe, is like what you used on your friend. The only additional ones are if there are burns to use the freely given dragon's blood mixed into a burn salve to help keep the corrosive properties of the poison from eating away at skin and muscle."

"We should make sure we have burn salves ready in the event we run into one," Thierren stated.

"I can begin work on that," Lysander volunteered. "I have the ingredients I need to work on them. Do you know how many groups we are planning to create?"

"Three, the plans are for a healer to be with each group," Thierren answered.

"Then I will create packs for each group with instructions just in the event we are unavailable," Lysander suggested.

"That would be most appreciative," Thierren agreed. He looked at Moira, who had also been making notes of their conversation. "You said you have other patients?"

"We have a broken leg, a bad cough, severe rash, and some other ailments," Moira told him.

"The broken leg is how recent?" Thierren asked her as they headed toward the teenager that had his leg wrapped up.

"Five days," Moira recalled. "He was helping chop wood for the fires when one goat got loose. He tried to help get it back in the pen but tripped over the axe and, well, the rest is history."

Moira smiled at the lad. "Tommy," Moira greeted the teen. "This is Thierren. He's a trained healer and friend of Sir Kaidan."

"You came in on the dragon?" The teen asked.

"I did," Thierren agreed. "Miss Moira here tells me you broke your leg."

"I tripped over my axe," Tommy groaned.

"Happens to us all," Thierren assured him. "I am going to look at it, if that's okay. I can use my sorcerer ability sometimes to help speed up healing."

Tommy looked nervous for a moment. "Is me being part elf going to affect it?"

"No, it might help me," Thierren told him. "Is that why you are running?"

"The Prime Chancellor, or whatever he is calling himself, believes all elves contain magic," Tommy explained, reiterating what Lysander had told him moments ago. "My parents hid my siblings and me when the guards came. After they were dragged out of the house, I grabbed my siblings and ran into the woods. We ran into Mr. Tolk a few days later and he's been helping us since."

"We have them as a family unit?" Thierren asked Moira.

"Yes, Tolk took care of it," Moira replied.

"All right, let's look at this leg," Thierren decided. "We'll give you a pain potion, then I'll unwrap it. You are going to feel your leg become warm and might feel something like prickles along the bone. It means my magic is working."

"Okay, but pain potions don't always work," Tommy warned.

Thierren nodded. He reached into his bag and rummaged around. He found a small container of the ground up herb he wanted. "Add this to the healing potion," Thierren instructs Moira. "It's a common herb, but it works well with helping part elves breakdown the pain potion better. Lysander should have some."

Moira did. "Every species reacts to potions differently," Thierren explained to Tommy. "So, if one knows herbs, they can make modifications to existing recipes to fit the needs of the patients. I make a special healing potion for a friend that is allergic to two of the most common ingredients in it."

"Really?" Tommy asked. "I kind of always thought learning about herbs was boring. My mom was teaching me."

"Oh, it can be," Thierren agreed with him as he finished checking his vitals. "But once you figure out how to create your own potions or change existing ones, it becomes less boring."

"That's actually kind of neat," Tommy admitted. "You don't need magic?"

"Nope," Thierren replied.

"It should be ready," Moira informed them. She handed Tommy the potion. "Lysander was using his own healing ointment on the leg. Could the herb be why?"

"Yes, but I only recently learned that it works in the potion as well," Thierren replied. "He might not know that."

After Tommy took it, he laid down and waited. Soon, he felt the effects of the potion. He felt relieved, as he could finally relax and not feel the pain.

"Now remember, you are going to feel heat and some prickling," Thierren reminded him.

Thierren unwrapped the leg, wincing at the bruising and the swelling. He laid a hand over it, moving it up and down the leg. The teen had broken the leg in two different locations. The one he could mend easily, the other was a bit more complicated. He could start the healing process, then finish once they were at the Tower.

"Remind me to have Tolk's group moved to my caravan or Lysander's," Thierren instructed to Moira. "I can mend the one, but the other will take a few times to do so."

Moira wrote the instructions down. She helped Thierren wrap the leg again. Thierren explained why he rubbed a healing ointment on the entire leg, then showed her how to wrap it better and where the splint should be. Moira was impressed with his skill and knowledge. He never talked down to her, his voice almost monotone, but she appreciated the information he will share with her. Not every doctor or healer would take the time to explain what they were doing to the patient or to another healer.

Tommy was deep asleep once they were done. Thierren wrote a recipe for his creation of the pain potion that would work on him so that Moira would have a copy. "This will work on any part, elf," Thierren told her. "Because of their longer lives, some components don't work as well. Adding the yellow ivy seems to make them work better."

"Thank you," Moira told him.

They worked on a few more patients. They were fit to go with the other two groups. Thierren then headed to the older man, who had been coughing on and off while he had been in the tent.

"Don't waste your time, boy," the man grumbled.

"I'll leave you two," Moira said. She gave Thierren a look that warned him this man was difficult.

"And if I want to waste my time?" Thierren asked the old man.

"Then you're a fool," he said. He coughed again.

Thierren helped him sit up. He handed the man a cloth to cough into. He let his magic listen to his pulse and lungs.

"How long did you work in the mines?" Thierren asked as he went and poured the man water. He handed him the glass.

"How do you know I worked in mines?"

"The dust in your lungs," Thierren informed him.

"You a sorcerer, aren't you?"

"Guilty," Thierren said. He sat on a stool near the bed. "So how long?"

148

"Thirty years, then the cough came. I was told not to come back by the human that ran the mine, for it scared the younger miners," the man stated. "The dwarves tried to help me."

"Can't have that, now can we?" Thierren said sarcastically. "Don't want them to see what could become of them."

"Isn't that the truth?" The old man looked at him. "You going to tell me you can fix me with some fancy tonic or spell?"

"No," Thierren said. "We both know there is no cure for black lung."

"She keeps thinking it's something else," he said, motioning to the tent flap. "Keep telling her to leave me in peace."

Thierren was studying the cloth he had the man cough into. "Going by the sample you left on the cloth, I'm guessing you are going into the final stages," Thierren replied.

"You know how to sugarcoat things."

"I can bring her back if you want something sugar coated."

The old man cackled at that. "Tell you what, I'll tell you my name. I'm Tobbin."

"I'm Thierren," Thierren replied. "Well, Tobbin, now that we introduced ourselves, let's have a conversation about what we can and can't do about your condition."

"Like I have options," Tobbin said almost bitterly.

"With me around, you do," Thierren informed him. "I'm not someone who bleeds a being dry of their money or their actual blood. I became a healer and a doctor to help people."

"Thought you said there wasn't a cure."

"I did, but I can help ease the symptoms, so what time you have will not be riddled with pain."

"We both know I am going to suffocate to death."

Thierren looked at the old man, a man the world forgot. "Look, I cannot stop death," Thierren began. "I tried once and almost lost myself in doing so. The final stages of black lung are not pretty, especially without doctor's care. But with care, we can work out a plan that can make it less painful, so your last moments won't be filled with panic and fear."

"If I refuse treatment?"

"Then you refuse. I won't force you into treatment," Thierren informed him.

"All right, let's talk."

#

An hour later, Thierren emerged from the tent. He headed to Kaidan's where everyone was meeting to go over the lists. Kaidan was talking with Grierr when he entered. He walked over to them. He knew he was pale; he had perhaps overdone it today after healing Tas last night. People were gathered around the table already. He was one of the last to arrive.

"Put Tobbin on my list," Thierren informed them.

"He finally talked," Kaidan said in disbelief.

"He has Black Lung, is entering the final phases," Thierren said. "We worked out a plan that will ease most of his suffering. We're talking probably less than a month before he's lungs will stop working."

"Moira has been trying to find other causes," Kaidan stated.

"I know, he told me, I'll talk with her and Lysander as well," Thierren promised. "When we get to the Tower, I'll go over his plans with you, so you know what needs to be done. We need to send letters to some dwarves he wants with him during the last stage."

"We'll have Verde pick a dragon to take the letters."

"You need a moment to clear your head?" Grierr asked Thierren.

"I didn't scan him too much. I pulled back once I saw what it was," Thierren assured him. "I've learned my lesson."

"And yet it happened again?" Grierr asked.

Thierren stared at him, then looked across the tent to where Tas was sitting, talked to Jonah. "I'd risk it all over again."

"You two are both idiots," Grierr mumbled.

Kaidan knew he was missing a story, one that Grierr and Thierren knew. He was not sure if he wanted to know the details. Kaidan decided to just get everyone's attention. Soon, about twelve people were around the table.

"Okay," Kaidan began. "Formal introductions: the man sitting with dark hair is Tas. He is a trained sorcerer. The red head is Edelberg. He is a trained battle mage. The tall one is Grierr, he is a rune smith and sorcerer. Then there is Thierren who is a mage healer and doctor. Last is Jonah. He is our guide. Questions?"

Those from the camp shook their heads. "Good," Kaidan said. "The blonde female is Rhea; she is an elf in case the ears didn't give her away."

"I'm from a water clan," Rhea stated. "I can find water sources without rods or tools."

"And they want to lock you up?" Edelberg asked. There was some doubt in his voice.

"They already have ten of my clan before we escaped. There are four here with me," Rhea answered.

"Next to Rhea, is Corkrin. He has been training whoever he can on how to wield a weapon. He isn't being hunted, but joined us to help protect those he can."

"I ran into Kaidan while protecting about twenty of these people," Corkrin said. His voice was deep.

Once the rest of the introductions had been made the meeting could begin. "All right, we are sending Josiah and his family with Thierren's group," Kaidan informed them. "Grierr is going to make a rune stone that will hide the fact that Josiah is coming into his sorcerer's abilities. Tas is also the best teacher among us and will teach him how to control his powers. Cork, I'm assuming you are going to want to go with his family?"

"I am, unless I am needed elsewhere."

"You have been with them the whole time, changing that now will terrify the kids," Rhea argued.

"Our thought as well," Kaidan replied. "Rhea, I am going to want you going with Jonah and myself. We will need your tracking to help with bandits."

"Do you want to split my clan between the three? That way, you have the best trackers divided amongst the three groups?"

"If you will part," Grierr answered. "We didn't want to separate you; I know how tight clans are and they don't separate unless they have to."

Rhea stared at the giant. "Thank you," she said with a bow of the head. "The knowledge we will meet up at the end of the journey will keep us focused on getting there."

"We'll have the five of you decide who should go where," Kaidan told her. "But you are with me."

"I always am," she teased. "Have Lysander go with Grierr's group. Otherwise, he will hover when I have to scout."

Kaidan rolled his eyes at her. "The few dwarves we have will go with Edelberg and Grierr. Edelberg has created documents to show they are from the clan outside of Rochleaux."

"Can he do that with everyone?" One of others asked.

"No," Edelberg answered. "Think of the paperwork as an illusion. I can keep it up for a few, but trying to keep it up for the entire group would have it falling apart in moments."

"Remember, there is a limit to what we can do and what we can maintain," Kaidan reminded them. He had this conversation with the group a few times to explain why he and the few other sorcerers with them were not always using their abilities. "Even with unique abilities, there is a limit and a consequence for using it."

Tas went to add something, but stopped. Thierren studied him as the others talked about which group would leave first and how they would stay in communication. Tas gripped the edge of the table as he tried to focus on what was being spoken, yet his brain was feeling foggy. His grip tightened on the table as the room seemed to swim around him. Tas did not see Thierren was moving toward him until Thierren was right there. Tas wanted to say something, but his blood felt as if it was on fire. Instead of speaking, he let go of the table with one hand and grabbed Thierren's forearm, his eyes wide with panic. He saw Thierren's mouth moving, but he could not hear the words.

"Tas!" Thierren yelled as he felt the strength leave Tas's grip. Grierr was right there to catch Tas as his body gave out.

"Our tent," Thierren instructed. "Jonah?"

"I am with you," Jonah said as he joined them.

Kaidan called for someone to get Moira and to see if a dragon was nearby as they hurried to the tent. Grierr laid Tas down on the cot while Thierren grabbed his bag and journal. Jonah was feeling Tas's forehead. He noted black ooze coming from Tas's nose.

"Thierren," Jonah said quietly.

Thierren froze at the tone that Jonah had used. He looked over and saw the ooze. "Talk to the dragons," Thierren instructed Jonah.

Jonah rushed out of the tent. Thierren stared at Tas, trying to figure out what he could do. "Treat the symptoms," he whispered to himself. "Grierr a bowl of cool water and a cloth, also have them prepare a kettle."

Grierr nodded and headed for the tent. He bumped into Moira. "What does he need?" Moira asked.

"Bowl of water, cloth, and boiling water," Grierr answered.

"Stay, I'll get it," Moira told him. "I'll send Lysander over. There are no patients in the medical tent if he wants to move him."

"I'll let him know."

Grierr headed back to where Tas lay. Thierren was kneeling next to him, taking his vitals. "Moira is getting what is needed," Grierr informed him. Thierren nodded. "Look, I know you can't ever make promises. But can you make me one?"

Thierren looked up at Grierr. "What?"

"If he is going to die and you need more energy to keep him alive, use mine," Grierr answered. "I have nothing to lose in this life. I have lost everything I had to lose."

Thierren just stared at Grierr for a few moments, not sure what to say. He stood up and walked over to the giant of a man and hugged him as tight as I could.

"You have lost more than most, but you're wrong," Thierren informed him. "You still have us, asshole."

Chapter 12

Thierren sat on the seat of the wagon. He was taking a break from steering the horses. His group had left at dawn, with Verde following them. They left two days early, but they needed to get Tas away from the camp. The only theory that Verde, Jonah, and Thierren could produce was that the blood dragon that had poisoned Tas was in the camp's area and was using his weak connection to Tas to attack him again. They knew little about the effects of blood dragons on Dragon Talkers, so everything was a theory. They had decided near midnight when Tas's fever spiked to dangerous levels, causing him to become delirious and have another fit.

"You could climb into the back and take a nap," Tolk informed Thierren. He studied the healer. "I can handle the wagon for many hours. Go rest, we need our healer healthy."

"You will wake me if I'm needed?" Thierren asked as Tolk slowed the wagon down.

"Yes, now rest," Tolk ordered.

Thierren steadied himself before he climbed over the wagon seat and into the covered wagon. Tas was lying on a makeshift bed in the wagon. His eyes were open, watching Thierren as he climbed into the wagon.

"How are you feeling?" Thierren asked him.

"The pressure on my mind is releasing," Tas informed him. "Ren, what are we going to do?"

"Grierr, Jonah, and I plan to make use of your grandfather's library. Lysander is researching everything in his clan's tome," Thierren admitted as he made a spot for himself. "For the moment, you are going to rest, and Grierr is going to work on a rune charm that will help to alert you to their presence."

"And if we can't?"

"Then I find a cure," Thierren said simply.

"You say that like it is no small task," Tas stated.

"Tas, rest," Thierren instructed. "Or we will have Tolk yelling at both of us to rest."

"Tell me the plan again?"

Thierren laid down and folded his arms underneath his head. "When we arrive at the Tower, we will help Kaidan get everyone settled," Thierren reminded him. "From there, we will send word to the Council and to your family. Once we are in Hruan, you should be fine. Kaidan suggested a library for me to check out, for there had been blood dragon attacks there during the tribal wars of the First Age. While you are in your meetings with Hruan and its navy, I'll research. Jonah is going to talk to some of his contacts and see if they know anything. Then we leave for Quinsenta where most likely the unofficial war council will be called."

"Thierren..."

"Tas go to sleep," Thierren yawned. "I'm too exhausted to hold a conversation right now."

"Do you think the others will be fine?"

"Tas," Thierren groaned. He heard Tas grumble as he let the movement from the wagon lull him to sleep.

\#

Edelberg was walking with Grierr as they scouted ahead with a few of their group. They were well within yelling distances if anything happened. They had left a day after Thierren and Tas. None of the groups wanted to wait longer than they had to, for fear of Tas's health. Edelberg knew it was killing Grierr not to be with Tas, with him being as ill as he was. They were more like brothers than friends.

"How do you think they're doing?" Edelberg asked.

"I am going to say they are fine since the dragons have not alerted us to anything different," Grierr answered. He looked to the sky that was mostly blocked by the overhang of the trees that lined the road. Though they were taking the old highway, it had been some time since anyone came through this way. If a dragon was up in the sky, it would be hard to see them or their outline.

"Jonah is more than what he says he is," Edelberg commented.

"We're all more than what we say we are," Grierr replied. He looked at his friend, who had made a sigh at his statement. "Yes, he is more. He isn't a sorcerer nor a god. Yet he means no harm. In fact, he has shown parts of himself that he has kept hidden to help us."

"And it doesn't bother you?"

"I hid who I was from all of you," Grierr reminded him. "Did that bother you?"

"There was a reason."

"Just like I am sure there is a reason for him to not tell us everything just yet," Grierr stated. "Like I said to Thierren earlier in this journey. We have had the luxury of knowing each other for years where Jonah is new, so we will not know everything about him as we do with each other."

"What of Moira?"

Grierr raised an eyebrow at the abrupt name change. "What about her?"

"There is something about her as well," Edelberg answered.

"You are just like the gossiping old women in my village," Grierr laughed, slapping him lightly on the back. "I could picture you having tea with them and swapping the latest town gossip."

"You exaggerate," Edelberg argued. He knew the women that Grierr spoke of and hated that he would often chat with them when he was in Emi.

They heard an approaching horse and saw it was Moira. "Mind if I join you?" She asked. "Our music trio is quite the gossips."

"Perhaps we could send Edelberg. They can exchange what they know," Grierr teased.

"Ignore him," Edelberg said to Moira, who was trying not to laugh at them both.

"I am sure Edelberg feels he needs to keep us well informed of what is going on around us," Moira suggested.

"You know what, I'm going to do a patrol," Edelberg retorted and led his horse in toward the woods.

"Was he like that in school?" Moira asked.

"Edelberg was the person you went to if you wanted to know what was happening," Grierr said fondly.

"Kaidan would speak of the group of you," Moira replied. "You all seem close, despite being out of school for ten years."

"I guess we graduated from the academy at 18, but some of us stayed for apprenticeships and further studies," Grierr admitted. "I worked on my apprenticeship on the Isle of Magic for a year and a half after graduation before I returned home. Most of them were still there, working on their training. Kaidan and Tas often work together as they both work for the Council."

"Which one were you in the group?" Moira inquired.

"In our group of four and then the larger group, I was often the peacekeeper," Grierr stated. "I was the quiet one who watched over everyone. When there was a problem or a fight, I often got dragged in to help solve the problem. Thierren was the hothead, and Tas was the academic. We balanced each other out."

"Do you still balance each other out?"

"In different ways," Grierr answered. "We're changing, so our dynamic is changing."

"Did Tas really have a dragon at school?"

"His dragon often was there even if it did not thrill our headmaster with the idea, but trying to separate the two back then when their bond was growing was impossible."

"But he's not here now?"

"Tas won't take him on long trips because Bart is not a long-distance flier," Grierr explained. "He is a fire and forest dragon. Not a common pairing, so he can go from Hruan to Greedin or Quinsenta to the Isle of Magi with a stop in Greedin. To fly to Emi would be too much for him. He is beautiful, though; he has bright red scales with a green iridescence to them. His eyes are this bright green that sees everything."

"He sounds breathtaking," Moira replied.

"He is," Grierr agreed. "He likes to show off when there are children around. He acts like a puppy around them."

"Making a memorable impression on the kids," Moira stated. "They'll be less terrified of them if they know they can be gentle and kind."

"It's a side benefit for him being a goof."

"I've always been confused. How does one become a Dragon Talker?" Moira asked.

"Well, one way is to become the ruler of Quinsenta," Grierr stated. Moira looked at him in confusion. "They go through a ritual with the ruler of the dragon herds so that they can communicate with each other."

"And the other way?"

"It's all up to chance, luck, or fate, depending on how you look about it," Grierr replied. "You need to be born the same moment a dragonling hatches from their egg. There are three currently at the moment."

"Do they have to be sorcerers or witches?"

"No. One actually is a blacksmith in one town in Quinsenta," Grierr recalled. "He's the first in his family. Then there is an older woman. She's in her 70s and trained Tas and the blacksmith. It's not inherited or passed down."

"How do you know, though, that one has been born?"

"The herd alerts the ruler of the dragon, who then notifies the king or queen of Quinsenta," Grierr tried to remember. "They send delegates to validate the claim."

"How did it begin?"

Grierr chuckled. "You want more information? You are going to need to ask Tas," he informed her.

"Sorry," Moira apologized. "I get excited when I'm learning something new."

"It's fine," Grierr assured her. "Thierren is a lot like you. Actually, he is another person you can ask about Dragon Talkers. He did a lot of research about them."

Moira went to ask a question when they heard a bird call. Grierr answered back to the call, then motioned for her to follow him. They rode to the lead horses.

"Guards approaching from the south," Grierr informed Clay.

Clay, one of the elves that rode with them, was silent for a moment to see if he could pick up the horses. "They're a few miles out," he confirmed. "I can just barely hear them. Get everyone ready."

Moira rode to inform everyone to remember their roles and what to say and do. Grierr waited for Edelberg to emerge from the woods as they rode on. There was no time to try to hide from the guards. It would only draw more suspicion if they tried. Edelberg emerged from the woods, riding up alongside Grierr. They nodded to each other.

They heard the whistle and then the order to stop. Edelberg and Grierr moved to the front of the group, where ten Rochleaux military guards were standing.

"Who is in charge?" One asked.

"I am," Edelberg stated as he climbed off his horse.

"I am Captain Larhode," the captain introduced himself. "What is the meaning of the size of such a group?"

"We are a theatre company," Edelberg informed him as he rummaged in his bag for papers. "We usually tour the southern section of Rochleaux this time of year."

"Papers?"

Edelberg handed him the papers to show them as a theatre company. The captain studied them as his own men walked up and down the wagon train.

"You have not picked a suitable time to return," Captain Larhode informed him.

"We have learned that," Edelberg assured him. "We picked up some supplies for horses and are headed back to Hruan as we speak."

"Captain, no one is permitted to cross the border," a soldier whispered.

The captain nodded to the soldier. "You all originate from Hruan?"

"Yes, that is where our company is based out of," Edelberg answered. He learned to keep lies simple and to only answer the question asked.

"That puts us in a tricky situation. As you see, the borders have been closed to all," Captain Larhode informed him.

"We have permission to travel across the border," Edelberg protested.

"If you have this proof, I would like to see it."

Edelberg nodded and returned to his satchel. He fumbled around until he found the folio that contained the document. He handed it to the captain.

The captain, being doubtful of any permission, took the folio with a smirk. He opened it and read the contents, his smirk vanishing when he saw the seal at the bottom of the document.

"I see," Captain Larhode said as he studied it a second time. "A few questions before you leave."

"Of course," Edelberg agreed.

"Rumors of a refugee camp in this area have been floating around. They sent us to investigate," the captain informed him.

"You can count the number of people in this caravan. You will see it matches what is on the document," Edelberg answered.

"Very well."

Captain Larhode called for a few soldiers to count. Grierr went with them so he could keep everyone calm.

"Is he part giant?" Captain Larhode inquired.

"That's part of his act," Edelberg confided.

"It is believable. No signs of refugees on your travels?"

"None," Edelberg replied. "We're a pretty large group. I'm sure if we were near them, they most likely fled the area."

"You would draw attention," Captain Larhode agreed.

The soldiers returned with Grierr. "Numbers match, sir."

"Very well," Captain Larhode said. "You are free to go."

"But, sir...."

"They have the personal seal of the President of Hruan so unless you want to start an international incident, I would be silent," Captain Larhode growled. He motioned to the two guards. "Bring him back to the barracks. Have him put in the stocks for questioning a superior."

The soldiers nodded, grabbing the stunned soldier. Captain Larhode smiled as he turned back to Edelberg. "I would hurry to the border if I were you. I cannot guarantee how much longer such paperwork will keep you safe here."

Edelberg nodded. They all watched as the captain and his men moved on down the road. The thought of breaking for lunch now vanished from their minds.

"Clay," Grierr said to the elf. "Inform everyone we eat while we ride."

Clay saluted him, then headed to pass the word on. Edelberg looked at his friend. "Was that a threat?"

"A warning," Grierr decided. "When word reaches the Lord Chancellor, or whatever he is calling himself, that we could cross the border because of the seal, he is going to make it harder to do so again."

****

Kaidan let out a sigh as he finally sat down on a log in front of the fire. He used the rune stones Grierr had given him that would conceal the smoke from others. Tents were up, they set wards, a scouting party was out, ensuring they were safe, and the dragons were resting nearby. He rolled his shoulders and just watched the flames for a few moments before a bowl of stew was handed him. He looked up and saw Rhea standing there with her own bowl.

"I was told you have not eaten yet," Rhea informed him as he sat down.

"Did Jonah get any?" Kaidan asked.

"I gave him a bowl before I came to find you."

Kaidan ate a few spoonfuls before he spoke again. "The other two groups are camping," Kaidan informed her. "Jonah was going to get more information from the dragons. So far, everyone is safe, and no one was hurt."

"Good," Rhea replied. "Do you know how he talks to them?"

"Haven't had the time to inquire," Kaidan admitted. "I am curious about it."

"How do you think Tas is doing?"

"He's with Thierren. If anyone will get him better, it's that asshole," Kaidan assured her. He laid a hand on her knee and squeezed it. "I promise he'll be okay."

"You and Thierren have a past," Rhea noted with a hint of a smile.

"A past you know about," Kaidan reminded her with a roll of the eye.

"I guess I get it after seeing him," Rhea went on with a bigger grin.

"You are annoying."

"Yet you keep me around."

Kaidan just chuckled before going back to his soup. He heard someone approach. Jonah sat down across from them. "Any word?"

"Taslan seems to improve the farther they get. They have camped for the night," Jonah answered. "They had no issue on their trail."

"Good," Kaidan said. He had been worried about what would have happened if Thierren's group was attacked.

"The other group ran into a group of guards. The paper from your father seems to have saved them," Jonah went on.

"Are they okay?" Kaidan asked. He knew Rhea was worried about her brother.

"They're fine, but they were warned that the paperwork might not work again."

Rhea looked at Kaidan, whose face was hard to read. "More to tell my father about," Kaidan sighed. "To think Tas and I had hoped there would be an easy solution to what was going on."

Rhea laid a hand on his arm. "This Watchtower, how is it different from the others?" She asked Jonah.

"It's still intact," Jonah began. "It was also one of the larger of the Towers with walls. At one point, a small village lived there to maintain it. It straddles the border of Hruan and Rochleaux, to one side woods, to the other is a lake."

"And we are sure it's neutral?"

"All Watchtowers are," Jonah reminded her.

"They say that, but we know some do not follow that," Rhea challenged.

"There was one time in history when a ruler tried to claim a Watchtower. It did not go well for him," Jonah said softly.

"What happened?" Rhea asked.

"It was during the First Age," Jonah recalled. "During the reign of the War King. He had conquered large parts of what were now Vulcan and Rochleaux before he set his sights on the fertile lands of Hruan. The Watchtower could warn the tribes of Hruan. His army took control of the Watchtower, claiming it for himself. This angered not just the tribes in the area, but all the tribes throughout the world. They had built the Towers as a symbol of peace and help. They were to warn of troubles, and grant safe passage to those that passed through their doors that needed aid. He believed he was better than all, a warrior king."

"You said it did not go well for him," Kaidan stated.

"He held control of the area for twenty years, but it was not an easy rule, for the tribes rebelled in ways that were undetected," Jonah answered. "The tribes worked on building alliances with other tribes so that when their number was greater than his, the rebels could take back the Watchtower, and then the tribes that he had held prisoner."

"So, it was controlled," Rhea argued.

"Depends on how you define controlled," Jonah countered. "The land that surrounded the Watchtower was rumored to be the most fertile in the area. Lush grazing land, fields filled with wildflowers. Plants of great healing properties, as well as rare animals that were forgotten, could be found on these lands."

"And the War king got control of this?"

166

"Not quite. It is said in Hruan the spirits of the land cried for the blood that had been shed on such sacred land. The spirits in their anguish made the land barren and hid the animals away from his blood thirst so that one day, when the people took back the Tower, the animals would return as a sign of rebirth."

"The First Age was when the spirits of nature were in abundance," Jonah answered.

Rhea studied Jonah for a few moments, watching as he ate his stew. "You can talk to dragons?"

"Not in a way that Taslan can," Jonah argued.

"But you can communicate."

"I can," he said simply. He looked up from his stew, sighing he set his bowl to the side. "I have a talent, one would say. I can hear a creature think by laying my hand on their head. They must be willing or ill for me to do so."

"You understand their language?"

"Only why I am connected to them," Jonah answered. "I cannot all of sudden speak the tongue of dragons or the dialects of the elves, but while connected, I can understand what is being said."

"And you are no sorcerer?" Kaidan asked him. They had been taught at the academy about such beings.

"One does not need to be a sorcerer to have a gift," Jonah reminded him. "We met an old man who knew everything about a person upon seeing them. He could see the path set out before them. Yet he was no sorcerer, no witch either. Just an old man with a gift."

"One would say you have a few yourself," Kaidan stated. "You seem to know places and trails that have long been forgotten."

Rhea gave out a startled cry as comprehension dawned on her. "You were there."

"He was where?" Kaidan asked, confused.

"You helped them take the Tower back," Rhea realized. "The clans tell stories of the old ways, of the beings that walked amongst us during the First Age."

"Rhea, he would be hundreds of years old," Kaidan said gently to her.

"Closer to thousands, but I could be off by a few years," Jonah answered. "We are meant to observe, to watch, only to aid when all other paths have failed."

Kaidan stared at the man before him. "Do the others know?"

"They have their ideas. There is an unspoken understanding," Jonah replied.

"You prefer not confirming their suspicion," Rhea realized.

"I like not being known," Jonah answered with a shrug.

Chapter 13

Tas stood staring out of the window of the top floor of the Watchtower as he leaned on his sorcerer staff. Tomorrow would be the Spring Equinox. It seemed fitting that the last of their group finally arrived. He watched the final carriages and wagons being brought in, saw Grierr and Edelberg conducting everyone through the gates. However, how he saw things was new and, according to Thierren was unheard of. The poison from the Blood Dragon had in sense destroyed his vision. Yet he could still see in a way. He saw impressions, shapes, shadows; he knew people based on their auras which had Thierren scrambling because there was a group among the magic community that did not believe in auras. While Thierren researched, Kaidan sparred with Tas to see how limiting his new sight was and found that Tas could hold his own in a fight. It had not thrilled Thierren with that idea, but agreed they needed to know if Tas could still defend himself. They learned he could, though he was going to need practice in dealing with his limited sight.

Tas cocked his head as he heard footsteps come up the stairs. He knew they were Grierr's and prepared for the hug.

Grierr stopped just at the top of the stairs when he saw Tas standing there. Deep down in his gut, Grierr had been worried that when he arrived at the Watchtower Tas would still be ill or dead. Kaidan had just laughed at Grierr's questions when he asked how Tas was doing. To see him standing, looking healthy, and grinning like a fool it made him want to cry in relief. He quickly covered the distance between them and pulled Tas into a tight embrace. He felt Tas patting him on the back as if he knew what Grierr's fears were.

"You are an asshole," Grierr informed Tas as he sat him back down on the ground.

"Thierren and Kaidan have already informed me of that fact," Tas assured him.

He knew Thierren had not told Grierr and Edelberg about his eyesight, as he wanted to do that after they settled the two. At the moment very few knew about it, Kaidan, Rhea, Jonah, and Corkrin were the only ones that knew.

"You lucky son of a bitch," Edelberg mumbled as he walked over and hugged Tas.

"I am," Tas agreed.

"Kaidan said you have contacted the Council already," Grierr stated.

"We did, on the second day we were here," Tas answered. "They are submitting forward the documents to state that the Watchtower is once again under the jurisdiction of the Council of Magi. Along with a clause stating that all who dwell here are under the protection of the Council."

"How will that help them?" Edelberg asked with a hint of doubt that the Council would do anything.

"It means if any country tries to force their way in, it will declare war against the Council, which means an army of pissed off Battle Mages will come to protect those that dwell here," Tas informed him.

"Oh."

"You think you would know this since you are a battle mage," Grierr reminded Edelberg.

Edelberg sent Grierr a glare. "How is the kid that is coming into his magic?"

"The Council is looking into how to get him and his family to the island," Tas answered. "Kaidan, Thierren, and I have been working with him and his family. Corkrin most likely will go with them as well."

"I thought I would find all of you up here," Thierren's voice said as he came up the stairs.

"Tas will always find the best spot in a tower to claim as his," Grierr joked. He got an elbow from Tas.

"It's time for dinner. Tolk has prepared a feast to welcome you all home," Thierren informed them.

"A home cooked meal will be amazing," Edelberg agreed.

Edelberg and Grierr headed for the stairs first. Kaidan had given them a quick tour when Kaidan showed them where their rooms were. Grierr turned back and saw Thierren was standing closer to Tas than normal. They were talking quietly; something was going on. Edelberg yelled something to him, and he hurried down the stairs after him. They met Kaidan at the bottom of the tower that Tas had claimed. Kaidan showed them toward the courtyard where people were spreading out blankets, tables were erected out of barrels and broken doors, and food was being brought out from the kitchen.

Rhea and Moira were already sitting at a rough table talking about what had delayed Grierr and Edelberg's groups. Rhea got up and hugged both men, surprising them as she did so. Kaidan came and joined, resting a hand on Rhea's back as he did so.

"How is Tas, really?" Grierr asked Kaidan quietly as Rhea and Edelberg were talking.

"He has surprised us all," Kaidan replied.

"How has Thierren been?"

"Quiet, he has been treating injuries and some colds while helping with Josiah teaching to control his magic," Kaidan answered.

"How much of this place is in ruins?"

"The main gate section is the most intact. We have been able to clear those rooms out on the first day here. Thierren set up an infirmary. The East gate walls are intact, but those rooms have seen the most damage," Kaidan replied. "Tolk, Jonah, and a few others could clear out the stables, the kitchens, and blacksmith shop. They aren't perfect, but they are workable for the time being. We're moving families with young kids into the rooms and suites that are livable. Jonah has been working on making pens to keep the animals we brought with us in."

"Edelberg and I can help now that we are here," Grierr assured him.

"We are also going to talk about what the guards said to you about the letter you had," Kaidan warned him.

They stopped talking when Thierren and Tas joined them. Moira greeted them both, asking Tas how he was feeling and Thierren about who was in the infirmary. Tobbin was resting in a private room off the infirmary. They sent a letter to a few dwarves he worked with. Kaidan was granting them refuge if they made the trip.

"At some point, Moira, I am going to show you and Lysander what Tobbin will need as the disease advances," Thierren informed her. "We wanted to wait until you were here. This way I only had to go through it once."

"Of course," Moira agreed. "Whatever we can do to help him not suffer, we will do."

"Kaidan, make a speech," Rhea suggested. "Tomorrow is the Spring Equinox, and we are all here."

"Do I have to?" Kaidan sighed.

"Welcome to leadership," Grierr teased.

Kaidan glared at him before standing up. He tapped his knife on his mug to get everyone's attention. "They have informed me I should say a few words," Kaidan began. "Our journey has been long. We have faced uncertainty, restless nights, leaky tents, and cold meals. It is going to take time for us to settle into this new home, knowing that for those who wish it, it is home for good. That we survived with only injuries is a testament to all of you and your will to continue despite what Rochleaux threw at you. With the coming of spring, it brings us into a season of re-birth and growth. Let us also see us coming here as a re-birth, a fresh start, a chance to start again. Hail the Great Mother, Hail Spring!"

Everyone clinked their mugs, goblets, stoneware as they joined in the blessing. Rhea kissed Kaidan on the cheek when he sat down, throwing an arm around him. "I'm proud of you," she whispered.

"You did good," Edelberg agreed, slapping him on the back.

From there, dinner was a lively event. Children were running between tables and out into the overgrown fields that would one day be crops. There was laughter as stories were told of their travels to the Watchtower. As the sun dipped down, the bonfires were lit to signify the coming of spring. There was hope that next spring, they would celebrate a spring planting season.

"How are the surrounding wards?" Grierr asked Kaidan.

"We re-activated a bunch of them our first full day here," Kaidan told him.

"Can I walk to them to see if there are any holes that need to be fixed?" Grierr asked.

"In the morning, we can plan," Kaidan replied.

Grierr went to say something, but a group of kids approached him. He bent down so the bravest of the group could whisper in his ear. He grinned and nodded, telling the boy to give him a moment.

"They want me to join their game," Grierr said.

"Have fun," Tas replied as Grierr pretended to be dragged by the group to the open field.

Someone picked up an instrument and soon Edelberg was dragged to dance and enjoyed dancing with every woman there. Once the moon was high and the stars were coming out, the families started to corral the children to their living spaces. Others made their way to the tents. Grierr drank a mug of water when he joined them. It had been good for him to play with children again; it was not as painful as he thought it would be.

Kaidan rose. "If the four of you would join me and Moira, if you want, you can go with Rhea. She and Jonah can show you around."

"I will take my leave," Jonah said as clapped Kaidan on the shoulder. "There is a horse ready to foal."

"Can I come help?" Moira inquired.

Jonah nodded. Moira excused herself and followed him toward the stables. Rhea also stood. "I have first watch," she informed them.

Kaidan squeezed her hand before she went to their room to change into her armor. Edelberg grinned at his friend. "Don't even," Kaidan warned. "She wears more knives on her than you expect, and I won't hold her back from impaling you with a few. Let alone the hexes I would throw at you."

Edelberg went to make a lewd joke but got a smack in the head from Grierr. He rubbed his head as they followed Kaidan to the main watchtower; they headed up to the second floor where there were four-bedroom suites. Jonah had taken up residency in the room off of the stable. Edelberg and Grier took the room that was not being used with the thought that Moira could bunk with Rhea. Thierren and Tas had taken the room with the back stairs to the infirmary. This also was the bigger suite of rooms, so they assembled in there.

"What aren't you guys telling us?" Grierr asked after he closed and warded the door.

"A lot has happened in the few days since we last saw each other," Tas began. "We spoke with the Council the day after we arrived. Edelberg, there was a huge earthquake in Friesen. Your family is fine, but there is much damage throughout the country and into Leneo."

"We aren't a country that has them," Edelberg said as he sat down in a chair.

"That isn't the only strange land occurrence," Tas warned. "The rumor Thierren heard about the volcano in the south of Greedin is true. It began erupting two nights ago and hasn't stopped."

"The cult is using this to gather more followers," Thierren informed them. Grierr looked at Thierren. "My parents apparently contacted the Council to see if they could locate me and force me to return to them."

"And what is their reply going to be?" Edelberg asked, waiting for Thierren to inform them of when he would be leaving.

"That they do not keep track of every mage in the world and do not know my location at the moment or soon," Thierren replied, looking right at Edelberg.

"That's a good line, because it's true," Grierr said.

"They want me to look into the Blood Dragon poison and their sudden appearance," Thierren continued. "Among other roles."

"You have until we leave Hruan to decide," Tas reminded him. "My grandfather has called for the War Summit for a week after the Hruan meetings. At the moment, with the exception of a few southern provinces of

Greedin and Rochleaux, all the other countries and tribes are sending delegates."

"What's our role?" Edelberg asked.

"Tas will represent the Council in Hruan and in Quinsenta," Kaidan stated.

"Aren't you usually the diplomat for these things?" Grierr asked Kaidan.

"They have given me a new position," Kaidan answered. "I am now the Keeper of the Watchtower and all who dwell here."

"There hasn't been one since the first age," Grierr stated.

"I know," Kaidan replied. "It's daunting, but also this is what I want. I can do good here."

"Did they tell you what they want us to do?" Grierr asked Tas.

"They want us to contact them after you arrived, but essentially Edelberg will be with us to help train what army we can gather and Grierr, you'll be helping with training and charming weapons and helping me in meetings."

Grierr groaned at the last part. "They know?"

"Apparently our headmaster always knew," Tas told him. "But when you walked into the family tomb, it apparently announced to the magic world that a descendent of Arkin had accepted his blood."

"Did you know that would happen?" Edelberg asked Grierr.

He nodded. "It's why I never went before; I didn't want the responsibility that came with it."

"So, are you a god now?" There was something in Edelberg's tone that caught the others off guard.

"No," Grierr assured him. "Or no more than I was before I walked into the tomb."

"Moving on," Thierren said as Tas nodded to him. "There is one more thing we must discuss. The only other two people that know are Rhea and Jonah."

"What is it?" Edelberg asked.

"It is Tas," Thierren said.

Grierr and Edelberg turned to look at Tas. Tas took a deep breath and removed the glamor he had placed on his eyes. His once hazel eyes now were a blue so pale, they were almost white as if somehow the color had been drained from his eyes. There was a cloudiness to them that had never been there before.

"What happened?" Grierr asked as he rested a hand on either side of Tas's face to study them.

"I am partially blind," Tas said and felt Grierr's hands fall away.

Grierr sat abruptly down in a chair next to Edelberg. "What do you mean 'partially' and how does one go partially blind?"

"It's all theory," Thierren warned. "The Library in Quinsenta might have more answers, but for now we're working on what both Jonah and I know about Blood Dragons mixed in with some knowledge from the dragons."

"I'm not defenseless," Tas assured them. "Kaidan and I sparred yesterday, and I took him down each time and he wasn't going easy on me because I could hear him cursing."

"How can you still defeat Kaidan?"

"I can make out blurry shapes, I get impressions of things in my mind, I also see the outlines of people and the auras of those I know."

"This is insane," Edelberg stated as he paced the room. "Kaidan, he's staying here with you, right?"

"Did you not hear the part about him going to Hruan and Quinsenta?" Kaidan asked Edelberg.

"You are going to send a blind man into a war?"

"I'm blind, not useless," Tas countered. There was a warning in his tone to not argue with him about this. "I can spar with you tomorrow if you need me to show you I am not defenseless. I might not see like the rest of you anymore, but I can fight, and my brain still works, as does my magic."

"Thierren, how is this possible?" Grierr asked.

"The poison from the Blood Dragon I theorize damaged his eyes and the muscles and brain that go with vision," Thierren answered. "It's why his vision isn't completely gone. We do not know if it is permanent, but I think it could be because of the change in his eye color."

"But you gave him the antidote," Edelberg argued.

"Yes, but not every antidote is a cure," Thierren reminded him. "There are some things that not even magic can fix."

"Then what good was it?"

"I'm alive, aren't I?" Tas stated. "I mean, unless I'm not and no one has gotten around to telling me."

Thierren hit him lightly on the shoulder. "Edelberg, right now I have tried everything I can. I have had to make do with the resources I have had access to. My hope is once we are in the capital at Hruan and I can research it even more and then more so once we're in Dracon."

"He's right, Edelberg," Kaidan added. "We have tried everything that we can."

"The rest of the camp doesn't know?" Grierr asked.

"Only Rhea and Jonah right now," Thierren said.

"The fear is if this became common knowledge and war comes, Tas would become an easy target," Kaidan answered.

"I wanted as few people to know," Tas told them. "Rhea knows because she was the one to notice the change in my eye color. Obviously, Jonah because Thierren and he discussed everything they know about Blood Dragons. So, when I am around everyone else, I glamor my eyes to look normal."

"The only thing really different is that he now takes his staff with him everywhere," Thierren added. "But Kaidan and I have been carrying ours around as well so that it doesn't seem odd, but it also helps training Josiah, so no one has really said anything or asked questions."

"How blind are we talking?" Edelberg asked, as if his mind could not get around this. "Like if I held my hand up, would you know how many fingers I'm holding?"

"All I would see is a vague arm shape moving," Tas informed him.

"How are you so calm about this?" Edelberg demanded, his anger boiling up inside of him.

Tas shrugged his shoulders. "I have had a few days longer than you to come to terms with it, but I also realize that I could be dead, so losing most of my sight seems a small price to pay for still living."

"Is there any pain?" Grierr asked.

"None," Tas admitted. "I am feeling no discomfort at all."

"That's something at least," Grierr admitted.

Thierren noted Tas was getting tense with how Edelberg was handling this all. "It's been a long day. We have dropped a lot on you," Thierren began. "We should all rest and get some sleep."

"When did you become the wise one?" Edelberg asked him.

"Since Tas was in and out of consciousness for a few days," Thierren reminded him.

Grierr stood up before Edelberg could pick a fight. "We will see you guys in the morning," Grierr said as he motioned with his head to follow him.

Kaidan let out a low whistle when the two had left. "I thought Edelberg was going to lose it," Kaidan admitted.

"We'll monitor him when he's around Thierren," Tas agreed.

"I don't need protection. I can handle myself just fine," Thierren reminded them both. "Maybe we need to spar so I can remind you of that!"

"And on that note, I'm heading to bed," Kaidan said with a grin as he headed toward the door.

Tas rolled his eyes at Kaidan. He listened to the retreating footsteps and the door to open and close. Once the door shut, Tas went to the bedroom, where he knew Thierren would join him. There was a bunk bed and a straw double bed in the room. Thierren had claimed the bunk bed, letting Tas have the double bed as Tas was taller than the two.

"Edelberg still believes I am going to betray all of you," Thierren said with a sigh as he entered the room and closed the door.

"He hasn't said that."

"He doesn't need to," Thierren snapped. He could feel it coming off of Edelberg in waves. "Now he will blame me for your blindness."

"Ren," Tas said as he laid a hand on his shoulder. "Don't worry about what he thinks. Edelberg has always been hot-headed, but he cools off quickly. I am sure by the time we leave for Hruan he will forget it all."

"The offer the Council made me. Do you think I can do it?" Thierren asked, changing topics. He knew why Edelberg would not let Thierren forget his shortcomings.

"I think you are one of the best medical healers around," Tas answered honestly. "Your understanding of how magic can aid in healing and traditional medicine. Your knowledge of anatomy and physiology is unparalleled. They asked you to teach your last year of medical school because that is how knowledgeable you are."

"But I do not know battle medical training and that is what they are asking," Thierren reminded him.

"But you know the injuries they cause, how to treat them. You have been in areas where you have had to treat many injuries at once," Tas stated. "You give yourself too little credit."

"And you give me too much," Thierren responded. He let out a long sigh. "I would go against my parents. There would be no going back for me."

"That is also true."

Thierren sighed again and sat next to Tas. "I don't know what to do."

"Whatever you decide, I will support you," Tas reassured him.

Thierren looked at him. "I know why you have all this faith in me," Thierren began. They never spoke about him knowing about how Tas felt for him. Thierren had never been comfortable will the idea of love and to have that conversation when he was unsure of his own feelings was terrifying. "But am I truly worth it?"

"To me, yes you are."

"Even if friendship is all I will ever be able to offer you?"

"Even then."

"What if I become a three-headed monster with six tails and I like to eat only mages that annoy me?"

"Then I might have to have some words with you," Tas admitted as he laughed. He shoved a pillow in Thierren's face. "Go to bed. You know Grierr is going to have us up early."

Chapter 14

Moira was up at dawn despite her sleep. She had been restless all night, as she had been since they arrived at the Watchtower a few days ago. Her dreams reminding her of her home, of why she left. She woke up each time, remembering she could never return to her home. Knowing that she could not go back to sleep, Moira climbed out of her bed. She grabbed a pair of leggings and a tunic before stepping behind the screen to wash and dress.

Once she was ready for the day, she stepped out of her room and headed down to the main floor of the tower her room was in. People were already up and getting ready for the day. There was smoke coming from the kitchen chimneys and the blacksmiths. Moira spotted some inhabitants getting breakfast ready for the animals as they mucked out the stalls. She saw Edelberg was practicing with a practice dummy made of branches and flower sacks.

"Couldn't sleep as well?" Moira asked when he saw her.

"A lot on my mind," Edelberg admitted. He took the water jug she handed him.

"Do you want to talk about it?" She inquired.

"Some things happened in my homeland while I was gone," he answered. Edelberg never had a problem talking with people.

"What occurred?"

"There were earthquakes. I know my family is fine, but I wish I were there."

"I know you're related to the king, but you talk little about your family," Moira realized. Not that she was one to talk, she never spoke of the life she left behind.

"My uncle is the king," Edelberg informed her. "He was crowned a year ago after my grandfather stepped down."

"What of your dad?"

"He is a lord, but he's also a farmer and is in charge of the largest group of farms in Friesen. He prefers being on the farm, working with farmers, inventing new techniques for farming."

"Any sorcerers?" Moira inquired.

"One uncle on my mom's side and several times over great-grandparent," Edelberg replied. "I'm the only one of my siblings to be born with it. A fact they hate, so of course I brag about it when we're together."

"You're close," Moira realized.

"You were wondering since I didn't talk about them, we weren't close," Edelberg stated. Moira nodded. "I guess I'm so used to people knowing my family that I do not really talk about them. Before you ask, I am the youngest of five. I have three older brothers, one sister, and two nephews."

"When was the last time you saw them?"

"A year ago, for my uncle's coronation," Edelberg realized. "I stayed there for a few months before the Council called for Tas and me. We stay connected through the mail and with an occasional orb."

Edelberg studied her for a moment. "What about you? I mean, I know you left on bad terms, but before that, were you close?"

Moira let out a sigh. "My two older sisters are identical twins," Moira informed him. "They have this amazing black hair with blue eyes. They resemble our mother. Then there is me. The brunette with boring eyes and the youngest."

"I've seen boring eyes. You do not have boring eyes," Edelberg informed her. "They are alive with your emotions."

Moira felt the blush rise on her cheeks. She tried to hide a smile as she went to continue talking. "I was always trying to tag along with them, but it was hard because they were so in tune with each other that they often left me out. Mom was always busy, running the farm, taking care of others."

"Grierr and Tas can be like that," Edelberg admitted. "They have been tight since they met. There are moments I think they can talk without words, just by looks."

"That's how my sisters are," Moira replied.

"It's easy to feel you're being left out despite knowing that they aren't doing it on purpose," Edelberg sighed.

"Yet sometimes I feel like it was intentional," Moira admitted. "It's horrible to think, I know. They just never understood or wanted to understand why I felt left out."

"That sucks," Edelberg admitted. "When the two were in one of their twin modes, I had my other friends to screw off with. What about you, friends?" Edelberg asked.

"We grew up on a small island," Moira admitted. "There were very few inhabitants that lived year round. So, while I made friends, they rarely stayed long. Mom taught us from home. She taught history and science as like this living thing that should be respected, understood, and appreciated."

"She sounds incredible."

"She is," Moira agreed, ignoring the pain that hit her. "She raised three girls on her own and while at the moment we are strained, I know we will be close again."

"You don't talk about the rift," Edelberg noted.

"I don't," Moira agreed. She looked around the area, then at Edelberg with the flaming red hair and a jovial smile. "My sisters and I, we each have a unique gift."

"That can happen with some families," Edelberg noted. "We went to school with four siblings who could each control an element."

"Don't all sorcerers control the elements?"

"To an extent," Edelberg answered. "We can use the raw energy that comes from nature and living things and funnel it into spells, charms, runes. We all have an elemental branch we are the strongest with and are taught how to use the different branches."

"And the siblings?"

"It was insane. Our headmaster said it had been almost a century since elementalists, as they are called, had been born. To have four in one family was unheard of. It wasn't just what they could conjure, but what they could control as well. There was a rainstorm our seventh year, it flooded parts of the campus. A first year had fallen running to the dorms. It was a bad fall; they could not move him until they stabilized him, but the rain was insane. You could barely see six feet in front of you. Kiera comes and not even needing her staff, she could stop the rain just above where they were and hold it so they could stabilize the kid, then she followed them so that as they walked, no rain fell on them. Any other sorcerer, it would have drained their mana to the point of coma or death. Kiera barely broke a sweat."

"That is amazing," Moira whispered in awe. "What does the staff you carry do?"

185

"It allows us to channel our intention to a specific spot," Edelberg said. "We can perform magic without, but we have more control over it, allowing us to control the power of the magic we are using and where it is going."

"Did your academy know what to do?"

Edelberg nodded. "The library at the academy has pretty much everything ever written," Edelberg informed her. "So, our headmaster found the journals from another head who was there the last time an elemental came through the door. The biggest thing with them is teaching their limits, so the power does not consume them, and not in the 'I can do anything' way, but in the literal sense of letting the element taking over until it kills them."

"Wow," Moira whispered. "I know Kaidan told me that there is a consequence for everything you do."

"There is. We are all taught our limit and the signs of what a mana drain entails," Edelberg replied. "Mild symptoms are nose bleeds, migraines, exhaustion. More severe cases can lead to falling unconscious, permanently weakening your core, and even death. Thierren has to be careful because he can actually use his magic to heal not just bones, but illnesses. He has come close to losing himself in a patient and not being able to pull himself back."

"As in, the patient was dying and was trying to stop it?" Moira inquired.

"We can't stop death, not even a healer like Thierren," Edelberg answered. "Thierren though, can get so caught up in his magic that he might not see the signs of death and if he stays connected too long, well, let's just say you end up with two dead people."

"Is that why he doesn't use his magic with Tobbin?"

"No, he knows he can't heal Tobbin so he won't use it," Edelberg assured her. "He shut his magic down with a patient like him because with how close he is to the end, Thierren will feel it and it will be painful to him."

"Do you have a gift?"

"The sword," Edelberg grinned. "I'm a battle mage because I am what they call a berserker. I can use the adrenaline from battle to strengthen my spells and blows from my swords."

"How would you lose yourself?"

"I would never come out of that mode," Edelberg said. His voice sounding neutral. He looked at Moira, wanting to steer the conversation away from him. "So, what's yours?"

"I can tell a person their future, or well, the different paths they have."

"Do they have similar abilities?" Edelberg inquired.

"In a way," Moira answered. There was a lot she could not tell him, things she was bound to secrecy. "Lu, my middle sister, she has a complex ability. It's hard to explain. It can be extremely dangerous; my mother has worked with her the hardest to control it. Lu can be very emotional, which doesn't help her control."

"Tas has a similar issue," Edelberg admitted. "When he gets angry, he can't control his spells. They become chaotic, unpredictable. The surrounding area will smell like the ocean during a storm."

"That might be their only similarities," Moira agreed. "She never wants to admit if she was wrong. Doesn't care if what she says hurts others. Yet we were raised to respect others, to care for those around us. Lu comes off sincere, but there is always something else going on with her motives."

"Is she why you left?"

"In part," Moira admitted. Words had to be chosen carefully. "We didn't agree completely with someone one of us fell in love with. We fought about it, how maybe their feelings of love were becoming more of an obsession with an individual."

"Love had turned to jealousy, I take it," Edelberg realized.

"And in a very twisted way, vengeance," Moira added as she went along with her version of what happened. "My mother and Lea, my other sister, they didn't cater to her wants, but they didn't dissuade her either. I became the voice of reason, a very unwanted voice of reason."

"Tas is usually our voice of reason," Edelberg noted. "I think it is part of the reason Thierren is often at odds with him."

"It's tough when no one wants to listen to you," Moira sighed. "I decided I couldn't live there anymore, so I left."

"Some would think that was very brave or very foolish."

"I like to think it's a bit of both," Moira admitted. "Lu is very much in the present. She can be rash, not think of what could happen because of something. Her emotions can control her. I know most of the things she said to me were said in rage, but they were still spoken."

"And what of Lea? Where does she fit in?"

"She is the queen of divination," Moira said with a smile. "Give her cards, stones, runes, and she could show how it has brought you to where you are now. She is the calm one, quiet, loyal, and fiercely protective of Lu."

"Meaning she sided with Lu instead of seeing reason," Edelberg stated. "I take it your mother stayed out of it."

"She wanted us to figure it out on our own. I don't blame her for that."

"Nor I," Edelberg agreed. "While it saddens me you had to leave your home, I am glad that you are here."

"So am I," Moira admitted. "I didn't see any of you after dinner. Did your reunion go well?"

"We caught up with things that have been happening around the world, what we have to do for the next stage in this journey," Edelberg admitted. "How have you been sleeping since we arrived? I've noted you have been lethargic during the day."

"Honestly, not well," Moria replied. "I'm not sure if it's being in a new place, but I feel like I'm on edge."

"How long were you on the run in Rochleaux?"

"A little over a month. I had been living in a village for almost a year," Moira replied. She looked at him. "Why?"

"Well, I can tell from experience that sometimes when we are used to sleeping in tents or because when we finally reach a destination, it can take time to get used to sleeping peacefully again," Edelberg informed her. "Our bodies are used to being hyper aware because of sleeping outside, add in the threat of being found, so when suddenly we find a place that is safe, our body and mind have to take time to acclimate to that. I bet you will find most people here are having some issues. Thierren has been handing out one of his teas left and right."

"What does it do?"

"Thierren is a genius with medicine," Edelberg replied. "He created this tea that helps your mind and body to relax enough to sleep but not feel that drugged feeling that often comes with some sleep aids."

"The healing tea he makes Tas. He says your friend has an allergy to one of the herbs?"

Edelberg nodded. "It can almost kill him," Edelberg answered. "Thierren was determined he would figure out a way to make a healing drought that would work on Tas and be just as effective as the regular one.

His recipe actually earned him placement in one of the hardest medical programs there is."

"Tas seems to have fully recovered," Moira noted.

"He has," Edelberg agreed. "Any other healer and Tas most likely would not be here."

"That is a sobering thought," Moria stated.

"Aye, we are lucky to have a friend as gifted as Thierren."

During the walk, they had made it to the main room of the complex that was just off the main gate. There was food set out for breakfast already, people were milling about. Edelberg noted two dwarves were grabbing plates of food as they talked to Kaidan. Edelberg realized they must be the friends of Tobbin. Grierr and Tas were already at a small table, talking. It amazed Edelberg as he watched how Tas moved with such ease. Grierr waved them over.

"We have plenty of food," Grierr told them as he handed them empty plates. "How did you sleep?"

"Moira has been having some issues," Edelberg answered as he made sure she took a seat first.

"You should talk to Thierren," Tas told her. "He was making a new batch of his tea this morning."

"Thank you, Edelberg told me about it," Moira said as she plated some eggs and a roll on her plate.

"You've been on the run long enough that your body is used to the threat of the unknown," Grierr explained to her. "Once it realizes it's safe, the sleep will come. And all you will want to do is sleep."

"Thierren can give you a whole explanation why," Tas added. "We tune him out when he goes off on topics."

Moira chuckled. "Where is Thierren?"

190

"He ate already," Tas assured her. "He wanted to check in on the foal and make sure that Tobbin was ready for his friends, who arrived late last night."

"You sure he grabbed food?" Grierr asked Tas. Thierren was known to lecture everyone about eating, but would forget to eat at times, if he was not reminded.

"I watched him," Tas promised Grierr.

Kaidan walked over to sit with them for a moment. "When you are done eating, I need to take these three gentlemen from you, Moira," Kaidan announced.

"I don't know. I kind of like having them around," Moira teased. "But I guess you can have them."

"You are too kind," Kaidan replied.

As they ate, people came and went. Several stopped to talk to them before heading to do various jobs that needed to be done around the keep. They impressed Grierr with how, in only a few days, people were acclimating to the place and working on improvements. The camp had created a tight community, and they were working together to make sure they would all be safe in the future. When they were finished, Moira went with them so she could talk to Thierren about the tea.

Grierr studied Tas as he led them through the main hallway of the keep. The Main Gate leading out into Rochleaux was locked and warded tightly. Later, he would see about how he can enhance the wards more. They headed through the first floor of the Tower that held their rooms. Moira went to the infirmary to speak with Thierren while Tas continued down the narrow passage. They walked into a large room where ancient maps were hung up. They had constructed a large table out of slabs of wood and crates. Kaidan was standing there with Jonah, looking over a map on the table. They both looked up when the trio entered.

"I know it's early," Kaidan began. "But there are some things we need to go over in greater detail than we did last night."

"Should we wait for Thierren?" Edelberg inquired.

"He'll be in shortly," Kaidan assured him. "I told him the first part, already. Jonah?"

Jonah nodded and motioned for them to move so they could see the map. "We have been communicating with the dragons to pinpoint other natural disasters that are happening," Jonah explained. "Friesen was hit first, about three days ago, with a big earthquake. The capital was spared but there is talk that one of the port towns just crumbled into the ocean."

"Was there any warning?" Edelberg asked as he tried to comprehend what that would entail.

"A minor tremor before it, but that was it. Survivors were still being pulled from some of the debris, but no one has searched underwater because the waves and undertow have been dangerous," Jonah assured him.

"And my family, Kaidan said they were safe?" Edelberg asked. He trusted Kaidan, but this was his family.

"Bart reached out to me," Tas informed Edelberg. "He arrived in Friesen yesterday and found your family. Many of the dragons that were living in a colony on the southern border of Friesen have fled to Quinsenta because of the earthquake."

"Your link wasn't damaged," Grierr stated, relieved. They had feared the poisoning from the Blood Dragon would interfere with Tas and Bart's connection.

"No, it's still as strong as it was," Tas confirmed.

"You said that Friesen and Greedin weren't the only countries affected," Edelberg recalled.

"The main volcano in Vulcan has stopped smoking and has appeared to have gone dormant overnight," Kaidan explained. "Both the provinces of Lynia and Silencia have also experienced natural oddities. Silencia has entered the rainy season a few months early, which is causing all the crops to be ruined. Lynia has seen a huge decline in fish along its coast. The fish that have been caught are diseased."

"On top of those two, the southern provinces in Greedin are seeing signs of a severe drought," Jonah added.

"The cults are going to be using this to strengthen their numbers," Thierren stated as he joined them. "They will use this to show people they are not pious enough, that they have fallen from the favor of Malforin and his children."

"You would know," Edelberg commented. He got a sharp look from Jonah, Grierr, Kaidan, and Tas. "What? He's the only one with family in a cult."

"Which is why I know how they are going to use these events to gain more followers," Thierren answered. "And those followers will become trained and become an army if need be."

"What's the plan?" Grierr asked as he looked at the maps and the notes.

"We will contact the Council. They want to speak with the six of us," Tas answered. "Then when we leave here for Hruan it's knowing that war with Mal and his children is going to be very much a real thing."

"You're serious?" Edelberg asked. "We're really going to be going up against gods?"

193

"We've been discussing this since before Emi, why are you all of sudden surprised at it?" Tas asked him.

"Because it's more real now, I guess," Edelberg admitted. "We're talking gods, Tas. How do we defeat gods?"

"We have to try," Thierren said. "Otherwise, we might as well surrender now and let the Greedin line destroy the world."

"So, you're on our side now?" Edelberg stated.

Thierren did not answer Edelberg's question. He looked at Tas. "If you are ready?"

Tas nodded. He took the orb out of the top of his staff and set it in the center of the table. Taking a deep breath, he focused on who he wished to speak to.

Chapter 15

Tas took the orb out of the top of his staff. He placed it carefully in the center of the table, laying his hand on it. He closed his eyes and focused on the orb. This had been his senior project. None of his teachers thought it would work - to forge an orb that could communicate between sorcerers. He had only made a handful at that point. Each time he used it, he still waited for it to fail. It began to glow, soon the room filled with the glow of the orb. There was a faint humming before the glow from the orb seemed to become more focused on a spot on the table.

"My boys," a familiar voice said as his image formed from the orb. Their old headmaster, Tobias Nord, now head of the Council, greeted them with a smile. "Ah, good Jonah is there as well."

"I see your orb works as well," Tas commented. He had given Tobias his own orb before Tas left the Isle of Magi a few months ago.

"These are amazing, Taslan. You have a gift for creating," Tobias stated. "Especially during times like these. Arngrierr and Edelberg it is good to see you. You had no more trouble?"

"None," Grierr stated, bowing his head to his mentor. Tobias was also a rune-smith and trained Grierr at the academy.

"Good," Tobias answered. "Have they told the two of you?"

"We have caught them up on the natural events," Kaidan answered. "We thought it best for you to explain the rest."

"Very well. The news I had hoped would be better. However, it is much as Taslan and Kaidan's notes had feared. At this moment in the last month, the Black Mist has claimed lives on every continent and country. We are talking about the thousands of deaths that result from it. Some are spreading rumors that the cause is a magical curse. However, one of our healers, Thierren your old mentor, has been examining the most recent deaths. He brought several healers and doctors to help with the investigation."

"What did they find?" Thierren asked. He had submitted his own findings to his mentor.

"No curse, spell, or poison caused the deaths," Tobias stated. He focused on Grierr. "There were no marks, no signs of a natural cause or illness. It is as if their life was just snuffed out."

"Sir," Grierr said, trying to keep his voice controlled. "We have questions about the victims."

"I would be surprised if you didn't," Tobias admitted. "What are they?"

"The victims were either related to someone in our community or were part of a smaller sect, correct?" Grierr inquired.

"At the moment, the only group of our community that is being hit is the natural witches," Tobias confirmed. "The rest are related to members of our community."

Grierr nodded to Thierren. "We have been working on a theory as to why the Black Mist is only targeting our community," Thierren began. Tobias motioned for him to continue. "If we go with the theory that the cause of what is happening is infighting amongst the Gods of Greedin, one could make the argument that the mundane would turn to us for aid. The idea being we would be the only group strong enough to go up against Gods."

"That would be a solid assumption," Tobias agreed. "We are seeing many in Greedin seeking refuge in magical communities. How does this explain our community being targeted?"

"What better population to attack than the very one that could wage a war against the very group that could pose a threat?" Grierr answered.

Tobias stared at Grierr and Thierren as he thought about what they had just theorized to him. "This would connect each together," Tobias realized.

"We were trying to work on an answer for each event," Tas agreed. "Then Thierren connected the dots, realizing that it was all intertwined."

"I also have told them we should start shortening the names of the Greedin Gods," Thierren added. "They might monitor when they feel the pull of their name being said. If they do that, they could overhear conversations they shouldn't."

"Can he do that?" Edelberg asked.

"It's said that all Gods know when their name is said. It's how they are to know how to aid," Grierr informed him.

"What do you know?" Tobias asked Thierren.

"I have not spoken with any of them since I left for Emi," Thierren stated. They all understood who he meant. "There is a division occurring between the Traditionalists and the Malfinites over whether they should continue to worship Mal or if his wife is the true leader."

"Any word into what has caused this supposed rift?"

"A letter from my brother while I was training in Gastion indicated one seer saw an argument between Mal and his wife," Thierren recalled. "Not just a regular fight, but accusations of cheating."

"That is an unusual rumor concerning those two," Tobias agreed. "I have known them to be the other's great love. If it were Malforin's oldest son, I would not pay attention to it, as they have always rumored him to be unfaithful and immoral."

Thierren noted Tas gripped his staff tighter and the mention of Taris, the oldest son of Malforin. "Precisely why I still recall it," Thierren agreed. "There are two versions: one is that it his wife received evidence of him being unfaithful, he denied it. The other is she cheated and denies it. From what I could learn, when the fight occurred, a huge storm tore across southern Greedin. The cult is stating the fight caused the volcano to form there. Even more so, it seems their children have picked sides. One in particular is looking at this as a way to overthrow his father."

"So, a family fight that has children picking sides with one wanting to take it all," Edelberg summed up. "It's like a royal drama, but with much more devastating effects."

"Instead of a country at war, they are destroying the world," Tas agreed.

"Could the other gods aid us?" Jonah inquired.

All eyes looked at Grierr. "I don't know," he answered honestly. "Everything that was passed down to me was that once a god ascends to the heavens, it is their final stage of their life. Arkos returned to the heavens to be with his children that were slaughtered."

"We saw him though in the tomb," Edelberg pointed out.

"We saw his spirit," Grierr reminded him. "I still don't know everything that I should. I have been delaying accepting my fate since a young teen. I wanted to wait until my children were older before I accepted it. This way, I would have time to learn."

"I know someone who can help," Tas said, though it looked as if saying those words pained him.

"Who?" Edelberg asked.

"My spy within the rebels in Greedin," Tas answered. "I can't say anymore but I will send word for them to meet us at Quinsenta. Grierr, I believe they will have answers."

"Unless they are a god, how can they help?" Edelberg demanded.

"Just trust me," Tas stated.

Grierr studied Tas for a moment. "I do."

"Grierr, I would like you to be with Tas in the negotiations at Hruan," Tobias replied. "I know you are not usually at these meetings, but I believe you will be able to help those still on the fence."

"I understand," Grierr replied.

"While in Hruan, Jonah will work with the dock workers, ship captains and navy to get a better picture of what is happening in the Ocean of Taris. We know sea monsters are being spotted daily in the Arkin Ocean, but we do not know the full details of what is happening in Taris," Tobias informed them. "Tas, Bart will meet you in the capital. He will conduct talks with the dragons there about helping with refugees and shipping issues."

"I look forward to seeing him," Tas admitted with a grin.

"Edelberg, I want you to talk with the army, see how many Battle Mages they have, work with them, and help with training," Tobias continued. "Thierren, have you thought more about what we discussed?"

"I have," Thierren answered. "I am planning to use their medical library at the university there to plan what I need. I will need others to help. If this comes to a full out war, I cannot be on the front line everywhere."

"Then plan, make a list of who you need and what you will need, and send it to me before you leave for Quinsenta," Tobias stated.

"I will," Thierren promised.

"Kaidan, one of the dragons here will be to you by the end of the week. They will have all the paperwork you need," Tobias informed Kaidan. "They will bring Josiah and his family here."

"Thank you, sir," Kaidan said, his voice full of gratitude.

"Gentleman, that is all," Tobias said.

They made their goodbyes before Tas deactivated the orb. Once the orb was done glowing, he placed it in his staff.

"Kaidan, can I talk to you for a moment?" Grierr asked as the others left.

"Sure," Kaidan said. They headed to a small office off of the main room. "What is it?"

"I need to have a widower's braid done," Grierr stated.

Kaidan looked at him with sorrow. This meant to Grierr was ready to begin the year of mourning. "My mother would be honored," Kaidan informed him.

"Are you sure she will do it?"

Kaidan walked to Grierr and took a hand in his and squeezed. "Grierr, you have been an honorary son to them. It would honor her to perform the ritual for you," Kaidan assured him.

"I... thank you," Grierr said softly. "I didn't know who I could have do it, knowing what it will entail and how I might be during it."

"There is no need for thanks, my brother in spirit," Kaidan said as they touched foreheads.

Kaidan heard a door open and saw that Rhea was standing in the doorway. She nodded to him and waited for them to finish. When they did, she walked to Grierr and handed him a small pouch.

"My brother speaks highly of you," Rhea informed Grierr. "He has suffered much since our clan split. Kaidan spoke of the tradition for those who have lost family, as my clan has a similar tradition. We would like to give you these to aid in your journey of morning."

Grierr was speechless as he took the pouch and opened it. Tears welled in his eyes as he stared at four beautifully crafted beads. There were no words he could say to Rhea, so he hugged her instead.

"The sorrow you carry, may the rain be your tears, the wind be your screams, the thunder be your anger, the stars guide you in the darkness, and when it is time may the sunrise be the start of the next path you will walk," Rhea whispered. It was a prayer said to those who lost people closest to them in her clan.

"Thank you," Grierr finally whispered, though the words seemed inadequate.

"Now let us walk the perimeter and figure out how to make this place well-fortified," Kaidan stated.

It thrilled Grierr for the distraction, otherwise he could see himself drowning in a wave of emotions and grief. Kaidan gave Grierr a few moments alone to calm himself. Once Grierr was sure his emotions were in check, he joined Kaidan and Corkrin to tour the perimeter of the keep and what seemed like land as well off the eastern wall. The keep was larger than Grierr originally thought when he was given the tour of the cellars and basement areas. Those would need to be warded, and there were several stones that could be imbued with runes to strengthen the foundation from any type of attack.

"I take it you can't prevent earthquakes or such things from happening," Corkrin asked as Grierr studied one of the main support walls.

"No, but I can place some Runes to strengthen against such things. It won't prevent them from occurring, but would limit the damage," Grierr answered.

"Isn't that the same thing?"

"Sorcerers work with nature," Grierr explained. "Everything around us gives off energy. Sorcerers can absorb that energy and then use it to perform spells, wards, charms, rituals, and to activate runes. Because we are, in a sense, tied to the energy of nature, we can't prevent natural events from happening. Even if it's a god causing them. What we can do though is help minimize the damage of the events. So, strengthen foundations with runes, use a wind spell to redirect water run off."

"You work with it instead of against it," Corkrin realized.

"Basically."

"That makes sense," Corkrin replied. "Instead of being offensive, magic works as defensive."

"Precisely," Grierr said. Corkrin impressed him with how quickly he was grasping the basic magical theory.

"What of the idea that women can't be sorcerers?"

Grierr chuckled at that. "We had three female sorcerers in our graduating class," Grierr informed him. "There were about fifteen female sorcerers by our last year there."

"Really?"

"You can ask Thierren. He has all the numbers and statistics," Kaidan told Corkrin. "Sorcerers on their own is an extremely rare occurrence. I think it's less than 5% of the population. No one really knows why there aren't more, but if you look at natural born witches, they have a higher number of females than males."

"How are they different from you?"

"They can't directly absorb the energy from nature," Kaidan stated. "They can wield it like we can, but they need a conduit to help summon it."

"When Josiah and his family settle, you can talk to the Academy. They often will give classes to families of students so they can better understand what is going on," Grierr informed Corkrin.

"I would like that."

They emerged out into the main courtyard and saw that Edelberg and Tas were finishing a sparring session. They were using the wooden practice swords. Grierr noted Thierren was watching closely. He assumed it was because of Tas, but realized the healer was focusing on Edelberg.

Grierr stopped next to Thierren just in time to watch Tas disarm Edelberg. For a moment there was a shimmer of red around Edelberg and Thierren tensed next to Grierr. But it faded before anyone could have noticed it. Tas held his hand out to help Edelberg stand. They clapped each other on the back before heading over to the gate. Edelberg must have said something funny because Tas was laughing at whatever it was.

"You were waiting for something," Grierr said quietly to Thierren.

Thierren looked at Grierr. "Just ensuring that no one gets injured."

"You are not the best liar," Grierr reminded him.

Thierren said nothing as he walked over to where Edelberg and Tas were talking. Edelberg spotted them and grinned. "Grierr you need to spar with him," Edelberg replied.

"I plan too," Grierr answered. "I want to see how he moves, where his weak areas are, so I can make runes to aid him in a fight."

"That is good thinking," Tas agreed. He stretched his arms. "I'm going to go wash up."

"Same," Edelberg said. He followed Tas toward the tower.

"You were worried the Rage was going to appear," Grierr realized.

"I wanted to ensure that neither of them got injured during the match," Thierren repeated.

Grierr studied him for a moment as he walked with him towards the infirmary. He grabbed his arm as he realized. "You've been asked to treat him, which means you can't say anything unless he poses a threat."

"I have other patients to see," Thierren said with a bow of his head before he headed into the infirmary.

Grierr took Thierren's comment as confirmation that he was attending to Edelberg's rage issue.

Chapter 16

It was their last day at the Watchtower. The five would leave tomorrow for Hruan. Kaidan was going to send letters and documents for his father to go over, as well as for Tas to send the Council. Tolk was ensuring they had enough food to go with them. He was going to help them cross the lake that separated them from Hruan, since the lake was part of Hruan they would be safe on it. Otherwise, they would have to chance to take the mountain passage, which involved stepping back into Rochleaux. No one wanted to risk the chance of being stopped by anyone from Rochleaux, so a few hours' boat ride was the best solution. He headed down the stairs toward Kaidan's office, where he heard voices arguing.

"What's up?" Tas asked as he entered the room.

The room contained Moira, Lysander, Rhea, Kaidan, Thierren, Grierr, Edelberg, Jonah, and Tolk. "Moira wants to go with the five of you," Kaidan explained.

"And the yelling?" Tas asked as he leaned against the door frame.

"It was a loud discussion," Lysander offered.

Tas stepped into the room. "Moira, please explain why you want to join us with no one interrupting her," Tas instructed.

"While I have loved being here with everyone, something is telling me I am needed with your group," Moira began. "I feel like I have done what I was set out to do, which was to ensure those I helped found safety."

"Do you understand what we are setting out to do?" Tas asked her. She had been in on some meetings that discussed Hruan and Quinsenta, but not all.

"I know it's a dangerous road you are going to be embarking on," Moira replied. "I don't have the power that you have, and I am not trained in fighting. But I can learn to fight, and I can help with healing and planning."

Tas looked at the others. His gaze falling on Thierren. "Thierren?"

"You know I don't want to bring more people into this than we have to," Thierren began. "However, with everything that I have to do, it would be beneficial to have another researcher who understands healing. She can help me while you and Grierr are dealing with politicians."

"Edelberg and I could help train her," Jonah added. "Even if it is just basic defense and how to disarm, not everyone needs to be a soldier."

"Moira knows some basic defense skills," Rhea spoke up. "Once the camp was established, I trained with the women and girls on how to defend themselves if the camp was attacked. Moira picked it up rather quickly."

"So, the basics are there. We would just strengthen that and add some more," Jonah suggested.

"Grierr?" Tas asked.

Grierr let out a breath. "I honestly agree with Thierren," he admitted. "While taking on another person for this cause is terrifying because of what we are going to be doing, her skills can be useful. If she can help Thierren that means more time for me to play politician and work on runes for you. I have a feeling her and Jonah won't be the only two that will join our merry band of misfits."

"Kaidan, what are your concerns?" Tas asked. "You know her and have worked with her for the longest."

"She is an asset. The camp would not have worked without having her as my second in command," Kaidan admitted. "She's organized, takes orders well, when she argues it's because she sees a flaw that I didn't see. She is a good healer. All the reasons I don't want her to go. But I can't force her to stay either."

"Lysander, are you okay taking on the role of only healer?" Tas asked.

Lysander nodded. "Our clan was about a hundred people when we were all together," Lysander said. "Before we split, I was pretty much in the final stages of my apprenticeship and tended to all the needs. I can also train a few others to help when it gets busy. Having Moira would be a boon, but I am not one to tell someone they cannot go if they feel they are needed elsewhere."

"So, who has the biggest issue?" Tas asked.

He was a bit surprised when all eyes fell on Edelberg. "Edelberg?" Tas asked, unsure of his reasoning. From what Tas had been seeing over the last week, Moira and Edelberg were getting quite close with each other.

Edelberg grumbled under his breath for a moment. He didn't enjoy having everyone looking at him. "Look, I had concerns about her traveling with us," Edelberg began. "Just like Thierren had concerns about Jonah joining us."

"Don't bring me into this," Jonah said, with his hands up.

"I doubt you referred to Jonah as an untrained female who could be a distraction," Rhea pointed out.

"Eddie, you didn't," Tas sighed. He looked at Moira. "Moira, I apologize for my friend, who can be a sexist asshole."

Moira tried to hide her smile as she coughed back a chuckle. She nodded to Tas. Tas then looked at Edelberg.

"If we are going to use the rationale that a companion is a danger because they could be a distraction, or weaker than the others, then those would point towards me," Tas stated. "Yes, I am good in a sparring ring, but I'm untested in an ambush. We also don't know if I'm going to have another spell at any moment. I think having a second healer with us might not be a bad idea. Because if I have another spell, then the second healer is free for any other injuries."

"He has a point," Thierren agreed. "It will also mean another person to rotate the watch if I have to monitor him. It would not be just the three of you having to stay up."

"She doesn't have armor," Edelberg pointed out. "Or weapons."

"She does," Rhea stated. "I changed one of my leather armors to fit Moira, and it fits her well. She also has a set of daggers, basic poison to use on the tips with instructions on how to use them and make them. None of them are lethal, but they will give her added time to get away."

"Corkrin also gave me his practice bow before he left with Josiah's family yesterday," Moria added. "He thought I might have some skill with it from the times he worked with me. I have survived on my own long enough that even if I can't kill a person, I know how to move about without being seen. If I were truly incapable of surviving on my own, none of you would have met me."

"She punches a mean right-hook," Kaidan said. Moira blushed at his words.

"Know this from personal experience, Kaidan?" Grierr asked with a grin.

208

"When we met, we didn't know if we were friend or foe. Moira punched me, telling the others to move deeper into the woods," Kaidan answered. "Leaving me on the ground in a muddy puddle."

"It's one of my favorite memories," Rhea teased.

"See Edelberg, she's not a helpless damsel in need of rescuing," Tas said to Edelberg.

"Fine, she can come," Edelberg replied.

"I'm so glad the decision of my future rested solely in your hands," Moira responded dryly. She looked at Tas. "What time we will leave?"

"Close to dawn, depending on the weather, it could take four hours to get across the lake," Tas told her. "We want to be to the mainland by noon. This will give us time to find a place for the evening and learn what has been happening in Hruan."

"Pack light," Grierr told her. "Thierren can give you a list or idea of what medical things you could bring."

"Trust me, I've been living out of one knapsack for months," Moira assured him.

It had been easy to forget that Moira was targeted by the Rochleaux regime and had fled from her home she had established there. That all the inhabitants here had left virtually everything they owned to escape.

"You are right, I apologize," Grierr told her.

"Don't forget to be in the courtyard for dinner," Kaidan warned all of them. "Everyone wants to be able to say goodbye to all of you before you depart. Tolk has planned a feast for tonight."

"We wouldn't miss it," Tas promised.

Chapter 17

Thierren had also spent time with Tobbin on the last day at the Watchtower. Lysander had already taken over the man's care. His dwarven friends had arrived shortly after the message went out. They were comfortable at the Tower and were proving to be good for Tobbin. When he died, the dwarves were going to take his ashes back to the mine, where they had all worked. They would bury him with their family with the honor of a dwarf despite being human.

Rhea and Kaidan were at the shore of the lake to see them off. Kaidan hugged each of his friends tightly before they stepped into the sailboat that was built from the remains of a boat they found. They stowed their packs underneath the hull as Grierr and Edelberg got the oars ready to push off from the shore. Rhea hugged each of them, giving them a good luck satchel. Kaidan spoke with Grierr and Tas, quietly going over last-minute politics. Once goodbyes were done, Moira, Jonah, Grierr, Tas, Edelberg, and Thierren entered the boat with Tolk.

"We're going to miss all of you," Tolk said as they lowered the sails. Jonah was helping him, as was Edelberg.

"We're going to miss your food," Grierr replied.

Tolk chuckled at that. The wind was picking up, allowing them to take breaks from rowing and let the wind do some of the work. It was still early, so they fell into a comfortable silence as they watched the sun rise. It was a cool spring day, with no cloud in sight, making it the perfect day to cross the lake. Tas sat with Moira. Now and then Tas would see a glimmer in the air, then he would feel the pull of a dragon and find himself lost in the language of them.

"Dragons?" Grierr asked.

"A small herd of water dragons," Tas answered. "They're friendly, curious who we are. They have seen no one cross the lake from the Watchtower before."

"That is an amazing ability," Tolk stated as he watched the air above them for a glimpse of the dragons. "What's it like when you are with your dragon?"

"Like having a twin that you talk to with your mind," Tas answered. "Actually, in dragon society, they view a Dragon Talker and their dragon as twin dragons. As they see it, we were born from the same egg in a way."

"Do dragons know you can talk to them?" Moira asked.

"Yes, in a way," Tas replied. "They are very curious but cautious creatures and when they realize I can communicate with them, they will either want to talk or throw a wall up in until they know me better. They also have different dialects, so it will take me a few moments to adjust to their language."

"Never thought much of them having different languages. Makes sense since humans, elves, and dwarves do," Tolk realized. "You should write a book about dragons, help people understand them better."

"Not a bad idea," Jonah agreed. "Many people know only what others have passed down. Magical creatures have a lot of folklore attached to them. A book explaining some of that might help relationships between us and them."

"Maybe when this is all done," Tas said.

To think of a life after what they were up against was an odd thought. It seemed almost foolish to think they could survive what was coming. There were moments where Tas felt the crushing weight of what they were up against and the grief of knowing hundreds were going to die before it was all over. A war against the Gods would not be without bloodshed. It wasn't just the war that worried Tas, but would their friendship survive all the harsh truths they were facing? He feared the coming months, the truths that would be learned, the sacrifices they were going to make.

"... Tas!" Grierr said loudly and snapped a finger in front of his face.

"What?" Tas asked as he shook his thoughts from his head.

"We were talking to you, and you were just out of it," Edelberg informed him, chuckling at his friend.

It was then that Tas noted both Tolk and Thierren were looking at him with concern. "Sorry, I was deep in thought."

"The water can do that to a person," Jonah replied. "There is something about it that allows a person to step back from everything going on, allowing the person to go through their thoughts without the chaos of the world."

"Jonah, I think that is the most I've heard you speak at one time," Tolk joked.

"And when he does, it's usually profound," Thierren replied. He looked at Tas. "Are you alright?"

"Was thinking about the road ahead, everything that needs to be done," Tas sighed. "It's a lot."

"War always is," Tolk stated. "It's why you make allies, like you did with me and the other refugees. You delegate roles, you focus on what you can control, you mourn those that are lost, while moving forward."

"You've seen war," Jonah observed.

"A few," Tolk replied. "Rochleaux has been falling apart for the past few years. I was in the army and saw what our Lord Chancellor doesn't want people to know about. There were small battles with some of the provinces that did not like the Chancellor and his new laws. It was hard because many of us didn't agree with the laws, yet it forced us to fight our own people."

"You left," Thierren said.

"I was injured, and they medically discharged me," Tolk answered. "So, I didn't desert. But they put me on the list because apparently my wounds healed too fast."

"What were your injuries?" Edelberg asked. He had not seen Tolk as a soldier, yet now as he studied him, part of him felt as if he should have known that.

"Concussion, broken knee, broken ribs, arrow wound to the shoulder," Tolk replied.

"How long did it take everything to heal?" Thierren inquired.

"Most were healed within three months. My knee won't be the same, but I didn't need a cane for short distances after four months."

Thierren paused from rowing as he calculated an estimated time for the healing of all those injuries. "Three months is on the short end with traditional methods," Thierren stated. "However, every patient is different and healing times are the average, which means people can heal faster or take longer to heal. With you being a solider, you would be in excellent shape, which would actually help speed up your recovery time. If you told me you were fully healed within two months, I might understand the thought that something else must have aided you."

"It was quite surprising when the letter arrives at your house with an armed guard to inform you they will return in two hours to escort you to your new home," Tolk replied.

"They give you two hours?" Tas asked. From what the others had said, there was no warning.

"No. The Lord Chancellor made a mistake and sent men from my unit. They gave me two hours," Tolk answered.

"They gave you enough time to grab what you could and vanish," Edelberg realized. It spoke highly of what his unit thought of Tolk, that they would give him the chance to escape. "Those are good friends."

"They are," Tolk agreed. "I could hit the woods near my village by nightfall. I stumbled upon the kids that night and vowed to protect them."

"They are very fortunate to have found you," Grierr told him. The bond that had formed between Tolk, Tomas, and his siblings was that of a family.

"I feel the same for myself," Tolk admitted. "Never wanted a family and now I'd give my life for them."

"That is how every parent feels," Grierr answered quietly.

"We should break here for a cooldown and a quick snack," Moira suggested. She saw the pain in Grierr's eyes and felt that a change of conversation might be due.

Moira ducked into the small cabin. She got out a loaf of brown bread, some cheese, and apples. Grabbing a knife, she headed back upstairs and sliced the bread and cheese for everyone. She hummed while she did so.

"I haven't heard that ballad in a while," Jonah stated as he recognized her tune. "Do you know the words?"

"My mother taught me," Moira informed him.

"Would you sing it for us?" Edelberg asked.

Moira smiled at him. "My humming is fine, but trust me, I do not have a voice for singing," Moira informed him. "Maybe at a tavern when there are more people to cover me being out of tune."

Thierren sat down next to Tas. Tas was so distracted by the dragons that he did not even notice that there was food. Thierren handed him a plate with apple slices, cheese, and a few slices of bread. Tas took the plate without saying a word.

"What are they saying?" Thierren asked Tas. He knew that look on Tas's face very well.

"The dragonling wants to know if they could push our boat the rest of the way," Tas stated. "Her brother doesn't think she can, and she wants to prove him wrong."

Tolk and Thierren chuckled at that. "If it means we don't have to row when the wind dies, I'm all for it," Tolk agreed.

They all saw the shimmer, then a stunning pale blue dragonling came out of the sky. She was small, a little bigger than the boat they were in. She was slender, her scales were pale blue with white edges. She did a few spins in the air before gently diving into the water. She perched her head lightly on the edge of the boat so she could get snout pets.

"You can call her Skye," Tas told them. "Her dragon name is more complicated, but she said that's what we can call her."

"Well, you are beautiful, Skye," Grierr informed the dragon. He got a friendly puff of air from her snout.

"What's her brother's name?" Thierren asked as he scratched near her ear flap.

Tas chuckled. "She says 'Jerk'. But if we don't want to call him by that name, we can call him Cobalt," Tas answered.

215

"It's refreshing to know that dragons act like my children as well," Tolk commented with a chuckle.

"I think we can find sibling rivalry throughout all species," Grierr agreed.

Once they were all situated, Skye vanished under the water to figure out how she was going to do this. They felt a bump, then the boat moved at a gentle pace. Jonah was looking over the edge to see how she was doing it. The boat was resting on the top of her head as she steered the boat. Jonah noted that unlike the forest dragons he had met, her feet had webbing between her claws, allowing her ease as she swam.

With the aid of Skye, they made it to the shore in half the time it would have taken them to finish rowing. They tied the boat to the dock as they gathered their gear. Tas had moved to stand on the edge of the dock as he talked to Skye. Thierren grabbed Tas's gear as Jonah, Moira, and Grierr headed toward the village. People had gathered when they docked.

"Tolk," Tas began. "When you are ready to return, whistle at the edge of the dock. Apparently, Cobalt now wants to prove that he can get you across the lake faster than his sister."

"It would mean I could return tonight," Tolk said. He had planned to stay the night in the village before having to row the lake tomorrow. Yet he was nervous about how Tomas and his siblings would handle the separation. They had lost so much already, he didn't want to worry them more about not being there.

"It would," Tas agreed. "Come on, let's catch up with the others."

Grierr was talking to a man as Tas approached. Edelberg helped Tolk tie the boat to the docks. Grierr turned and smiled at them. "Mayor Hancock, these are Tolk, Thierren, and Tas. Tas is the Dragon Talker."

"Ah, we were wondering what had the dragon family out and about today," Mayor Hancock said with a chuckle. "Welcome to Haven Spring. It surprised us when a boat was spotted coming across the lake."

"I can imagine that does not happen often," Tas replied.

"You can say that," the mayor agreed. "Come, we can talk in the inn."

They followed the mayor to the small inn that was attached to the general store. The mayor headed to a table in the back corner that could fit all of them. Tas grabbed a few letters from his satchel before he sat down.

"These are for you," Tas said as he handed the documents to the mayor. "Kaidan Hunt is in charge of the Watchtower. He wasn't sure if you were still mayor or not."

"Ah, Kaidan," the mayor said, smiling. "His mother's family is from our village. He's a good lad."

"He is," Grierr agreed. "Tolk here is the cook at the keep. He also volunteered to be a liaison between the village and the tower."

"Henry Hancock," Henry introduced himself to Tolk. "We can set up some accounts for you. If you have a list of supplies, we can figure out the best way to go about getting the supplies."

"That would be much appreciated," Tolk replied.

"How many are at the keep?" Henry inquired.

"Fifty refugees from Rochleaux, myself included," Tolk answered.

"We have a few here as well," Henry informed them. "I'll get you their names and see if any of your people know them."

"Any elves?" Tolk inquired.

"Yes," Henry answered. "About ten."

"Let them know the adult children of their clan leader are at the keep and Kaidan is calling it a haven for their clan," Tolk told them.

"Kaidan has said it all in one of those letters," Tas told Henry.

"They will be relieved to know," Henry informed them. "One of them was badly injured when they arrived. Jasper had come running into the village asking for help. He had dragged his friend across the border but was out of energy. He had carried Willow the last several miles to the border."

"How is Willow now?" Thierren asked. "I'm a healer, as is Moira."

"If you want to look her over, we can ask her. She's on crutches, but is improving each day," Henry replied. "Are the six of you going to the capital?"

"Yes," Tas answered.

"We'll get you rooms for the night, take the day to rest and we can discuss details further," Henry offered. "Tolk, you are welcome to stay as long as you need before heading on the water again. We will have to figure out a system for communication that is easier than the boats."

"Birds can be trained to carry messages," Thierren replied.

"That could be a solution," Tolk agreed. He looked at Henry. "Do you have a blacksmith? Ours gave me a list of equipment she wants to order?"

"Why don't you all stay and eat some lunch? I'll grab our blacksmith and the general store owner," Henry told them. "Then I need to head out and check on a few things. We can meet up at dinner."

"Thank you, Henry," Tas said to the mayor.

He nodded, then headed out of the taproom. A serving woman came over with a tray of mugs and some fresh bread. Their meals would be out in a little bit. They thanked her.

"Your thoughts?" Grierr asked Tas once the serving woman was out of earshot.

"All good people," Tas answered. "Mayor is genuine. He wants to help. This village has seen the brunt of the lockdowns in Rochleaux. If we did not ally with Kaidan, he would not have informed us of the refugees here."

"I like him," Tolk decided. It said something that the mayor will protect those they took in.

"He will be a good ally," Tas agreed.

"And you get this all with your gift?" Moira asked. She had heard that Tas could see through falsehoods in people.

"Pretty much."

"That is a handy gift," Tolk stated.

The serving girl returned. "Willow says the healers can meet her once they are done with their meal, says she'll be the elf on crutches in front of the meeting house. Meeting house is the stone building on this block."

"Thank you," Thierren said to her. "I guess we might have a slightly busy afternoon."

"Jonah, Edelberg, and I will get the supplies we'll need for the ride to the capital," Tas replied. "Grierr, you can help Tolk with the blacksmith."

"Yes, please," Tolk said. "I know very little about your craft."

"Don't worry," Grierr assured Tolk. "I promised Martha I would oversee the order. She wants you to do it, since you will probably do the supply runs."

"It makes sense. I'm still uncomfortable ordering stuff I know nothing about."

"You are in good hands with Grierr," Tas promised him. "He'll having you understanding the basics by the end of the day."

Their food arrived with the blacksmith. Grierr and Tolk took their food to a different table so they could talk to the blacksmith and go over details.

Chapter 18

Ursa, Hruan

They had left the village two days ago and thankfully they had beautiful spring weather for their days on the road. They would reach the capital city of Ursa around lunchtime that day. Then they would have a break from riding on horses for a while and sleeping on the ground. The trip was quiet, and they were not on edge about guards demanding papers or asking why they were traveling. Jonah could observe the interaction between the four sorcerers, he could see how close they were. It was interesting to see how Moira was now fitting into their group. She brought a calmness to the group.

In the beginning, he worried about the group dynamics and how they would handle his presence in their group. It had taken Thierren the longest to open up, but as Jonah learned of his past; he understood why the blonde sorcerer was unsure of strangers. He had even apologized to Jonah last night for his previous behavior. That act made Jonah respect him much more. It seemed, though, that Thierren was learning to open up more.

"We're going to head to the presidential residence when we get to the capital," Tas informed Jonah.

"Ah, you have all decided," Jonah said.

"We figure Kaidan's parents will summon us if we don't and Kaidan's dad would take offense for us not going straight to him," Tas replied.

"His father uses a different last name," Jonah realized.

"In Hruan the first born gets the oldest parent's last name, then second then gets the younger parent's last name," Tas explained. "They lost so many people during the Tribal Wars that it was a way to rebuild the tribe numbers and pay homage to those that had died. Kaidan has his mom's last name, and his sister Kaia has his dad's. His younger brother also has his dad's, as it continues the pattern for each child."

"I wasn't sure if it was because of his dad's political position."

"His dad wasn't in politics when we were in school," Tas replied. "But Kaidan is happy that he has his mom's last name, as he can move easier than his siblings."

"I can imagine," Jonah stated.

"Can I ask you a question?" Tas began. Jonah nodded. "You speak of a Dragon Talker you once knew. What was he like?"

Jonah smiled fondly. "He was the best first mate I have ever had," Jonah began. "We met toward the end of the First Age. He sailed with me for five, almost six years."

"Did his dragon come with him?"

"He was not a Dragon Talker like you."

"What do you mean?" Tas inquired.

"He and his brother were tinkerers, inventors," Jonah began. "He always wanted to talk to dragons, to hear their language. They created an amulet that would allow him to communicate with them. But only when he wore the amulet."

Tas studied Jonah. "That is impressive skill and impressive use of magic."

"He was impressive with his magic," Jonah agreed. "He was twenty when I met him at a port. I forget which one. I don't think it's around anymore. I needed to take on a few more people. He came told me he wanted to see the world, explore customs, languages. When I met him, he had this urgency as if he had limited time."

"Was he sick?"

"No," Jonah answered. He was quiet for a moment. "He was the oldest child and was going to be taking up the family mantle, so to speak. It made him nervous. He wanted to see the world before he accepted his fate, as he said."

"He didn't want to take up the family role for him?" Tas inquired. He was realizing who they were talking about.

"He was worried the power of his role would get to him, that it would corrupt him," Jonah recalled. "We spent many evenings discussing his fears. He said he didn't have to do it, that it was his choice, but he worried what his younger siblings would think if he didn't accept it."

"So, he wanted to cram as much life into the time he had before he had to decide," Tas stated.

Jonah nodded. "He was a good man. There was always an edge to him that would come out when he was angry, but he worked hard to keep it under control," Jonah continued. "He loved women, didn't care if they were elf, dwarf, or human. If they were willing, then he was willing. He despised men that abused woman, that forced themselves on woman."

"You mean he had a conscience once?" Tas asked.

"He did," Jonah said. He looked at Tas sadly. "What he became occurred after he agreed to take on his role in his family. It wasn't sudden, it was a gradual change to where, when I would see him, I no longer saw the friend I once knew. When he attacked my ship, there was a moment our eyes made contact. I saw it then that he had succumbed to his worst fears, the monster he has become killed the man he once was."

"Is that why you came with us?"

"There is regret that perhaps I could have guided him better, helped him realize he was more than just the power that ran through him," Jonah sighed.

"Are you hopeful we could help him?"

Jonah chuckled sadly at that. "No. My friend is long dead. I need to make sure that what he did to my crew never happens again. I know I will be of use. My abilities, life experiences will be of use when the battles begin."

"You said I looked like him."

"Let me rephrase that. You look like he did once a long time ago," Jonah answered. "He altered how he looked when he became what he is. Only those that knew him before would know."

"So, my mother..."

"Would not see him when she looked at you." It was the only comfort that Jonah could offer Tas.

A wave of relief washed over him at those words. He could feel himself becoming choked up and need a moment to regain control of his emotions. "I... thank you."

"Your friends do not know, do they?"

Tas shook his head. "For years we weren't certain if it was him or someone else who attacked her, if it was him or one of his people," Tas admitted. "No one had ever lived through one of his attacks on a ship. A few years ago, I met someone, well two people actually, they could fill in the gaps."

"Ah, they would be your contacts in Greedin," Jonah realized. He had an idea who the two people could be, but did not ask.

"Yes, we nicknamed ourselves the Black Sheep. Sounded better than the unwanted," Tas replied.

"Your friends will not be repulsed by who you truly are," Jonah told him, realizing the lad's fear that his friends would leave him. "I think Grierr would take comfort knowing he was not alone. Thierren will be shocked, but he will stand by you."

"It's not fear of how they will react, it's saying the words that have me not finding the words to tell them," Tas confided.

"Words are always the hardest, for they have a lasting impact," Jonah agreed.

Tas nodded. They rode in silence for a while. Jonah would tell stories of his time on the sea and Tas telling his own tales of cases he worked on for the Council, mischief that he and Bart would get into.

"Why Bart?" Jonah asked suddenly.

Tas shrugged. "It's the best I could do at producing his name when I was three," Tas replied. "He won't let me change it. They gave him a more human sounding name when it was known we were bound. His actually name is Gilaebart, or that's the closest to how the dragons pronounce it."

"A bright pledge," Jonah said with approval. "It's a good name for your twin mate."

Their conversations soon ended as they merged onto the main highway that would take them to the entry gates of Ursa. They joined other travelers and merchants, making their way to the capital of Hruan. Eventually, they dismounted and walked their horses to the gates and into the city. For Jonah, it had been many years since he had walked through the gates. He had been here for the rebuilding after the great Tribal War, his ships bringing much needed supplies and aid. He saw that they kept the red pillars at the front of the houses to honor those long dead. During the Tribal Wars, when bodies could not be sent home, the families would paint a pillar red on the front of their house to show they had lost someone. To see it flourishing now with life and trade helped ease the harsh memories of that war.

Grierr navigated them toward the Presidential residence after he saw the look on Jonah's face. He knew it was important for Jonah to see the city as it was now. Perhaps it would help replace some memories the ancient man had of this place. Thierren was now walking beside Jonah, as Tas took his spot next to Grierr. Moira was talking with Edelberg about the history of the architecture, what the red pillars meant, and how much tragedy the capital city had seen during the Tribal Wars.

"I wonder what this is like for him?" Tas asked Grierr quietly.

"I hope therapeutic," Grierr answered. "He seemed at peace at the Tower, seeing how much of it was still standing. The amount of information he gave Kaidan will help them rebuild."

"And we thought he was an ordinary sea captain," Tas chuckled.

"Oh, I think he is also an ordinary sea captain," Grierr replied. "In fact, I think that is the role he prefers the most."

"True."

Their conversation ended with the roar of a thrilled dragon. Soon, a brilliant red dragon came out of the clouds and landed before them. Tas handed the reins for his horse to Grierr as he ran to the dragon. The dragon used its snout to pull Tas up against its broad chest and hug him with his snout. Thierren and Jonah joined Grierr as they observed and enjoyed the reunion before them.

"I take it that this is Bart," Jonah replied with a smile as Moira stared in awe at the sight.

"You would be correct," Thierren replied. He was glad that Bart chose the large gathering courtyard to do the reunion. If it had been the market area, some stalls would have been damaged in the reunion of a dragon and it's human.

"He's beautiful," Jonah declared as he saw some scales had a bright green at the edge of them, giving the dragon an almost iridescent look.

Thierren saw Bart releasing Tas and motioned for Jonah and Moira to follow him. "Bart, this is our good friend Jonah," Thierren informed Bart. "And this is Moira."

The dragon, the size of a small cottage, rested his snout on the ground so that Jonah and Moria could pet it and he could get accustomed to the new scents. Tas stood right there, grinning from ear to ear, and looking like he was finally complete. Once Jonah and Moira had imprinted on the dragon, Grierr came over to greet the dragon. The dragon hugged him much like Tas, but shed a single tear to show his grief over what Grierr had lost. A dragon's tear was a rare thing and the person to whom the tear was given was said to be blessed for it. Edelberg was next. He got an exaggerated huff, then was nudged away.

When it was Thierren's turn, Bart seemed to sniff him again and let out a huff as he stared at the mage. Tas motioned for Grierr and Jonah to move to the side. Thierren approached Bart, resting a hand on the dragon's chest.

"Yes, you read me right," Thierren informed Bart. He let Bart sniff him as he kept his hand on the dragon's chest. "I finally made my choice."

He felt the rumble in the dragon's chest. "Ok, yes, I made both choices. No, I have not told him the other choice yet."

A deeper rumbled had Thierren laughing. "No, you can't tell him."

Bart stomped his front leg, letting Thierren know he didn't think that was fair. "Yes, I will let you help," Thierren sighed. A tail twitch told him that Bart was happy with that.

Bart then did something he never did before. He lowered his body completely to the ground as a show of submission to Thierren.

"I didn't mean right now," Thierren groaned.

Bart used his front paw to keep Thierren at his chest. Thierren felt something fall into his palm and he glanced down to see a small-scale laying in his hand.

"You can't give me this," he whispered. "I know what you are doing."

Bart said nothing as he seemed to snuggle the snarky sorcerer closer to him. "Gilaebart!" Thierren exclaimed over the display. "I am not a stuffed bear to snuggle!"

"I think he disagrees," Grierr said, trying hard not to laugh. "You have always been his favorite."

"I'm glad you all are finding it amusing," Thierren snapped, though it was not really an angry snap, as it was hard to be mad when a dragon was giving you a hug. Dragons only showed affection to people they trusted. "Must you show Jonah and Moira this side of me?"

There was a huff and a tail twitch. Thierren rolled his eyes and tried ignoring the crowd that was forming.

"I wondered what the delay was, but I forgot about Bart's love of Thierren," a deep voice said.

Thierren turned and saw Kaidan's father walking their way with a small group of guards and a redheaded female he did not know. "Sorry," Thierren said.

"It's fine," President Raymond Moan stated as he greeted Grierr and Tas with a hug.

"Mr. Moan, this is Jonah," Tas introduced the two men. "This is Moira."

"Mr. President," Jonah said, with a slight bow of a head. Moira curtseyed to the leader.

"Please, you may call me Ray," Ray informed the sea captain he had heard much about him. "You both have helped my boys out. That means no need for formalities."

"Tas," Thierren finally said with a pleading edge to it.

"Fine," Tas said. "Bart, we really need to head back to the presidential estate."

Tas turned, finally seeing the female standing there. "Lia!" Tas exclaimed in shock as he rushed to hug her tightly. "What are you doing here?"

"I came with Bart, your grandfather asked if I would attend the meetings," Lia told him.

Tas heard a cough behind him and saw Grierr and a now dragon free Thierren behind him. "Oh, right," Tas said. "Um, Grierr, Thierren, Edelberg, Moira, and Jonah, this is my ... what did we decide?"

"I don't think we ever decided if we are actually related," Lia answered. It was true. They shared relatives, but in a very convoluted way. "I'm Lia."

She shook hands with them and saw the questioning looks she was getting from Grierr and the skeptical ones from Thierren. The sea captain was neutral as he observed her. Jonah noted Moira seemed to withdraw a bit in the presence of Lia.

"Why don't we all make our way there? I have food ready for lunch. We can talk, then I can show you to your rooms," Ray stated. He turned to Grierr. "My wife said she will meet with you when you are ready."

"Thank you," Grierr said. He had Kaidan write to his parents before Grierr left the Tower so that Maya would not be caught by surprise by Grierr's request.

With that, the unusual group followed the President of Hruan through the gates that led to the main estate of the Presidents. Each Hruan President ruled for eight years, they served only one term. Half-way through their term, a vote of confidence was called to ensure that the country and parliament were happy with the sitting President. They took the lessons they learned from the great Tribal Wars and built a government that ensured an event like that could not happen again. Tas had always enjoyed coming to Hruan. It was one of the more diverse countries as many tribes helped win back the land from the War King. Many stayed after the war, leading to a rich and diverse country.

Bart had taken to the skies, flying in large loops as he circled back and forth between them and their destination. Once they were close enough to the house, he settled back in the garden area that he was told could be his for his stay.

"Maya gave him a garden?" Tas asked as he noted where the dragon had settled.

"We were planning to redo it anyway, so he is helping the gardeners," Ray assured him. "We had talked it over with them before offering it to him."

"Good, then I don't have to worry about being run out by pitchforks and mad gardeners," Tas said.

"Has that happened?" Jonah asked.

"A few times," Tas admitted. "He destroyed my grandmother's rose garden when he was a youngling. I don't think the head gardener has forgiven him for that. My grandparents thought it was hysterical, which only encouraged him more."

"Don't forget the central garden in Friesen," Edelberg added.

"I am realizing just how much trouble the two of you are," Jonah realized.

"Destruction everywhere they go," Thierren informed him.

"You can be such a grump, you know that," Grierr said to Thierren.

Thierren said nothing as he followed the group into the main house. The guards seemed to go to different posts as they headed toward the family wing. Thierren was curious about this Lia person. He had not heard of her, and he knew all of Tas's family. Then there was the uncertainty of how Tas should introduce her. Part of Thierren wondered if this was the informant that Tas had mentioned. She was young, maybe early twenties at most. She was wearing leather leggings, a woven tunic, and a bright green vest over it. Her red hair was braided into a series of intricate braids that were then woven into a larger one.

"You don't know her?" Grierr whispered softly.

"No," Thierren answered.

"She the informant?" Edelberg asked.

"That's what I'm wondering as well."

"I guess we'll find out," Grierr replied. "Look, we know she has to be good and means no harm to Tas or Bart."

"How do you know that?" Moira asked. She wondered if they had conversations like this about her.

"Bart would not have flown with her on his back," Thierren answered. "If she meant harm, he would have tossed her off as soon as they were over the ocean."

That had Edelberg chuckling. "He did it once to a bully back at the Academy," Edelberg recalled. "Though it wasn't from high up and it was into the lake off campus."

"Was the bully okay?" Moira asked.

"He learned to not pick on people, especially a Dragon Talker," Thierren replied.

Grierr then looked at Thierren. "What was going on with you and Bart?"

"I'll tell you later," Thierren assured him. "In confidence."

Grierr nodded. He then smiled as Maya Hunt-Moan appeared from the hallway. "My boys," she said as she went and hugged them. "This would only be better if Kaidan was here."

"Kaidan, he has found his place," Grierr told her.

"That makes my soul happy," Maya replied.

"Maya, these are our other companions," Grierr began. "This is Jonah. He is a sea captain and Moira is a healer."

"Welcome," Maya said to both of them. "If we were back at our farm, things would be much less formal, but here, we have to follow a certain decorum."

"Now please, follow me, as we have dinner ready for all of you," Maya told them.

She squeezed Grierr's hand tightly before taking his arm. Grierr had been like another son as they worked with Tas's parents on who would have Grierr for which holiday and break. "How is Rhea?"

"Trying to get word to her clan when we left," Tas replied as she escorted them into the informal dining room they used for family.

"We will get word out as well," Ray promised, joining them at the entrance to the dining room.

"Everyone, please take a seat," Maya instructed. She noted how Grierr looked at the spots his family would sit at during visits. "Grierr, you can sit next to me."

"Thank you for including Jonah and myself into your home," Moira began as the staff brought out trays of food for the table.

"It is no trouble," Ray assured the young woman. "All our children are out of the house, so we enjoy visits."

"Lia has been keeping us abreast of what is happening in Greedin," Maya replied. "It's nice having another female around. They notice things that men sometimes overlook."

"You are just fascinated with her daggers," Ray pointed out.

Maya laughed. "Jonah, tell us about yourself. You are a sea captain?"

"Yes," Jonah began. "I am based out of Vulcan, but sail all around the globe. With the madness that is going on, I unfortunately lost my crew and ship."

"I am sorry," Maya said. "You survived?"

He nodded. Jonah did not wish to talk more of the incident but did not want to be rude. Grierr noted his hesitation and spoke before Maya or Ray could ask for more detail.

"His knowledge of maps is unparalleled," Grierr stated. "He can find any route, even if has been long forgotten. He was critical in helping us all get to the Watchtower safely."

"There are many that have forgotten about that Tower," Ray replied, studying the sea captain. "Hruan has been looking after it since the Tribal Wars. How was it?"

"Flourishing when we left," Tas replied. "Most of it was livable. They were making plans for fields, crops, and housing when we left."

233

"The ground should be fertile," Maya replied. "The only time it wasn't was during the wars."

"The ground knows those that live there mean no harm," Jonah said. He saw Maya react to his words.

"Oh, my..." Maya began as she stared at Jonah. Pieces slid into place as to who was sitting at thier table.

"Dear?" Ray asked as he saw her eyes widen.

"All is fine," Jonah answered. He knew at some point someone would recognize him in Hruan.

"There are many alive today because of you," Maya whispered. "My tribe is among them."

"Then I am honored to know the amazing people that came from it," Jonah answered.

"Maya?" Ray inquired.

Jonah bowed his head. "I should explain," he admitted. He saw the encouraging looks from the three friends that smiled at him. "I am a sea captain; I have been for many years. I am also what the tribes once referred to as a nature guide or spirit."

"He is a water guide. He was one of the ones that helped save the tribes from the War King," Maya finished for him.

Ray looked at him in awe. Jonah raised a hand. "Please, I do not want attention for it or accolades. I did what every spirit should have done," Jonah answered.

"Very well," Ray said. He understood the sentiment very well. "Then let us eat."

"Thierren, Lia is also from Lynia," Maya informed Thierren turning the topic away from Jonah.

"How are things there?" Thierren inquired.

"Tense, as I am sure you can imagine," Lia answered. "The duke is reluctant to do anything to help those being displaced due to what is going on."

"That would be because one of his advisors is a Traditionalist," Thierren stated, almost shocking everyone at the table.

"I have heard that they have gotten more... devout," Lia replied.

"I would have used the term 'crazy' but devout is good," Thierren stated. "They believe that in this 'judgement for the sins of the people', only those truly devout will win favor of Malforin."

Tas studied Thierren for a moment. "You know the advisor."

"My uncle, which means you will have to work around him," Thierren advised.

"We've been trying to get an ear in the inner circle there for months," Lia admitted.

"I know only names of those my uncle distrusts. Those would be the best place to start," Thierren suggested. Edelberg stared at him from across the table in shock at his words. "I would not use my name at the moment. They could see it as a trap."

"That would be amazing," Lia admitted.

The food was delicious as they kept the conversation light. Talk of war and tragedies ended. Now was the time to enjoy conversation and company. Lunch ended when Ray had to leave for a meeting with a parliament committee, leaving Maya to show them to their rooms. With that, she let them settle in, telling them she or Ray would come for them for dinner and that the estate was open to them to use. She promised Thierren that he and Moira would have access to any archive or library they would need by the morning.

Tas headed into his room, noting that Lia had followed him. He sat his bag down on the small table in front of the fireplace. Balcony doors were open already, letting in the springtime air. Bart could be seen in the garden getting comfortable under a tree. He stepped out onto the balcony with Lia following, both standing there and taking in the view. Tas studied Lia as she watched Bart. She wore a simple cream tunic and leather pants. She stood just barely to his shoulders in her simple boots.

"Were you sparring before we arrived?" Tas asked her.

"I was," Lia replied. "Some of the soldiers here are also trained in their tribal fighting traditions. We've been teaching each other our fighting styles."

"How was Cal when you left?"

"Strategizing with our top people on where to set up some new camps," Lia replied. "Lynia is the only one giving us trouble and calling us rebels. The other provinces have appreciated our aid and help."

Lia looked at Tas. "I thought you were going to tell them."

"I was, I am," Tas said. "There really hasn't been a moment where I could just sit down with them and tell them about who my biological father actually is."

Tas let out a sigh as he turned from the balcony and headed into the room. "Jonah knew him," Tas informed Lia.

"Really?"

"It was before he made the choice to become a god. He had joined Jonah's crew so he could see the world before he went through with the ceremony."

"What was he like as a mortal?" Lia asked.

"He was Jonah's best friend. It conflicted him about becoming a god. He enjoyed being with women of all kinds and only those willingly," Tas told her. "He said I looked like he did before he became a god."

"Did him becoming a god change him that much?" Lia asked. To her, Tas' resemblance to her stepbrother was tiny. Lia had recognized Tas by his magic, not by any physical resemblance.

"Jonah believes that because he did not go in with a clear mind, it corrupted him," Tas told her.

"Zola has said that to Cal and me," Lia replied. "That one must go in willingly and with a clear mind."

"Could we get her on our side?"

"We're working on it," Lia informed him. "Cal has been communicating with one of her main messengers. We know she has not been corrupted nor has she chosen a side in the fight between my family."

"Even if she stays out of of it, it would be fine," Tas replied. "I honestly do not know what we would do if we had to go up against the goddess of death."

Chapter 19

The morning came far too soon for any of them. But the smell of food and coffee had them all meeting in the family dining room. Ray had already left for a day of meetings. Maya had yet to leave for the temple. She sat with them and talked while they all got food and drinks. As sleep faded from them, they each started talking. Jonah asked her who would be the best to talk with first. Edelberg was going to join him for the day.

"Ezekiel," Maya decided. "He was in our navy for twenty years. He now runs a cargo company that does land and shipping routes. Zeke won't be in his office before ten, as he helps his daughter with her children. Tell him I sent you and that will get you to see him without an appointment."

"Is there anything I should know about him?"

"He is an honest man. He is frank in how he talks. He sugarcoats nothing," Maya answered. "You two should get along just fine."

"Thierren, are you going to the libraries today?" Tas asked.

"I really need to sit down and make a list of our questions, and what particular information I need," Thierren replied with a sigh. "Right now, it's written on various pieces of paper. I need to organize it before I can start really researching what we need to know."

"Tas, talk with the housekeeper and butler," Maya realized. "Let them know what they can do to help you move about more freely."

"I am going to want to spar with you to see how you have changed your fighting," Lia added.

"Grierr what are your plans?" Maya asked him.

"I was going to check out some of the blacksmith workshops in the city, see if they would lend me space if I had an urge or need to forge," Grierr replied. "There are some projects I want to complete before we leave for Quinsenta."

"Talk with our blacksmith as well. He often lets others use his workshop near the stables to work," Maya suggested. "Lia, are you training with the guards again?"

"No, I have to do some research for my brother," Lia answered.

"Then I will make sure the private library is available to both you and Thierren," Maya told them. "If you need anything, I will be at the children's temple today."

"Moira, you can join me," Thierren said. He noted Moira had been more quiet than usual since they arrived in the capital city. "If you have nothing planned?"

"Or I can play tour guide," Maya suggested.

"I... that would be lovely," Moira replied. "I have not been to Hruan before."

"Then it is settled, Moira and I will explore the city," Maya began. "The rest of you are more than welcome to join if you need a break from your duties."

After that, they all talked for a little longer before they split up to go about their day. Lia headed right for the library as she had already used it before. It was one space in the estate that each president got to decorate how they saw fit. This room was one that anyone could get comfortable in. Warm tones covered the walls behind floor to ceiling bookshelves. The furniture was leather, with blankets draped over the arms for added comfort. They spread family pictures and items throughout the room. This was a room where one could retreat to and escape the pressures of the day. The large windows were open a bit, letting in the early spring air when Lia walked in.

She headed over to the rough farm table she knew was where Maya and Ray took their meals when they had no visitors. Lia set her bag down and took out the cylinder container that contained her maps. She grabbed the one of Greedin and unrolled it. The resistance, as the supporters of Malforin called them, was having some supply issues, and she needed to figure out a way around it. Cal had sent her some notes on what their contacts learned and, hopefully, from that she could figure out a solution.

She heard Tas and Thierren's voices before Thierren stepped into the library. "Hi," Lia greeted him.

"You don't mind sharing?" Thierren asked her.

"There is plenty of room," she promised him.

He nodded, then found one of the comfier chairs and set his satchel down. Thierren had never been one to work at a desk. He thought better in a comfortable chair. Thierren noted Lia was staring at a map. "Can I help?"

Lia looked at him. "Actually, you might be able to," she realized, and motioned for him to join her. "We're running into supply issues. Supporters of Mal are ambushing not just us but other caravans as well. We don't know where they are coming from or how they even know when we are going to be moving goods."

Thierren nodded. "Where are your holdings?"

"I marked them with the symbol for Gaiaa," Lia told him. "Our Allies have the rune for a friend."

Thierren studied the map, identifying the current routes they were using, and saw her notes about where the attacks were taking place. "Can I use your quill?"

Lia handed it to him as he was focused on the map. "Do you see a pattern?"

"I do," Thierren answered. He looked at her with a kind smile. "You would never have seen it because you would have to know cult locations."

Lia watched as Thierren drew on certain locations on the map. She noted he was using an M and another symbol she could not recognize. She did not ask questions as he studied the map and made marks on it. Lia took the time to study him as he worked. Lia had heard much about him from Tas. Now it was her time to get to know this person who meant so much to Tas.

He was easy to look at with his curly blonde hair that framed his face to give him an almost innocent look. His eyes were intense as they roamed over the map as if they took in every detail. He was tall and thin but not lanky, which people would make the mistake of thinking he was weak. There was muscle hidden under his clothes. Lia knew one part of being a sorcerer needed to control the excess energy they had. Exercise, sparring, running were all methods many used to keep the energy from building too much.

"I think I have made some routes for you," Thierren finally said as he stood up from the map. Lia moved to stand next to him again. "The places marked with the M are towns or villages with a large population of Traditionalists and Malfinites. They are going to have eyes and ears on everything happening in the area. This is probably where they get information on caravans and such."

"Some of these are main centers of trade," Lia noted, as she studied the province of Lynia.

"Lynia will be the hardest to maneuver around, as the cult has people high in government," Thierren warned her. "They could not infiltrate Corin's government."

"Should we move completely out of Lynia?" Lia inquired.

"I wouldn't. I would keep a few places open, so people know they have somewhere safe to go. If your main base is there, I would move it into Corin."

"We have contacts in the government," Lia replied.

"Then I would focus on building up your group and supplies there," Thierren suggested. "You can run smaller supply routes to the Lynia camps from Corin. It's also more centrally located among the northern provinces, so it would be better for a base of operations."

"We can avoid the water easier that way as well," Lia noted. She looked at the symbols. "What are these?"

"Those who you absolutely trust can only see this map," Thierren warned her as he was putting his very life on the line for the information he drew on the map. "If word got to the cult that I showed you this, I will be on the top of their hit list if I'm not already."

"These are my personal maps," Lia assured him. "Only Cal and Tas see them. Cal is my twin brother."

"The symbol is for the cult," Thierren informed her. "If you see it anywhere, it essentially means they control that place. These are areas you are going to want to stay clear of. The fanatics will be here, with their army they are raising."

"None are in Corin," Lia noted.

"Corin and much of the northern provinces are proving to be a disappointing endeavor for them," Thierren replied. "They will not pull out, but if you can gain a footing, it will hurt them a lot."

"How big of an army?" Lia asked him.

"Every child, when they turn 13, starts being trained in basic sword fighting."

"And if someone is bad at fighting?"

Thierren looked at her. "There is no being bad at fighting. Weakness is a sign that you are weak in your devotion," he informed her. "Those deemed weak go to special camps to be trained in a more intense environment and mandatory prayer and scripture study."

"That is insane," Lia stated.

"Everything about it is insane," Thierren agreed.

"What will happen to you?" Lia asked. "I mean, if you decide to leave, I mean..."

"It's fine," Thierren assured her, as she floundered for how to finish her statement. He sat down in one chair by the table. "I honestly don't know. Grierr and Tas are working on ways to keep me safe. At the moment, I am fine because they won't know until we leave here."

"Are you scared?"

"Terrified," Thierren admitted. "I've heard the rumors of what happens to those that leave and knowing what they are capable of has me on me edge."

"Always having to look over your shoulders, it can be exhausting and draining in the mind," Lia sighed.

Thierren looked at her. "I would imagine doing what you do has made you enemies."

"Even before we got involved, I feel like my brother and I have had a target on our backs," Lia sighed. She looked at Thierren and tried to decide if she could trust him or to keep silent. He said nothing, as if waiting for her to decide. "Cal and I were born into a family that was already fighting and falling apart. Siblings picking sides or staying out of it. Our mother tried to keep us away from it. She had moved to her family's farm in Corin by the time we were born. But she couldn't keep the truth away from us forever and eventually we had to flee if we wanted to live."

"What happened?"

"Several things," Lia admitted. "We assumed our parents were our mother and the person we called father. Our oldest brother is an asshole and on our twentieth birthday informed us that the man we thought as father was not."

"That's kind of brutal timing," Thierren admitted.

"He laughed at our reactions, at our mother scrambling to explain," Lia recalled. "He is a horrible person, violent, ruthless, always has to be right. He saw Cal as weak, an easy target. Cal could defeat him, but his injuries were bad, and we knew if we stayed, he would come back while Cal was recovering. So, we fled."

"And your mother?"

"She had stopped acting like a mother long before we left," Lia replied. "We were being hopeful she would see the surrounding chaos. By the time Cal was attacked, we already had plans in place."

"It's the hardest thing making that decision that this is the time to go. The knowledge that I can never step foot in the town I grew up in or go to another family event," Thierren said, understanding. "You question yourself a million times before you take that first step. Then a million times more after the first step."

"It's been almost six years and I still wonder if we did the right thing," Lia admitted.

"Is there ever a moment when you know it was the right choice?"

"A million little ones," Lia said. "When laughter is heard in one of our spots, when something goes right, when Cal and I have a moment to just be twins, to just enjoy the moment. That's when it's all worth it."

Thierren studied her for a few moments. "There's this tale that has been floating around the Traditionalists about the 'Lost Twins' of Malforin' and how they will either burn the world at our feet or unite our world."

"Huh, that is very interesting," Lia agreed.

"My family obviously believes you'll be burning the world to the ground, but they are often wrong."

"In some weird way, I kind of want to meet your family," Lia stated.

Thierren chuckled at her comment. "Sadly, I have a feeling you will meet a few of them as we continue with our path."

Lia looked at him with a faint smile, wanting to change the conversation from the depressing thoughts that were hitting both of them. There was an understanding now between them that during this war, the two of them would fight their own family.

"What did Bart give you?" Lia inquired trying to change the conversation.

Thierren arched an eyebrow at her. While grateful for the topic change, he did not want to get into the conversation she was starting. "What do you mean?"

"He essentially greeted you and showed everyone watching that he sees you as an equal, like Tas."

"Ah, well, that would be between Tas and myself," Thierren replied with a secretive grin.

She narrowed her eyes at him. "You hurt him and..."

"And what? You'll hurt me, torture me?" Thierren inquired. "If I hurt him, it will be the end of me. There would be nothing left of me for you to kill, torture, or hit. Also, he can take care of himself."

"Even now?"

"Even now," Thierren assured her. "Spar with him and you will see, but then you have to get in line because Grierr wants to spar with him, and Edelberg wants a rematch from their last match in Hruan."

"I will," Lia answered.

From there, they spent the day in the library, helping each other with their tasks. They found they could work comfortably with each other and also in the same space. It was rare that Thierren found someone that he could research with and not get frustrated with their work ethic. They took lunch in the library, which led to an intense discussion on the mythology surrounding the Malforin gods. After lunch, Lia took a break from her maps and helped Thierren organize his thoughts into lists and questions. When dinner approached, it took Tas and Grierr to drag the two of them out of the library and away from their work.

Tomorrow would be a busy day for Tas, Edelberg, and Jonah. They were going to work with Ray outlining the council meetings about the war. Jonah would help with the shipping issues. As they continued talking after dinner finished, Thierren followed Grierr up to their rooms. Grierr kept his door open so that Thierren could enter first. He realized Grierr was staying in the room that Kaidan and his siblings would use when they visited.

"You have something on your mind," Grierr noted as he took a seat on one of the leather chairs.

"How can you tell?" Thierren inquired.

"Your fingers tap on the top of surfaces," Grierr answered. "Or you twirl a piece of hair. Edelberg taps his foot and Tas cracks his knuckles."

Thierren reached into his pocket to pull out the scale and walked toward Grierr. Even sitting, the man was still taller than Thierren. He handed the item to Grierr and stepped back.

Grierr raised an eyebrow, then looked down in his palm and just stared. He almost dropped it when he jerked in surprise. This was a scale, a scale from Bart. But not just any scale, this was an inner scale. Dragons had two sets of scales that protected their bodies. There was the outer scale. This was mainly for defense, as a dragon could shed one in battle if damaged. These were the scales that were often found when a dragon grew or after a dragon fight. They were some of the strongest materials in the world. These scales grew back fast. The inner scales truly protected the dragon's skin and internal organs and bones.

Many did not know about the inner scales. These were a rare find. The only way one would have one is if a dragon had freely given it to them. For it took much longer for an inner scale to grow back, meaning that the area would be defenseless. Any scale given to a person from a dragon was a treasure, but this was more than that. Verde had given Grierr an outer scale. It showed their trust in him and they accepted him as an ally. The inner scale meant much more than that. It was essentially claiming the person as an equal to the dragon.

"Bart gave you this?" Grierr said when speech and thought finally returned.

"Yes," Thierren answered.

"Shit."

"My reaction as well," Thierren replied. He sat down on the small couch, otherwise he would pace.

"You understand how insane and important this is, right?" Grierr asked Thierren.

"I do," Thierren assured him.

"What the bloody hell did you tell him?"

"That I have made my choices," Thierren answered.

"You made your choices," Grierr repeated. It took a moment for him to understand. "You are not returning home."

"I sent them a response. They should have it in a week or two," Thierren informed him. "I mailed it out at Haven Spring."

"Does Tas know?"

"He knows I was writing a letter to them to inform them of my decision; he does not know everything I said in the letter," Thierren replied.

"Why did you give me this scale?" Grierr asked cautiously. If Thierren was going to reject the gift, it would destroy Tas and Bart.

Thierren stared at the unlit fireplace. He tried to find the words to explain what he wanted. He ran a hand through his hair, sending his curls into chaos, and closed his eyes. He was never good with emotions, with showing them.

"I don't know what I'm doing," Thierren finally whispered.

"No one ever does," Grierr said with a chuckle as he sat down next to his friend. He had rarely ever seen Thierren this stressed out. "How about instead of why you gave it to me, you explain to me what you want done with it, because I'm guessing you want me to create something with this?"

Thierren nodded. He tried to find his voice but could not. Grierr sat with him patiently, not rushing him, not listing all the things he could do with this. Because there were many things that could be forged from the inner scale of a dragon. Items that would brag of one's connection to a dragon, ornaments to be displayed, things that did not matter to Tas. Tas was not a man who could be courted with frivolity.

"I want two rings made," Thierren finally said.

Grierr smiled with true happiness for the first time in an exceedingly long time. "It would honor me to forge them. When?"

"Before we leave for Quinsenta," Thierren answered.

"I can do that," Grierr agreed said with the biggest grin he had worn in a long time.

Chapter 20

The following morning had Thierren and Moira leaving after breakfast to begin his research. Lia would join them later but at the moment she and Jonah were playing an odd game of do not ask too many questions while Tas was talking with Ray about the upcoming meeting. They set the meeting for tomorrow. This left Grierr with too much time on his hands, as Edelberg was already off with the soldiers' training. The scale that Thierren had given him was secure in his room. He had secured the use of the blacksmith shop at the estate here, which would be perfect. He could make the rings with no one seeing. He took a deep breath borrowing some of the bravery that Thierren had shown yesterday afternoon and made his way to one of the temples.

Maya's temple was the main one in the memorial gardens. She was the High Priestess there, had been since before her husband was president. Grierr made sure before he left he had everything he would need, then headed off toward the garden. Tas was the only one who knew where he was headed. He had gotten a silent nod from Tas as he had left. The memorial garden was near the river that ran along the western side of the capital. Large cherry and apple trees were in full blossom, adding a sweet scent to the air as he walked down the path. A tinkling of bells could be heard from the trees. They hung small bells for each victim of the Tribal Wars in the trees of the garden. The site of the garden was where one of the bloodiest battles was fought.

There were people spread out on blankets on the grass or sitting on benches looking out on the river. If anyone noticed him, they did not show, allowing him to walk in peace to his destination. He was relieved when he saw the doors to the temple were wide open. Maya dressed in her priestess robes, purple today, with flowers embroidered along the seams of it. She was watering the plants and flowers that were in pots all over the steps of the temple. Grierr ascended them and waited for her to finish.

She smiled sadly as she set the watering can on its shelf, then turned to study Grierr. "It is time?"

"It is," Grierr whispered. His words choked and filled with sorrow.

She motioned for him to enter the temple. "Sul, I will be in the small ritual room," she informed the male high priest.

"If you are needed?" Sul asked. He recognized Grierr and bowed his head to him.

"A widower's braid with beads," Maya replied.

Sul bowed his head in sympathy. "I will handle all that comes this way," he assured them. "If you need help, ring the bell."

Maya nodded. In silence, she led Grierr to one of the small ritual chambers that were off the main room. They painted the walls in cream colors, pillows lined the floor. Candles were placed on most of the surfaces. In the center was a small cleansing pool that used rainwater to fill it. It was purified through rocks, pebbles, and sand underneath the temple before going into the ritual pools.

"Undress to your underclothes," Maya said softly.

Grierr went behind the screen to undress as Maya situated pillows in front of the pool. She brought a small table over to be next to the pillows. Maya gathered the lotions, oils, and soaps she would need, along with the tools for the braid. When Grierr emerged, he carried two small pouches.

"These are small things that were ... they remind me of them," Grierr explained, ignoring the tears that fell. He handed her the second. "The second contains a scale from a dragon that will watch over the Tower, the beads from Rhea's clan."

Maya smiled sadly as she took both from him. "Lay on the pillows so your neck is on the edge of the pool," Maya instructed. Once the large man was laying, she draped the top half of him in a soft woven towel. "We wash the hair first. This symbolizes the start of renewal, of starting on the new path. It does not wash away the memories."

Grierr nodded. He closed his eyes as Maya lit candles and rubbed oil into her hands. She began softly to sing a funeral song as she used a pitcher to wet his hair with water from the pool. As she stood, he thought of his family. Luna laughing at something he did, the twins fighting over who was better at something, Jacob using the wooden sword to practice. And the baby talking excitedly in baby talk. He loved them with all he had. Now he felt empty in a way.

He tried not to shake as he cried; it did not bother Maya as she continued with washing his long black hair. It had gotten long before the deaths and after that he did not want to cut it, knowing at some point, this would be happening. Maya worked through the tangles, continuing her song as she did. She rinsed his hair free of the soap. Without speaking, she signaled for him to sit up. Positioning the towel around his shoulders, Maya used another to begin the process of drying his hair enough that she could work with it.

"After the braid, what do you want me to do with the rest?"

"The braid of the Arkonites."

Maya smiled and nodded. She slowly and carefully dried his hair. From there, she used a small string to section the hair for the larger braid.

Once it was sectioned, she took the smallest of sections, just behind the left ear, and began the braid. Her singing changed to a chant for the dead as her fingers gently wove his hair. The small charm from Luna's favorite necklace was woven into the braid. She tied the tip with a thin piece of string.

This was the hardest part, as the beads for each child would now be added. Her heart grieved and broke for all that Grierr had endured. With a prayer for each, she carefully added each of the four beads to the tip of the braid. When the last one was set, she sat back.

"I will give you some time to grieve before I return to begin the rest," Maya informed him. She added scents to the water. "When I leave, undress and step into the pool, letting the waters aid you in your grief. You may talk to them. When you are done, you may ring the bell."

Maya gave him a hug before she slipped out of the room. Sul said nothing as she walked to the private garden reserved for the priests and priestesses. This was their private sanctuary, where they could work through the things they saw as religious leaders. Maya lit the lantern to signal that someone was in the garden and wished to be alone. She walked to the small statue of Arkos and kneeled before him.

"May their journey to you be of peace," Maya began. "I know he is in your line. He has been a light in our world since he met Kaidan. We have watched him grow, fall in love, become a father, and we will stand with him as he grieves, letting him know he is not alone. Tell Luna, his children, that we surround him with love. That we will help him, we will not let him lose himself to the grief."

Maya then closed her eyes and allowed her own grief to be released. When they had heard the news, it was like losing grandchildren that were her own. Then to not be able to be there because the ports were closed added to the sorrow. To not be with Grierr as he was crippled with grief devastated

Maya as it did with Anya, Tas's mother. This was her time to grieve before having to be strong for Grierr. No parent should have to bury their child. Yet with war on the horizon, Maya feared many will share in Grierr's pain.

A few hours later, the bell was heard, and Maya went to the ritual room. Grierr sat on the edge of the pool with his feet still in it. He was dressed in his underclothes already. Maya was silent as she entered the room. She kneeled next to Grierr, resting a hand on his shoulder.

"They loved coming to visit you and Ray," Grierr informed her.

"We loved your visits," Maya replied. "They filled the world with laughter and light."

"Now they fill the heavens," Grierr answered.

Maya squeezed his shoulder. "Are you ready?"

Grierr nodded. "It's time to embrace who I am."

"You can stay where you are," Maya told him. "If you need a break, let me know. This will take a bit to do."

From there, Maya began the process. Three sections on each side of his head were made. The thickest two being those in the center of the head, with the thinnest being down toward the neckline. Each braided into its own braid, each having its own song as Maya's fingers wove the hair together. Once the six braids were there, she then created one main braid from the six. She took the widower's braid and wove it between the main braid so the beaded section could be seen at the end of the braid. As she secured everything, she looked at Grierr and realized that this was the first time she had seen a true Arkonite. Pride filled her as she showed him the braid with mirrors.

"Thank you," he whispered.

"Hang onto every memory," Maya told him. "They will always be alive in our hearts and in our memories."

"I will."

"Promise you will not forget to live for yourself?"

"I believe my friends will make sure that I don't fall to the grief," Grierr answered.

"Nor will your family."

Grierr hugged Maya. "Thank you for everything."

She bowed her head to him. They exited the ritual room together; Maya noticed several people see Grierr and once they recognized the braid, realized who he truly was. Grierr walked on as if not noticing.

"I will see you all at dinner," Maya told him as she bid him goodbye at the temple steps. "This day is for you, live."

He nodded and descended the stairs. Grierr headed for the presidential estate. When he saw Bart was laying under a tree, he headed to him. The dragon opened a brilliant green eye at Grierr before he shifted a front paw so that Grierr could sit and lean against him. Here he could be left to his thoughts, for no one would approach a sleeping dragon.

#

Tas found them a few hours later, after a meeting with Lia and Jonah over the list of names that Thierren had given them before breakfast. That was before Thierren had squeezed his shoulder before heading to the library. Thierren had Tas questioning every interaction they had since their stay at the Watchtower. Since Thierren wrote the letter to his parents, something had changed in him, like it had lifted a weight off his shoulders. Tas was sure that was true. Tas sat down next to where Grierr was sitting.

"It's a good look," Tas said. "Though I'm not sure if I should say that because of the other braid."

255

"It's fine," Grierr assured him. "How was your planning session?"

"Good, Lia is using my orb to contact someone so we can get the ball rolling in Lynia," Tas replied. "The list of names Thierren gave us is amazing."

"It seems once he decided, he goes all in."

"I guess," Tas answered as he stroked Bart's wing. "I.. this is going to sound weird."

Grierr opened up an eye and looked at his friend. "What is it?"

"Has Thierren been touchier lately?"

"Not with me. Why?" Grierr asked, trying to hide a grin.

"I'm over thinking things."

"Knowing you, that is probably true," Grierr agreed. "Why are you over thinking things?"

Tas let out a long sigh of frustration. "It started at the Watchtower," he admitted. "He flirted with me when no one would notice," Tas admitted.

"Oh, we noticed, we just had a bet going on about how long it would take you to notice," Grierr answered. Tas just stared at him in shock. "It was between Kaidan, Edelberg, Rhea, and Me. Moira wanted nothing to do with it. Jonah holds the money, since he didn't want to partake in the actual bet."

"You bet on me?"

Grierr chuckled at the face Tas was making. "May I remind you of the bet that was made of how long it would take me to straighten out and ask Luna to marry me?"

"I know nothing about any bet like that," Tas said innocently.

"You are a horrible liar."

"Why are you my best friend?" Tas asked.

"Because we were both awkward eleven-year-olds who decided on our first night at the academy, we would be friends forever and now, nearly

18 years later, here we are," Grierr reminded him. Grierr looked at Tas. "I have not asked, but how are you coping with their deaths?"

Tas was the godfather to his twins, but had been deemed uncle to all his children, an honorary brother to Luna, and had always been his rock. He was a brother to him in every way but blood.

"I see her, especially when I'm fretting about something and that look she would give me," Tas admitted.

"It was the only thing that would get you out of one of your moods," Grierr recalled with a fond smile.

"I can't talk about the ..." Tas voice broke. He closed his eyes as he thought of the twins. "I don't know how you function?"

"I think part of me still feels like it is a nightmare, that I will wake up with a bed filled with children and Luna laughing at me," Grierr confessed. "And then are the moments where it's paralyzing, and I don't know how to move one foot in front of the other. At the temple today, I sobbed for what felt like an eternity. I wanted to punch something, the wall, the pool, anything. "

"Do you want to spar?"

"How's your vision?"

Tas groaned. "It would be good for me to fight in an area I am not used to," Tas replied.

"Didn't answer the question."

"I might have almost shattered a five-hundred-year-old vase this morning because I didn't see it or feel it with my staff," Tas admitted. "But that doesn't mean I can't take you in a fight."

"I will spar with you on two conditions: the first is you have to explain to me how you see while we are fighting," Grierr began. "I want to understand how you see or sense an attack so I can figure out defensive runes for you. The second is the moment you feel overwhelmed. You let me know. I know that in war we can't choose our battles, but you don't have to overdo it. We can build to it."

"Deal," Tas agreed.

"Let's change into something comfortable and talk to the estate guards for a place we can use," Grierr answered.

It would be good for both of them. Instead of them both brooding, they could be productive and work towards getting Tas ready for what was coming. Tas would be crucial in their war, between his connections and his strategic mind, which meant they had to help him become accustomed to his sight. If it meant sparring with him, pushing him to his limits, then that is what they would do.

Chapter 21

Lia walked with Thierren back to the estate. Moira had found a healer that sold some rare plants and had gone to place an order for herself and Thierren. Lia had been spending the last few days in the library with him and Moira doing research alongside him, as well as getting more information on the people she should talk to. Thierren was brilliant. It was amazing to see how fast his mind could connect things or process information. While they might have more questions about how to battle gods or how to treat Tas' poisoning, they still had walked away with more information than they did before that day.

"How do you think they will handle what we found out?" Lia asked. Some of what they learned was unsettling.

"That he should be dead or a blood sorcerer?" Thierren asked. "Or that I know who you are?"

"Both," Lia replied.

Thierren shrugged. "I want to hear what Tas has to say because I know there is something you two are holding back from us," Thierren began. "Not out of maliciousness but out of fear of if word gets out."

"You should be a spy."

Thierren laughed at that. "Tas has said the same thing to me several times."

"Well, if you tire of healing, I'd recruit you," Lia informed him.

"I'll take that into consideration, but I think Tas might have a problem with that."

"And why is that?" Lia asked with a sly grin.

"Because as he told Micah, if I was to be a spy, I would be part of his network because I would co-run it with him, that I work under no one," Thierren replied.

"He is such a romantic in a weird way," Lia said with a laugh. Thierren sent her a look, but could not help but chuckle as well.

They reached the estate; the housekeeper greeted them. "I have a letter from Kaidan for you, Mr. Haas," she informed Thierren.

He took the envelope from her, fearing what would be in the letter. He thanked the housekeeper before heading to the family sitting room. Grierr was there, looking fresh from a bath. He knew Grierr said something to him, but he was silent as he walked to a corner chair and sat in it. Thierren opened the envelope and slid the paper out.

He passed two nights ago in his sleep. Lysander and his friends were with him. We are going to build a pyre and celebrate his life as a family, then his remains will be brought back to the dwarves' clan. He was in no pain at the end.

Thierren stared at the words, ignoring that they were getting blurry. He almost jumped when Tas kneeled in front of him and took the paper from his hand. Thierren pulled Tas toward him. Tas immediately wrapped his arms around Thierren to comfort him. As a healer, death was part of his duty. Yet there were some deaths that were hard to move past. Training would say to focus on how one eased the suffering of the patient. Tobbin was one of the hard deaths. The cranky old man had seen through all of Thierren's walls, and gave him advice that no one else could.

"When?" Tas asked quietly.

"A few nights ago," Thierren whispered, his voice with emotion. "I knew it would be soon..."

"But he was a cranky asshole that everyone loved," Tas finished for him. "Grierr and Lia went to see when dinner would be."

Thierren nodded, taking comfort in his head resting against Tas's chest. At the moment, he did not want to move. Tas' scent was calming, as was hearing his heartbeat.

"Where's Jonah and Edelberg?" Thierren asked as he lifted his head.

"He is having dinner with several suppliers about deals that could be made with the aid of dragons. Edelberg is eating at the barracks," Tas told him. "We could say a prayer for him tonight on the balcony?"

"He would prefer us getting drunk on ale and laughing," Thierren answered.

"Then we'll do that," Tas stated.

Thierren moved back and out of Tas's embrace. "Okay," he said, taking a deep breath.

"You sure?"

"No, but we need to eat, and I have questions to ask you and Grierr," Thierren admitted. "I wish Jonah were here, but we can tell him when he returns. We need to send word to Edelberg; he needs to be here for the conversation."

Thierren then noted that Tas also looked like he had just come from a bath. "Did you spar with Grierr?"

"Yes, I need to learn how to fight in new surroundings," Tas replied as they headed out of the sitting room. "Grierr is also figuring out how I fight, what is the limitation with my vision, so he can make defensive runes for me."

"Any injuries?"

"I'm sure just sore muscles in the morning," Tas assured him.

Thierren headed into the dining room first, making sure any obstacles were removed before allowing Tas to enter. The conversation that Tas had with the staff a few days ago seemed to work as Thierren noted there were clear paths for Tas to move freely...

Grierr came over and squeezed his shoulder. "The asshole will be missed," Grierr replied.

"He will," Thierren agreed. He spotted Moira, who must have arrived and learned of Tobbin.

She walked over and hugged him tightly. "You gave him a better outcome," she whispered.

"And you would not give up on him," Thierren reminded her.

Maya arrived, smiling at all of them. "Ray is eating with the assembly, so we are to eat without him," she informed them. "They are ironing out some details for tomorrow's meeting."

With what both Grierr and Thierren had dealt with that day, dinner was a calmer affair. It did not stop Maya from telling Lia and Moira stories about them when they were in school, all the trouble the group of them caused. Now and then, one of them would object to telling their version of events. After the plates were cleared, they enjoyed a light dessert before Maya excused herself for the night.

Edelberg appeared toward the end of dinner. He took a seat next to Tas. "I heard I was needed?"

"Thierren wants a meeting with all of us. Jonah is at dinner with suppliers, so we will fill him in tomorrow," Tas told him.

"Knowing Jonah, he probably already knows it all," Edelberg pointed out.

"That is true," Tas agreed.

"Why don't we all meet in my rooms?" Tas suggested. "I believe Thierren wants to talk to us about some things he learned over the last few days."

"Agreed," Grierr replied. "I can also discuss my plans for Tas and the runes that will aid him."

They got up from the table and headed out of the dining room. Tas saw the outline of one of the staff. Recognizing his aura, he walked over to him.

"Mathias, if Jonah returns, send him to my rooms," Tas asked.

"Of course," Mathias replied. "Also, the staff had made clear paths for you, so you should be okay. However, if you ever want to 'accidentally' knock over that vase you almost did this morning, we will not say a word."

"No one likes that vase, I take it," Thierren commented.

"It's a leftover from the collection held by the mad War King," Mathias informed them. "It's been here as a show of us accepting our past. No leader wants to remove it because of fear of outrage from a small political group."

"Consider it broken before I leave," Tas replied.

"Trouble is attracted to you," Thierren mumbled.

"You can be no fun," Tas said to him as they headed toward their rooms.

"Only because I usually have to clean up your mess," Thierren commented.

Moira watched them as she walked with Lia and Grierr. "Are they always like this?"

"Since school," Grierr answered.

Tas opened the door to his rooms and let the three of them in before he closed it. He placed a silencing barrier around the room so what they talked about could not be overheard by anyone or anything. Grierr had taken a chair closest to the balcony doors, Lia was walking around looking at his decor, Moira settled on the floor cushion in front of the fireplace while Edelberg leaned against a bookcase. Thierren had settled on the couch. Tas took the chair across from Grierr.

"What did you learn?" Grierr asked Thierren.

"A lot, but I also have more questions," Thierren warned them. "I started with the big question we need to solve at some point: how do we defeat gods?"

"Did you find anything?" Grierr asked. He did not think there could be much on that topic.

"Honestly, I searched your family history," Thierren admitted. "It's pretty grim. As far as I know, they were the only gods or descendants of gods that were murdered."

"That is a bad place to start," Grierr agreed.

His parents had been killed when he was two. With no living relatives alive, the Priests from Emi rescued him from the orphanage he had been sent to and brought him to Emi. An older couple took him in. The whole island helped raise him. They were aware of who he was, but no one spoke the words, understanding the danger he would be in. The priests had started a rumor that he had died on the journey from the orphanage to his new home to ensure his protection.

"Grierr," Moira said softly. "How I reacted when we first met, I didn't understand the connotation to the word. I am so sorry."

"It's water under the bridge," Grierr assured her. "Most who use that word currently don't know that it once was a death sentence when used. I know you meant no ill will toward me."

"Still, I apologize."

"Did my family tree help?" Grierr asked Thierren.

"It proved to be a fruitful starting point as there are ways to weaken and even kill a god," Thierren continued. "It isn't clear in the texts I could access. I think I need access to the Cult of Prophecy archives."

"Good luck with that," Lia replied.

"Why?" Moira inquired.

"How much do you know about them?" Tas asked her.

"As much as anyone, I guess," Moira replied with a shrug. "They store all the prophecies that are made by the Fates, they protect them, and see them as the word of the gods who ascended back to the heavens."

"They are also a violent group," Lia replied. "They are very selective in their membership. You can't be born into their cult. They choose you, usually because you will serve a purpose or goal for them. They will destroy any document that contradicts any of the prophecies."

"But prophecies aren't set in stone," Moira argued. "They are simply warnings of what could be."

"To the Cult, the prophecies are infallible," Thierren answered. "They destroy any writing that speaks of discord between the gods. It's one of the few things they and the Malfinites agree on: gods are infallible and to speak negative of them is a sin worthy of torture and death."

"And you think what we need is in their vault?" Moira asked.

"I do, but Lia is right. I won't be able to get in," Thierren replied. "I am sure by the time we reach Quinsenta I will be on their list of enemies."

Tas thought while they discussed the Cult of Prophecy, when the idea formed in his head. "My grandfather might have some of their tomes in his personal library," Tas stated. "If you give me the list of what you need, I can send it and see if he has it. Otherwise, I know someone who could get them to you from the archives."

"Do you have people everywhere?" Grierr asked Tas.

"Between Kaidan, Micah and me, yes," Tas admitted.

Grierr knew the network of spies that Tas had was large, but he was only figuring out how large that network really was. Moira raised an eyebrow, but Edelberg gave her a subtle shake of the head. She had a feeling he would fill her in later.

Thierren continued. "While I don't know methods yet, there is some hope that there are ways we can actually defeat them," Thierren replied.

"Maybe for some of them, the knowledge we can defeat them could be enough to sway them to step down," Lia commented.

"Can a god step down?" Thierren asked her.

"It's all theoretical," she warned. "Just like they can refuse the power, there is the theory that they could ask for their powers of a god to be removed. Though the question of what would happen to them is severe. The longer they had the power, the worse the consequence."

"What are we talking about?" Tas asked.

"Well, for example, Malforin or Olga would suffer a slow, painful death because they have been with the power for so long, especially Malforin. He was born with it. The body would slowly shut down."

"I don't see either of them willingly stepping down," Grierr commented.

"I agree," Lia assured him. "But not every one of their children is completely behind this war, so if we can get them to stand down with the knowledge we gain, it would help."

"What else did you learn?" Grierr asked.

"I also delved into some of the medical journals and creature records on the Blood Dragon poison," Thierren began. He took a deep breath and ran a hand through his hair. "So, what I learned is that Tas should either be dead or a blood sorcerer."

The room was silent at his words. Tas just stared at Thierren unsure of what to think. "I'm not dead and I'm not a blood sorcerer."

"I know," Thierren answered.

"Is it because you pushed some of yourself into him?" Grierr asked Thierren.

Thierren shot Grierr a look, but it was too late. Tas stared at him. "I told you not to do that ever again!" Tas exclaimed.

"And I told you it's my ability. I can use it how I want," Thierren shot back.

Lia held a hand up. "I'm sorry, you lost me somewhere," she interrupted. "Thierren pushed a part of himself into Tas?"

"Thierren is what the Academy called a Natural healer," Grierr explained, knowing Thierren wouldn't. "He can actually use his magic to heal people. Death is the only thing he can't heal. However, sometimes when a person is near death, Thierren can push himself to the brink of exhaustion to strengthen the person's connection to the living."

"It's not a big deal," Thierren assured her.

"I watched him do it with a broken leg," Moira replied. "It is a big deal."

"He's magically exhausted for several days," Grierr countered.

"And he's done this before with Tas?" Lia inquired.

Tas let out a long sigh as he realized at the moment what they were discussing was about who he truly was. It was time to tell them the truth.

"I was twenty. It was a really low point in my life," Tas began. He never spoke of this with anyone. Only Edelberg, Grierr, and Thierren knew of the events. Grierr and Thierren had found him. Edelberg had come as soon as they sent word to him. "I swallowed a bunch of health tonics that had the herb I'm allergic to in them."

Lia and Moira stared at him in shock. She did not know how to respond. Grierr spoke up next. "Thierren and I knew something was up. We hadn't heard from him in a few weeks. When I contacted his mom, she had said the same," Grierr continued. "We didn't hesitate. We went to his flat he keeps in Gastion. We found him. We knew it was bad. We sent word to Edelberg to get to us as fast as he could."

"Honestly, his body had already started the purge," Thierren told Lia and Moira. "He would have survived it, but it would have been worse."

"His heart stopped," Grierr reminded Thierren. Then looked at the women. "When it did, Thierren hit him with a bolt of electricity and used his magic to heal the damage as it was occurring."

"He gave no warning," Edelberg recalled. "I was holding Tas down and suddenly this surge of power hits Tas and I'm flung across the room. It worked, though, Tas began to breathe on his own."

"We stayed with him for a month after until he got it through his thick skull. He was not alone," Thierren replied.

"As I said, it was a dark time," Tas answered.

Lia looked at him for a moment. "You were twenty," she realized.

Thierren, Edelberg, and Grierr looked at each other, knowing they were missing something. Thierren then looked at Tas.

Tas stood up and walked to the balcony doors. "I know why I survived the blood poisoning," Tas said. His tone was neutral. "It's tied to what happened almost ten years ago."

Tas let out a long sigh before he talked. "Take your time," Thierren said softly.

"At the age a twenty, a child of a god goes through one of their first power surges," Tas began. "It is the first inclination of their power base."

"I went through it. It can be brutal," Grierr recalled. "But you are not the son of a god."

Tas laughed bitterly at that. "Turns out I am."

Silence filled the room. It was Grierr that spoke first. "Tas, I have met and lived with your family for years. There is no way your mother would ever have an affair. Your parents are madly in love with each other."

"Unless it wasn't an affair," Edelberg realized as dread filled his stomach.

"My mother had gone to visit her family in Silencia," Tas began. "My father stayed with my three brothers, allowing her to get away from everything in Quinsenta. She stayed for a month, on her return her ship vanished during a freak storm. They searched for months for her. Three months after the ship vanished, they spotted it a few miles off the shore of Quinsenta. My mother was the only survivor. She had been savagely beaten, assaulted. It was bad."

He felt a glass press into his hand and saw it was water that Moira had poured for him. He drank it before continuing. "She almost died from her wounds several times. During one of these times, they realized she was pregnant."

"Shit," Thierren whispered as Grierr mumbled a series of curses.

"They all knew it couldn't be my dad's, which confirmed their biggest fears," Tas went on. "My father never batted an eye; I was his son, no matter what. It didn't matter how I came about; I was his and they would love me. My mother almost died carrying me and during my birth. They named me after the doctor that they credit for saving both of our lives. They shielded me from the truth, then I turned twenty."

Grierr closed his eyes as understanding dawned on him. "Your second powers came into play," Grierr whispered.

"If you're not a sorcerer, you suddenly wake up at twenty with these abilities you never had before," Lia added with a vivid memory of her twentieth birthday.

"So, no matter what, it's a huge transition," Thierren stated. "Then for someone who doesn't know that they're related to one, it has to be a huge shock to everything."

"Tas, who raped your mom?" Grierr asked gently.

"She never said. She never really could recall what he looked like. He kept his face shadowed," Tas answered. "She had a feeling deep down; she only told my father. I turned twenty, and I saved a child from drowning by controlling the water."

"You've never had that ability," Grierr stated.

"I know," Tas agreed.

"How did you control it?" Edelberg asked.

"I walked into the ocean and the water parted. I picked up the child and somehow summoned the water out of his lungs. I felt like I had been run over by a carriage several times afterwards."

"Well, shit," Thierren said as it slid into place. "You smell like the ocean as it's about to storm when you lose control of your powers. Your eyes change to the color of the stormy sea."

Edelberg looked at Thierren then at Tas. "Taris?"

"I've wanted his head on a platter since then," Tas answered. "I went into the spiral; how could my mother see me and not recall those three months of hell? How could my dad see me and not blame me for what happened to her? Am I going to turn into him?"

"You will not turn into him," Thierren declared.

"How do you know that?" Tas challenged him.

"Because we won't let you," Thierren answered. "Why didn't you tell us sooner?"

"How do you tell your friends a god raped your mom, and you are the product of it?" Tas asked. "Where does that ever come up in a conversation?"

Grierr leaned forward in his chair, letting his face rest in his hands for a few moments. "We're asking you to fight your..."

"He is NOT my father!" Tas yelled, his voice rolling like thunder as the scent of the ocean filled the room. "My father is Crown Prince Trion of Quinsenta, that is my father. The other person is a monster and deserves to pay for all the pain and suffering he has caused the world."

Thierren stood up. He walked over and laid a hand on Tas's arm. "You're right," he said softly. "Grierr just wanted to make sure you are truly okay with everything we are going to be doing."

"I want his head on the points of his trident so I can feed it to sharks," Tas stated.

"Then that is what we will do," Thierren agreed.

Edelberg realized they had to steer the conversation away from this. "Grierr, you said you figured out runes that could help Tas?"

"Huh? Oh yeah," Grierr replied, noting with appreciation how Edelberg easily changed the topic. "So, we sparred today. I had Tas explain to me how he was seeing me, how he was fighting, where he had blind spots in his vision."

"What did you learn?" Lia asked.

"Tas is adapting quickly to his new way of seeing," Grierr replied. "I've made runes for the blind before. There are different levels of blindness: complete loss of sight, some can see light, others can see vague outlines, and anywhere in between. So I have some idea of what to play with."

"I see you all as fuzzy shapes, but I can identify you because of your auras," Tas explained as he sat on the couch with Thierren. "Just like I know some of the staff's because I have been here before. Also, the center of my vision is clear, but I compare it to the size of the head of a pin. From there it gets blurrier until it fades to black where my peripheral vision would be."

"He can fight, though?" Lia inquired.

"He disarmed me a few times. He's fast and nimble. I really had to plan my attacks ahead to get near him," Grierr confirmed. "His weak zone is pretty obvious: it's coming from the back and the sides."

"That makes sense," Edelberg agreed. "What are you planning?"

"Tas and I are going to work on his armor, placing runes on it that would help him be aware of people around him," Grierr confirmed. "I don't know if I can get them to help him identify friend from foe, but if we can get it to him knowing there is someone approaching from behind on the sides, that would be a huge step for him."

"We could train a small unit with him so they can work with his weak areas," Lia suggested. She knew many who would jump at the chance to aid Tas.

"That is not a bad idea," Tas agreed. "I would learn their auras, but would anyone be willing to do so?"

"I can think of dozens of the people you have helped who would jump at the chance to give back," Lia informed him.

"I think you exaggerate," Tas answered.

"He has never believed the impact he has on people," Edelberg informed Lia.

"Well, he's a moron," Lia stated.

"He is right here," Tas reminded the two of them.

"We know," the two said in unison.

Grierr chuckled. "Look, why don't we take a break for the evening? We've had some pretty intense discussions," Grierr suggested. He could tell that Tas was drained.

"That sounds good," Tas agreed.

Grierr got up and walked over to Tas, where he gave him a hug. "I love you, brother."

"I love you too," Tas replied.

Lia came over and hugged him before following Grierr out of the room. Edelberg hugged Tas tightly before telling him he was a moron. Moira told him she had a tea to help with depressive thoughts. She would show Thierren the recipe tomorrow. Thierren stayed sitting on the couch. Tas looked at him, not sure what was going through his mind.

"I'm sorry I didn't tell you sooner," Tas said to him as he sat down next to him.

Thierren turned and looked at him with a slight smile. "You could have saved me some grief if you had," he replied.

"And how is that?" Tas inquired, intrigued by the comment.

"Because I could have told my parents in the letter I sent them that the guy I chose is a descendant of their god's son," Thierren said. "They would have been at war with their beliefs."

"That would have been fun to see..." Tas began, then stopped. "Wait. 'The guy you chose'?"

Thierren reached into his pocket and handed him a small pouch. Tas looked at it before he opened it and dumped out its contents. It was a scale, a deep burned red with black around the edges. It was stunning, and he knew who it came from.

"How did you get this?" Tas asked him, his voice cracking as he did.

"Bart gave it to me the day we arrived here," Thierren informed him. "I have asked Grierr to make two rings from it."

Tas just stared at it, then looked at Thierren. If Bart gave this to Thierren it meant his feelings were true. Dragons only shared their inner scales with those who were true to their feelings and intent.

"You know what this means in dragon cultures?" Tas asked quietly.

"Yes," Thierren answered.

"You told Grierr?"

"The night after we arrived," Thierren informed him.

"You told your parents that..."

"I was choosing you, choosing my path, choosing freedom," Thierren replied. "I told them in the letter I sent before we arrived here."

"Right," Tas said as his hands trembled.

"You're shaking," Thierren noted.

"I hadn't noticed," Tas answered dryly.

Thierren laid a hand on top of one of Tas's and squeezed. "Talk to me."

"I knew you've been flirting with me the last few weeks," Tas said. "I was babbling about it to Grierr. He would just roll his eyes at me, then told me about a bet he has with a few people on how long it would take me to realize."

"You can be oblivious sometimes," Thierren agreed.

"I can be," Tas agreed. He looked at Thierren. "Are you sure you want this? Want me? I come with a lot of baggage."

"So do I," Thierren reminded him. "I'm going to have a cult that wants me dead."

"I like to see them try to lay a hand on you," Tas challenged.

Thierren looked at him. "What do you want?"

"I mean, it's been you since our second to last year," Tas admitted. "It's always been you. I was happy with you as my friend. I would never force it."

"Hence me showing you the scale," Thierren added.

"With everything going on, I want to say this is probably a bad time to start this," Tas said honestly. "Yet maybe it's the perfect time to start it."

"So, can I kiss you now?"

Tas pulled Thierren to him until their lips touched. "Yes."

Chapter 22

Tas had never been one who had patience dealing with politicians. Kaidan had been the one to handle the politics and the grandstanding, getting support. He enjoyed the word games and half truths he had to work through to get people on his side. It drove Tas up the wall. He hated how long it always took to get to the point.

However, it turned out that Grierr had a way of getting people to talk without trying. Grierr was also having a grand time teasing him that while he was raised as a Prince, it was the orphan who could talk to politicians. Tas would fire back with the fact that Grierr was seven feet tall, and his height intimidated people, leading them to just agree with him. For Lia, Thierren, and Jonah they were simply happy they were not involved in the meetings.

There was one block of senators that were refusing to listen to anything that was happening outside of their county. Refugees entering Hruan were not their problem, earthquakes in odd locations did not impact them, and who cares about a volcano that suddenly emerged over days. Tas was ready to bash their heads together as they entered the fourth day of meetings.

"How do we know these Black Mists are not fever dreams or hallucinations?" Senator Hawthorn demanded. "For all we know, this is a made-up scenario to strike fear in the populace."

"Then my wife and children died from a made-up scenario?" Grierr challenged, rising from his seat. There were shouts of support for him.

"Did you witness their deaths?" Hawthorn challenged.

"I did not, but my neighbors saw the Black Mist, saw it stop at each door until it reached mine, watched in horror as it seemed to melt into the door," Grierr recounted what he had been told.

"But you did not witness it yourself. All we have is a secondhand account."

"Excuse me," a voice said as the door to the parliament room opened.

"Dr. Haas," Ray said as he stood. "What brings you to our session?"

"They informed me that today you would discuss the rumors of the Black Mist," Thierren began. "I'm sorry I did not arrive with Prince Taslan and Lord Arngrierr, but I had to pick up someone."

Tas walked over to Thierren greeting him and his guest. "Just in time," Tas whispered in his ear as he brought him to their table.

The young woman with Thierren took a seat next to him as they sat. One clerk had them sign in on the parliament log for the day. Once signed in, the session continued.

"Dr. Haas, perhaps you could explain to us the rumors swirling around the Black Mist," Senator Hawthorn suggested.

"Of course," Thierren agreed as he stood up to speak. "A year ago, when the rumors of such a thing began, many in the medical community thought it was nonsense, this idea of a mist that targets specific people and kills them instantly. Many of us dismissed the idea entirely."

Hawthorn looked incredibly pleased with this statement. Thierren continued. "However, as the months continued, we were being presented with unknown deaths that made no sense," Thierren explained. "People that were healthy with no ailments dead with no sign of foul play, self-inflicted wounds, or an accidental death. Many families gave permission for autopsies, which showed nothing. No poisons, no allergic reactions, nothing to explain why their heart just stopped beating."

"You said there were no signs of foul play," Senator Hun stated. "Can you explain that?"

"Of course," Thierren replied. "In situations where we are unsure of the cause of death, we will look for any sign of a struggle. An example would be bruises, especially around the neck. We look for places where a needle could be injected into the body, rope marks suggesting strangling."

"So, this unknown death, you would rule out foul play and self-inflicted wounds," the same senator stated for clarification.

"Correct," Thierren replied. "We would look for natural causes with samples from the body. These samples could be hair, skin, fingernails, blood even."

"And those samples also came back normal?"

"Correct," Thierren agreed.

"What were you looking for?"

"Different potions will indicate different causes, such as poison, drugs, substances that could explain why a seemingly healthy person is dead. We also use the samples to look for health issues that had gone undiagnosed."

"From these samples, could your rule out health conditions and other causes?"

"Yes," Thierren answered. "I have copies of the reports if you need to look at them."

"If we have need of them, we will ask," the senator assured him.

"Currently, what is the medical opinion on the Black Mist?" Ray asked Thierren.

"The consensus of the top medical schools in the world, and top experts in disease and plagues, all agree that whatever the Black Mist is, it is very much a real thing," Thierren answered. He saw the glare aimed at him from Hawthorn. "It was not an easy decision, as we have no sample that shows what it is. All we know, based on witness testimonies and the location of the deaths, is that whatever it is kills instantly and leaves no traces."

"Is it being signed on death certificates as a cause?" Senator Hun asked, trying not to smile at Hawthorn's outrage.

"Within the last six months, we have been signing it as a cause of death," Tas confirmed.

Hawthorn and his block of supporters looked furious at this statement. Hawthorn stood and spoke. "Dr. Haas, you are a well-regarded healer and doctor. Your papers show impeccable research skill and a clear understanding of your field," he began. "What is your medical opinion on this Black Mist?"

"That it is very much a real and lethal organism that we need to take seriously," Thierren declared.

"I am surprised that someone in your field with your expertise would follow along with the propaganda," Hawthorn sighed dramatically.

"Senator Hawthorn, have you ever performed an autopsy on a victim of the Black Mist?" Thierren asked the Senator.

"Of course not. I am not a medical professional."

"Good, I'm glad you said that," Thierren said with a slight smile. "Because I am a medical professional and I have performed eight autopsies on the victims of the Mist. I have spoken with those who watched the Mist float from door to door until it found its target. I have seen firsthand what it does."

"This is all based on secondhand accounts," Hawthorn challenged.

"Which is why I have brought my guest with me," Thierren said. "Mr. President, I would like to introduce Emaya Hurst. She apprenticed with my Aunt Amelia for two years. She was there the night the Mist killed my aunt. She is a certified healer and trained with my aunt to further her studies in herbal lore and pathogens."

"Healer Hurst, welcome," Ray said with a kind smile.

"Thank you," Emaya said quietly. She was now glad for Lia helping her look more presentable. Lia had helped her place her hair in a bun, she traded in her travel clothes for a simple light blue day dress.

"You were an apprentice for the late Dr. Haas?" Ray asked. "I know her apprenticeship was one of the hardest to get."

"Yes," Emaya answered. "Amelia was very selective with who she takes and because of how long we are with her, it must fit with her schedule as well."

"Where did you live while you were an apprentice to her?"

"Because of how intensive it is, we stay with her," Emaya explained. "Amelia only took one apprentice at a time. Because of this, she allowed us to live with her. She had a loft in her home that was set up as a study and sleeping area for us. There have been a few that lived near her as they had a family, but mostly, we lived with her."

"I'm sorry if these questions will seem rather odd, but it is to gather information so we can understand what happened," Ray warned her gently. "Can you explain the layout of her home where it was located?"

"She had a two-floor cottage right on the outskirts of the village, Fleure in Gastion," Emaya replied. "We had neighbors, we were not as isolated as some would think."

"I think we sometimes think of these healers as isolated women who live in the woods, like you hear in the stories," one senator stated. "Thank you for clearing that up."

"Amelia's home was off a quiet street, but close enough to town that people could come for emergencies or for potions," Emaya replied. "Her office was an old barn on her property. It had a small exam room, a small washroom, and her office. This is where she would see patients."

"Then they never entered the main house?"

"No," Emaya answered. "She stated a variety of reason. The main being it helped prevent contamination of her home if she treated them in a separate space. The other was it separated her workspace from her home. Something very much needed in our profession."

"I can't count how many times I am dragged out of my home office because it's late or dinner is getting cold," Ray chuckled. "My wife would agree with your aunt."

Emaya smiled. She accepted the glass of water from Tas. "Her cottage was not large, but two people could live in it without being in the other's way. The main floor was a large main room comprising a living area and kitchen with a washroom off it, as well as a storage room. There was a basement, that was her lab, but to enter it you had to exit the house. The second floor contained the loft, her bedroom, and a closet."

"How close to her bedroom was your sleeping area?" Ray asked her.

"I could see her bedroom door from my bed," Emaya answered.

Hawthorn did not like her answer. "You were there the night she died?"

"Yes," Emaya answered.

"Can you walk us through that day and night?"

"Of course," she replied. "It was her day off from seeing patients. She always had a scheduled day off during the week. For me, it meant a day to study and review what we had discussed over the past few days. Amelia would use it as a day to visit the market, have tea with friends, and relax."

"Was she stressed about any cases?"

"No, we weren't working on any serious or complicated cases," Emaya replied. "We had been seeing mostly colds and common illnesses that happen around the Winter Solstice. It was a relatively easy week."

"You remember this, how?" Hawthorn inquired, wanting to poke a hole in her story.

"Every healer, doctor, and apprentice keeps a log of patients' ailments, so that we have it to keep a history of their health, or if I ever needed it for court or schooling," Emayla explained. "I can tell you that on the day she died, I was researching the properties of herbal plants on aiding mental illnesses."

"That is impressive," Hawthorn admitted. "I take it she looked over your notes?"

"It was how we were graded in an apprenticeship with her," Emaya clarified. "Our logbooks were our textbook, our homework, exams, everything. It is one of my most valuable possessions."

Hawthorn nodded. "How was Amelia that day?"

"She was planning for the Solstice celebration in the village, what we would bring, working with other businesses to ensure those that those who had little would have plenty for the twelve-day festival. She wasn't ill or showing signs of an illness."

"Emaya, were you there when the Black Mist came?" Ray asked in a gentle tone. He knew this would be difficult for anyone that bore witness to a death.

Grierr reached over and laid a hand on hers to show support. "I was," Emaya answered, her voice almost cracking with emotion.

"Can you explain what happened that day?"

Emaya nodded as she took a deep breath. "She had gone to bed at her normal time. I was reading in my bed. I wanted to finish the chapter I was reading. We did not have an early morning the next day, so I could sleep a little later than normal. It was close to midnight. I remember it became silent. All the noise from outside just went quiet. The air seemed still. I thought it odd because around midnight, the farmer down the road had a rooster who would go off at midnight and he was silent. It's something you always wished would happen, but when it did, it made me nervous."

"Did Amelia notice this?"

"Amelia was a very sound sleeper," Emaya answered.

"It's true," Thierren confirmed. "We joked she could sleep through a massive storm."

"I take it she was the only one the rooster didn't bother," Ray commented.

"Yes," Emaya said with a sad smile.

"When you didn't hear him or the other night sounds, what did you do?"

"I took my lantern and went to see if there was anything wrong," Emaya answered. "The windows and doors were all locked. We had banked the fire for the night. There was no storm going on. I opened the back door and saw nothing. I looked out the front window and..."

"It's okay," Thierren whispered to her. He handed her a handkerchief, knowing she would need it.

"Sorry," Emaya whispered, as she took a moment to compose herself.

"Take your time. We know this is tough to discuss," Ray assured her. Grierr had spoken earlier about his own experience with the Black Mist. He could only imagine what it was like to have actually witnessed it happen. "If you need a few moments, let us know."

"Thank you," Emaya replied. She just wanted to get this over with. "When I looked out the front windows, there was this black shadow moving down the street. It made little sense, it had no real shape, it just floated, yet it stopped by each gate as if it were looking for something."

"What did you do?"

"I double checked all the locks, then went back up to the loft," Emaya answered. "I turned off my lantern and grabbed a book. I figured if it were an intruder I could throw a book at them, silly now to think of, but at the time it seemed like a clever idea."

"Anything can be a weapon when used right," a senator informed her. "That is what I tell my daughters all the time."

"What happened then?" Ray asked. He was thankful to the few senators who were trying to comfort her.

"The temperature dropped suddenly, as if the fire had gone out, but I could still see the embers going in the hearth. I could see my breath in front of my face," Emaya recalled. "I knew when it stopped in front of our door, for this darkness fell over the cottage, as if it had snuffed all the light out. The only light I could see was the sliver of the moon coming in through the window near my bed."

She gave herself a moment. Thierren held her hand, squeezing it in support. "I watched the front door as this black formless mist just seemed to melt out of the door and into the main room. It lingered there for a moment before moving throughout the first floor, searching for something. It floated up the stairs, and it came to the loft area it...it stopped right in front of me. I could see my breath. It was so cold as it just hovered there. I can't explain how it felt to have it hovering in front of you, realizing that all the stories of the Black Mist of death were real. Terrified I was its target, that there is nothing you can do. There's this scream that you want to let out, but you can't because you're frozen."

"Yet obviously you're still here, Miss Hurst," Hawthorn said, sounding bored.

"Because I was not its victim," she snapped. "You wanted to know what happened from a firsthand account, and here I am explaining it. I'm sorry if my details are boring to you. That it isn't gory enough for you!"

"That is out of line," Hawthorn challenged.

"I'm sorry," Emaya said, as she checked her emotions.

"Do you want a break, or do you want to continue?" Ray asked her, ignoring Hawthorn.

"I would like to continue," Emaya answered. Ray nodded. "The mist moved, and I felt relief that I was still alive until I saw it go toward Amelia's door. I threw a book at it to watch it sail through it and hit the wall. I yelled. I tried to get up but couldn't. I watched it vanish into the door. For minutes, which felt like hours, I couldn't move. Then suddenly the night noise returned, the coldness vanished, and I could move again. I knew deep down that it meant Amelia was dead. I rushed to her room, and she lay there as if she was still asleep, her eyes closed, her blankets undisturbed. I kneeled in front of her bed and felt no pulse, her skin it was like ice. I must have screamed because I heard pounding on the door and then our neighbor was sitting with me on the floor telling me it would be okay."

"And did this neighbor witness the Black Mist?" Hawthorn asked.

"That would be secondhand information, wouldn't it?" Emayla asked him.

He stared at her. "Did he make a comment to you?"

"He did," Emayla answered. "He had been up with his youngest and saw this black shadow pass by the windows of his bedroom. He watched it stop in front of our house but found he could not get his doors to open."

"That matches with other accounts we heard," Ray stated. "That those who witness the Mist can't move or alert the victim."

"If there is nothing medically that can be done, why are we even bothering to discuss this?" Hawthorn inquired, as he seemed bored by the conversation.

Tas was ready to explode. He took a deep breath as Thierren rested a hand on his knee to keep him calm. "I understand the fear that we all share," he began. "Much of what we have discussed over the last few days seems beyond what we can control. What we are discussing, what we are thinking of doing, seems to be insane. The last time the world seemed to unite was in the First Age to depose of a mad king. But we aren't going up against a mad ruler. We're talking about going up against the very beings that take an oath to protect those under their dominion. We might not stop the natural disasters that are happening or this Mist that kills, but can we really just sit back and do nothing, to just accept what is coming? This problem is not just in Greedin, it has spread to all the continents."

Tas stopped for a moment and stared at the men, women, at everyone that made up the parliament. "I leave for Quinsenta in two days," Tas reminded them all. "Where I will meet with leaders from other countries to begin the preparation that will be needed to orchestrate such a massive front. Each one of you needs to decide what I will tell those leaders: Am I telling them that Hruan will send aid, will help with refugees, with medical care, with whatever they can give? Or am I telling them that there are politicians in Hruan who refused to hear the world's cry for help, who would turn their backs on allies because in their mind there is nothing we can do? I don't know about all of you, but I would rather go down fighting than do nothing."

There was silence for a moment before applause began. Ray banged the gavel a few times after the applause went on for a bit to get everyone's attention. "Once our guests have left, we will begin the voting procedures," Ray informed everyone. "To our guests, thank you for all the information you have given us over the last three days."

It took them a few moments to gather up their notes and journals they had brought. One guard helped them with the doors as the four exited the chamber rooms. Lia and Jonah were leaning against the wall, waiting for them.

"Come, let's head to the tavern. I have a private room reserved," Jonah stated.

Matthias was there with a few of his workers to bring back their things to the estate. He promised it would all be in Tas's rooms when they returned. Once they were free of their items, they followed Jonah out of the parliament building.

The *Thorn and Dragon* was located on the edge of the government section of the city and one of the residential sections. It occupied one of the few buildings in the capital that predated the Tribal Wars of the First Age. The tavern had occupied the building for several centuries already; it was one of the oldest taverns in the world. It was a commonplace for those working in the government to go after hours to talk and relax. The barkeep nodded to Jonah when they entered the place, the old doors creaking from use. A serving woman escorted the group of six to one of the small dining rooms off the main tap room that was used for private affairs.

"Food and drinks will be right out," she told them as she got them settled.

"I have to say, Tas, for the fact you hate politics, that was one hell of a speech," Grierr informed Tas as he took the pitcher of water that was already on the table and poured them all a glass.

"It was amazing," Emaya agreed as she sipped her glass, glad to get away from the senators.

"It could be the greatest speech in the world for all I care," Tas stated. "But if they don't listen and vote against us, then what was it for?"

"It was to warn them, to give them the information, so they had it," Thierren reminded him as he squeezed his hand. "Some might not want to listen now, but down the road they might."

"Look, I might not know Ray as long as the rest of you," Lia began. "But even with what limitations his powers have about war and aid, I feel like even if they vote against us, he will do everything within his powers to prepare his country and aid others."

"Just so you know, Tas," Jonah started. "The dragons are with us, despite how the vote turns out."

"How does that work?" Emaya asked. She knew dragons had their own leader and laws.

Their serving woman came in with a tray of drinks, fresh bread, and bowls of soup. She set everything on the table, checked to see if anyone needed anything, then left.

"Dragons are protected in the countries they live," Tas explained. "Who they listen to depends on the scenario. Country issues, they will listen to their Herd Leader. In situations like this, then the ultimate decision is made by Drache, the current Dragon King.

"The herds here are ready to help. All their leaders are in an agreement. We've worked out trade routes, refugee routes. It's all ready to go no matter how the parliament votes," Jonah replied.

"Has the Dragon King said anything?" Emaya inquired.

"He won't until I'm in Quinsenta," Tas answered.

"Why?" Lia asked.

"Because they could see it as a conflict of interest if I was to talk to the Hruan Parliament when the Dragon King made his word known," Tas stated. "Since I'm a Dragon Talker, I'm kind of tied to his word as well."

"Hence conflict of interest," Emaya realized.

"Drache and my grandfather will do a joint announcement. This is something they usually do when it's something big and involving both worlds."

"Will I be dressed appropriately in Quinsenta?" Emaya asked, suddenly realizing she would live in a palace.

There were chuckles around the table at that. "My family is very low key with formality," Tas assured her. "Formal wear is strictly for balls and ceremonies. Work attire is for when in meetings, but around the palace when there are no duties, then as long as you are presentable, no one really worries about it."

"Well, your mother did not like my rogue armor," Lia reminded Tas.

"Because you wore it to dinner," Tas countered. "There is a strict no armor and no weapon rule at any dinner table in the palace."

"This has to be an interesting story," Emayla said to Jonah.

"I will have you know I had nothing to do with it," Tas informed them all. He saw the dubious looks. "I'm serious. It happened while I was at the Academy. My two oldest brothers got in a fight during a sparring match, they refused to change, brought the fight to dinner, ended up breaking the table, a set of china, a priceless vase, and a dagger ended up embedded in the portrait of my great-grandmother."

"And there are four of you?" Jonah asked.

"Four boys and I'm the youngest by six years," Tas sighed.

"And the palace still stands?" Emaya teases.

"You should meet my cousins," Tas informed her. "They are far more chaotic than my brothers and I."

"He's right, especially Helena," Grierr agreed. "Helena and Heath are twins. They hate their names, and the two are an entire legion on their own."

"Helena is a sweetheart," Thierren argued.

"To you," Tas and Grierr said at the same time.

"It's because she obviously has taste in who she wants to associate with," Thierren informed Emayla and Jonah.

"I guess you will be out of luck when we arrive in Quinsenta," Grierr teased. "Since you paired yourself up with Tas, your standing has probably fallen."

"Or my standing will go up," Tas replied as he grinned at Thierren who just rolled his eyes at him.

They continued with the conversation as they finished their soups. Lia was telling Emaya about Quinsenta, the Dragon Keep, the elves and dwarves as well. Tas promised to bring Jonah and Emayla to the Dragon Keep so they could meet Drache, the Dragon King.

Dinner was a roast lamb, with carrots, potatoes and other root vegetables. There was a thick gravy to go with it, as well as more drinks and a freshwater pitcher. During dinner, Jonah talked of some of his journeys while Grierr, Tas, and Thierren spoke of their school days. Once dinner was over, tea and coffee were brought, the stories fading as they got anxious about the vote that was happening. When it was asked where Moira and Edelberg were, Lia had a smirk on her face saying they wanted some time to unwind.

It was an hour before midnight when Ray walked into their private room. Thierren stood and gave him his seat while Lia poured him a mug of tea. Tas went out to the bar for a plate of food to be brought to their room for Ray, and for his guards that were standing outside of the room.

"The resolution to send aid passed," Ray informed them. "Hawthorn being the only Senator to vote against it. Even his bloc voted for it."

Tas let out a huge sigh of relief as the words sunk in. Thierren placed a hand on his shoulder as he moved to stand behind Tas.

"I warned them before they voted that if the resolution did not pass, any district that did not vote would be on the bottom of the list for aid when things get bad here," Ray explained. "I had a feeling Hawthorn would have had his bloc not vote otherwise. I can't punish for no votes, but I can have consequences for not voting."

"Ray..." Tas began and stopped. He didn't know what to say.

"The amount of trust you placed in us honors us," Grierr finished for him.

"It is I who am honored that we have people that will speak out and do what we need even when it seems impossible," Ray answered. "Tas, I will have paperwork for you to bring to your grandfather for when you leave. Tomorrow, I think we can all use a day off and some well-deserved rest."

They all agreed. Ray smiled at Emaya. "You should know, your testimony swayed many that were on the fence about the whole thing. Hearing someone's firsthand experience made them realize that everything they were hearing was true. I believe it shamed many of them that in order to believe in what was happening, people had to tell a traumatic event for them to realize it."

"I... thank you," Emaya answered, bowing her head. "I'm glad that I could help."

"What is next for you?"

"I'll be joining Thierren and training people to run field hospitals," Emaya told him.

"Then you will join them in Quinsenta," Ray realized.

"Yes, I have experience with trauma situations. When Thierren asked, I had to say yes," Emaya replied.

"Then we are fortunate to have you," Ray said. He stood up. "I am heading back. I wanted you to know the news first."

They stood as he left. Once he was out of the room, they all collapsed into their chairs. Tas felt utterly drained.

"We should probably all head back as well," Thierren stated, as he noted Tas was exhausted. "It has been a very long few days and Ray was correct that we all deserve some rest."

"Always the healer, having to look out for us," Grierr joked.

"Someone has to," Thierren replied.

Chapter 23

They would leave in a few days. Tas would be happy if he never had to argue with politicians again, but knew he was facing more in Quinsenta. It was why when Edelberg asked if he would spar with him, Tas jumped at the chance. It would get him out of being dragged into last-minute meetings or discussions from senators visiting the President's estate. They changed into light leather armor before meeting at the sparring ring at the barracks. Their friends joined them to watch. Grabbing the sparring staffs, they headed into the ring. They both agreed: no magic. Edelberg wanted to see how Tas moved so he could help train a unit to protect his weak areas.

Tas looked as if he was enjoying the fight. There was a slight grin on his face as he could dodge Edelberg's attacks. Edelberg looked frustrated, as if he forgot how fast on his feet Tas was despite them only sparring a week ago. Grierr figured Edelberg was counting on Tas' limited sight to slow him down. Lia was now understanding what Grierr and Thierren had tried to tell her. Tas was not helpless and would not be a weak link on their journey.

"Edelberg doesn't look happy," Grierr commented to Thierren.

"You sound worried," Lia stated.

"He never does when he isn't winning," Thierren reminded him. He did not make a comment to Lia.

"It is amazing what he can do," Moira stated, referring to Tas.

Tas did a complicated move that knocked Edelberg down on one knee. He never turned his back to Edelberg. He instead walked backwards, keeping his eyes on his target. A lesson to the soldiers that were watching. Even when your opponent is down, one did not take their eyes off of them. It was the only way Tas had the time to pull up a shield of magic around him as a bolt of electricity was sent his way. There was a yell of "No magic!" by Lia and Jonah, but it seemed Edelberg did not hear that as the surrounding air was crackling with his magic. Grierr and Thierren both rushed to the fence.

Before they could hop into the ring, Tas had thrown up a magical barrier to keep Edelberg's uncontrolled magic from hitting innocents. Lia, quickly sensing something was wrong, yelled for everyone to back up. Moira ran to the main house to grab her medical supplies and inform Mathias to keep the staff inside.

"Edelberg, stand down!" Grierr yelled. He knew Edelberg could lose himself in a battle. He had seen teachers having to stun Edelberg when it would happen during sparring sessions.

Tas deflected another spell as he tried to get his sparring stick in a defensive position to block Edelberg if he surged forward. Tas dropped to the ground in a roll as a bolt of lightning struck the spot where he had been standing. He could feel the magic radiating off of Edelberg alerting him to his location. Tas tried not to be distracted by what appeared to be a colored trail of energy that tied the spell from where it landed back to where Edelberg stood. He was seeing red bleed into Edelberg's aura.

"Edelberg, don't let the rage control you!" Tas yelled, trying to break through the rage that had taken over his friend.

Edelberg charged him. Tas blocked the blow of Edelberg's sparring staff with his own. He heard the wood crack and quickly let go, side stepping the rest of the swing. The edge of Edelberg's staff caught his calf, but he ignored the pain as he set up a few defensive spells to give him time to scramble away. He heard Thierren call out his name; he saw something being thrown his way. It had his magic in it. Reaching out his hand, he caught his sorcerer's staff. He slammed the bottom into the ground and caused a slight shake of the ground right under where Edelberg was standing.

They all heard a loud roar before Bart landed in the middle of the ring, his tail slamming on the ground in a warning as he stood on all fours. The air crackled around him as he stared down Edelberg.

"Lia, back up," Thierren said quietly to her, as she was the closest to the ring.

Moira returned with the satchel. She stood in shock when she saw Bart had appeared. The playful and friendly dragon was gone. In its place was a predatory animal, ready to pounce.

"Edelberg, it's just me Tas," Tas reminded him, wondering if he could get through to him. He had never seen Edelberg this bad before.

Grierr tried to slip into the ring, but Edelberg must have sensed him and lashed out. The bolt of electricity sent Grierr flying into the fence. Moira rushed toward Grierr with Thierren at her heels. Lia helped keep the other soldiers back.

Tas tried to ignore the still form that was Grierr lying on the ground beyond the ring. Bart moved his position so he could protect the injured friend, leaving a slight opening for Edelberg. Edelberg just growled as he cracked his neck before he surged toward Tas. Tas quickly got out of the way, scrambling as he slid over some pebbles. Edelberg pounded the bottom of his practice staff into the ground but was soon air born as Bart flung him away with his tail.

"Come on, Eddie," Tas said calmly. "It's just us in a practice ring."

Tas was sweating from all the spell casting he had done. He was drained, his body was aching, and he did not know how much more he could handle this. Tas could not pay attention to anything else but Edelberg. One wrong step and that would be it.

"Edelberg, Grierr is injured," Tas said calmly. "We need to check on him."

Another growl came from Edelberg. This time he could grab Tas by the arm, pulling him toward him. He tossed him to the ground like a rag doll, then stormed toward him. Tas curled into a defensive ball, waiting for the hit. It never came. Instead, he heard Edelberg howl, followed by a body crumbling to the ground as the surrounding air seemed to ignite with dragon fire. Uncurling from the ball, Tas slowly sat up and saw that Edelberg was splayed out on the ground, unconscious. The green translucent fire was circled around where Tas lay as Bart kept a paw on Edelberg keeping the unconscious man from moving. Thierren was in the ring looking furious and glowing with anger, though Tas doubted anyone else saw the glowing.

Thierren walked to where Tas lay on the ground. He extended a hand and helped him stand up. Thierren looked around. "Jonah, can you help get Grierr up? Moira, see if we can use the barrack's infirmary," Thierren instructed.

"What should I do?" Lia asked.

"Stay with Bart. I'll see if some soldiers can bring Edelberg. I just want to know where first," Thierren directed as he steadied Tas, who was weaving.

A soldier came running toward them. "We have the infirmary set up and instructed Moira where to go with Sir Grierr," the soldier informed Thierren.

"Can you instruct your fellow soldiers to bring the man the dragon is holding there as well?"

"If the dragon will let us."

"Bart," Tas called to the dragon. His voice strained with exhaustion. "When these good soldiers approach, let them have Edelberg."

There was an answering rumble from Bart, Tas answered it with a stern look. Bart stomped a paw but seemed to nod with his head. "Lia will escort him," Tas assured the dragon.

"I need to get you to the infirmary," Thierren said. He pulled one of Tas's arms over his shoulder.

Once everyone had orders, Thierren followed behind them, helping Tas. They entered the infirmary and saw that Grierr was already sitting up, Moira was checking his pulse. There were vials of potions and bandages on a table next to her, along with one of Thierren's bruising balms. Thierren got Tas settled on a medical bed before walking over to her.

"How is he?" Thierren asked as he saw her notes.

"Frazzled," Moira admitted. "Jonah went to inform Ray and Maya what happened. He will be back with more of our things."

"Grierr, how do you feel?" Thierren asked as he raised the tunic Grierr wore. There was bruising on his back.

"Like I was struck by lightning," Grierr answered. He winced as Thierren poked his ribs and shoulders.

"His pulse is slowly going back to normal," Moira informed Thierren.

"Ringing in the ears?" Thierren asked Grierr.

"No," Grierr answered.

"If that changes, let one of us know, or if your nose or ears bleed," Thierren told him. He turned to Moira, "When Jonah returns, have him help you wrap Grierr's ribs."

Lia entered with the soldiers carrying the stretcher with Edelberg on it. He noted how Lia was in charge as she instructed the men furthest from them to place him and for the two of them to stay on guard. Thierren went to Tas finally.

"Where does it hurt?" Thierren asked Tas as he stood in front of him.

"Everywhere," Tas answered. His voice was weary. His glamor was failing, he had no energy left. "He got me in the right leg and the back."

Thierren nodded. He rolled up Tas's pants leg and saw the nasty bruise already forming on the back of his calf. He grabbed some salve and bandages. With his magic, he searched to see if there were any breaks or fractures. Thankfully, there were none. He applied the salve and the bandages.

"I need your shirt off," Thierren informed Tas.

"I usually require dinner first," Tas joked.

"Raincheck on dinner," Thierren replied. He saw the surprise flash in Tas's eyes as he helped him get the tunic off. "Not how I thought the first time undressing you would go."

Tas just stared at him, unsure of what to think or say. This side of Thierren was still new to Tas. He felt Thierren's fingers softly travel over his back; he felt a pulse of magic as Thierren searched for injuries.

"Your back is a mess," Thierren commented as he applied more salve.

Jonah returned and immediately helped Moira with wrapping Grierr's ribs. Thierren finished with Tas before he moved to where Edelberg lay. He was still unconscious. Thierren checked him over for any major injuries. He treated the bruises, wrapping his right arm as it had a small fracture from when Bart threw him. He told the guards they could leave. Edelberg would be out of commission for a few hours.

"What happened out there?" Lia asked.

"That wasn't Edelberg out there," Moira replied. "He wouldn't attack a friend like that."

"You're right, in most cases he wouldn't," Grierr agreed with her. "He is one of the most loyal people I know. He can be hardheaded and a gossip, but he would never harm a friend without reason."

"So, what happened?" Lia asked.

Thierren ran a hand over his face as he tried to decide how to handle this. "Right now isn't the time to get into the details," he began. "The easiest way to explain it is that Battle Mages, especially ones like Edelberg, can develop a rare condition. Simply speaking, there are moments when he loses himself into the violence. On a battlefield, it's great. But in a sparring ring when it happens, well, you saw the outcome. And this was a good outcome because we have handled this before."

"So why let him spar with Tas?" Moira asked. She was not accusing anyone, but wanted to understand what was happening. Thankfully, no one took her question as her accusing them.

"Because most Battle Mages learn to control it, they learn to use it to their benefit in battle, and to control it during sparring," Thierren told her.

"If they don't?" It was Lia that spoke this time.

"When the signs first appear, they go through a physical and a check of the mind. From there, they work out a training plan," Thierren explained. "This is a very condensed answer, remember? They get one more chance to show they can handle it once they passed the training."

"And if they fail?"

"They are expelled from the Battle Mages," Thierren said simply. "Edelberg had told us he passed his training and was in control of it."

"I take it this isn't an isolated event," Lia said as she saw the look on Tas, Grierr, and Thierren's face.

"Lia and Jonah, can you help Grierr to his room?" Thierren asked. "Moira, can you help Tas get comfortable in his rooms?"

"What about you?" Tas asked.

"This isn't the first time I have had to clean up his mess," Thierren admitted sadly.

When everyone had left, Thierren sighed as he sat in an old rickety chair. He rubbed his tired eyes and wished he braided his hair early as it was already escaping the quick bun; he had rolled it up when he heard the uproar outside. Knowing Edelberg would be out for another hour, Thierren updated his logs and drafted the report that he would need to send to the Council of Magi.

An hour later, Edelberg stirred. Thierren set his journal down and stood up, taking a step or two back from the cot his friend had laid on. In his hand was his own sorcerer's staff. Edelberg slowly opened his eyes, looking around to see where he was. Thierren watched him as the red head slowly sat up, wincing slightly as he did. When Edelberg spotted Thierren he stared at him.

"What happened?" Edelberg asked him.

"What do you remember?" Thierren asked cautiously.

Edelberg was quiet for a moment. "I was sparring with Tas," Edelberg recalled. "The slippery bastard was winning."

"What else?"

"I ..." Edelberg focused on the sparring session. The images were unclear. He smelled electricity and remembered hearing the rushing of his blood and how hard his heart was beating. "Shit. How is everyone?"

"Tas will have some pretty intense bruising on his back from where he landed on the ground. Grierr has four broken ribs from a boulder being thrown at him," Thierren stated.

"Shit."

"You told me it was under control," Thierren reminded him. "You told me that the techniques they taught you, the potions I make you, were helping."

"I do and they are," Edelberg said as he sat up fully and swung his legs from the cot.

"So then, how did two of our friends get injured?" Thierren asked angrily.

"It was a onetime thing," Edelberg told him.

Thierren stared at him. "I thought the last incident was a onetime thing," Thierren replied. He paced the infirmary. "Bloody hell, Edelberg. They gave you a third chance after that instead of being thrown into a cell. Today you almost killed Grierr! Bart will never trust you again with Tas!"

"I know!" Edelberg half yelled. "I screwed up, okay? It won't happen again."

"It won't," Thierren agreed.

Edelberg stared at for a moment, thinking he had won, but then he realized what Thierren meant. "You can't, Thierren, you can't tell them!"

"If I don't, they will take my license. You know this."

"And there it is. This is all about you, just like it always is," Edelberg laughed bitterly.

"Oh, grow up!" Thierren exclaimed. "This is about more than just me. It's about me, as a doctor, saying that you are still fit to be a Battle Mage, despite knowing you aren't. What's going to happen next time?"

"There won't be a next time," Edelberg pleaded.

"I have heard that one too many times coming from you," Thierren answered wearily. "I'm done keeping your secrets."

He should have seen it coming, but the moment the words were out of his mouth, he was up against the wall with a hand around his throat.

"You will ruin me!" Edelberg growled out. "I can't have everyone knowing!"

Thierren was seeing spots in his vision, which was never a good sign, as his fingers tried to loosen Edelberg's grip. He vaguely thought he heard feet running toward them and a door being thrown open.

"I will not have my secrets told!" Edelberg roared as he tightened his grip.

"Too...bad!" Thierren wheezed as he brought his knee up and slammed it into Edelberg's groin.

Edelberg immediately let go as he crumbled to his knees. Hands were on Thierren, telling him to steady while he heard voices yelling at Edelberg. The world swayed, and arms scooped him up and brought him out of the room as he let the darkness win.

Chapter 24

Thierren woke to his throat burning and his head pounding. But he was alive, so that was a bonus. He was laying in Tas' bed in the room they shared. He could hear quiet voices in the small sitting room off the bedroom. He tried to sit up, but his body did not like that decision. There was a glass of water in it sitting on the bedside table. Thierren went to grab it, but it crashed to the ground. The voices stopped and footsteps came.

"You're awake," Tas said. The relief was clear in his voice.

Thierren wanted to talk, but knew his throat would not be ready for it. Tas came to the bed and sat on the edge. He handed him a piece of parchment and a charcoal pencil. He wanted to know how long he had been out.

"Three hours," Tas answered. "Moira has been checking in every hour. She just went to see how Grierr was doing."

Tas watched as Thierren wrote on the paper again. Tas looked at Lia, who was in the sitting room. "Can you have Moira and Grierr come over?"

Lia nodded as she slipped from the room. "Jonah is with Ray. They have my orb and are talking with Tobias," Tas informed Thierren. "You know, if this is how you wanted to end up in my bed, there are other ways."

Thierren chuckled at that, then regretted it as it led to a coughing fit. Tas handed him a new glass of water, which he took gladly. The door to the suite opened, Moira came in first and immediately went to Thierren, checking his pupils, pulse, and then had him open wide so she can see his throat.

"Maya is going to have dinner served up here," Lia told Tas. "She is going to have broth sent up for Thierren as well."

Thierren wrote something on his paper for Tas to see. Tas read, then grabbed Thierren's medical satchel and handed it to him. Thierren grabbed a small vial of purple color. He popped the cork, then downed the contents. He grimaced as he swallowed it.

"Okay," Thierren said with a hoarse voice. "I have a bit of time to talk. I will be dead to the world for the rest of the day and evening. First: where is Edelberg?"

"Currently being housed in one of the barrack's cells with a rotation of guards and a pissed off dragon," Lia stated.

"I saw to his injuries once he was in his cell," Moira assured Thierren. "As it took several soldiers to get him off of you."

"Is that why I ache?" Thierren asked.

"He almost shattered your larynx," Moira informed him. "You have severe bruising to your neck. After this potion wears off, I would prefer if you don't talk for at least a day to allow the swelling to go down. You also have blood vessels that burst in your eyes, so don't freak out when you look in a mirror."

Thierren nodded. Grierr spoke up. "When we talked to Tobias earlier, it seemed like there have been other occasions," he said.

"There have been," Thierren confirmed. He sipped the water to focus on where to start. "Edelberg's form of blood lust is severe. He completely dissociates himself when he enters one state to the point where he recalls nothing of the episode. He can recall everything right up to it. Then he might get glimpses, impressions, but no recollection of what happened. He doesn't recall who he hurt or how bad it was."

"That's bad," Moira stated. She had never heard of it being that severe.

"It is," Thierren agreed. "Most of the prior incidents had occurred during training or on assignment where it was easy to brush it off as no civilians were injured."

"The last time wasn't one of those times," Tas realized with a sickening feeling hitting his stomach.

"No, it's why they called me in," Thierren confirmed. "I told none of you because I was called in as a doctor, but also there was hope that the face of a friend would help."

"How bad?" Grierr asked.

"It was in a tavern," Thierren said. "He was drinking with some of his buddies from his squad. Pretty woman enters, he flirts with her, she flirts back. They drink together. Then the husband enters. He was not too thrilled that Edelberg was flirting with his wife and that his wife was flirting back. They exchange some words, then the husband punches him. From all accounts, the husband threw the first punch, but that's all it took to trigger Edelberg."

"Bloody hell," Lia mumbled.

"The wife tried to intervene but thankfully was pulled away. Edelberg beats the husband into unconsciousness. It takes his entire squad to get him off the guy. The wife was terrified when he went for her. If his squad had not been there, if mages had not been there, he would have raped her. When I arrived, it was the following morning, and they locked him in a cell guarded by his squad because they had to keep him under a sleeping spell because he still was raging."

"Did he remember you?"

"Two days later when his head finally cleared," Thierren replied. "He shows remorse at first, but then it fades into how it was not his fault if he can't remember or if someone triggers him. They pulled him from the front line and were supposed to be working on a strict training and conditioning program. I have been making potions for him to help him calm his mind."

"Is what happened with you a leftover from the sparring ring?" Tas asked.

Thierren shook his head. "Edelberg can't communicate when he's in one of these states, but downstairs with me, he was coherent. He knew what he was doing."

"Shit," Lia said. "Even if we wanted to say it was another episode, it's still bad. He tried to kill you an hour after he lost it on the training field."

"What did Tobias say?"

"He will go before the Council, but the laws are weird regarding where the Council can step in and where they have no authority," Tas admitted. "The tavern event would technically be under the law of the country it happened in. Since they did not file charges, it can only show a pattern of behavior."

"What about today?" Moira asked.

"Today involved sorcerers, which means the Council has full jurisdiction to try him," Tas answered.

"But can a mundane government actually have the facility to keep a sorcerer from escaping?" Lia asked.

"A few have signed treaties with the Council to give the Council jurisdiction over any crime committed by a magical being," Tas replied.

"I'm going to bet the country the tavern incident happened in was not one of them."

"Edelberg is also royalty, so it complicates things," Grierr added. "It shouldn't, but it does."

"They won't punish him," Thierren said almost bitterly. "It's the same reason he had more chances than any other in his position. The council will get a letter from his father or grandfather. Friesen doesn't have a treaty with the Council, so they have used it to their advantage."

"That's insane," Lia stated.

"Many of the laws regarding the magical community were written at the start of this Age," Grierr replied. "Many countries were just being formed and starting their own government. They created the Council of Magi at that time to help moderate and protect the magical community, but no one really knew what to do with it. It can declare a Watchtower as protected land and those who dwell there. Crimes perpetrated by sorcerers against the mundane are so rare that no one thought to create laws on what to do."

"So, first we wage war with gods, then we can change how the Council and laws are run," Tas stated. "For the moment, once Edelberg is at the Isle he will be in a cell where he will stay until trial."

"Thierren, is this what has been the issue between the two of you?" Grierr asked.

"I know his secrets and he hates that," Thierren replied. "He has been waiting for me to use them against him to get my way. Not sure what way I was going to be getting, but yeah. For me, it was how do I trust him fully when I know what he can do."

"With your oath as a doctor and healer, there is not much you can tell us," Tas added.

"Why tell us now?" Lia inquired.

"Because you need to know what kind of person you are traveling with," Thierren answered. "My oath allows me to speak out against a patient if I believe he is a danger to himself or others."

"He is definitely a danger to those around him," Grierr agreed.

"Do you think one of us should write to his parents?" Tas asked. "Maybe if they hear it from us, they will understand more of what is going on."

"I would run it by Tobias before doing so," Thierren said. He then let out a huge yawn. "I think the potion is running out."

"Rest, we will keep an eye on you," Tas assured him. He had a feeling that Tas would not be leaving soon.

#

Thierren was not looking forward to what he was about to do. Today the commander of the Battle Mages would arrive to begin the process of taking Edelberg into custody and bringing him to the Isle of Magi. Thierren was the one that would explain all this to Edelberg. As he approached the barrack's cells, he noted how the soldiers snapped into attention. He entered the cells, signed himself in when he was handed the log, then headed to where Edelberg was being held.

"Dismissed," Thierren told the soldiers standing guard. They nodded and headed down the hallway toward the small room for the soldiers working.

Edelberg had sat up at the sound of Thierren's voice. He had been laying on the cell cot staring at the ceiling. When the door had opened to the cell block, he thought it was soldiers changing shifts. He was not expecting Thierren to be entering.

"Why are you here?" Edelberg snapped.

"To ensure you are healing from your injuries," Thierren stated. "Also, to inform you of what will happen over the course of today and tomorrow."

"You called the Council," Edelberg realized. "Nice to see our friendship meant nothing."

"I actually did not notify the Council," Thierren replied. "While I was unconscious, Grierr, Jonah, and Tas did."

"I bet you are glad we brought Jonah along," Edelberg said darkly. "Have him eating out of your hands."

"Edelberg," Thierren sighed. There was nothing he could say that could make any of this better. "How are your injuries?"

"Your balm worked. My arm is better, still stiff," Edelberg stated. "The bruises from the soldiers are all healed."

"You will need to keep the arm in the sling for another three days until you can move it without pain," Thierren suggested.

"So, what are the plans?"

"Samuel will arrive shortly," Thierren answered. He saw a flash of recognition in Edelberg's eyes at the name. "He will review the documents of what happened. He will talk to you as well. Then at some point tomorrow you will leave with him to the Isle of Magi. We are still working out which one of us is going with you."

"Why would any of you want to go with me?"

"Because despite it all, you are still our friend," Thierren reminded him. He looked at Edelberg. "Why didn't you reach out to me? You know I would have come to you to see if I needed to change something?"

"I was feeling good, the tea was working, the counselor was good," Edelberg replied.

"You stopped seeing them four months ago," Thierren stated.

Edelberg stared at him. He laughed bitterly. "Of course you would check. Did you count my vials as well?"

"If I could find them, I would have," Thierren answered.

"You really are a piece of work," Edelberg said.

"You knew this when we all agreed upon this path," Thierren reminded him. "You agreed I would check in with who you were seeing, checking vials if there was concern you weren't taking them. So, I guess the question is when?"

"Four months ago," Edelberg answered. There was no use in lying to Thierren. He would find out anyway.

Thierren closed his eyes. "Why?"

"I didn't like how I was feeling."

"And you didn't think to contact me to see if I could change the tea around to make you feel differently?" Thierren inquired. "You know I would have. How many times have I done that for Tas and his allergies or Luna for each of her pregnancies? By the gods, I must reformulate everything for Grierr because he's huge. Did you think I would not do that for you?"

"I knew you would do it," Edelberg told him. "I just didn't want to feel like these potions were controlling me."

Thierren stared at him. "Edelberg."

"I'm the warrior, the tough guy, the guy that likes to have fun," Edelberg continued. "But using that tea, the Rage was gone, the edge wasn't there."

"Because that is what it was supposed to do," Thierren said. "The Rage in you acts as a poison. The more it lingers, the less control you have over it. You know this. I explained everything to you, as did the other healers and your therapist."

"And I didn't expect to miss the rage and the violence!"

Thierren just stared at him. "Well, you certainly showed your need for violence, haven't you?" he commented.

"I didn't mean to hurt any of you," Edelberg said sadly. "I just, I thought I could control it."

"The good news is you are going to have a lot of time thinking about why you like feeling the rage and the violence," Thierren said. He turned and rang the bell for the soldiers to return.

"You are just leaving me here?"

"For another night, tomorrow you leave for the Isle," Thierren reminded him.

Edelberg grabbed the bars and glowered at Thierren. "You will pay for this!"

Thierren did not acknowledge the threat as he left the cells. He found Grierr waiting for him as he stepped out of the building. They walked in silence to the landing spot for the dragons. Bart was there with Tas.

"Jonah thought it should just be the three of us," Grierr informed him. Thierren nodded. "How was he?"

"Angry," Thierren said. "He thinks I am enjoying this."

"Yes, I can tell how much you are enjoying it," Tas commented. "You are waking up in the middle of the night in a panic. This is fun for all to experience."

"Don't you make a tea for that?" Grierr inquired.

"I do and I have been drinking it, but I wake up feeling like there are hands on my throat and that this time they are going to finish the job," Thierren admitted.

Grierr stared at him for a moment before laying a hand on his shoulder. "It will take time for it to fade enough that you won't be in fear."

"He went off the tea four months ago," Thierren informed them.

"What?" Tas asked.

"He says he missed the rage and the violence," Thierren replied.

"What did you say?" Grierr asked.

"What could I say that wouldn't be antagonistic towards him?" Thierren inquired. "He will not take responsibility for any of it. I am out to ruin him. I have somehow manipulated Jonah into following me."

"I love him like a brother," Tas began. "But sometimes the best course of action is letting them hit rock bottom. It might be the only way for him to learn what we have been trying to say to him."

"I hope so," Thierren said.

They noted Bart was more alert, meaning the dragons from the Isle of Magi were close. When Bart's tail twitched, Tas realized he must recognize one of the dragons that was coming.

"Do we know who else is coming with Samuel?" Grierr asked Thierren.

"A few of his top soldiers," Thierren answered. "He wanted to ensure there was enough power in the event Edelberg attempts something they could contain him."

"Smart," Grierr said.

They fell into silence once again as the dragons came into view. There were three, each carrying three people. There was plenty of room in the open courtyard in front of the manor for them to land. Bart got excited as the dark green one landed, Tas realized as soon as the dragon touched down.

"She's his cousin," Tas informed Thierren and Grierr.

The two dragons waiting patiently for the riders to slide off her back before they greeted each other. Commander Samuel Winter could not help but chuckle at the two dragons.

"Gentleman," he said as he approached three of his former students. He taught defensive magic at the Academy.

"Commander Winters," Tas said, stepping forward and shaking his hands.

Thierren and Grierr followed. Samuel introduced the eight soldiers he brought with them. "Captain Rua has planned for your soldiers to stay in the barracks," Grierr informed him. "She has the guest quarters ready for you as well."

"Excellent," Samuel said.

"I can take you to meet her and show you where everything is," Grierr suggested. He looked at Tas. "We'll meet in a half hour?"

"Ray has given us use of his personal office," Tas reminded Grierr. "Meet us there."

Grierr nodded and motioned for Samuel and his people to follow him. Tas laid a hand on Bart's side. "Can you show the dragons where they can feed and rest?"

Bart gave a nod before signaling to the others. Within moments, the four dragons were in the air. Tas watched for a few seconds before he took Thierren's hand as they walked back to the presidential manor. They walked in silence, nodding to staff as they walked by. Entering through the family entrance, they found Jonah, Moira, and Lia in the family sitting room.

"Well?" Lia asked when she spotted them.

"Grierr is showing Samuel and his people to where they will stay," Tas said as he sat in a chair next to the one Thierren sat in.

"How was Edelberg?" Moira inquired.

"The same," Thierren answered. "I'll fill you in when we talk with Samuel."

313

"I'm sorry, this must be so hard for the three of you," Moira replied. "In the brief time I have been with you, I can tell how amazing Edelberg is."

"He is," Tas agreed. "I think it's why it makes it so hard. If he was a complete asshole, then you could almost understand it."

"We're here for all of you," Jonah told them. "Don't carry this burden alone."

"The three of us have been talking," Lia began. "We know the three of you don't want Edelberg to go to the Isle alone. So, the three of us have been talking about how we could help, if there was anything we could do to help."

Lia looked at Moira, who nodded. Moira smiled sadly at them. "I feel like out of the six of us, I would be the one that would be missed the least," Moira began. She held up a hand before any of them could argue. "Jonah is vital due to his ability to see routes that don't exist. Lia is valuable for a whole list of reasons. They bring to the table skills and abilities that no one else can. I am a healer. There are many of us around, many who will join your cause. I need to be with Edelberg. This is the path I am supposed to take."

"Did you see this?" Tas asked gently.

Moira looked at him in surprise. "Did Edelberg tell you?"

"No," Tas said. "Your mind is very loud and out there. I picked it up by accident."

"Oh, I'm sorry," Moira replied. "My mother told me I had a challenging time shielding my mind."

"It's not an easy skill," Tas assured her.

"I... it's not so much that I saw anything," Moira told him. "It's more this intense feeling that I need to take this path. I have only ignored this feeling once and I regret not listening to it."

"Are you sure?" Thierren asked her.

Moira nodded. "Jonah, Lia and I have been going back and forth since yesterday about this," Moira assured them. "I am not making this decision lightly."

Thierren Tas looked at each other. "After our meeting with Samuel, I will notify Tobias," Tas told Moira.

"If you change your mind at all once you arrive, let Tobias know," Tas told Moira. "He knows how to get a hold of us."

"He is going to lash out, Moira," Thierren warned her. "Ignore what he says in those moments. He has not been taking the tea for four months now, so beware of his mood swings, especially now. You do not need to tolerate him when he is like this. Do not feel as if you cannot leave the room when he is in such a state."

"Should I try to reason with him?"

"No," Thierren replied. "He won't hear you. It's why it is better to just leave him at those moments."

"Okay," Moira said.

"Treat it as you would any patient is dealing with mental illness," Thierren instructed. "If you need anything, talk to Tobias. He will be able to help you."

"We can never repay you for this," Tas admitted to Moira. "Knowing someone who knows Edelberg is going with him, it takes a lot of weight off our shoulders that he won't be alone."

"I'm glad that I can do that for all of you," Moira said.

Tas noted the time on the mantle clock. "We should head to Ray's office. Samuel and Grierr should join us soon."

Chapter 25

Thierren rode with Tas on Bart as they flew to Quinsenta. They had left late in the evening, the day before they were supposed to leave. Moira had left the day before with Edelberg. Tobias had let them know they settled her in one of his guest suites. They needed to leave earlier than planned, for there had been a horrible ship attack during the daylight hours. Many feared for the group's safety if they traveled by sea. When night had fallen, Ray and Maya saw the six off on three dragons. Two of the dragons Bart had selected. He knew them and trusted them. Thierren could feel the rage in Tas as he held onto him as they flew. Rage at what they had done to the ship and passengers. Knowing the full story of Tas's past, he understood the emotions that coursed through Tas's veins.

They landed a few hours before sunrise. Trion stood there at the landing area for dragons, waiting for their arrival. Tas was the first to get off, going to his father, who hugged him tightly. They spoke quietly for a few moments, no one approaching them as the father and son spoke. Trion rested his forehead against Tas's forehead before they parted.

"Welcome, I am sure you all are exhausted," Trion said to the group. "We have a late breakfast planned for you, so do not feel you need to be up early. The staff knows not to disturb any of you until you are out of your rooms."

"Grierr, Thierren, and Lia, we set your usual rooms up," Trion stated.

"Actually, Thierren will be with me," Tas informed his father.

Trion stood straighter at the news; he could not help a grin at this bit of information. His wife was going to be so mad at him for knowing before she did. He also saw the look of determination on his son's face, as if he was daring his father to challenge his request.

"Very well," Trion said, trying to conceal a smile. "Jonah and Emaya, your rooms are right next to theirs."

He motioned for all of them to follow them. As they walked, he paid attention to Thierren and Tas as the group talked quietly. Most of the staff were still asleep. The only people awake were the night watchmen. They turned lanterns down low as they made their way to the family wing of the castle. Tas's family had the second floor of the wing. Trion bid them all to sleep well and he would see them when they woke later in the day. He hugged Tas again before giving Thierren a stern look, as if to inform him they would have a discussion.

"I'm 29 not 16," Tas reminded his dad when he thought the stare down went on for too long. He grabbed Thierren's hand and dragged him into his rooms.

Exhaustion was settling in as they stripped down to their undergarments before collapsing into Tas' bed. Thierren had been in Tas's rooms before, they all had. They had all camped out on the bed several times when they were in school. But this was different because now Tas had himself wrapped around Thierren, his hand resting over Thierren's heart. Sleep came immediately to both of them.

When morning came, Thierren woke to someone running their fingers over his dragon tattoo he had on his back shoulder blade. He had gotten it from a tribe while he visited their village in the Northern arctic tundra. As payment for his service and aid, they made him an honorary member, giving him a traditional tattoo according to their customs. Sunlight had filled the room, letting him know it was late morning. He rolled over so he could face Tas and saw a huge grin on his face.

"You seem happy," Thierren commented.

"I had to pinch myself a few times when I woke up this morning," Tas admitted as he brushed his hands through Thierren's curls. "I've dreamed of this for so long that to have you in my bed, it's beyond anything I could ever expect."

"You are a sap," Thierren informed him as he kissed his nose.

"You knew this before," Tas reminded him.

Thierren rolled his eyes. "What are the plans for the day?"

"Nothing," Tas informed him. "Well, we should check in with Tobias, let him know we're here. But I think that's it."

"I think we could all use a day to do nothing," Thierren agreed. They had been on the move since Emi.

"Is that the healer talking?"

"The healer and your lover," Thierren grinned as he rolled so that he had Tas pinned to the bed.

"I'm okay with that," Tas said.

Thierren bent down to kiss him. Tas already had his fingers threaded through his hair, pulling him down so their bodies were flush against each other. Thierren was taking the lead, and Tas was fine with that. They were still learning about each other's bodies, their likes, as well as their dislikes.

The first knock they both ignored. Then a loud bang followed. "Oh Taslan! It's your brothers!"

"I am going to murder them slowly," Tas groaned as Thierren rested his forehead on Tas's shoulder. "GO AWAY!"

"Nope," Thaddeus answered back.

"They will not go away, will they?" Thierren realized.

"No, because I think Sebastian is already picking the lock on the main door," Tas answered.

Thierren rolled off him. Tas slid out of bed and pulled on a pair of pants from his pack and a shirt before he stormed through the bedchambers and into the sitting room. He opened his door, glaring at his three brothers. Sebastian had been kneeling on the ground but was now sitting on it with an innocent grin. Thaddeus was leaning against the door frame while Richard was reading a book, trying to look innocent.

"What?" Tas inquired.

"Someone woke up on the wrong side of the bed," Thaddeus declared.

"I would have been in a much better mood if you left me alone," Tas pointed out. "What do you want?"

"We wanted to say hello to Thierren," Sebastian stated as he brushed off his pants after he stood up. "We have not seen him in so many years and would like to catch up with our comrade."

"You saw him last year at your wedding," Tas reminded him. He eyed his three brothers. "Nope. You will not do that thing you do when you find out I have a boyfriend."

"And what thing is that, oh dear brother, of ours?" Thaddeus asked, pretending he knew nothing.

"The whole drag him to the training ring to show him how good the three of you are with weapons," Tas said.

"Do we do that?" Thaddeus asked Sebastian.

"I am sure our youngest brother is very mistaken," Sebastian answered.

"Don't worry, I'll just cast a fire storm on them," Thierren said as he joined Tas in the doorway. "Gentlemen."

"Thierren," the three brothers said in unison.

Richard marked the place in his book. "Good, we're done with the intimidation part," he decided. "There is a lunch spread in the family dining room, mom is there along with your companion Jonah, and I believe I saw Lia headed there on our way here."

"You're no fun," Sebastian informed Richard.

"You know I can tell both of your wives," Tas pointed out and then looked at Richard. "And I'll have grandfather ban you from the private archives for a week."

"You wouldn't!" Richard exclaimed, but knew that Tas very much would. "Brothers, I believe our baby brother has out-matched us. Thierren, welcome to the family. Just remember, you joined this insanity."

"Thank you, Richard," Thierren said. He looked at Tas. "I'll meet you at the table. I want to check on Grierr."

Tas nodded. Thierren slipped past him and the brothers. Tas watched him leave. "Who won the bet?" Tas inquired as he headed to the family dining room with his brothers.

"What bet?" Sebastian asked.

"The bet I know you all have had about when this would finally happen," Tas answered.

"You think we would place a bet on such a thing?" Thaddeus stated, pretending to be upset. Tas arched an eyebrow at him, causing Thaddeus to let out a sigh of defeat. "Gramps."

"We think he is cheating because he can talk to dragons and I'm sure they were already gossiping about this," Sebastian pointed out.

Tas had to laugh as they walked. "When did he pick?"

321

"Well, we started the bet after you and Thierren had the fight, after the Council sent you on your mission," Sebastian informed him. "I had it after the first battle, Thad had it after one of you were wounded in battle. Richard figured when you first saw each other, which would have been Emi."

Richard shrugged. "I figured it had been the longest you had gone without seeing each other," he replied.

"To be fair, part of me was hoping for that as well," Tas told him.

Tas heard footsteps rushing to catch up to them. He smiled when he saw it was Emaya. "How did you sleep?" He asked her as he kissed her on the cheek.

"Good," Emaya said. She was incredibly nervous about being in a palace and not knowing how to act.

"Emaya, let me introduce you to my brothers," Tas replied. "The one with the brown hair and broad shoulders is Thad. He is the oldest. The tallest of the three is Sebastian, and then one with his nose in the book is Richard. Gentleman, this is Emaya."

"You were Amelia's apprentice," Richard noted.

"I was," Emaya answered.

"We are thankful that you were with her, and she was not alone," Sebastian replied. "She was a dear friend of our grandfather."

"I... thank you," Emaya replied, unsure of how to act amongst royalty.

"Are you heading to breakfast?" Tas asked her. She nodded, overwhelmed. "That's where we are headed right now."

Sebastian noticed her nervousness. "Don't be nervous," he said calmly. "We are a very informal group. Titles and honorifics only happen during official visits, ceremonies, and when in the public areas during events. In the family section, we don't use titles, ranks, or anything like that."

"Should I bow or curtsey?" She asked.

"If Gramps arrives during the meal, you could bow your head if you feel you must, same as our father," Sebastian suggested. "But they do not expect it and will tell you that."

"What if I see you on the streets?" Emaya asked. "Or in a public space and I forget..."

"You will be fine," Tas assured her. "You are a guest here. No one will reprimand you or throw you into jail."

The scent of food filtered through the halls as they walked. Tas noted how his brothers seemed to make sure that one of them was always on either side of him. He knew it was not for protection, which meant they knew about his eyes and did not want those working for the household to know until Tas informed them. Sebastian must have noticed him staring and sent him a quick wink as he talked to Emayla about places in the palace she should visit while staying there. A hand on his back guided him in a different direction, but he could still tell they were heading in the right direction.

"They are redecorating the main hall we use," Thaddeus whispered. "We thought it best to steer you away from there."

"Thank you," Tas answered. "Though if there are any vases we want destroyed, I'm sure I can help with that."

Thaddeus laughed at that. "How are you adjusting?"

"I'm... adapting," Tas admitted. He could always be honest with Thaddeus. "I can still see in some weird way of seeing. It's just the world is fuzzy and slowly fades to black with this really narrow window of clarity in the center."

"If I could take this burden on for you, I would do so in a heartbeat."

"I know, brother," Tas whispered. His brothers never changed how they treated him when they had learned the truth of his parentage.

"We are going to want to see how you fight so we can work on defenses for your weak spots."

"Grierr and I have been doing that," Tas replied.

"Good, he can join us," Thaddeus replied.

"How are mom and dad handling it?"

Thaddeus sighed. "They are relieved Thierren is with you and trying to figure out what happened," he answered. "Dad will joke that he has more gray hair because of you, but I think when they see how easily you move about, they will breathe easier."

They could hear laughter as they neared the family dining room. Sebastian led Emayla into the room first, hoping the decor of the room would ease some of the young woman's concerns. The walls were in a warm yellow. They hung portraits of the family above the stone fireplace. The wood was all a honey wood color. The long dining table in the center of the room could easily fit twenty comfortably. Instead of being set with fine porcelain, they had set out everyday pottery in earth tones. The food laid out on the buffet was in matching serving dishes. The floor was wood covered in rugs, where a dog lay sleeping at the head of the house by a distinguished gentleman with silver hair. A cat was lying perched on top of the dish's hutch, licking its paw.

"You're awake," a female voice said, coming from a door at the other end of the room. Her chestnut brown hair had silver highlighting it. She wore a simple day dress as she approached Emaya. "You must be Emaya. I'm Nora. I hope my sons have behaved."

"Yes, they have," Emaya said, as they guided her to a seat where Lia was. She saw that Jonah and the other man were deep in conversation.

"That is my husband, Trion," Nora informed her. "The dog at his feet is Ash. He's old and has become hard of hearing."

Soon, a servant had arrived and asked Emaya what she would want to drink. Nora told her to help herself to the food on the table and the buffet before she turned to fuss over Tas.

"Finally realized I'm here," he teased as she hugged him and kissed him on the cheek.

"You lost me ten gold, so I believe I'm allowed to ignore you for a bit," Nora teased as she looped her arm through his and guided him to his usual chair. "Where's Thierren?"

"He wanted to check on Grierr," Tas said as he sat down.

Tas focused on the table and the auras that surrounded it. "Where are my two honorary sisters and Gramps?"

Trion looked up from his conversation with Jonah. He smiled at his son. "Your grandfather and Sienna are at the Three Sisters," Trion answered.

"Bre is taking Marissa to the zoo as she is finally over her morning sickness," Thaddeus replied as he set a plate in front of Tas. He left the seat on the other side of Tas empty and took one across from him.

"What's the *Three Sisters*?" Emaya asked.

"It's a charity," Sebastian informed her, taking his seat. "My wife, Sienna, is one of the teachers there. It's our grandfather's favorite charity, something about being around well-behaved children."

"I wonder what that's like," Nora commented.

"What type of charity is it?"

"It's a haven for at-risk children and teens," Sebastian explained. "Orphans with no family, a child whose family is abusive, runaways. They live on campus, go to school, they can get apprenticeships or apply for universities during their final years."

"That sounds amazing," Lia commented. "Is it just for those in Quinsenta?"

325

"No, they are open to all the countries," Tas replied as he ate a strip of bacon. "Some of my people drop orphans or runaways off at the campus."

"Just how many do you have now?" Sebastian asked Tas.

"Are you counting mine and Kaidan's combined forces or just mine?"

Emaya looked confused. "Tas here runs his own spy network," Thaddeus informed her.

"Yes, go right ahead and just announce it to the world," Tas sighed. He looked at Emaya. "My work for the Council means having eyes and ears everywhere. My brothers like to tease me about how I am the least assuming person to run a spy network."

"Hence why it's perfect," Richard answered.

"I have a quick question," Emaya said, looking at Sebastian. "Why do they call it the Three Sisters?"

"After the Three Sisters myth," Sebastian answered.

"Explain it to the Greedinites," Thierren said as he entered. "We don't learn about them." He kissed Tas's forehead before greeting Nora and Trion.

"He's right," Lia admitted. She was a bit surprised she was not aware of the legend.

"Do you want to tell it, Thierren?" Tas asked him. Tas knew that the moment that Thierren had arrived at the Academy, he raided the library to learn everything he could that his conservative parents had hid from him.

"No, Richard is the renowned expert on early mythology," Thierren said as he sat down in the seat next to Tas with his plate of food.

"How's Grierr?" Nora asked before Richard could speak.

"He is exhausted and is sleeping," Thierren answered. "I have instructed the cook that when he does wake, to give him simple broth and the tea I gave her. He's run down and just needs a few days to recover."

"That is understandable," Trion replied. "Did you tell Emmiline to have the staff leave his suite alone?"

"Yes, she is going to see to his rooms personally," Thierren replied. Emmiline was the main housekeeper for the family wing. A second mother to them all.

"Good, she'll take care of him and see to what he needs," Nora agreed.

"Emaya," Richard said. "If you would like, we can discuss the myth after lunch. As my brothers say, myths are my area of expertise."

"Thank you, that would be amazing," Emaya admitted. "I fear I need more caffeine in me before I could fully appreciate it."

Richard looked at Jonah. "Jonah, do you know of the tale?"

"I do," Jonah replied. "I have heard several variations."

"I would be interested in hearing them at some point," Richard replied.

Jonah chuckled. "I would be happy to help expand your knowledge."

"He can keep coming around," Richard informed Tas.

"Sebastian, does Sienna want me to come visit campus while I am here?" Thierren asked.

"You know she would love it," Sebastien told Thierren.

Tas smiled at Emaya. "Thierren volunteers his time at the charity to help with medical care."

"Do you think I could see the campus? I would love to see how it all works." She asked.

"Of course," Sebastian told her. "When she comes back today, I can have Sienna figure out a time where you can visit. Thierren usually goes over there as well to help in the health clinic."

"We are going to work it around my research schedule," Thierren admitted. "This time I am going to be doing heavy research on what the hell your brother did to himself."

Tas hit him on the shoulder. "I got poisoned by a Blood Dragon. I didn't do that to myself," Tas argued.

"That reminds me," Trion said. "I have the passes for you, Thierren. They will add you to the family list, allowing you full access to everything."

"You did not need to do that," Thierren replied.

"It's his way of saying you have his blessing," Tas informed Thierren.

"Oh, well, if I had known this, I would have dated you years ago," Thierren teased.

This had Tas's brothers laughing and Tas just shaking his head. Even Lia was chuckling as Tas tried to keep a look of annoyance on his face.

#

Later in the afternoon, Nora walked with Tas through one of the gardens. They walked arm in arm as she filled him in on family gossip. His cousins, Helena and Heath, were returning to the capital to act as guards for the family. He had not seen them in over a year as they deployed when Sebastian got married. Nora stopped at her favorite bench under the pear tree and waited for Tas to sit next to her.

"How are you really doing?" Nora asked her youngest child. The child she worried most about since the day he was born.

"With my vision? With Edelberg? With what I must do?"

"Yes."

Tas turned and looked at his mother before letting out a sigh. "We knew, we've known since they diagnosed him with the Blood Lust that at some point we would lose him to it," Tas began. "But how it happened, then him attacking Thierren while in control of himself, it... hurts."

"When he is one of this Blood Lust modes, does he remember?" Nora inquired. The boys never told them much of what it entailed.

"It's one of the first signs of someone having it," Tas said. "They don't remember the moment, sometimes they don't remember the few hours after the episode."

"Thierren said he was in treatment."

Tas nodded. "The moment they diagnose a Battle Mage with it, they pull the mage from active duty," Tas informed her. "The treatment is long because every mage is different, so finding the right dose or version of the potion can take time. For Edelberg it was in a tea, it was how his body best took the potion. Some take it in a tincture, others in a capsule. Edelberg didn't want anyone knowing, so for him the tea was the best solution."

"And they are monitored?"

"Closely," Tas assured her. "They can spar while closely monitored to see if flare-ups occur and then dosage is altered if needed. They also work with a therapist to help isolate the moments before the episode occurs. If they can figure out what could set it off, then they can work a better plan out."

"Did Edelberg get to that point?"

"He stopped taking the potion four months ago and stopped seeing his counselor three months ago."

Nora placed a hand on Tas'. "As a healer, one of the hardest things to watch is a patient who walks away from treatment," Nora began. "We think of all the things we could have done differently, words we could have said instead. While also remembering that it is the patient's choice in the end. As his friend, you must understand that none of you did anything wrong. It was his decision. And while these sounds harsh, he needs to see the consequences of it."

"Maya told Thierren that, and us as well," Tas sighed.

"This will not go away easily, Tas," Nora told him. "You will all go through a kind of mourning phase. But remember, this is not the end. This could be what he needs to realize he needs help. I know you will be there for him."

"We sent Moira with him because none of us wanted him to feel like we abandoned him," Tas told her.

"A wise decision," Nora agreed. "While he might lash out at her in the beginning, he'll in time realize that her being there will be a comfort."

"I think you will like Moira," Tas admitted.

"I think I will as well," Nora agreed. "I always like a woman who forges her own path."

Tas smiled at his mother. Nora would not marry Trion until she had finished her medical training and had a job. Once she settled at the hospital in the capital, they married. Until his grandfather's health started declined a few years ago, they had lived in a townhome near the hospital that his mother purchased with her salary. Sebastian and Sienna now lived there, as it was close to the *Three Sisters*.

"How are you handling your eyesight?"

Tas looked at his mother. "Did Thierren share his notes?"

"He handed them to me after lunch," Nora replied. "I have yet to go over them, as I wanted to talk to you about it first."

"It sucks," Tas confessed. "Especially with Thierren and I being together, and I can't fully appreciate his... appearance."

Nora laughed at what her son was trying to say without saying it. "But you are managing?"

"I am," Tas assured her. "We are working as a group on my limitations. Grierr is planning some runes to help me get around more independently, and I focus on how I could be dead or a blood sorcerer. Somewhat blind is positive in that context."

"Do you know how you were less affected?" Nora asked. Her youngest had already been through so much in his life that another hurdle was hard for her, but she rather him alive than dead.

Tas did not answer right away as he looked at the surrounding garden. Nora allowed him time to gather his thoughts. She had never been one to rush someone into speaking. He ran a hand through his hair as he thought of what he was going to say.

"Thierren researched some old tribal records back in Hruan that mentioned Blood Dragons, and what their blood could do," Tas began. "When he explained what should have happened, I realized why it didn't."

He stopped and looked at his mother. "I had to tell them," Tas confessed to her. "About all of it, what happened when I was 20, why I spiraled after it, what happened with you. It was the only reason I'm not dead or a monster."

Nora saw the pain in his eyes, and she looped her arm through his. "You and I have seen so much in our life," Nora whispered. "I don't what you to look at me and feel shame for what happened."

"How can you be so calm about it? I want to rip his head off and serve it to a shark."

"Can I watch when you do?" Nora asked. She smiled when Tas chuckled. "It took many years of therapy to reach the point I am at. Those first few months were horrible. I told your father I would not blame him if he left me. I was a mess; I couldn't stand to be touched. When we realized I was pregnant, I screamed. I broke a vase that was a few centuries old. When you were born, I was afraid to hold because I feared all I would see was his face. I won't lie. There were moments when I did. Your father was there every step of the way. He let me scream, throw things, he let me do what I needed to do to heal. You and I would not be here if your father did not believe in either of us."

"Jonah says I look like he did before he became what he is now," Tas informed her.

That shocked her. "Jonah knew him?"

"He joined his crew before he had to make the choice," Tas recalled. "Jonah said that he wanted to see the world and experience it before they forced him into his position. Jonah believes that because he did not go willing, his power was corrupted."

"I can tell you, you look at nothing of my attacker," Nora assured him.

"Jonah told me that too," Tas said. "He said the only people who would know who I was would have to have known him before he chose to be a god."

Nora held his hand in hers. "Taslan," Nora began. "Do not use what he did to prevent you from living your fullest life. If you decide you want to accept the power that comes with your birthright, your father and I will not be disappointed. All we have ever wanted for our children is to be happy and to be fulfilled. Do not hold back from who you could be because of what that monster did to me."

Tas kissed her forehead. "You have to be the strongest being I have ever met."

"I had to be. I had to handle you and your brothers," Nora reminded him with a chuckle. "The four of you were difficult to handle at times. Unless you forget trying to join Richard in his sword training when you were four."

"I could hold the sword!" Tas argued. "You said I could learn to fight if I could pick up the sword. And I did."

"And this is why I have gray hair," Nora replied. "As well as why we have the no weapons rule at the table."

Chapter 26

Thierren stared. He did not care if his mouth was agape or what. He was standing in the private section of the Library of Quinsenta, where only academics and researchers could access the tomes kept here. Richard stood next to him and let Thierren take in the library's beauty. The walls that were not covered with shelves were wood paneling that had aged. There were seating areas near fireplaces with private reading rooms built into one wall. The windows were stained glass, showing the story of the gods descending to the earth.

"Are you ready?" Richard asked Thierren.

"The question should be am I worthy," Thierren commented.

Richard laughed. "It is my honor to welcome you to the Repository of Knowledge and Learning," Richard stated. "It was the original name of the library. When it was expanded several hundred years ago, they kept the name for what we call the inner sanctum: the academic and archives area."

"How did your family collect all of this, Richard?" Thierren asked as he tried to take in the collection's scope. Even the public section was impressive.

"Centuries," Richard stated. "It started with one of the first rulers of Quinsenta wanting to share our knowledge. He traded what we knew with local tribes. That knowledge was written and kept. Then, as countries formed, if a scholar from somewhere else wanted permission to study here, they needed to bring translated editions of some of their culture's great works. There were purchases as well, auctions, gifts. Gramps had the oldest editions copied and the originals are in vaults with charms to preserve their contents. He feels it is our legacy to ensure that knowledge is available to all, as his ancestors did."

"It's amazing," Thierren replied.

Richard nodded as he guided Thierren to the archivist desk that was in the center of the room. "Hiram, this is Dr. Thierren Haas," Richard said to the archivist. "Thierren this is Archivist Hiram Salt; he keeps all of us academics in line."

Hiram chuckled as he shook hands with Thierren. "It is a pleasure to meet you, Thierren," Hiram stated. "The king has left me what they granted you access to. I will get that ready. First thought, Richard and I will add you to the family archives wards."

Thierren arched an eyebrow at this. "Kierra," Hiram called. A young woman walked over to them with a smile. "You are in charge until I return. We will be in the Family archives."

"Of course," Kierra replied. "I'm allowed to kick the old goats out if they complain?"

"Absolutely with the threat their access will be revoked if they continue with their nonsense," Hiram added. He then looked at the two gentlemen in front of him. "Follow me, lads."

Thierren absorbed it all as they walked through the library towards two beautifully carved wooden pillars. He should not have been surprised to realize that dragons were carved into the pillars. A large black oak door stood in the center of the wall. Thierren noted a brass podium next to the door with an unusual box standing on it.

"Grierr designed the box," Richard informed Thierren.

Hiram took out a ring of keys and found the one that unlocked the box. A glow came from within once the lid was off. Hiram motioned for Thierren to come stand next to him. A small orb sat in the box.

"Tas created it," Hiram informed Thierren. "It is how we allow access to the private archive behind the door. We used to have another archivist sit here just to allow access to a few people. Tas and Grierr figured out a better system."

"How does it work?" Thierren asked.

"If you lay your hand on the orb and push some of your magic into it," Hiram instructed. "For us mundane folk, we state our name while our hand is on the orb. It recognizes our aura, but it will recognize your magic."

"Of course, Tas would create something like this," Thierren stated.

Thierren laid his hand on the orb and felt a hum as soon as his skin touched the smooth glass of the orb. He felt Tas's magic all around him as he pushed his magic into the orb. When it glowed brighter, Hiram told him to remove his hand.

"You're grinning like a fool," Richard informed Thierren.

"I felt his magic all around me," Thierren answered.

"What does it feel like?"

"Home," Thierren said simply.

#

Thierren was pacing as he talked through a theory while Tas sat on the couch, listening. They were in Tas's suite, or their suite. Thierren was going over what he was hoping to find in the archives and libraries. Tas always loved watching Thierren as he talked out theories or problems. Nora and Thierren had been reviewing his notes on the blood poisoning, which of course had Thierren's mind working overtime. It was this rare glimpse into how Thierren's mind works.

"I need to talk to the dragons," Thierren stated. He had turned to look at Tas.

"I'll send word," Tas replied. "The meetings don't start for a few days, so I have the time."

"We should also talk to them about the scale and the rings," Thierren said quietly.

Tas smiled. "We can do that as well."

Thierren went back to pacing and talking to himself as he made a mental list of what he needed to do. There was a knock on the door, causing Thierren to stop. Tas motioned for him to continue while he got up to answer it. He grinned when he opened and saw his grandfather standing there. The older man pulled Tas into a hug.

"I am sorry I could not meet you all yesterday when you woke up," Artur told his grandson. He smiled when he saw Thierren. "Thierren, it's good to see you."

Thierren walked over to greet the king and was pulled into a hug. "You too, Artur."

"If you need to talk, my door is always open," Artur told him.

"I appreciate it," Thierren answered.

"If you don't mind, I need to borrow my grandson," Artur informed both of them.

"We'll go to the balcony," Tas replied. "You can keep pacing."

"I'm not pacing, I'm thinking," Thierren countered.

Tas rolled his eyes as he led his grandfather to the balcony that ran the length of his suites. He closed the large glass doors, then placed a barrier around them.

"You look content, happy, at ease," Artur noted. "As does Thierren."

"I am. I hope he is," Tas replied. "You wanted to talk to me?"

"Just a few things," Artur assured him. "I had my people go over the laws to make sure I would not be overstepping. I also consulted with Tobias. Once you are bonded you both will receive titles, and if Thierren would like, he can take our name or the last name of Magus."

Tas stared at his grandfather in shock. Magus was one of the oldest last names in their family lineage, and it belonged to the first sorcerer born in their family.

"Both of your brothers and your cousins received titles on their wedding day. I did not want the two of you excluded," Artur went on. "Drache is helping with selecting the title."

"I... thank you," Tas replied. "I am going to be taking Thierren in the next few days so he can meet Drache and show him the rings."

"Good," Artur said as he looked out on the garden that could be seen from the balcony. "This brings me to the second reason I'm here."

"What's wrong?"

"My advisors made the final list of leaders and representatives who will be at the meetings," Artur began. "They brought it to my attention who the Duke of Lynia is sending."

Dread filled Tas. "I will not like this, will I?"

"We just got his list, which means we can't ask for a change with the limited time we have," Artur continued. "As Thorin says, it was probably intentional."

Tas cursed under his breath as he leaned his elbows on the balcony railing. He hung his head down as tried to produce thoughts. "Any of his siblings?"

"Just Oberon and his security detail," Artur answered.

Tas shook his head as he tried not to panic. He felt his grandfather rest a hand on his shoulder. "I am going to call Sebastian, Thaddeus, your cousins, as well as Grierr into a meeting with Thorin," Artur began. "Oberon is terrified of him. We will notify the staff tonight. Everyone will be on high alert when they arrive."

"Will he be staying in the palace?"

Artur grinned slowly. "No," he said. " He is one of the lower rankings. He will stay at one of the guest houses in the city. There are a few that will also stay within the city."

Tas nodded. "He will accept nothing I tell him," Tas informed his grandfather.

"Would he accept bonding rings?"

"He would have to," Tas replied. He then looked at his grandfather. "What are you thinking?"

"It would be fast, but a small bonding ceremony before the meetings begin," Artur suggested.

"Gramps, we've been together maybe for two weeks," Tas began.

"And you have been in love with each other for far longer than that," Artur reminded him. "Does Thierren know everything?"

"No," Tas sighed. "I didn't want to add more stress to him."

"You should tell him, then the two of you decide what you want to do," Artur replied. "Your grandmother's garden is stunning this time of year for a small garden ceremony."

Tas had to chuckle. "You have it all planned, don't you?"

"Your mother and I have had it planned for years," Artur informed him. He squeezed Tas's shoulder. "I will take my leave and send him out here."

Tas nodded. He focused on the blurry images of the garden that lay beneath him. He heard the muffled words of his grandfather and Thierren then the closing of his suite door. The moment Thierren stepped onto the balcony, he felt a sense of calm wash over him.

"Hey," Thierren said quietly. "Your grandfather looked serious when he left."

"Yea," Tas answered. He looked at Thierren, then took his hand and walked him to the doors that led to the bedroom. "We need to talk."

"He's against our bond?"

"No," Tas assured him as he pulled him to sit next to him on the bed. "You are going to have to decide on what last name you want. You can take mine or the last name, Magus."

"That's one of the oldest sorcerer surnames," Thierren informed Tas.

"I know," Tas replied. "Gramps is one of his descendants."

Thierren was speechless at that. "Okay, if that's not the issue, then what is?"

"The Duke of Lynia is sending his youngest son to the meeting," Tas said.

It took a moment for Thierren to realize which son that was. "Oberon? He's a pompous asshole who cares nothing for the government or his people," Thierren stated. "He also has been bothering you for several years. I am not going to like what I hear, am I?"

"No, you aren't," Tas answered. He stood up and walked to the balcony doors. "For the last four years, Oberon has been attempting to court me."

"I had heard rumors he's attracted to all kinds. Though his father and the cult try to stop any rumors about him with elves or dwarves," Thierren replied as he watched Tas. "Rumors of one-night stands in dingy taverns, cover-ups, things like that."

"His grand plan is that we will marry. I would be his consort," Tas informed Thierren. "He plans that once we are settled, and he has risen in his political career, he would then select a woman that he would bed to produce children."

"What an amazing plan," Thierren said dryly. "Your thoughts?"

"I have told him no, repeatedly," Tas assured him. "However, he does not like rejection."

Thierren stared at Tas. He stood up and walked over to him. "Tas, what did he do?"

"He has done nothing, but he tries," Tas assured Thierren. "He will try to corner me, get me alone, demand an audience with just me. He gets angry. He tried to start a rumor that we were together, but that I didn't want anyone to know."

"How will he react to us?"

"He will not acknowledge it," Tas answered. "He thinks I am the piece that he needs to rise in the world of politics. To outshine his older siblings."

"Because you are the higher title," Thierren realized. "So, what are we going to do?"

"Gramps is going to have a meeting with Thorin, Grierr, and my brothers to go over security protocols. They will inform the staff tonight. Thankfully, he will not be staying on palace grounds," Tas answered.

"Is that enough?"

"Gramps had a suggestion," Tas began. "There is one thing that he would have to accept, that he could not ignore..."

"Our rings," Thierren said.

Tas nodded. "He thought if we did the ceremony before the meetings, it would grant us more protection and avenues that we can pursue if he keeps ignoring it."

"Okay."

Tas looked at him. "Okay?"

"I love you; you are it," Thierren said. "Really, when you look back over our past, haven't we been in some form of a relationship for years now? Unless you don't want to?"

"Honestly, I would rather have the small ceremony in a garden than have to go through with the pomp and circumstance of a royal wedding," Tas agreed. He stared at Thierren for a few moments. "We're doing this?"

"Let's go meet with Drache and then we will talk to your family tonight," Thierren suggested. "But yes, we're doing this."

Tas pulled him into a deep kiss. "I love you," he whispered. "Let's go see some dragons."

"Wait, now?"

Tas just grinned as he pulled Thierren out to the balcony and looked up at the sky. Within moments, Thierren heard the flapping of wings and soon Bart appeared. Thierren looked at Tas like he was out of his mind before he followed Tas over the railings and onto the dragon. Tas had Thierren sit in front, since they were flying without a harness.

"Trust me," Tas whispered as he told Bart to bring them to the Dragon Keep.

Thierren let out a small scream as Bart took off into the sky. Soon they were above the palace grounds and the city of Dracon lay before them.

They built the city and palace on the mesa of Mount Draconis. The volcano now laid dormant. Most of the inside of it had exploded during its last eruption centuries ago. The dragons, with the aid of dwarves, created the Dragon Keep. It was where the dragon rulers lived, as well as those in their family. It was the seat of power for all dragon herds.

Thierren had been there only twice before. Both times, Tas had them take the walking path that led up to a giant door that covered the main hole from where the volcano exploded. Dwarves had used stones and carved welcome to all in the Draconic language into the stones that created the door frame. They carved the door from wood, with scenes showing the friendship between dragons and dwarves. This time it seemed as they were going to be entering how dragons did, which was through the top of the dormant volcano. Tas tightened his hold on Thierren as Bart flew to the top of the keep and then plummeted down through the top of the volcano.

Tas was laughing as they flew through the top, knowing Thierren probably had his eyes closed for the whole descent. Large torches were lit as they passed the various levels of the keep. Even with his limited eyesight, Tas felt as though he was seeing it all perfectly, as if there had been no damage to his sight. Bart slowed as he neared where Drache, the Dragon King, sat on a large platform. Bart landed in front of the large, almost black dragon. Laying on his stomach, he let Tas and Thierren slide off of him.

Tas cocked a head toward Drache, then he smiled at Thierren. "Take my hand," Tas replied. "You will be able to understand Drache."

Thierren looked at him in surprise, but did as the King of Dragons suggested. *"Welcome, Thierren,"* Drache's deep booming voice greeted. *"You may speak in common; I will understand what you are saying."*

"Uh, thank you," Thierren replied, not sure what to say.

"May I see the rings that Arngrierr forged from the scale of my grandson?" Drache inquired.

Thierren let go of Tas' hand and walked to where a table sat. He took the small pouch from his pocket and emptied its contents into his hands. He placed the rings on the table.

With one of his claws, Drache picked up the rings and examined them closely for a few moments before setting them back on the table.

"Stand back," Tas instructed Thierren.

Thierren followed his orders. Drache opened his mouth and a blue flame came forward and engulfed the rings. Thierren could have sworn he heard singing for a moment before Drache finished. The rings were still intact, there was no damage to them.

"You can pick them up," Tas told him.

Thierren cautiously walked toward the table and picked up the ring, surprised they were not hot. He slipped them into the pouch and placed it in his pocket. Thierren walked back to Tas and took his hand.

"Tell Arngrierr that he did an exceptional job. Not all rune smiths can work with inner dragon scales," Drache told them. *"Thierren, what is it you wish to do with these rings?"*

Thierren felt nervous for the first time in a long time as he looked at Tas and then at the King of Dragons. This was even more nerve-wracking than the conversation he had with Trion earlier in the morning.

"I ...," he stopped and took a deep breath. He knew Drache was not the only dragon that would hear what he had to say. Loyalty and love were important to dragons. "The moment that Bart gifted me with the scale, I knew there was only one thing I wanted to do with them. That was a ring for Tas and a ring for me to remind each other of everything we've been through and everything we will go through together. I know that dragon marriage bonds are the strongest bond amongst creatures. There is no breaking it. Both must go into it without hesitation. Until now, I have been hesitant about everything, every choice, every decision. The one thing I have never hesitated about was the knowledge that I needed Tas to be in my life. I just needed to take time to figure out where in my life I wanted him."

"And where is that?"

"I want him as my friend, my lover, my confidant," Thierren admitted. He felt Tas tighten the grip on his hand. "He let me be free to make mistakes, to be with others. He never forced his love on me, never made me feel guilt that I couldn't return it yet. Once I chose the path I have, I knew it was time to no longer hide behind my fear."

"I know what it is like to make a choice between the family we are born into and the family that we found," Drache confided. *"I belonged to a herd of volcano dragons in the arctic north. My father was the leader of the herd. He had plans, plans for each of his children. Yet I wanted to see the world, to meet the other herds, to learn about the other dragon cultures, other creatures. He saw this foolish, a waste of time. He wanted no association with those outside our herd. He saw any alliance with anyone outside of one's herd as a sign of weakness."*

"Sounds like him and my father would get along," Thierren commented.

A low rumble was the chuckle of Drache. *"I believe you are right. Like you, it took me many years to build the courage to leave. He told me when he learned of my wish that once I left the herd territory, they would never welcome me back. I still left. There are moments now where I don't know how I had that courage."*

"What did you do?" Thierren asked.

"I traveled, visited the herds near ours that we never met, met elves, humans, dwarves, other creatures," Drache recalled. *"I learned cultures, customs, languages. As I traveled, a dragon here or there would join me. Either they were outcast or had wanted to explore the world. I soon made my herd. We ended up here in Quinsenta, welcomed by the Dragon Queen, who had co-ruled with Artur's grandfather. She had no children and took my herd and myself under her wing. None of us were born here, but the dragons here accepted us simply because we meant no harm, and we were dragons. The herd I came from was all about order and your place in the herd. I had learned what freedom was in my travels, but it was not until here that I truly knew what it meant."*

"I am learning," Thierren admitted.

"The Dragon Bond is not just a symbol of our devotion to our partner, but it allows us to be connected in ways that are unique to the pairing," Drache informed them. He saw the surprise flash over the two sorcerer's faces. *"There has never been a dragon bond between a Dragon Talker and his mate, which, Thierren, is how you are seen, as Bart gave you the scale. Bart accepted you as a dragon, and you are now part of our herd. I am unsure of what bond you will form, but it will not harm you."*

"Will Thierren gain my damaged sight?" Tas asked in the tongue of dragons.

"No, the bond only exchanges the strength, not the weaknesses," Drache informed him.

"My grandfather said something about how this is a bond that no one can contest," Tas stated in common.

"For non-dragons to be given the blessing of such a bond, it is a universally recognized bonding. No one can contest it because both partners must be willing with good and pure intentions, not even in human court."

"It would protect you from Oberon," Thierren said to Tas.

"I don't need the bond to protect me," Tas argued.

"Oberon is coming to Quinsenta?"

The tone of the King of Dragons was not friendly. The growl in it reminded one of how dangerous these gentle beings could be. "Yes," Thierren said. "He is being sent as part of the Lynia delegation for the war meetings."

Thierren could not understand what was being said, but he saw Tas wince and realized Drache was not happy with this news.

"You wish to have the bond soon?"

"Before the meetings," Thierren answered. He ignored the looks Tas was sending him. "Is that even possible?"

"We do not require a length of courtship because individuals cannot fake what it entails for such a ceremony, for such a gift to be given," Drache informed them. *"I would suggest the full moon in two nights. A place I can fit."*

"My grandmother's garden," Tas said quietly.

If a dragon could smile, Thierren swore it would be Drache now. *"I have fond memories of that garden; your grandmother often would yell at the gardeners when I arrived, and they would try to make me leave. I have not been there since she returned to the universe."*

"What do we need to do?" Thierren asked.

"Just let Artur know, and he will ensure all we need will be there," Drache answered. *"When you showed me the rings, I blew my flame on them to give my blessing and protection. To show others you are part of my herd now. I already had made my decision before you entered, for I have known for years that you two are mates."*

"Thank you, Drache."

"It is I who thank you for allowing us to be part of this." Drache stared at Thierren. *"We are honored you will join our herd."*

Chapter 27

Artur was not sure the last time there were this many people in his private office. His oldest son, daughter-in-law, four of his grandsons, two granddaughters in-law, Thierren, Grierr, Jonah, Lia, and Emaya were all sitting or standing in his sanctuary. Usually there was a combination of the above group, but not all of them at one time. He was also certain that Bart was outside his windows listening in on what was being said. They were here to discuss Oberon, the Bonding Ceremony, and he was about to let them in on something he had not told Tas. Helena and Heath were standing guard outside to ensure no one overheard what was being discussed inside.

"I did not want to tell you this when we spoke, Tas," Artur began as he looked for a slip of paper. "I wanted the decision that you and Thierren made to be one that you were not fully forced into making."

"Kind of impossible to force a Dragon Bond," Tas pointed out. "But what didn't you tell me?"

Artur handed him the sheet of paper. Tas took it and walked a few steps away, putting up a barrier so no one could grab it from him, which, knowing his brothers, one of them would.

"What's he reading?" Thaddeus asked, annoyed that Tas had prevented any of them from spying.

"A draft of a marriage contract," Tas answered before his grandfather could.

"What?" cried the group.

"Along with Duke Lynus of Lynia's list of who would attend the war meetings, he also sent along a marriage contract he would like to file and a letter," Artur explained. "He feels that the games that Oberon and Tas have been playing these last four years have run their course. It is time for them to settle down, as they are nearly past their prime. The union of his Dukedom with our kingdom would be a great alliance for both."

"What do we get out of it?" Thaddeus asked, ignoring the punch to the arm from Sebastian.

"Nothing," Tas said as he lowered the barrier. "However, what we would have to give them is insane."

"I want to see," Bre said. She was a barrister and knew laws better than most.

Tas handed it to his sister-in-law before sitting on the arm of the chair that Thierren was occupying. Thaddeus looked at Tas. "You can read with your vision?"

"Bart read it for me," Tas answered. Everyone just looked at Tas. "What?"

"We'll discuss it later," Thierren promised. "What did it state?"

"That I would wed Oberon by the next solstice. We would get a title of a dukedom here. Then, after two years for us to settle into our new life, Oberon would select a female to father children with. Those children would be heirs to the throne of Quinsenta."

"Is that all?" Trion stated with an amused tone.

"Breanna, may I read it after you?" Thierren asked her.

"I didn't know you knew the law?" Sebastian asked, surprised.

"I don't, but I know the language of cults," Thierren stated. He thanked Bre when she handed it to him.

"If they challenged it in court, he would lose," Bre told them. "Marriage contracts like these are political alliances. Which means both parties must bring things to the table. Tas is correct when he says they list nothing for what they would bring."

"That is because you are thinking with the mind of a lawyer," Thierren informed Bre as he finished reading it.

"The cult?" Grierr asked Thierren.

"My uncle's wording," Thierren answered as he looked it over. "It's close to the one that was drawn up for me and whichever of the three women I would have chosen as a bride. Except in my case, my family would get nothing. It was the bride's family that would give to us because they would get status by having their daughter wed to me."

"Glad you jumped that hurdle," Thaddeus replied. The more he learned about Thierren's family, the more he wanted to hurt them.

"Yes, but it seems by doing so they are dragging you all into this mess," Thierren said. "I stated in my letter home my intentions toward Tas, that it would be pointless for them to change my mind."

"Instead of changing your mind, they move to take him out of the picture entirely," Thaddeus replied.

"Thierren, it's not only that, but Oberon has also been after me for four years," Tas reminded him. "Maybe your letter prompted them to take action, but we all had a feeling at some point Oberon would have his father try something like this."

"Bre, how would we reject it?" Artur asked Bre.

"Well, I would state the obvious that it does not follow the code of law regarding political marriages," Bre replied. "Since the Duke has not publicly declared the Malconites the official religion of Lynia, which he can't do without King Harold's approval, he could not use their rules as justification. Thierren, I'm assuming this is normal for the cult."

"Yes," Thierren said. "It is shocking that they would even write something like this, allowing Oberon to marry a male, as they cannot biologically produce children."

"You forgot the section where two years after our marriage, Oberon is to take on a mistress to produce the children," Tas reminded Thierren.

"Of course, how could I forget," Thierren said dryly. He saw a look on Grierr's face. "What?"

"Bre," Grierr began. "Does the contract include clauses of what happens if one dies?"

Thierren handed her back the contract. She took out her glasses and began to re-read the document more carefully. "If Oberon is to pre-decease Taslan, Taslan must wait a full year before entering society to re-marry. If they have children, then the new spouse must meet with the approval of Oberon's family."

"What if Taslan dies first?"

Bre continued reading. "If Taslan is to pre-decease Oberon," she began. "Oberon will keep all titles given upon him during their marriage, and any wealth and properties either gifted or purchased. If children have been born at the time of death, Oberon may marry after a three-month mourning period."

"I guess it will take him only three months to get over me," Tas sighed dramatically as he sipped his tea.

"I'd never be over you," Thierren assured as he kissed his free hand. He ignored the groans from the brothers.

"Okay, so if Oberon died first then Tas would in theory have to wait a year, and get permission from his in-laws to remarry," Lia summed up. "Yet Oberon, after three months, can essentially marry who-ever the hell he wants? I've never heard of that."

"Most cultures have a one-year mourning period as protocol," Grierr agreed, trying not to finger his own widow's braid. "It's more of a custom than anything else. Luna and I had a contract because of who my family is."

This news surprised everyone. "You did?" Tas asked.

"It was to protect her family," Grierr explained. "They hunted my line to the brink of extinction. It would grant those willing to marry in a haven at any temple of Arkos. They also would be allowed certain burial rites, as well as a key to a hidden chamber if being hunted."

"Was there anything about how long mourning would have to be for?" Bre asked delicately.

He shook his head. "But for those who follow the Arkon religion, we mourn for a minimum of a year," He answered. "We grieve, we remember, we commit ourselves to serving our god during that time. Then, at the end of the year, we can continue our mourning process or take the first steps on this new path in life. When one is ready to move to the next path, they cut off the widow's braid, burn it, then release the ashes to the wind."

"That's beautiful," Lia said. "Too often grief is a kind of brushed to the side and will force a person to move on before they are ready. To have such a practice built into your religion, your culture, it says much about your ways."

Grierr nodded to her in response. Nora reached over and squeezed his hand. "Can I ask why you all want to know what happens if Tas dies?"

"Because they are thinking the worst," Tas answered. "Essentially, the contract is written so if I suddenly die after, let's say, three years, Oberon

353

walks away with titles, money, and properties. Thierren is this the cult or is this Lynus?"

"A mixture of both," Thierren replied. "In the last few years, the cult has been trying to get a firm footing in regional and national government. The hope is that with these allies, they have their religion made an official religion, giving them protection of the government. It is not working well for them. They will use the alliance with Lynus to gain the footing they lack elsewhere."

"He's right," Lia agreed. "The Rebellion has been running into roadblocks because of local leaders in Lynia and Corin, making it hard for us to move freely throughout those districts."

"Add to that Lynus is power hungry and wants to prove to the king of Greedin that Lynia is the most important province, and you have a perfect contract that spells my untimely death."

"Does he not think we wouldn't do something?" Trion asked.

"You are thinking of a happily married man," Sienna reminded him. "Not every royal family out there is like this. It's well known that Lynus and his wife hate each other. They sent each child to boarding school in Rochleaux not because they were the best schools, but so the children would not be near them."

"She's right," Lia and Thierren agreed.

"I went to school with Oberon," Emaya admitted. They all looked at her. She had been silent for most of the meeting. "He was five years above me. I had gotten a scholarship to the same boarding school. It was a huge honor for my family."

"What was he like?" Lia asked.

"Obnoxious," Emaya answered. "The rumors about him were disgusting. He flirted with anything that moved. But most rumors circled around girls."

"They always frowned upon it at cult meetings when he was seeing a guy," Thierren recalled.

"Do they really call them cult meetings?" Thaddeus asked Thierren.

Thierren snorted. "No, they refer to them as Meetings of Truth or Class of Enlightenment," Thierren answered.

"I like cult meetings better," Richard commented.

"So do I," Thierren agreed.

"Your parents wouldn't pawn you off onto Oberon?" Sebastian asked.

"The very idea of me being with anyone other than a human female repulses my parents. They would rather think I was dead than have me marry a son of the duke," Thierren replied. "They are purist Traditionalists to the extreme."

"They would have you marry a woman?" Nora asked.

Thierren ran a hand through his curls. "I do like both," he answered. "I have been... I have dated both. I just prefer Tas above everyone else."

"Why?" Sebastian asked. He yelped when Richard hit him upside the head with the book he was reading.

"What was your contract?" Bre asked, ignoring Sebastian. Then realized what she was asking. "I mean, you don't have to tell us."

"They had selected three women, so they gave me a biography of each of them, though I knew one of them," Thierren answered. "The contract I would have filled out with the chosen name. But her family would give my parents 1000 gold pieces, a portion of their crops or livestock. If I were to die before her, she would return to her family. She would have to wait one year

355

before being able to marry. If we had children, she would have to wait until the youngest child was of the age of five. Her new husband would also have to be from the cult. Our children could not take his name. I was also to have to select a specific career that would benefit the family and show that I could support my growing family."

"And if she died?"

"Then I would mourn for three months and start the selection process over," Thierren answered.

"Thierren, I really hate your parents," Thaddeus stated.

"As do I," Thierren agreed. "The only difference between Tas's contract and mine is the parts about Oberon selecting a mistress. Otherwise, it's very much the same contract."

"Bre, when they go through with the bond, it would erase this?" Sienna asked.

"Nothing surpasses a Dragon Bond," Bre answered.

"Can I ask a question?" Emaya inquired. Artur nodded. "What is the big deal with this bond?"

"That is a good question," Lia agreed as she studied Tas. "How is it so important?"

"They are very rare, even among dragons it is rare," Artur answered. "Dragons do not need to mate for life. They can choose a partner to mate with for life, but some do not feel the need to perform a bond. The Dragon Bond is special because of what it entails. Some dragons do not feel the danger involved is reason enough to do it."

"What kind of danger?" Emaya asked.

"When a dragon bonds, they actually remove an inner scale and give it to their dragon of choice," Tas replied. "During their ceremony, they will actually take this inner scale of the other and place it in the vacant spot of where their own scale piece had once been."

"This spot, I take it, makes them vulnerable until they have the scale back?" Emaya realized.

"The outer scales grow back within a few months," Artur explained. "It can take up to a year for an inner scale to grow back. That spot would be defenseless against an attack."

"When Bart gave Thierren one of his inner scales, it showed that he acknowledges Thierren as part of his herd, that Thierren would protect him and his herd," Tas added.

"But other creatures can have this bond," Lia said.

"Only if they have been gifted an inner scale, can they have the bond," Artur corrected her. "Most would have such an item crafted into a protection amulet, mounted to their armor, or placed in their coat of arms."

"And then there is Thierren who had it crafted into two rings," Thaddeus teased.

"Well, it seemed fitting, since he's a Dragon Talker," Thierren pointed out. "And his dragon gave it to me because he knew of my intentions and feelings concerning Tas."

"You two are almost too perfect," Thaddeus groaned.

"You could take lessons," Bre teased.

Thaddeus rolled his eyes at her. "So, what do we need to do for this ceremony?"

"Grandma's garden," Tas said. "Drache recommends that it be performed during the full moon. Everyone in this room, along with Bart, we want there."

"I will want your favorite foods, and what you want for dessert," Nora informed them. "You will both want to wear your formal sorcerer robes."

"The big question is, who marries us?" Thierren answered. "I know Drache has to be part of it."

"I cannot," Artur replied. "I can give a blessing, but I cannot preside over marriages of families. I also figure you do not want a religious leader, Thierren."

"Yea, I'm kind of not a fan at the moment."

There was a clearing of the throat. They all turned to Jonah. "I am an actual captain," Jonah reminded them. "If you both are willing, it would honor me to perform a ceremony for the two of you."

"While everyone works on the ceremony tomorrow, I will draft a letter to Lynus," Bre stated. "Artur, if I may, I can work on it here so you can sign it once we have a final draft."

"I'll have Emaya and Lia go through our wardrobes for something to wear," Sienna suggested. "Between our clothes, we should have something to work for a moonlit ceremony."

Thierren looked at Grierr. "Would you escort me down the aisle?"

Grierr looked absolutely shocked at the questions. "You know I will."

"Thank you," Thierren said. He then looked at Artur. "If you agree to it, I would like the last name, Magus."

"It is yours," Artur told him with a nod.

Chapter 28

The Isle of Magi

 Moira was exploring one of the medicinal gardens outside of the library on the Isle of Magi. One of the archivists had told her about it. The archivists thought as a healer she should spend some time studying the plants that were planted in it. During the school year, the upper years at the Academy maintained the garden, during the holidays, the groundskeepers took over. It had become one of her favorite spots on the island, especially after a visit with Edelberg when he was not very welcoming.

 Tobias found her sketching some plants. He sat next to her, not wanting to bother her until she was done. He had heard that Edelberg was not in the best of moods.

 "I heard a rumor I would find you here," Tobias said as she closed her notebook.

 "It's peaceful," Moira admitted.

 "It's why I am sure you have noticed that many of us use the library gardens as a place to get away," Tobias commented. "I heard he was not agreeable to anyone today."

 "Usually, I read out loud whatever I'm reading to block him out, but today nothing worked," Moira sighed. "Was I needed?"

"I needed to stretch my legs after a Council meeting and heard from Samuel that Edelberg was a bit more venomous today with his words."

"How was the meeting?" Moira inquired.

"A headache," Tobias chuckled.

Moira looked around at the garden. "How did this all start? Tas told me some of it."

"The Isle or the Council?" Tobias asked.

"Both I guess," Moira admitted.

"The island became a refuge during the Tribal Wars," Tobias answered. "The mad War King was hunting down any who held magical abilities and executed them in the main square of his capital. A small clan of elves had inhabited this island; they spread word through the clans that they would offer refuge to any of the magical community who needed it. The villages were the first to be built, then the Academy to help teach the youngsters. After the Tribal Wars ended, countries asked if the island would take students from all over here were sorcerers to teach. The elves renamed the island the Isle of Magi. They became our protectors and still are. They established the training grounds where we train our Battle Mages. They were some of our first teachers. They planted this garden."

"And the Council?"

"That is relatively newer," Tobias admitted. "Roughly, the Council started shortly after the Tribal War ended. Though it has gone through some big changes in the last century."

"How so?" Moira asked.

"About a hundred years ago, there was a rise in Blood Sorcerers. Countries didn't know what to do," Tobias explained. "They reached out to us. We always had a council that would meet regularly, but no presiding officer. We decided we needed a governing body with a head. We still have not really agreed on what to call the head. I am labeled as President, but some think the Prime Minister is better or even Minister. But 'minister' reminds one of the church I was dragged to at a young age."

Moira chuckled. "Well, I think you are excellent no matter what title they use," Moira noted.

They spotted a dragon flying overhead. "Ah, it seems our other guest is arriving," Tobias noted. "I will introduce you."

Moira nodded. She slid her notebook into her bag and followed Tobias to the carriage that awaited them. They rode toward the Council building. Tobias and his family lived in a cottage on the property. His wife was a healer who helped train healers after they graduated from the Academy. They rode in the back silently. As they neared the Council building, Moira spotted some guards. She had become friendly talking with a man. A dragon was sitting nearby, getting rubbed down from the flight.

"Micah," Tobias said as he stepped down from the carriage. "I wasn't expecting you in person."

"I am here on official Crown business and Council," Micah replied, spotting the young woman standing next to him.

"Micah this Moira," Tobias introduced. "Moira, Micah is one of Edelberg's brothers."

"It's a pleasure to meet you," Moira said, as they shook hands.

"I would like to thank you for being here with Edelberg," Micah stated. "While a huge weight has been placed on your shoulders, know it has allowed those of us who care for him to breathe a sigh of relief that he is not alone."

"There is no need to thank me," Moira assured him.

"What do you need to do, Micah?" Tobias asked him.

"First, I need to speak with my brother, then we need to meet to go over the security council mission you had me do," Micah informed him.

"After you are done with Edelberg, you can find me in the cottage," Tobias told him. "You know the way to the prison."

Micah nodded. He bowed his head, then headed toward the small building that was the prison for those who committed atrocities in the magical community.

"Micah is one of our Blood Sorcerer experts," Tobias informed Moira. "When we hear rumors or a leader notifies us, Micah is usually the one to go out to gather the information for us before we decide on the best way to approach the situation."

"Is he a sorcerer as well?" Moira asked, already knowing he was not.

"No, but his family is unusual. There have been several sorcerers in the last few generations," Tobias admitted.

"That's unusual?"

"From what the latest research shows us is that it does not get passed on," Tobias replied. "If you want to read the study, you will find it in the library."

#

Edelberg sat in his cell. He had finished his morning workout and was now contemplating what to do to kill time. The cell was not horrible. He had a private wash area, a bed, there was a desk crammed into a corner with a chair. There were books for him to read, three meals a day, Moira could only visit during mealtime. The rest of the time was waiting for someone to come talk to him about what happened, if he understood the charges against him. He still could not believe that Thierren had done this to him. He was not sure if

Moira was here to remind him of everything he lost or if she was here as a curtesy. No one was blaming Tas for taunting him, for triggering his episode. It was more proof that they were out to get him.

He heard the main door open and footsteps entering. It was not Moira, as it was not dinner time yet. It was too late in the day for a lawyer to bother with him, so he was curious if another prisoner was coming or if it was something else. He saw his brother Micah stop in front of the cell door.

"Ten minutes," the guard said to Micah. "I'll be on the other side of the door."

Micah nodded. The guard stepped out, shut the door, and locked it behind him. Micah turned and stared at his brother. For the fact Edelberg was in prison, he looked good.

"Micah," Edelberg began, but stopped when Micah held up a hand.

"Wait to give me any gratitude," Micah warned. His tone was neutral as he studied his brother before him. "Eddie, you swore you had it under control. That the therapy was working, as was the medicine."

"I had it under control," Edelberg growled.

"So, what the hell happened in Hruan at the Presidential Palace?" Micah inquired.

"I lost my temper. It was a onetime thing," Edelberg stated. "Look, they are making this into a bigger deal than it is."

"Explain how they do that," Micah demanded as he folded his arms across his chest.

"Tas didn't want me to hold back. Once I unleashed everything I had, he freaked out, realized he couldn't handle it," Edelberg answered.

"And Thierren?"

"So, I shoved him into a wall and yelled, look, he's been looking to ruin me for years," Edelberg snapped.

363

"You didn't just shove him into a wall, you strangled him to the point he lost consciousness, you crushed his vocal cords, you almost killed him!"

"But I didn't!"

"Because he kneed you in the balls!" Micah yelled. "You almost crushed Grierr."

"I know!"

Micah took a deep breath and steadied himself, reminding himself why he was here. "I am not here to argue with you."

"Then why are you here?" Edelberg asked with a glare at his brother.

"They have sent me on behalf of the Royal family of Friesen," Micah said, drawing himself up to his full height.

"Are they sending a lawyer?"

Micah stared at him so he would stop talking. "The Royal Family of Friesen will not be involving itself in matters that the fall under the Council of Magi," Micah began. "They will not contest any verdict that comes from the trial of Edelberg Smythe. They will not be sending a legal representative as this is a matter of the Council and not of the mundane."

"You can't be serious," Edelberg said, his voice choked. "Dad would never do this."

"You're right, he wouldn't," Micah snapped. "Uncle was not happy when he found out what Dad would do to get you out of sentences. Our father is now under investigation for using the seal of the Royal House fraudulently, all to keep your ass safe."

"Come on, Mike, you can't be okay with me being here."

"I'm not," Micah admitted. "Seeing you here, seeing you like this, it makes me sick. But you did this to yourself!"

"How can you side with them?"

"You stopped seeing your therapist, you stopped taking the tinctures that you needed to take," Micah replied. "You won't accept responsibility for any of it."

"Because it's all bullshit!" Edelberg yelled. He laughed as he walked around his cell. "Nice to know uncle will turn his back on family, reputation is everything right?"

Micah shook his head. "It has destroyed him having to do this. Do you think this is easy on any of us?" Micah challenged. "He was in tears when he stripped you of your titles, but if this is the only way you will realize you need help, then we do whatever it takes."

Edelberg charged the gates; the only way Micah knew Edelberg attempted to use magic was the runes glowed around the cell door and guards came rushing in. Micah turned and walked down the hallway as the guards handled Edelberg. Micah headed out of the prison and headed toward the cottage that housed the leader of the Council of Magi. Tobias was sitting on a bench in front of the cottage, reading a book as Micah approached.

"How did it go?" Tobias asked.

"Not well," Micah admitted. "He tried to use magic."

Tobias sighed as he closed the book. "That would be the third time since his arrival."

Tobias stood up. "Come, we have the house to ourselves," Tobias informed Micah. "Cynthia is at our daughter's house and our son is on a training mission."

Micah followed Tobias into the cottage. He could smell a roast cooking and fresh bread. They moved through the main room and into what had once been a summer kitchen; it was attached to the house during an extension of the home. Micah sat at the table as Tobias moved about the kitchen.

"You have not failed him," Tobias informed Micah. "This is a path he has chosen on his own."

"Have you been telling yourself this as well?"

"My wife," Tobias admitted. "She keeps reminding me we have all done everything we could."

"My uncle thanks you for the letter, alerting him to what had happened before he took the crown," Micah told him.

"It is a letter I never wanted to write, but I had a feeling that he might not know everything," Tobias sighed as he brought plates piled high with food.

Micah took his plate from Tobias and set it on the table. He poured them wine before he settled into the food. They did not speak of anything important during dinner. Once the meal was done, plates were washed, they poured tea and sat.

"What did you learn about Moira?" Tobias asked.

Micah stared at the tea in his mug before he answered. "The only record of a Moira Minoris I found was of a twenty-three-year-old woman who died in a horrible fire fifty years ago," Micah stated. "She lived on a small island off Toroand, with only one village on it. There was a terrible fire that burned and destroyed the village. Most of the inhabitants died during the fire. Those that survived would die later from burns."

Chapter 29

Tas stood in his suite while his mother fussed. Every sorcerer had formal robes to wear at events. They were colored based on the discipline chosen. Thierren's would be a deep green with herbs embroidered along the hems of it to represent him as a healer. Grierr's would be a deep silver with runes along the hem to show he was a rune smith. Tas' were black, silver and gold embroidery lined his robes in the shapes of planets and constellations to show he worked for the Council. Under the robes, which he wore open, he wore black dress pants and his royal doublet. His father wore a similar doublet, as would all the males. Everyone agreed, no crowns or tiaras. Bart wanted to wear something, so Nora worked with Marissa. They made him a garland of flowers to wear. Bart had seemed thrilled with the idea, especially when Marissa presented it to him and Tas helped her place it on him.

"You, okay?" Trion asked as he watched his wife fuss.

"Excited," Tas said. "I dreamed of this, but never thought we would be here."

"You don't feel forced, or rushed?"

"It's faster than what I thought, but Drache was right. We could not do the bond if we were not committed," Tas answered. "And with what is on the horizon, the uncertainty, I enjoy knowing we are walking into it together."

"He's been in love with you for years," Nora informed Tas. "He just needed to figure out it was a future he could have."

There was a knock on the door. Trion walked over and opened it. Thaddeus stepped in. "We are ready in the garden," he informed them. He grinned at his brother. "Looking sharp, baby brother."

"Thank you," Tas said. He took a deep breath. "Alright, let's do this."

Nora took his arm, then they followed Trion and Thaddeus out into the halls. The staff would watch as well. Tas had invited all of them to watch with their families, and take part in the dinner afterwards. They headed down to the main floor. The doors to the garden were near the family library. Sebastian was blocking the door with a grin.

"Grierr and Thierren are having a moment," Sebastian explained. "I will let you through once they are ready."

"Is he okay?" Tas asked.

"They're fine," Sebastian assured his brother. "Everyone is sitting, and Marissa is dancing about around Bart. She now has a matching garland for her hair."

"Of course she does," Tas said with a smile. His niece adored Bart and Bart adored the five-year-old just as much.

"Was the letter sent?" Trion asked Sebastian.

"With Drache's commander," Sebastian replied.

"That should get the point across," Tas agreed. The commander of the dragons was a huge mountain dragon that looked every bit the part of a commander of an army of dragons.

There was a knock on the garden door, and Sebastian grinned. "All right, it's time," Sebastian said. "Let's get Tas married off."

Thaddeus rolled his eyes at Sebastian as they opened the door. Harp music had started, Tas noted the staff were lining the edge of the garden as

Emmiline's granddaughter played the harp. Artur was standing at the end of the aisle with Jonah and Drache. Tas grinned as Marissa danced down the aisle in front of Thierren and Grierr spreading rose petals. When she was done, she headed right back to where Bart was sitting near Drache. Tas wanted to know what Grierr and Thierren were whispering about as they walked to the front of the aisle. Grierr hugged Thierren tightly before sitting next to Emaya and Lia. Thaddeus, Sebastian and Richard walked down next before taking their seats next to Sienna and Bre. His cousins Heath and Helena were also sitting, both ready to spring to action if necessary but otherwise enjoying being with the family.

Nora and Trion stood on either side of Tas as they began their march. Thierren tried to keep his neutral face, but by the time Tas joined him, Thierren was grinning. Trion and Nora hugged both before taking their seats.

Tas took Thierren's hands in both of his. He was bouncing on his toes as his grandfather began his blessing. Tas did not care what his grandfather was saying. He was focused on watching Thierren and just seeing him so free with his emotions meant everything to him.

"Taslan," Artur said. He laughed at his grandson's face. "I do need you to pay attention."

"Sorry," Tas said with a grin. "But he distracts me."

"And that has been the sum of their relationship since they met," Artur informed everyone. "What are you learning about at the Academy? Sorry Gramps, but there is this boy, and he distracts me sometimes. When we first met Thierren, my wife knew. She told me that night that this was the boy that had our Tas distracted and all a flutter."

Thierren blushed a bit. "I know she is watching over us tonight," Artur said with a smile. "With that, it is my honor not just as a King, but as a grandfather to give my blessing of the union of Taslan Sturm and Thierren Magus."

Artur hugged Tas tightly before doing the same with Thierren. He went and sat with his son and daughter-in-law. Jonah took Artur's place and smiled at the two men in front of him. He had only known them for two months, yet he had rarely seen two people so well-matched for each other.

"I will keep this as brief as we can," Jonah began. "It is my honor to preside over this union of two people I can call friends. Thierren was unsure of me at first, but I now understand his hesitance in me. He does not trust many, but when he does, you realize how precious that trust is. Tas welcomed me immediately. He never doubted my word. When I met all of you, I realized why. Tas was raised with love, with a family that supports each other. Over the last two months, I have watched Thierren go from being closed off out of fear to who he is now. When he reached for the future that he wanted, it opened him to being the person he kept locked away. Hidden, yet Tas always saw that person. He saw who Thierren could be. To watch Thierren open that door, to embracing the possibilities, is one of the most empowering moments I have seen. So, it is my honor to marry them."

Jonah nodded to Drache. Jonah placed a hand on Drache's front leg so that he could vocalize what Drache would be saying.

"The union of dragons is sacred," Jonah stated. "It is more than the union of two but the sharing of strengths and accepting of weaknesses. It is unbreakable, it is why we use our scales to show our commitment to each other. That we weaken ourselves only to strengthen who we are at the same time."

Jonah motioned to Thaddeus, who stood up and brought the pouch with the rings in them. He emptied the contents into his palm, then placed a hand back on Drache.

"These rings symbolize the exchanging of scales," Jonah began. "They can only be accepted if the feelings are true, the intentions honest, and the devotion equal. In the union of dragons, no one dragon is greater than the other partner."

Jonah had Thierren take the ring for Tas. "Taslan, I ask you to accept this ring as you have accepted me," Thierren said.

Tas nodded. "Yes," Tas whispered. Thierren's hands were trembling as he slid the ring on Tas's left ring finger. There was a glow that came around his finger as it slid into place. He felt a warmth spread over him.

"Your turn," Jonah told Tas as he handed him the ring for Thierren.

"Thierren, I ask you to accept this ring as you have accepted me," Tas said.

"Yes," Thierren said, his voice cracking with emotion.

Tas took Thierren's hand and slid the ring on his finger. The same glow emitted on Thierren's finger.

"As the King of Dragons, or the voice for him," Jonah began. "I am pleased to announce the bonds have been accepted and have the blessing of my herd and all dragon herds."

Jonah then smiled at the two. "You may kiss each other."

"Gladly," Tas commented before pulling Thierren to him. "Hello, husband."

Chapter 30

Over the centuries, the palace of Quinsenta had been added to and rebuilt several times from when it had been first constructed. They had built its present format after a fire had torn through a huge section of the palace just over a hundred years ago. The main section was what the family referred to as the museum. It held the throne room, the picture gallery, music room, a two-story library, and a grand ballroom. The East Wing was the family wing, which was the most used wing of the palace as the immediate family lived there. Along with the bedroom suites, there was the family dining room, sitting room, smaller library, as well as a few private offices.

The West Wing was the governmental wing. It contained the parliament chambers, public offices, meeting rooms, a dining room for official functions that did not require the ballroom, as well as official guest rooms for political visitors. Like the family wing, they used it daily and had its own entrance. They could lock the doors to cut the West Wing off from the Main section, just as the doors were locked to the East Wing, so only family, staff, and family guests had access.

At the moment, the dining room of the West Wing was open with buffets set up with breakfast, tea, and coffee. Leaders from all over the globe were mingling, catching up before the war meetings started. They had started to arrive at 9 in the morning, some staying in the official guest rooms the evening before. Many were arriving throughout the morning by dragons. Tas and his brothers were mingling with a few of the leaders they knew and were friendly with. Thorin was standing near Tas, monitoring for when Oberon would arrive.

Tas grinned as he spotted a dark-skinned woman walking toward them. Her hair was arranged in an intricate braid, she wore a bright gown with patterns from the tribe her family came from. "Queen Larissa," Tas said as he walked over and greeted her.

"Taslan," she said, accepting the hug. "How are you?"

"Much better since you last saw me," Tas assured her. "How are things in Gastion?"

"The same as most places," Larissa responded. She guided Tas away from ears. "I hear Oberon will be here?"

"Thorin has a plan in place," Tas assured her.

"I will have Bryon and Sasha speak with him," Larissa replied. "I'm staying here in the West Wing, so my guard can aid yours."

"I am sure Thorin will appreciate the aid," Tas informed her.

"Where are your grandfather and father?" Larissa inquired.

"In the dining room, Volpe had them in a discussion," Tas answered, referring to the Duke of Leneo.

"Then I will have to join," Larissa said. She glanced at his left hand. He was hiding. "Congratulations, my dear. I was excited to hear it finally happened."

"And this is why you are my best informant," Tas laughed.

"Or your grandfather's favorite drinking companion," Larissa stated with a smile. She squeezed his shoulder before saying hello to his brothers.

Thorin approached Tas. "She knows, also Bryon and Sasha will approach you," Tas told him.

"Good, your cousin has lent her unit as well," Thorin replied. "How is your navigation?"

"Your people did good," Tas told him.

"Grierr worked with them and the staff to streamline where everything should be to give you clear access," Thorin answered.

"Has Benton forgiven me for beating him yesterday morning?"

"Yes, though he is getting some ribbing from the rest, but he is challenging them to take you on before teasing him," Thorin grinned.

Tas laughed. He returned to where Sebastian and Grierr were standing. "Thad went to escort Larissa into the dining room," Sebastian told Tas.

"She's one of yours, isn't she?" Grierr inquired.

"My lips are sealed," Tas replied. He then spotted Lia walking in with Micah. "Micah!"

Grierr and Tas both went over to him, each giving him a hug. "You're the rep from Friesen?" Tas asked.

"We figured it was easier than me having to fill someone else in on everything I know," Micah said. "Lia and I were just catching up."

"Have you seen Edelberg?" Grierr asked solemnly.

Micah took a deep breath. "We'll discuss that meeting and what I've learned later," Micah promised them. "Thierren and Jonah should be there as well."

"We can arrange that," Tas assured him. "You're staying in the family wing, correct?"

"Yes, your mom had my things already brought there," Micah replied. "I also hear congratulations are in order."

"The formal announcement will be at the ball," Tas told him.

"Won't stop us from teasing the two of you when we're in private," Micah stated with a sly grin.

Tas rolled his eyes. He heard a loud voice coming from the entrance hall and went rigid as he saw who had entered. Oberon, Count of Lycan, had arrived with his guard. Grierr saw him as well and stood to his full height. He also allowed some of his power to ooze out of him.

Oberon was wearing a bright turquoise tunic with the coat of arms for his house embroidered on it. His pants were a bright yellow tucked into black leather boots. They cut his brown hair short and seemed to be styled to the popular trend. His hazel eyes latched on to where Tas stood and headed straight to him.

"Taslan," Oberon greeted. He took his arm in his hands. "I need to speak with him. Excuse us."

Tas removed Oberon's hand from his arm. "You can speak with me here," Tas informed him.

"This is a personal matter," Oberon clarified. "Now stop being difficult."

Tas shared a look with Grierr then moved a few feet away from the group. "What do you want to discuss?"

"I am sure your grandfather has informed you of the marriage contract that my father sent," Oberon began. "Now, I know he would like us married before the next solstice. However, I was thinking perhaps, with all the leaders here, we could have a ceremony here on the last night of the meetings."

"We received the contract," Tas confirmed. "My grandfather sent a response a day ago."

"Well, that was unnecessary," Oberon stated. "Since I am here, with the blessing of my family, we can go through with signing the marriage contract."

"Oberon, I'm not marrying you."

Oberon stared at him, then let out a laugh that rang out around the room. "Really, Taslan? You really must stop playing whatever game you have been playing for years," Oberon sighed. "It is getting rather tiresome; it is not something that I want to continue when we are married."

"Oberon, this is not a game. I have never been interested in you. I am not marrying you," Tas stated. "You refusing to accept any of this will not change that fact."

Rage flashed through Oberon's eyes. "You are mine."

"I am no one's," Tas stated. "If you must know, I am already married."

Tas did not wait for the response. He turned on his heels and walked back to where his friends were waiting. "He looks like he could kill you," Lia commented as she sipped her tea casually. "And now he's calling over his guards and talking to them harshly."

"How does she do that and barely move her lips?" Grierr asked Tas in amazement.

"I have not figured it out yet," Tas told him. "What now?"

"A few are leaving, and he is talking to the leader of his men," Lia replied.

"Good thing I finished the rune stones for you and Thierren," Grierr said. "If they try to poison either of you, the stone will pick up on it."

"Once he learns of your eyesight, he will use that to his advantage," Micah warned.

"I'm working on that as well," Grierr told Micah. "At the moment, Thorin and I have things figured out. A few leaders have offered their guard to aid us as well. Oberon is not a well-liked individual."

"No, he's not. He has made many enemies," Micah confirmed. "I'll talk to Thorin during a break."

Sebastian saw people were leaving the dining room. "It looks like we're being herded to the Parliament chambers," Sebastian stated. "Lia, you will be with Tas and myself at the table. Grierr will be at the table next to you. Grandfather has the tables set up by closest to our borders. This way, no one can claim we are playing favorites. Thaddeus, our father, uncle, and grandfather will be up on the dais."

"Right," Lia whispered. They had taken their time the night before to go through the layout of the room and where she would be, so she would be comfortable today.

Sebastian gave her a reassuring smile as he escorted her toward the council chambers. The table for Quinsenta was in the center of the room with tables spreading out in half circle rows. Lia had met Reed the night before. He was Commander of the Quinsenta military and lived on the base at the southern point of the island nation with his family. Reed had promised her she would be fine during the meetings.

Lia took a seat in-between Sebastian and Tas. Grierr took the seat for Hruan as their representative. Tas filled her in on who was who, making notes for her so she could remember later if she needed it. Sienna and Bre had helped her with her clothing for the next few days so that she looked the part. As Sienna said, mostly it was all about first impressions. When it seemed like all but four tables had people sitting at them, Artur banged the gavel.

"Welcome everyone," Artur greeted the room. "I wish we were meeting under better circumstances. Only one country and three provinces did not send representation, so I thank all of you who came to understand the urgency of the situation."

"Artur," King Harold of Greedin stood up. "I would like the names of those from my provinces that did not send people. I see who is missing, but I want to say to them I saw the invitations."

"I will have me secretary provide you with all of that," Artur assured him. "The only country that refused was Rochleaux."

"Rochleaux has shut all borders," Micah stated as he stood to speak. "No one can enter the country nor exit the country. Even if they are citizens of another country, they are not allowed to leave."

"Has anyone had contact with the royal family?" Artur inquired.

Tas stood up. "I last had contact with Princess Anya six months ago," Tas stated. "Her letter was very formal and did not match what we had been discussing in prior letters."

"Anyone else?"

"I lost contact with my people who worked with the royal family," Duke Volpe of Leneo added. "Our Prime Minister has tried to communicate with theirs, but they have not returned all responses."

"Hruan has been flooded with refugees fleeing Rochleaux," Grierr stated, standing up.

"Do we know why they are fleeing?" Harold asked Grierr.

"From what we could learn, and witness for ourselves, anyone that is deemed to have any magical ability is apparently being placed in camps," Grierr replied. "They are being told it is for their own protection."

"You recently traveled through Rochleaux, did you not?" Oberon asked.

"I did," Grierr replied. "And that should tell you how much attention they are paying if we were allowed to exit the capital. Though we almost did not make it to the border."

"Do you have examples?" Larissa inquired.

Grierr looked at Tas. Neither was sure who should answer. "I believe Lord Taslan should answer, as it involves refugees. We aided them in getting to the Watchtower on the border of Hruan."

"The Council of Magi has ensured protection for all who inhabit the properties of the Watchtower," Tas began. "For example, there are two that jump out because neither individual has any ability what so ever. The first was in the Rochleaux army, the man was badly injured in an attack on a village. They deemed him magical because his healers thought he healed too fast."

"Did he?" someone asked.

"Our healer asked him about his injuries and said he healed on the faster end of the estimate given to him, but magic was not the cause," Tas answer did not aid it. "The soldier was told three to six months to heal fully. He was healed within four months. Our healer, who is a sorcerer, said he could understand if he had been healed in two months. But being he was in good health and fit before the injury, he said that would aid in a quicker recovery."

"Can I ask who your healer was?" Volpe asked.

"Dr. Thierren Haas," Grierr answered for Tas. "Taslan, Thierren, and I, as well as a few others, helped with the refugees."

"He is an expert in his field," Volpe replied, impressed with who their healer was. "I would believe his word. What of this second case?"

"A young lad, thirteen is his age," Tas replied. "He's half elf. His mother is an elf. She is part of one of the forest clans. They would visit her clan on weekends. They made a decree in Rochleaux that declared elves magical beings. Therefore, because he was half elf, they deemed him magical, as were his two siblings. His parents were taken from them the day before as they lied to the guard about the location of their children, giving them time to flee into the woods."

"Are they safe?" Trion asked.

"Yes," Tas assured those concerned. "They met the soldier in the woods, and he has taken them under his wing."

"What of the forest clans that live in Rochleaux?" Harold asked, making notes to speak with the clans in his territory.

"Those not captured have split off into smaller groups," Tas explained. "A group could join up with mage Kaidan Hunt, who is now head of the Watchtower. Word is slowly being spread for those dispersed to go there."

"I will contact the clans in Silencia and Tarsina to see if they would be willing to take on some of the dispersed elves," Harold said. He looked at the representatives for those two provinces. "We can meet after dinner to discuss details and who to contact."

"Does Hruan need help with the refugees?" Reed inquired. He knew that a country could quickly become overwhelmed.

"At the moment, they are handling the situation," Grierr answered. "But I have some requests from the President and the Parliament. If it gets to be above a certain number, they will need help with relocation and resources."

"We should have those plans in place before the number gets there," Reed suggested.

"Agreed," Artur stated. "I would like names of people who could form a refugee committee to help Hruan and the Watchtower."

Artur looked at his notes before speaking. "King Harold, you wished to pose a question?"

"Oberon," Harold began as he stood up to speak. "Do you know why the three southern provinces below you are not here?"

Oberon, almost bored, stood up. "They have given Lynia, and my father, permission to be their voice in such matters," he answered.

There was a moment of silence. This was unheard of for if a province could not send a representative, then arrangements are made with the ruler of the country. Tas, Lia, and Grierr shared a look with each other that this followed their theory.

"Is there a reason that they did not notify me of this?" Harold inquired.

"They felt my father was more than capable of securing representation for them," Oberon stated.

"Your father did not see fit to inform us of such a request?" Duchess Amelia of Fluth inquired. "Such a matter should have been brought up at our provincial meeting earlier this month, to which Duke Lynus was present."

"I am unsure of the reasoning behind the decision," Oberon said, trying to hide the annoyance in his voice. "They informed me only that Lynia would be the voice for our southern allies."

"I will reach out to him them," Harold stated.

"Harold, what do you know of the group of refugees in central Greedin?" Artur replied. "Do you know of them?"

"I have knowledge of them," Harold said. "I have told the national army to aid them if they need help near outposts. I know some provinces have issues with them, but I have not heard of them creating any disturbances."

"Can you do more?" Lia asked. Everyone looked at her. "For the group, I mean? While the national army has been of help, there are some areas where there is no aid to those who lost everything in the attacks and natural disasters."

"The last vote to give national aid failed by four votes," Harold said. "Unfortunately, my hands are tied on this matter. May I ask who you are?"

Lia took a deep breath. "I represent the group," Lia answered.

"So you admit to treason," Oberon stated.

"How am I admitting to treason?" Lia asked him.

"You are terrorizing villages, spreading fear, tales of horror," Oberon replied. "Lynia has outlawed your organization."

"I didn't know that trying to help those who have lost everything is treason," Lia commented.

"It's not," Harold assured her. He turned with narrow eyes to look at Oberon. "Oberon, I hope you have evidence of this?"

"I am shocked that the representative from Corin has not spoken up," Oberon began. "As the terrorists burned an entire village down to get people to join their cause."

"I am not sure what our neighbor has heard," Joslin, Duchess of Corin, began. "But the group that this young woman represents aided the army of Corin greatly in helping get villagers out and fighting off the actual terrorists that were burning the villages."

"What is happening in Greedin?" Larissa asked.

"The gods of Greedin have gathered their own forces," Joslin began. Harold gave her a nod. "There were rumors, rumors many of us in Greedin were foolish to ignore. It is more than just the Black Mist, the earthquakes, sudden appearances of volcanos. We are dealing with villages burning to ground with fire that can't be extinguished."

"That's preposterous," Oberon replied. "Fire that can't be put out? There is no such thing."

"Actually, there is," Tas stated grimly. "The amount of power behind it would be more than any sorcerer could handle. It would require rune stones to ground the person. It is ancient and dangerous magic that violates all laws sorcerers swear to uphold."

"Would a god have this power?" Harold asked.

"Yes," Grierr replied. "If cast correctly, it would burn until it had no more fuel to consume. The god Leo created it for destroying creations or experiments that were too dangerous. But he had a specific room built to contain such a fire."

"If they cast it wrong?"

"It is a spell that you want to be cast wrong," Tas answered this time. "When it is cast wrong, it will burn itself out. The moment the caster loses control or drops the spell, the fire will weaken, for it needs magic to feed it. It still will burn everything in its path, but that path with not be as wide if it was cast correctly."

"How long was the fire in Corin burning for?" Someone asked.

"It lasted for twelve hours," Lia whispered, her voice sounding haunted. "It was all-consuming, hot enough to melt metal, to burn flesh."

Tas laid a hand on her shoulder. The room was silent. "You were there?" Joslin asked gently.

Lia nodded. "We had gotten word that a group loyal to Mara would be near the village," Lia explained, trying to control her emotions. "We had just evacuated the children... when she arrived."

Lia closed her eyes, which she regretted as she could see it all over again. "Take your time," Tas told her. He handed her a handkerchief while Sebastian asked an attendant for tea and water. "There is no rush."

"I close my eyes and I still see it," Lia confided to them all. "She came in on a black horse, her hair flames, her eyes filled with excitement. It

383

was a nightmare come to life. The goddess of beauty, of love and beauty, had become a goddess of vengeance and hatred. People crumbled as they tried to flee from her destruction. It was no use. They were there one moment and then they were nothing but ash. Our soldiers bought us time to get as many people as possible out. They knew there was no surviving the battle. Her soldiers torched the buildings with her fire, not caring if people were still in them or not. We were able to get all the children out of the village along with most of the adults, but... there were those that we couldn't save."

"We always regret those we could not save," Reed stated as he saw the anguish on her face. "But we must force ourselves to remember those we saved, the lives that continue because we helped. Though it is not always easy to remember that."

"We are taking the word of this person who we don't know?" Oberon asked.

Tas looked at her, unsure of how she wanted to handle this. "I'm done hiding," she whispered to him.

Standing up, Lia tossed off the glamor that concealed her power and had changed her looks. "My name is Calia Arkoson," she declared. "Though I prefer Lia."

Gasps filled the room as the members realized who she was. She looked at Oberon with a slight smile. "I hope the word of the youngest daughter of Olga is good enough for you, my lord."

"You vanished," he stammered. "You're supposed to be missing."

"A rumor my brother created to cover our movement," Lia assured him.

"Your... holiness..." Larissa began, as others bowed their head in a show of honor and respect.

Lia almost cringed. "Please, just Lia."

"Very well," Larissa said. "Lia, you and your twin, you have moved against your family."

"We have," Lia answered. "It was not a decision we took lightly. At first, we hoped we could reason with them, or with some of them. Show them what was happening with the discord that was forming in the family. But we are young babies to them. They did not want to see or hear what we had to say. We knew we could never side with them. How could we turn our backs on the people we are supposed to serve, to protect?"

"Yet you turned your backs on your family," Oberon reminded her.

"Because my oldest brother threw my twin off the top of his tower," Lia declared. "We left because if we stayed, we would be dead."

"Your twin, is he all right?" Trion asked. He knew the answer already. He knew that Cal, or Callum, was fine and healed from his injuries.

She nodded. "We already had a plan in place. I could get him to an ally who risked their life to heal him with no one knowing," Lia replied. "I'm sure you know well that five years ago there was quite the search for us."

"Quite an extensive one," Joslin recalled.

"The villagers you aided, I do not need to know where they are," Harold began. "But they are safe?"

"Yes," Lia promised him.

"Lia, do you know how many of your family members have started their own armies?" Volpe inquired.

"At the moment, only my oldest sister has not raised an army," Lia replied. Lia feared for when Zola raised an army, for Zola was the Goddess of Death.

"Have any united?"

"Right now, there seem to be three factions," Lia stated. "The first is my father; Leto and Doulas have sided with him. We have seen the least amount of movement from them, but they have been staying in the southern section and, as I'm sure King Harold is aware, word from there is limited."

"Yes, it feels as if they have shut themselves off from the rest of the country," Harold agreed.

"Mara has sided with my mother," Lia continued. "I believe my mother is holding up in the lake area of southern Tarsina and northern Corin. She is from that area and used to tell us that her old home was still there but protected from all but her."

"That would make sense," Duke Rolland replied. "There has been much activity in that area. I believe her hut to be near where the lake, mountain and forest meet."

"I have noticed that as well," Joslin agreed, as that was by her northern border. "Rolland and I have been working with each other's armies to have more patrols in that area."

"At the moment, Zola is staying out of it," Lia informed all of them. "The third fraction is Taris. Taris at the moment has the larger force. We believe he is using this moment to make himself the head of the family by, well, killing all of us."

Reed drummed his fingers on his table. "So, we're talking about three different armies," Reed surmised. "Each after a different purpose. Are they fighting each other or staying away from each other?"

"They are fighting each other," Lia told him.

"You're already forming a strategy, aren't you?" Volpe said to Reed.

"If they united under one force, it would be disastrous," Reed admitted. "But if they stay fractured into three, possibly four groups that will fight each other, that gives us a decent shot. I would like to talk with your strategist, Lia. But if we can coordinate three main armies, we can control some of the battles."

"I would suggest a fourth as well," Tas added. "We will need a smaller force to help get key people close to the gods."

"And when you meet them, what are you going to do with them, plead for them to stop?" Oberon asked sarcastically.

"We can try that," Lia said dryly. "But I believe killing them is a better idea."

"You want to kill gods?" Oberon yelled. "Are you out of your mind? Gods can't be killed!"

"My family line would beg to differ," Grierr pointed out as he stood to his full height. "They killed Arkos's sons and daughters, along with most of the family line. The Black Mist killed my own children. Just because we're gods doesn't mean we can't die or be killed."

Oberon stared at him in shock. "What are you talking about?"

"My name is Arngrierr Thodeson. I am the last of the Arkonites, and the several times over grandson of Arkos," Grierr declared.

"Are there any other gods hiding amongst us?" Larissa inquired.

"I think we're good," Tas assured her, ignoring the elbow from Lia. "Oberon, do you have any other protests or complaints? Or can we continue?"

Chapter 31

The meeting ended earlier than usual, as there was a formal dinner later that evening to welcome all the delegates. Tas quickly got word to their companions to meet them in his and Thierren's room so that Micah could catch them up on what he had learned since they last saw him. Emaya had received a quick rundown of the conversation, for she would not be in the meeting. Emaya had volunteered to not attend the ball. She felt out of place. Instead, she would stay at the orphanage so that Sienna and several others could attend the ball. Jonah was the last to arrive. It turned out he had to lose one of Oberon's men on his way to the family wing.

"We're all here, Micah," Tas noted.

Micah nodded. "I'll start with Edelberg," Micah began. "Certain things have come to light over the last few weeks. Apparently, the president before Tobias, and my grandfather and father, had arrangements made that would keep Edelberg out of trouble. Arrangements that neither Tobias nor my uncle were aware of until they asked questions."

"Your father?" Tas and Grierr asked in shock.

"Trust me, they have caught many of us off guard," Micah replied.

Edelberg and Micah's father had always talked about how titles should not be used to escape one's problems. To hear he had done so was shocking.

"It's caused a big scandal within the family," Micah admitted." My mother wasn't even aware of the arrangements. She is furious with my father."

"What has your uncle done since learning the truth?" Grierr inquired.

"My father has lost several titles as a result; I hand delivered a statement that the Crown of Friesen will no longer turn a blind eye about this. Essentially, Edelberg will be tried as a citizen of the magical community and the Crown will not interfere in the Council's authority."

"Lawyer?" Grierr asked.

"One that was appointed by the Council," Micah replied. He looked at Thierren for a moment. "They might call to have you testify; Tobias is seeing if a statement will be enough."

"I figured as much," Thierren answered. "It's why he has been short with me; I know too much, and he sees that as danger."

"At the moment, he goes between blaming you or Tas," Micah informed them. "Tas instigated the whole thing, was provoking him to lose his temper. He claims that if Grierr hadn't gotten involved, nothing would have happened."

"Does he remember any of it?" Thierren inquired.

"He remembers the start of the spar and then waking up in the infirmary," Micah answered. "He remembers attacking Thierren clearly. He remembers their conversation and what he accused Thierren of. He remembers little of attacking Grierr and Tas."

"Which shows that he was in a rage during that part," Thierren stated. "When one is in that blood rage, they usually have very little memory of the events that occurred during it."

"Which is why they are going to use the statements from all the witnesses and the medical reports," Micah replied.

"You said you had to talk to us about Moira," Tas reminded him. They were short on time. He did not want Micah to leave any important information out.

"She is the bigger issue," Micah replied.

"Well, that's terrifying," Lia admitted. She was a bit surprised Moira could be a bigger issue than Edelberg.

"How so?" Tas asked, just as confused as Lia.

"Tobias asked me to look into her past when he heard her name linked with Kaiden's," Micah began. "I took the information that Kaidan and you had on her and researched her. The person she is saying she is would be impossible."

"How so?" Jonah inquired.

Micah pulled out a map. "Moria claims she comes from this island near Toroand," Micah showed them as he pointed to the island near the arctic tundra in the North.

"That can't be right," Jonah argued as he stared at the map. He knew that island very well.

"Why?" Grierr asked Jonah.

"No one has lived on that island for almost fifty years," Jonah answered. "It's a small island, only had one main settlement. There were a few year-round residents, but most were stragglers. A woman oversaw the village. She ran it with her three daughters."

"Do you remember their names?" Micah inquired.

Jonah shook his head. "The few times I dropped supplies off, it was always at night and at a dock out of sight of the village," he replied. "But there were rumors and stories that had circled about the island for centuries. Many shippers would not go there."

"Zola told me about this place," Lia realized. "Our mother would go there on vacation with my siblings. If it's the same island, I think the woman was related to Malforin somehow. It was never clear, as it depended on who you asked."

"Did you ever go?" Tas asked Lia.

She shook her head. "No, Zola said a brutal fire had leveled it to the ground before we were born. The was nothing left of it the village."

"That matches what I learned," Micah confirmed. "A passing ship noticed the smoke. They went to investigate and found the village engulfed in a fire that was so hot they could feel the heat on the ship. It took two weeks before anyone could reach the island. When they did, there was nothing left of the village but piles of ashes and ruined structures and some bones."

"How does this tie into Moira?" Thierren asked.

"The woman had three daughters," Micah reminded them. "The name Moira is using belongs to the youngest."

"That's impossible!" Lia argued. "She would be over fifty years old, and she would have to be a sorcerer or something."

Micah looked at Jonah. "You said there were tales of the island?"

"It never had a name, or if it did, no one ever spoke of it," Jonah recalled. "We only talked about it based on its coordinates. I was always told that if you spoke the name, it would curse you."

"Did you ever know it?" Tas asked him.

Jonah shook his head. "It was never on any map," Jonah answered. "For as long as I remember, a woman was always in charge of the island. You hear tales. It was the same woman all the time, which would mean she is some being of magic."

"What did the tales say about her?" Lia asked.

"She would take in anyone that was injured, running from a horrible situation," Jonah recalled. "Some tales say you never saw them again, other tales say very few were allowed to live there year round."

"Why couldn't you drop the deliveries off at the island?" Grierr inquired.

"It was said to protect those on the island that were hiding from people," Jonah replied. "It was strange. As you approached, it was like entering a space that should not exist but does because the island is on maps but not the name. We would always rush to get the goods off as quickly as we could, so we did not have to spend a night docked there."

"And you never heard names?" Thierren asked.

"It always seemed as if you were given a name of someone on the island, you would forget it as soon as you left the vicinity of the island," Jonah admitted. "It definitely had magic protecting it."

"Powerful magic, from what it sounds like," Grierr stated. "Those have to be powerful charms or runes to keep an island's name or inhabitants from being remembered."

"Why create charms like that?" Lia asked. "Are you protecting something?"

"Or are you protecting someone, including yourself?" Tas added. "You don't just settle an island and ward it from being found by anyone meaning harm just because you feel like it. You do it because you're hiding something that could be in danger."

"Or dangerous," Thierren added.

"Would Zola give us more information?" Tas asked her.

"If we can get her to talk to us," Lia reminded him. "But why would Moira give us a name of someone dead?"

"Because she's running herself," Thierren suggested. "She told me and Edelberg on separate occasions she had to leave her family because it was too dangerous for her to stay. Maybe she knew someone from the island and used the name of a person long dead to hide herself from being found."

"I can delve deeper," Micah promised.

"Micah, there is a naval library in Inglisia," Jonah informed him. "You will find information on every island off Toroand there, as well as maps of them all. If you need a place to start, that would be it."

"Once the meetings are over, I'll head there next," Micah replied. "Do I need permission?"

"Tell them Captain Jonah advised you to visit," Jonah answered. "That should get you clearance."

The chime of the clock had them all looking at what time it was. "We need to get ready for the dinner," Tas realized. "Micah, we'll look into this more. I'll send some of my people to look into the island to see if they can find out anything."

"I have mine looking into it as well," Micah answered. "Lia, do you want me to write to Cal about any of this?"

"No, I would worry about anyone getting the missive," Lia replied. "I'll communicate with him."

"Very well," Micah agreed, standing up.

"I guess we will see each other in a little bit," Grierr said with a grin.

"Yes, all of you have fun while they drag me around doing my princely duties," Tas groaned.

"Oh yes, the poor prince," Thierren teased.

Tas raised an eyebrow at him. "You realize they will drag you around with me, right?"

Thierren paled at the comment. "Bloody hell."

#

Thierren stood leaning against a wall as he watched the ballroom. He was taking a quiet moment for himself while Tas handled the well wishes and promises of alliances if Oberon were to act out. When Artur had introduced them as the Duke and Duke of Draconia, Oberon has not handled the news well. He had stormed out shortly after they descended the stairs into the ballroom and had only shortly returned to the ball. Thierren sipped his champagne as his eyes found Tas, who was telling an exciting story based on how his hands were moving. Tas must have felt him watching because his hazel eyes locked with Thierren's. He flashed a quick grin at Thierren before returning to his tale.

Thierren spotted Lia and Grierr talking with one of the King of Greedin's people. The two were becoming good friends. Thierren had been to functions before. Being friends with both Edelberg and Tas meant their friends had the privilege of being invited to balls and dinner parties. He knew the protocol; he knew what they expected of guests, how to greet royalty and nobility. How to make polite conversations, what topics to avoid, and who to avoid. Yet that had all changed, for he was now married to a Prince, which meant he would be there with Tas, and they would scrutinize any fumble.

"A moment to yourself?" Jonah asked as he came to stand next to Thierren.

"Tas took pity on my lack of etiquette," Thierren responded, getting a chuckle from the man. "I recognized your date."

Jonah grinned. "She demanded that she be my date, and she is not one to be told no," Jonah replied.

"I take it she has a tavern here as well," Thierren said dryly.

"That she does," Jonah confirmed. "She has them spread around so she can be where she is needed to be."

"And she needed to be here?"

"Something about seeing where we are on our journey," Jonah answered. "I don't argue with her when she gets like this."

"She sees things?"

Jonah watched as someone led Heathyre onto a dance around the dance floor. Her iridescent green dress changing colors, the peacock feathers in her hair dancing with her as she seemed to float about. She was laughing at something her partner told her.

"She is better at explaining it," Jonah admitted. "I have never understood what she can and can't do. I think she prefers us not knowing."

"To be fair, I agree with her. Not knowing means people can't take advantage," Thierren answered. "If people knew my full healing abilities, they would ask me to do the impossible."

"And you would do it because under the steel exterior is a kind heart," Heathyre stated, appearing at his side.

A server passed by with a tray of champagne and each took a glass. "Are you having fun, Lady Heathyre?"

"I always love events like these," Heathyre answered with a grin. "The gossip, lies, scandals that one can learn is always an enjoyable time."

"That would explain why Tas and Micah were excited for tonight," Thierren realized.

"Oh yes, for people like them this is like waking up on the first day of the winter solstice as a child," Heathyre laughed. She smiled at Thierren. "Seeing you here was like that for me."

"Are you flirting with me?" Thierren asked in mock aghast. "I am a married man!"

"I think I will leave you two and join Lia and Grierr with whatever conversation they are having," Jonah informed them, as he slipped away.

"I am proud of you," Heathyre informed Thierren.

"Did you think I would betray them as well?" Thierren inquired.

She shook her head. "I had a feeling I knew which path you would end up on, even if you had gone the other way you would have done everything to protect them," Heathyre answered. "You were never the one to betray them."

Thierren stared at her as comprehension dawned on him. "You saw what Edelberg did?"

"His path was always heading to that point in time," Heathyre answered. "There was no deviating from it. Even if you had left, he still would have fallen to the Blood Rage. It would have been worse because you would have not been there to stop it."

Something eased in Thierren, for he feared that him being there at the Watchtower had led Edelberg to act out. Knowing somehow that it would have happened no matter what eased some of the guilt he had been feeling.

"You worried you were the trigger," Heathyre observed. He nodded. "Even if you were the trigger, his actions are still his own. You are not responsible for his failing to control his anger and rage. He is the only one who is wrong, for he lied to everyone about his control. He set his path forward, and he is now facing the consequences of doing so."

Thierren stared at her for a moment. "What are you?"

"A guide, a barmaid, tavern owner, friend, and more," she answered. "You might want to rescue your husband in a few moments, for Oberon is heading toward him. But give them a moment to speak."

Thierren turned to look and watched as Oberon approached Tas. Tas caught Thierren's gaze and gave a quick look to say he had it under control for now.

Tas made quick goodbyes from the people he was talking to so that he could see what Oberon wanted without him intruding on conversations. Tas watched the brunette stalk towards him with a neutral expression on his face. Tas did not miss how Oberon's people spread out throughout the crowd.

"Oberon, I hope you are enjoying the dinner and reception," Tas said with a slight bow of greeting with his head.

"The introductions of the Royal Family really set the stage," Oberon answered. "Congratulations on your new title."

"Thank you," Tas replied.

"Though I feel we must discuss this marriage of yours," Oberon said as he accepted a champagne flute from a passing server.

"I am not sure what there is to discuss," Tas replied.

"You have broken our own marriage contract," Oberon informed him. "I have already sent..."

Tas held up a hand to stop Oberon from continuing. "I am not sure what reality you are living in," Tas began. "However, I have never agreed, nor have I or any of my relatives signed a marriage contract that promises a marriage between us. Whatever relationship you think we have is not real."

"You want more rights in our contract? That is what this must be about," Oberon stated with a chuckle. "You are feisty, I will give you that. But this act needs to end."

"No, this stops here. I will signal my guards to escort you out if you persist with this conversation."

"You have led me on."

"Enough!" Tas yelled, surprising himself and everyone near them. "I have said no. I have explained that I am not interested. Whatever rise to political rank you are after, I have never wanted to be a part of."

"I know you love me."

Tas laughed. "The only person who I have ever loved I now call husband," Tas informed him. "You have become obsessed with this idea that I somehow belong to you. I am not a trophy, a prize, or a reward. And if you do not leave now with your people, then I will have you escorted out."

"You will make an enemy of Lynia and Greedin," Oberon snarled.

"No, not of Greedin," King Harold of Greedin stated. "Oberon, we will escort you out of here with your people and return you to Lynia. I will have some conversations with your father about what I have learned today."

Oberon stared at the gathering of people. "You have all made an enemy today."

"When you return, Oberon, tell my uncle I say hello," Thierren stated as he stood next to Tas. "Please inform him of my recent marriage and my resignation from the cult he is a part of."

Oberon spit at Thierren's feet before storming out of the ballroom, his people following in his wake.

Artur moved to the center of the room. "I think perhaps we should end this evening's festivities," Artur said apologetically. "I would like to meet with my security people to ensure the safety of those here and under my protection."

"I will also join you," Harold said to Artur.

"Micah?" Artur asked.

"I want to escort Tas and Thierren back to their room and secure it before I join you," Micah informed Artur.

"I will go to the ports," Jonah told Artur. "Ensure his ship is ready."

"Thank you all. We will start tomorrow's meeting at ten in the morning to give us all the time to recover from tonight," Artur announced. "If any wish to be escorted to their rooms or lodgings, you may speak with my head of guards, Thorin."

Micah then motioned for Tas and Thierren to follow him. Grierr and Lia joined them as they headed up the stairs. "There is an old disused servant's passage we can use," Tas said quietly to Micah. "Grierr knows of it. He can lead us to it."

"Grierr you take point," Micah informed the tall god.

Grierr looked at Tas and seemed to understand. He nodded, casting a quick spell on them so that no one would notice them. As they headed down one of the side halls, a servant noticed them. Thierren and Tas stared at each other, knowing they should not have been noticed with the spells they had placed around them. Tas gripped the pendant he wore, knowing Grierr would feel if it worked the way Grierr had designed it. Grierr had gifted one to him, Thierren, and Jonah. If Tas needed aid, he could grip it and the others would feel it and know where he was.

"Can I help you?" The servant asked, looking nervous, as she was in the presence of royalty.

"We are just escorting Tas and Thierren to safety," Micah assured the woman as he noted the looks the three sorcerers were giving each other.

"I can offer my assistance," the servant replied. "You are heading toward a dead end; it appears you must have gotten lost."

"We are following an old path," Tas informed the servant. "If you could head back to the servant quarters until the guards clear the area, that would be good."

"I'm not sure that is a promising idea," she stated, her voice taking on an odd edge to it that had not been there before. "I believe I should ensure your safe arrival at your destination."

Micah slowly placed his hand on one of his hidden blades. "Ma'am, I think it's time you tell us your name."

She smiled at him. "I think not," she answered.

Tas felt her magic before she cast the spell. Ignoring the corruption of it, he threw up a shield barrier in front of Micah before the fireball hit him. The ball of flames extinguished the moment it hit the barrier. Lia shot up a barrier of ice as Grierr grabbed Micah while Tas handled the blood sorceress in front of them.

"Stay back," Grierr whispered to Micah. "Let us handle this. If you see a path to safety, alert the guard."

"I can help," Micah promised.

"I'll stay with him," Lia stated as the ice shattered, sending shards back at them.

"I know, but something is off with her," Grierr warned. "I think she is a blood sorcerer."

He erected a barrier around Micah and Lia before stepping back. Grierr stood to his full height and lashed out at the female with electricity. Thierren was warding the area so others could not enter. The female was laughing as she dodged their attacks. Lia created ice patches near where the woman was fighting.

"We can play here all you want," she taunted as she melted the ice. "The little princess over there will be of no help to you!"

Tas sent her a spell that had her body contorting, causing her to fall to the ground. She screamed as she went down. She shot out a stream of fire from her fingers as she crashed to the ground. The fire was hot enough it burned the floor; the heat became almost suffocating to those in the area. The spell was enough to confirm they were dealing with a blood sorcerer.

"Micah, if she bleeds, stay away from her blood," Thierren hissed as he created wind to counter the heat coming from the flames.

"Poor blind Tas," she teased. "Can't see where I am, must rely on your friends. Should have chosen Oberon."

"Oh, why is that?" Tas asked as he focused on his ring.

"He could have healed you," she whispered in a sinister way. "Made your eyes see all there was to see in the world."

"Really? And how would he do that?" Tas asked, as his vision seemed to clear. It was disorienting at first, but soon he could see clearly. He realized he was using Thierren's sight to see clearly.

"Our secret, one you can never appreciate now that you have rejected the way," she answered.

"And if I was to want to hear more, to make a different choice?" Tas asked, as if he was even thinking that.

She slowly got to her feet and went to speak, but was cut off as Tas charged right at her. He swiped a leg, knocking her back to the ground. She went to counter his move but was frozen to the ground. Tas stood behind her now with her arms pinned to her back. She did not know how he could move that fast.

Thierren created vines to wrap around her wrists that Grierr charmed into metal. The charm would last long enough to get her into more secure bindings. Micah came over to them as they heard feet rushing toward them. Thorin appeared with Thaddeus and several other trusted people.

"Four attacks, one night," Thorin stated.

"Grierr will go with you with her," Tas informed Thorin. "She's a blood sorcerer. I'll notify the Council."

"Micah, get them to their rooms," Thorin instructed. "Thad, go with them."

Once everyone was ready, Tas took the lead and headed for the tapestry that concealed the old passage. He unlocked it with a quick spell and waited for everyone to enter before he locked the door. They were all silent as they made their way through the narrow passage, Thaddeus and Tas in the lead as Micah took the rear. They were let out in the family sitting area on the second floor. Thaddeus waited for everyone to exit before locking the door.

He pulled Tas into a huge hug. "You're safe."

"Who else?" Tas asked his brother.

"Harold, Larissa, and Volpe," Thaddeus answered. "Jonah was the one to signal the alarm."

"Each one who spoke out against him at the meeting," Lia realized. "Someone planned this. It could not be a spur of the moment attack. This had to have been in place before they arrived."

"I agree," Micah replied. "The organization, the places the attackers were waiting, they had people waiting for tonight."

"Waiting for me to say no, or yes?" Tas inquired.

"The marriage contract was a ruse," Artur answered as he entered the room. He hugged his two grandsons and then Thierren. "It was a serious contract, but we are seeing a bigger plot, one that Thierren warned us of. The Traditionalist sects are preparing for war. I believe they would have used the marriage as a ruse to gain more power. Tonight was a demonstration of what they are capable of and what lengths they will go to in order to achieve their goals."

"Knowing the enemy is a benefit," Micah reminded them all. "Artur, go to your rooms."

"I wanted to make sure my family is accounted for before turning in," Artur informed the spy. "You will send word to your uncle?"

"After I get them to their rooms," Micah promised.

Artur walked with them until they reached the narrow hall to his own rooms. The hall was now lined with well trusted guards. Artur hugged them all before heading to his door. Thaddeus took his own leave as he hugged Tas tightly before retreating. Thierren opened the door to their rooms and held it open for Tas. He felt Tas use his magic to check the room for any traps or other people hiding in the room. Tas gave a quick nod with his head to signal it was clear to enter.

Once in, they closed the connection between them. Thierren reached out an arm immediately, catching Tas as his knees went weak. Thierren got his arm around his waist and helped him walk into their bedroom. Tas was sweating all over and his body was trembling. Thierren kept reassuring him as he took on most of Tas's weight as they walked. Thierren helped him sit down on the edge of the bed. Thierren gripped his pendant really quickly before he looked at Tas. His eyes were no longer clear, they had become cloudy once again.

"Talk to me," Thierren whispered as he kneeled in front of Tas.

"She tried to enter my mind," Tas answered. "She was trying to follow the path the Blood Dragon created."

"Did she?" Thierren asked him. Tas shook his head. "It drained you keeping her out, though."

"Towards the end it was like a faint burning at the edge of my mind," Tas said.

Thierren rested his forehead against Tas as they both took the moment to calm their emotions. "We will figure it out," Thierren whispered.

"And if we don't?"

"Then we learn to adapt," Thierren replied.

"Ren," Tas said wearily. "If this kills me..."

"It won't," Thierren assured him. Tas went to argue, but Thierren shook his head. "Tas, I might not know how to cure it or fix it at the moment, but I know one thing. And that one thing is you won't die from it."

Any conversation ended when the floor seemed to shake. Both sorcerers looked at each other, not sure what was happening. Tas could hear the dragons.

"Waves are coming!" Tas yelled as he rushed to the balcony where Bart was waiting. "Thierren, alert the castle. I need to head to the ports and evacuate them before the waves reach us!"

Thierren watched Tas take off on the back of his dragon as the surrounding ground shook again.

Chapter 32

The ground shook for two days. The waves came at dawn on the second day, wiping out a port town and doing damage to most of the northern coastline. Thierren had not seen Tas at all. Instead of worrying, he helped with injuries, setting up field hospitals throughout the city of Dracon and helping where he could. Lia and Emaya also lent their hands, allowing Thierren to be where he was needed the most. Grierr was working with Jonah trying to coordinate rescues while also trying to find out what happened. They knew a massive earthquake must have triggered what happened, but they did not know where.

In the chaos, Oberon could slip out on a ship in the dead of the night. Reports were that no waves touched the ship as it sailed into the mayhem around them. Thierren knew Tas was okay because of the bond. One of his in-laws would approach him and he would just nod, letting them know he could still feel the bond. The rulers that were here for the meetings were lending what people they could to help with rescue and recovery. The palace was on lock down from the attacks, but everyone inside was busy with creating schedules and helping areas that needed it.

On the fourth day, dragons were arriving with survivors and some news. A massive earthquake on the border of Tarsina and Silencia had occurred. Harold left on one dragon with Tanis and Rolland to assess the damage when he heard it was his kingdom. Quinsenta had sections of land washed away in the twenty-foot waves that hit the shores. It was too soon yet to know what the total number of dead was for Quinsenta and Greedin and the small north arctic islands. Thierren was in the city hospital doing evaluations to help sort who were priority and who could wait. Volunteers from all over were coming in to help, Lia was helping organize the volunteers while Emaya oversaw those who needed training.

The ball room in the palace had become a disaster relief center with staff from the palace and volunteers working with information they had and maps to figure out where rescues and where supplies were needed. Jonah was helping to translate for the dragons and their aid in the relief. Most of the news they were getting was coming from the dragons. Micah, Heath, and Thaddeus were working with Thorin to figure out who was in on Oberon's plan. Richard and Heather had taken the lead in helping organize shifts and where resources should go.

Thierren finished his last patient for the day when he spotted Sebastian heading toward him. Sebastian had been on the coast the last day, overseeing how badly the structures were damaged.

"You're back," Thierren noted.

"Just arrived and told to come get you," Sebastian said. "You look as exhausted as I feel."

"If your mother wasn't also working at the hospital, I would have just been sleeping here," Thierren commented. "But she's been dragging me back with her each night."

"And no one is going to argue because she's their future queen," Sebastian laughed.

"Very true," Thierren agreed.

Sebastian looked over at Thierren noting the bags under his eyes and the exhaustion setting into his shoulders. "How are you holding up?"

"Part of me is furious with him. The other part knows I would have done the same thing," Thierren admitted.

"Sienna and I had the same fight when she rushed to the orphanage during the tremors," Sebastian recalled. "Meanwhile, I was packing my gear to see how structures were holding up. We ended up laughing as we used the same arguments on each other."

"That sounds like what we will be like," Thierren answered. He looked out at the streets as they rode. "Do we know the damage and totals yet?"

"I think that is what this meeting is for," Sebastian admitted. "From what I've seen, we have lost most of our southern port and one of the western shores is now under water."

"That's what I heard," Thierren confirmed. "Any confirmation on Silencia?"

"Nothing more than what the dragons have told us."

They fell into silence as they approached the now heavily guarded palace gates. Once the carriage was checked, they passed through the gates and headed toward the private wing. A group of guards were waiting to escort them into the palace. From there, they headed to the one of the smaller dining rooms they would use for guests. They spread out maps over the dining room tables. Leaders and close advisors were talking. Richard spotted Sebastian and Thierren and walked to them.

"Dad and Gramps are coming. They have some information that's been confirmed," Richard told them. "Grab some food while we wait."

"I think a moment to sit will be enough," Thierren admitted.

Thierren took a seat at a small table in a corner. It was covered with Richard's notes and empty mugs of tea. Richard joined him with a plate of food that he subtly set in front of Thierren. Neither spoke as Richard looked over his notes, hiding the smile behind the paper when Thierren grabbed some of the food on the plate to eat. Both were fine with silence; they did not need to fill it with senseless chatter.

They both stood straighter when they heard a group of people heading towards the dining room they were in. The royal guard stopped at the door, both Trion and Artur entered. There was no display of bows or curtseys, Artur had been enforcing a no formality rule when a crisis was at hand.

"We have confirmation that the mountain range along the border of Tarsina and Silencia is gone," Artur began. "Parts crumbled into the sea while water surrounded the other sections. Silencia is becoming an island. The North Arctic Islands of Gastion have also seen severe damage and land change."

Larissa gave out a cry as she stared in disbelief at Trion. A few of her aids were at her side.

"Larissa," Trion began. "We have a dragon waiting to take you."

Larissa rushed forward, hugging both men before she went with her people to follow a guard to the waiting dragon. There was silence for a moment. "We don't know numbers yet," Artur stated. "But we expect them to be... large."

"Any word of destruction on the other continents?" Volpe asked.

"The North Arctic Islands at the moment are the only other area impacted largely besides Silencia and Tarsina," Trion answered. "Grierr, we are trying to get word on your brother-in-law. We have confirmation that most of the duke's family has been accounted for."

Artur went to speak, but froze for a moment. He rested a hand on Trion's arm as Drache spoke to him through their connection. His face paling as the moments went by.

"A huge tidal wave is heading toward our northern shores," Artur began. "It will hit within the next few hours."

"That's barely enough time to evacuate the coastal towns," Trion answered.

"It's enough time to evacuate those we can," Thaddeus answered as he joined them.

Grierr looked at Thierren as they had a conversation with looks. "Grierr and I can try to slow it," Thierren replied. "But we won't be able to do it for long."

"How?" Artur asked.

"We can use our mana to slow the wave. It will still hit at the size it is. We can't change that, but we can give you time to get more to safety," Grierr explained.

"We will wait until the last moment then, rescue as many as we can before we have to use you both," Thaddeus decided.

"Jonah, are you aware of routes we could use?" Sebastian asked the sea captain.

"A few that will cut the time," Jonah replied. "I can lead a group to secure them."

"Drache is sending us dragons," Trion replied. "I will be on Sasha."

"Dad, stay," Thaddeus argued.

"I'm coming," Trion stated. "You will need me to translate."

"Stay on Sasha, don't come on ground, fly off when the wave is too near," Thierren instructed Trion as he grabbed some food from the buffet. He tossed some rolls to Grierr. They were both going to need fuel to power what they would be doing. "We can keep Thaddeus and Sebastian safe and warn them with plenty of time."

"I can handle myself," Trion reminded them.

"Yes, and I'm married to Tas, which means if you get hurt, I'll get yelled at," Thierren pointed out. "So, either do that or I bind you to a chair."

"I knew I liked him," Artur said to Thaddeus.

"Fine," Trion replied.

"Everyone coming, let's move," Thaddeus ordered.

Thierren ran to his rooms to grab his medical bag and staff. Grierr waited for him outside the door. They nodded to each other than ran to where everyone was meeting. Dragons, carriages, and horses were being organized, along with which groups were going where. Thaddeus was working with Jonah on where people would be needed. Thaddeus motioned for Grierr and Thierren to join them.

"You are going to follow Dad to the northern most shoreline," Thaddeus explained. "We have a dragon ready to follow. We are going to being evacuating those towns first as it will take the longest for them to get to safety."

"Do we know how big the waves are?" Grierr asked.

"That if they hit at the rate they are building, it could reach as high as the Low Mountain Road," Jonah stated.

Grierr and Thierren stared at him in shock. "All right," Thierren replied. "Let's do this."

Jonah clapped the two sorcerers on the shoulder. "Be safe. Do not sacrifice your lives, for we will have bigger battles to fight," Jonah whispered. "You are my brothers in spirit. Do not be reckless."

The two headed to where Trion stood with his dragon, Sasha. She was a water dragon. Another water dragon was waiting next to them.

"This is her brother," Trion introduced them. "He says you may call him Azure."

After a quick introduction to the dragon, Thierren and Grierr both climbed on. They would fly ahead of everyone else to the northernmost point of the coastline. The plan was to start evacuating the towns there, as it would take them the longest to reach the Low Mountain Road. They would also try to gauge the height and width of the tidal wave that was forming off the coast. From the air, they saw the ground began to roll with another earthquake.

"This is not good," Grierr stated as he stared as roads crumbled into the earth. "It's like we are watching the end of the world."

"It's the end of something," Thierren agreed as they watched in horror at the destruction happening around them.

"Trion, if you want to go back, we will understand," Thierren called to Trion. The conflict the future king must feel had to be unimaginable.

"No, I will continue with you," Trion decided. "I can save the people on the coast while my people aid those in the cities."

Their dragons flew with urgency as they soon could see the coastline in view. Off in the distance, they could see the giant wave that was heading towards them. The wave was large enough to erase the entire northern shore and all its buildings and it would only get bigger as it traveled.

"The low road might not be high enough," Grierr realized as he gauged the wave and the distance it would travel once it hit land.

"I'll spread word to get everyone higher," Trion yelled to them. "You both stay on course. Start evacuating."

The two nodded as Azure flew lower to pick up speed. They could hear him call out in the air to other dragons. Thierren was hoping it was for aid. Right now, they needed a miracle if they were going to save anyone. The mountains gave way to forests that blended into the sandy shoreline of northern Quinsenta. Many villages were scattered throughout the forests.

There were several fishing villages and a bustling port. All would need to be evacuated.

Azure landed near the port town; people were already rushing about. Someone spotted the dragon landing, for a group of town guards walked toward them.

"Are you here to help?" One of them inquired.

"We are," Grierr assured him. "Your mayor?"

"Ran off at the first sign of trouble," another spat.

"Who is in charge?" Thierren asked.

"Owner of the tavern near the docks," the first said. "She's been ordering everyone to pack what they could carry, and that wagons should carry children, the elderly, and the infirm."

"Sounds like Heathyre," Grierr said to Thierren.

"Go to her," Thierren told Grierr. "I'll talk with the guards and get them under control."

Grierr nodded. "Signal if you need me."

Thierren saluted him before turning to the guards. "Gather up your fellow guards. I'll fill you in on the plan."

When Thaddeus arrived with more people, the evacuation was in full swing, wagons had already left. "How bad?" Thaddeus asked.

"We need to get them to a higher place," Thierren told him.

"Dad is working with Jonah on new locations," Thaddeus answered. "We're going to keep moving them toward the low road as that leads everywhere. Jonah is already working on a higher location with the help of one of the dragonlings."

Thierren nodded. "We sent our friend Heathyre ahead with some of the guard here to start on the villages," he told Thaddeus. "Grierr has the port under control."

They heard a familiar dragon trill, both turned to watch a red dragon come into view. Bart landed near them, lying low to the ground so that Tas could slide off. A few days' worth of beard growth covered his face as he headed toward Thierren and Thaddeus. He greeted his husband with a quick kiss before turning serious.

"Good, you have started evacuation," Tas said with relief.

"Only just," Thaddeus admitted as he looked at his exhausted brother.

"Better than nothing," Tas assured his brother. "Is Grierr here?"

"Yes, he's overseeing the evacuation of the party. Heathyre is here as well. She has gone to start on the villages," Thierren filled him in as they walked to the part. "How much time?"

"Two hours at most," Tas said grimly.

"We won't save everyone," Thaddeus realized.

"No, but we will save the ones we can," Tas promised, laying a hand on his oldest brother's shoulder. He had already seen enough death and grief over the last few days. "We have the chance to save lives, which is better than in Silencia."

"How bad?" Thierren asked Tas as they walked toward the entrance to the Port town.

"The capital city is now a coastal city," Tas answered.

"By the gods," Thaddeus cursed. "The city was ten miles inland."

"The entire mountain range either crumbled into water or is now submerged underwater. Silencia is now an island."

"Tarsina?"

"Its border to Silencia is destroyed, villages swallowed up before anyone could do anything," Tas replied. His voice was void of emotion, for if he thought of the number of lives lost already, he would crumble. Now was not the time for that.

"From an earthquake?" Thierren asked in disbelief.

"This wasn't a normal earthquake, just like the wave heading toward us isn't normal," Tas replied.

Grierr spotted them and rushed forward. "You've arrived," Grierr said, hugging him.

"I have," Tas answered. "How are we doing here?"

"Last few houses are being evacuated," Grierr replied. "Once we clear the port, we'll seal it with a barrier spell. The guards from this village will follow the people to the mountain road."

"Thad, move to the next places," Tas said to his brother.

"The three of you will be fine?" Thaddeus asked.

"We'll be fine," Tas promised his brother. "We will buy you enough time to get most of the area evacuated. Don't be worried about dragons showing up to speed the process along. They will help. They know their own limit."

"I'll pass the word on," Thaddeus replied. He pulled Tas into a tight embrace. "Don't go playing hero. You are the heart of this family; nothing can happen to you."

Tas nodded as they pulled apart. "Keep dad in line."

"I'll try," Thaddeus said with a laugh. He nodded to Thierren and Grierr before heading off with his men.

The three friends watched as Thaddeus got on his horse and rode off to the nearest villages. When his men and he were out of sight, they headed to the beach.

"We're not surviving this, are we?" Grierr asked Tas.

"We might," Tas said. "I mean, the odds aren't great, but think of the tales they will tell of us."

"The three idiots that tried to stand down a wave big enough to swallow half an island," Thierren scoffed. "They thought they could beat the odds, but the odds beat them."

"Always the pessimist," Grierr chuckled.

"Realist," Thierren corrected. "If it's the end, at least I get to spend it with you two."

Tas grinned foolishly as he reached out and took Thierren's hand in his. Grierr slung an arm around Tas's shoulders as they watched the wave come closer. Bart approached them, ready to take them off into the air as soon as the water broke. All knowing there was a good chance it would sweep them up when the wave hit land. Tas had already told Azure to leave, but the dragon stayed, making his stand with the three humans he had only met that day. Bart or Azure would update Tas on the evacuation as they received word from other dragons. The earth trembled as the water drew closer.

"Well, gentleman, the time approaches," Tas replied.

"So, containment spell?" Grierr inquired, just to make sure they were on the same page.

"Until we get word that the last wagon is on the low road," Thierren added.

With the three of them, they should be able to hold it for that long. They could not be on Bart to cast, as with the magnitude of the spell, they would need to be in direct contact with the ground to channel energy from the earth. Tas squeezed Thierren's hand as they got soaked from the mist of the wave that was barreling down toward them. There was no turning back. They waited until the wave made its descent, as the whitecaps curled over the three men, as if they had practiced this a million times prior, wordlessly cast the spell at the same moment. The wave seemed to shudder for a moment as the spell hit it, parts of it spilling over but it held. Now they would wait for a signal or for their mana to run out.

The only noise was Bart's voice in Tas' head informing him of updates, of giving him encouragement. They were performing something dangerous, trying to bend nature to their will. They frowned upon it. They were taught the ramifications of such an act. Yet in this moment, the ramifications were worth it if they could save thousands of lives.

Tas was not sure how long they stood there. Thierren was the first to start with the nosebleed, the first symptom of dangerously low mana. The blackouts would start soon. Tas turned slightly to look at Grierr. He was pale and sweating. Tas knew soon Grierr would also have a nosebleed. They had to hold out longer for the signal, even as Bart warned him it was getting too dangerous. There were signs of the spell crumbling, of water breaking through in spots.

Tas felt the world tremble under his feet and knew in that moment they had lost control. He wondered if it threw him off his feet. It was the only thing to explain why the world went black for a moment. When he stood, he stared at the figure who stood before him and froze. Panic seized him as he realized he must be dead, unconscious, or dying.

"You are none of those three," the deep voice replied. "I have ... stopped everything for a moment."

"How... what are you doing here?" Tas asked in awe, noting the water was frozen, standing still as if the world had indeed just stopped.

"To talk to you," Arkos answered.

"Heck of a time to want to have a conversation with me," Tas informed him.

"It was the time for this conversation," Arkos replied. He studied the scene before him. "The three of you would risk it all to save the lives of others, no matter the cost to yourselves."

"Many would do the same," Tas answered.

"I'm not so sure," Arkos admitted. He smiled at Tas; he had watched over them since they left Emi months ago. "I am here for a reason. You have reached a point where you will need to make a choice in who you are."

"I know who I am," Tas stated. He was not sure where Arkos was going with this.

"But do you accept all of you?" Arkos challenged. Tas stared at him in confusion. "There is a part of you that you have been ignoring. It comes out from time to time, but you shove it away. You fear that by accepting it you will become him, that you would denounce the family you have despite the assurance of your mother."

"He is not my father."

Arkos sighed as he created a large rock to sit on and motioned for Tas to join him. "You are right, he is no father," Arkos agreed. "The man that raised you is an amazing father and more than deserving of his title. Trion has raised all of you with love, acceptance, and support. It is not blood that unites you as a family, but love, love that is strong and understanding. That will never change, even if you accept who you are. They will not love you less, they will not be disappointed in who you are meant to be."

"I feel like I would say it was okay what he did to my mother," Tas confided as he stared at his hands. "That he will think I forgive him for it."

Arkos placed an arm around the young male. He allowed a moment for Tas to come to terms with what he said. When he felt Tas was ready, he spoke.

"He will not know who you are," Arkos informed him. "All he will know is that someone of his blood has accepted the call. A call he had never wanted to feel. It will infuriate him, anger him. For he has gone to horrible lengths to ensure he has no children."

"Why did he go to these lengths?"

"He would see any child of his as a threat to his power, to his control," Arkos admitted. "He sees family as a hurdle to keep his power and for him to gain more power. He has every right to fear you and what you could become."

"Why?"

"Because when a god accepts their power, they accept their responsibility to those that follow them," Arkos explained. "We are to serve our followers, guide them, aid them when it is called upon to do so. He was never comfortable with would be asked of him by accepting the power. The uncertainty has corrupted him. He has violated that pact he made with the universe and nature, as have several of his family. In doing so, his power has become corrupt. It is not working like it once had."

"What happens if I accept all of me?" Tas asked.

"You will feel a surge in your power," Arkos explained. "You will need to learn to control that surge. You will gain certain abilities you did not have before, such as controlling waves and water. You are a sorcerer, so for you it will not be as life altering as it was for Calia when she went through it. Your body has been dealing with magic since you were born. You will just need to learn and discover the new raw power you have."

"If I don't?"

"Nothing would change. You won't lose what you have," Arkos assured him. "You will continue as you are."

"Why not ask this of Grierr?" Tas asked. He turned to see his friend standing frozen in the moment.

"Because my grandson is not ready," Arkos answered as he stared at his grandson. "He must work through his grief and much more before he could decide without a clouded mind."

"Yet I am?"

"You have been ready since you were twenty," Arkos informed him. "It's why you could use the power that you did that day. If you weren't ready, it would never have happened."

"Yet you didn't come to me then," Tas pointed out.

"Your power was ready at that point," Arkos stated. "You were not mentally ready for what we would ask of you."

Tas nodded. "Yea, I didn't handle it well."

"Which is why it was not asked of you to commit," Arkos replied. "We would not risk another god being corrupted because of uncertainty."

"And you think I'm ready now?"

"Correct."

Tas nodded. He looked at Grierr and Thierren frozen in time. "If I choose this, will I save more lives?"

"You cannot save every life," Arkos warned him. "But you will give those already near the Low Mountain Road the time needed to get to higher ground. You will also ensure the two with you will survive."

"Will his family and he know I have chosen this path?"

"Those who share the blood of Malforin will feel the activation," Arkos said.

"If I chose not to do this now?"

"You will have other moments where you can change your mind if you survive this moment," Arkin answered. "But those not yet near the Low

419

Mountain Road will die. The destruction to the land will be devastating for the country."

"What do I have to do?" Tas asked.

He knew this was what he needed to do. His mother had told him that when this moment arrived, to not shy away out of fear of what she would think. This moment had been building since he rescued the boy back when he was twenty. He had felt it growing over the last few months, as if his power and body knew what would be coming.

"You state who you are," Arkos said simply.

"That's it?" Tas asked, surprised at how simple it was.

"Not everything has to have a complicated ritual that involves candles and chanting," Arkos replied. "Plus, we do not have the time for that."

Tas had to chuckle at that. "I am Taslan Strum, youngest son of the Crown Prince of Quinsenta. I am the Duke of Draconia. I am husband to Thierren Magus," Tas began as Arkos nodded. "I am a Dragon Talker, a sorcerer. I am a spy, assassin, and representative to the Council of Magi."

"Very good," Arkos said encouragingly.

Tas closed his eyes, as the next statement would be the hardest thing he ever had to say. "I am by birth the son of Taris, god of the Oceans," Tas stated. "I accept the birthrights bestowed upon me."

Chapter 33

The earth around Tas seemed to tremble for a moment, but not from an earthquake or anything. It was just where he stood. It was as if nature was answering his statement with floating specks of light surrounding him. He felt a breeze surround him, as if his words were accepted. He looked up and saw that Arkos had vanished. A rush of noise and spray of water alerted him that time was no longer stopped. Tas saw the spell crumbling as Thierren fell to his knees.

    Tas stepped forward and raised his hand, canceling the spell. He heard Grierr and Thierren call out to him as he continued to walk toward the edge of the shoreline. The water parted where he walked as if the ocean already knew and accepted who he was. He could not erase the wave, nor could he send it in one direction, for another country would suffer what would have been Quinsenta's fate. The wave, towering well over a hundred feet, seemed to tremble as he walked toward it. In his mind, he imagined what he needed the wave to do: split it into three parts. It would mean parts of Leneo, Greedin and Quinsenta would get the wave, but it would not be as destructive as this one monster of a wave. He felt some resistance, the tail end of a spell or curse sent by the man whose blood ran through him, the anger that fed the spell. Tas grinned at the thought of what Taris would think when he realizes someone of his blood could now undo his carnage. As Tas undid it, he could feel the rage that Taris felt at whoever was undoing the spell. It made Tas grin as he continued to unravel it. The wave was torn between two forces who battled for control of the spell that destroyed.

Tas could feel the new power that was surging through his veins. He felt as if he now breathed in time with the current of the ocean, as if he could sense the creatures that dwell below the surface of the ocean. The power was unlike anything he wielded before, as it had him staggering forward into the surf. The moment his knees hit the sand, the water vanished around him, allowing him to land in the wet sand. As his command won out, his spell canceling out the original command, he watched in awe as the wave split into three sections.

He knew that this all happened in a moment, but for him, it felt like time had slowed for him to do this. Tas sat kneeling in the wet sand, watching as the wave crashed around him. As the scents and sounds returned to normal around him, he became aware of Grierr and Thierren. It was then he noticed that a barrier of water had encircled him.

"They can come through," Tas said to the water.

He did not hear them approach. Instead, he could feel their power buzzing around him as they walked toward him. Thierren crouched down next to him, looking around in wonder as the water stayed away from them. Grierr stood next to them, trying to find the words for what he and Thierren witnessed moments ago.

"How?" Grierr finally asked once words could be formed.

"I don't know if you would believe me if I told you," Tas answered honestly as Thierren helped him stand up.

"Try me, because you're glowing right now," Grierr replied.

"I accepted my birthright," Tas said, simply leaning against Thierren.

Thierren turned to look at him in surprise. He squeezed Tas's hand, knowing the decision had to be emotional for him. "We should make sure everyone got out," Thierren stated

But first, Thierren pulled Tas into a bone-crushing hug as he let his fear be replaced with relief that they had survived.

"I'm fine," Tas promised him as he kissed him quickly. "A little tired, but fine."

"You are going to learn how to control that power that is buzzing around you," Thierren noted.

"We can help him," Grierr replied as he pulled Tas into a hug.

They walked to the original shoreline that was now submerged in water, two dragons hovering just above the water. Grierr was in awe that as they walked, the water disappeared around them. He had to laugh at how amazing it was to witness. They had watched their friend become a god. Grierr let out a victory cry as he spun in a circle.

"Did he get hit by a rock that I didn't know about?" Tas asked Thierren.

"We just watched you become a god. We are allowed to act euphoric about that and also about surviving," Thierren pointed out.

"Fair point," Tas admitted. He kissed the side of Thierren's head as they walked.

Bart and Azure waited for them. Grierr grabbed on Azure's wing and pulled himself up onto the saddle. "Meet you on higher ground!"

Bart helped Thierren and Tas up on to his back, letting out a purr and rumble at their survival. Thierren held on tightly to Tas. Then they were off. The waves had washed out large sections of the port. Piers, docks, and even some buildings were sticking up at odd angles in the water. Some villages on the edge of the water were fully submerged, with the roofs of the taller buildings the only things above water.

They would need to wait a day or two to see if the water receded before the recovery of bodies could begin. As they flew inland, the destruction was less and less. When they reached the original meeting point, they saw the water had not reached it. Tas almost sagged in relief at seeing his choice had been the right one. If he had not, the whole road and everyone on it would have been washed away and under water. Instead, only trees had been uprooted and were floating in the areas of high water.

"This could have been much worse," Thierren realized as he took in the destruction of the surrounding woods.

Tas nodded as Bart took them higher to the main caravan road that connected to the highway. As they got to where the wagons would have met to be directed to final spots, they saw several soldiers and Sebastian standing, talking to a few villagers. Bart landed first, allowing both Tas and Thierren to slide off of him. There wasn't room for two dragons to land, so he flew back into the air so that Azure could drop off Grierr. Tas walked over to Azure and rubbed his snout.

"Tell your herd to rest. We will call on you when the water recedes or in two days to aid in recovery," Tas instructed in the dragon. Azure nodded before flying off towards the waters.

Sebastian came rushing over to them and pulled Tas into a tight hug. The moment they saw the wave hit, Sebastian feared he had watched his brother die. He did not care that the villagers could see his tears of relief as they hugged. Tas, sensing the urgency, hugged back just as hard.

"You three assholes did it," Sebastian said after he hugged Thierren and Grierr.

"It was Tas at the end," Grierr corrected him.

Sebastian studied his brother for a moment and noted the energy that vibrating around him. "You accepted it," Sebastian realized.

"I'll explain when we are all together," Tas promised. "Dad and Thaddeus?"

"Dad and he led two of the larger groups to their temporary lodgings," Sebastian answered. "I promised I would wait for word on the three of you."

Tas nodded, then looked at Bart. *"Tell Sasha we will meet them at the palace,"* Tas instructed.

Bart gave out a sigh before he sent off the message to Sasha. "Do you want a lift?" Tas asked Sebastian.

"Can Bart carry the four of us?" Sebastian asked.

Bart pawed the ground as if insulted at the questions. "He says yes and is demanding snout scratches from you for a week for the insult," Tas informed Sebastian.

"I am sorry, my good Bart. I will gladly tend to you," Sebastian said with a grin, bowing before the red dragon.

Sebastian turned to one soldier, letting them know they can head to the camps. He also told them to spread word that the three sorcerers survived. Once he was done with his orders, he joined the three on the back of Bart. They were all exhausted as Bart flew toward the palace. They could see some of the destruction from the earthquake and the tremors that came from it.

"This will be a long recovery," Sebastian realized as he looked at the smoke and collapsed buildings.

"But we will recover," Tas assured him.

"I hope so," Sebastian said.

Bart flew straight toward the palace. Drache was there in the main garden, most likely consulting with Artur. The older dragon looked up at the sky as they neared. A few more people seemed to join Drache and Artur as the dragon descended from the sky. Artur was the first to greet them, hugging each of them as they slid off the dragon.

"If the three of you ever do that again, I will have you arrested for giving the king whiter hairs," Artur threatened the three sorcerers. He then hugged each of them again before letting Nora fret over them.

"How did you split the wave?" Reed asked as he walked toward them with a grin.

"That was Tas," Grierr answered. "We could hold the wave, but it was Tas that somehow broke it apart."

Artur turned to look at Tas. He saw hesitancy in his grandson's eyes. He walked over and took him by the shoulders, resting his forehead against Tas.

"Blood does not make a family a family," Artur said quietly. "Accepting what belongs to you does not make you no longer my grandson. Becoming who you are meant to be is all I have ever wanted for you. I will always be proud to call you grandson."

Tas hugged his grandfather tightly. "I couldn't save everyone."

"You saved those you could," Reed said, clapping Tas on his back. "Many people owe their lives to the three of you. You all gave us enough time to evacuate the area, time we would never have had."

"Let's get the three of you into dry clothes and some hot food," Nora said as she took in their waterlogged state. "Over food, you can tell us everything."

As the group headed toward the doors to the palace, Lia spotted them and came running. She hugged Tas tightly, pulling away slightly to look at him. He simply nodded before she moved on to Thierren and Grierr.

"Jonah has arrived with some numbers," Lia informed Artur. "Micah is with Heathyre at Applehills town hall, helping get everyone settled there. Thaddeus is on his way back with Richard."

"Good," Artur said as he took the arm Lia offered.

Nora gave out instructions to staff and other visitors that the family would be in the family dining room. It was her way of saying give them some time as a family before we were ready to talk about everything. Nora had very much believed one of her sons would be dead by the end of the day. She ushered the three of them to their rooms to shower in warm water and to change into dry clothes.

#

Thierren finished towel drying his hair as he walked out of their washroom. He saw Tas standing on the balcony. He laid the towel over a chair before stepping out and wrapping his arms around Tas. They stood like that for a few moments, just taking in the moment of quiet, enjoying the calmness that they felt.

"Whatever you are thinking about, you are thinking about it too hard," Thierren informed him.

"Isn't that what I usually tell you?" Tas chuckled as he turned around. "You ready for food and the chaos that will happen when they learn everything?"

"There is always chaos when you are involved," Thierren reminded him.

There was a knock on the door. Thierren walked through the suite to open it. Grierr was waiting for them. Grierr had pulled his hair back into a bun, leaving the widow's braid to hang free.

"Ready?" Grierr asked them.

"Ready," they both said.

As they walked, the staff would stop and thank them for what they did. Emmeline gave them each a huge hug when she saw them head toward the dining room. She then ushered them toward the room so they could eat to regain the energy they had spent saving the island nation from utter destruction. Tas saw his mother at the entrance to the room and stopped to speak to her.

"I had a choice to make," he began. "Are you okay with it?"

"It is not my opinion that matters," Nora answered with a smile as she brushed a strand of hair out of his face. "Are you okay with it?"

"I can undo the damage he wants to create. I might stop him," Tas said. "But it meant accepting who he is and who I fully am."

"All I care about is that you are my son. I love you. All I want is for you to be happy," Nora told him.

Tas hugged her before they entered the room. Thaddeus came through the doors and pulled Tas into a hug before Tas could sit. Tas felt his oldest brother tremble in their embrace as he tried to regain his composure.

"I believed I was leaving you for death," Thaddeus whispered. "That I would bury you."

"I told you, you can't get rid of me that easily," Tas reminded him with a grin.

"Don't do that again," Thaddeus instructed.

"I'll try not to," Tas promised.

Nora walked over to her sons, placing her hands on their shoulders. "Let's eat," she told them.

Tas took a seat in-between Grierr and Thierren. He felt Thierren rest a hand on his back as they loaded their plates with food. As other family came in, there were more hugs and tears, everyone relieved to see who survived. No one spoke of the destruction or what it was going to take to rebuild. For now, it was about family. Jonah arrived with Emaya. Emaya hugged them each tightly before she let Jonah have them. He clapped the three of them on the back of the shoulders, nodding at Tas, understanding the decision he must have made.

After they were done eating, they all stayed at the table talking and enjoying this moment. Tas felt the buzz in the air first, standing up as it intensified. Lia and Grierr were next, followed by Jonah and Thierren. Without realizing it, Tas immediately cast a barrier in front of the table that would protect everyone in the room.

"What?" Artur asked quietly as he felt the ripple of his grandson's power. A shimmer around the table informed him a spell had been cast.

Tas raised a hand to silent the question. The air seemed to move near the door to the dining room. In a blink of an eye, a woman appeared. She wore a black leather rogue uniform. Her black hair had red streaks in it, it was cut short along her jawline. Her dark colored eyes took in the room and its inhabitants until they landed on Tas.

"Hello nephew," the woman spoke.

Appendix

The Universal Gods:

Arkos: God of the Weather, married Elidi. Returned to the Heavens.

Cresica: Goddess of Medicine, comes and goes from the heavens and mortal realm.

Leo: God of the hunt. Unknown where he is.

Cala: Goddess of Astronomy, returned to the Heavens after she traveled all over Izar.

Toran: God of the Oceans, settled on Toroand. Is rumored to be seen there by ships passing the arctic tundra.

Malforin: becomes God of Weather when Arkos returns to the Heavens. He will settle on Greedin.

#

The Gods of Greedin:
- Malforin: God of Weather
- Olga: Demi-god of the hearth and home
- Taris: Oldest Child of Taris, God of the Ocean

Zola: Goddess of the Dead, Queen of the Underworld, Collector of Lost Souls.

Mara: Oldest of Malforin and Olga's children. Goddess of Love and Beauty.

    Aru: God of War

    Doulas: God of the Hunt

    Leto: God of Illusions and Tricks

    The twins: not yet gods: Callum and Calia

#

Other Demi-Gods and Spirits:

    Elidi

    The three Fates

    Heathyre, Lady Feathyre

    Captain Jonah

Made in the USA
Middletown, DE
24 July 2023